THE
FIFTH
DENTIST

THE
FIFTH
DENTIST

Edward Gretz

ISBN: 978-10-79758-80-1

Imprint: Independently published

www.edwardgretz.com

Cover photograph and layout by
Adrijus Guscia / RockingBookCovers.com

for Susan

CHAPTER 1

New Q

"We might discover meaningful purpose while we sleep."
— *Cadence Ng*

I had gradually awoken to the day-start vibrations from my personal reinforcement wearables, recalling appointments and work assignments that composed the framework of my local reality, reluctantly accepting that the dream I'd been having, in which my job was to discover hidden rooms in other people's homes, was not part of the received, accepted world. I felt no compulsion to sit up, as I had lately begun to enjoy the intended-to-be-irritating pulsing sensations from my microdevs and wearables.

As I welcomed and absorbed the benign kinetic energy from day-start quivering, I indulged in the fantasy that I had stopped the flow of time, heroically, omnipotently delaying the start of the day and its intricacies, not merely for myself but for everyone living on overly entangled Earth. With time paused thusly, I forced myself to think only about what would be required of me that Tuesday morning, the likely agenda of activities and with whom I must interact. Only briefly did I allow myself to agonize over whether I would face the horrors of public scrutiny and condemnation because of my new work assignment.

It seemed a particularly dark morning, even for late February, based upon the ominous view through the window near my bed. There in my temporary efficiency suite in Manhattan, I continued to recline on the bed, imagining that I could safely and indestructibly drift away into that vast gray sky, that I could disengage from all work and personal commitments, from new physics, new engineering, new wellness, famine, politics, unexpected biological malignancies and other unsettling world events. After a minute I accepted that time still flowed. I would try to behave as though it mattered.

Stretching, I reached over to the nightstand and retrieved my smarts. I always used smart eyeglasses, since the smart contact lens technology, in my opinion, did not yet measure up to eyeglass features. As the main displays activated, I semiconsciously dubblinked on "Career Day wrap-up" in the list of recent activities displayed in the lower left quadrant, triggering text to begin scrolling up my field of view. It was the first part of the wrap-up segment of my speech from a "career day" event held the previous day at a high school in the County of Santa Clara, California:

Recently, my career has shifted from biotechnology to a focus *on confidence and certainty. Think about the evolution of transportation, communication, medicine, agriculture, manufacturing, energy sources and so on. All growing more complex and entangled, making certainty harder to achieve. How can we make a decision without certainty? We take the <u>next best action</u>. Yes. We do that today.*

But what if there were a source for <u>certainty</u> in deciding on the best career for you ... or choosing a place to live ... or even a life partner? What would it take for you to <u>trust</u> that source? What if <u>you</u> were the source? Yes! What if your own brain could be augmented to reach a state of certainty in making a decision? How much would it be worth to you?

I had paused there and stood center-stage, my arms extended slightly away from my hips, palms forward in the way that questioning and welcoming gestures converge. Every few seconds, I turned to face a different section of the audience. Sensing uneasiness, I resumed:

In the next few years, new technologies could enable what I like to call "pervasive certainty". By that I mean the creation, allocation and dispersal of algorithms and biological implants enabling pure objectivity for artificial intelligence and, yes, even human brains. Experimental work going on now in several parts of the globe could very well lead to pervasive certainty, building upon recent progress in augmenting brain growth in infants.

That's the focus of my life now. Creating, validating, marketing and monetizing certainty. I'm all about certainty. Guess that makes me a confidence man.

That was the summary of my career day script, which I read to them as it displayed on my smarts as I wandered about the stage. There were a few scattered chuckles after the "confidence man" reference, mostly from faculty members, followed by a bit of polite applause as the attendees gradually realized my speech was over.

I had been invited to join three other business professionals in an auditorium to speak to roughly two hundred senior students ... the graduating class of 2034. The intent, of course, was to expose the students to "real life" examples of actual career paths: how each of us started out, how we became "inspired to choose" the path we did and what value, if any, we believe we contribute to the world.

I have no idea how many students were actually paying any attention to what I said. Were any of them wondering if it is truly possible for humans to objectively assess information? ... to dispassionately draw conclusions from information without adding subconscious bias?

Perhaps some were tempted to call out such a question while I stood there, miming my willingness to respond to questions or comments. In that public setting, I would have responded reassuringly.

Privately? No. It is impossible. At least, that's what I've concluded. Since my conclusion was based upon analysis I did for my employer, the TFD corporation, it was a TFD proprietary conclusion at the time. Publicly, I had to support the possibility of total objectivity and certainty.

Confidence is my deliverable. I am acutely aware of the irony.

After the career day event, I had returned to my condo in Cupertino, packed and took a car to the San Jose airport that afternoon to catch a plane to New York City where TFD's "transitional quarterly meeting" ... a "New Q" as we had come to call them ... would be held. I had received a message earlier that day from my boss, Astrid Ekland, that I was being temporarily assigned to lead a team to assess the feasibility of a controversial (and possibly apocalyptic) international project, referred to as the "Gravity Train" or simply "GT". Instead of returning after the usual two days of New Q meetings, Astrid requested I stay and work in mid-town Manhattan for at least two weeks to get the team off to a good start. TFD would provide an "agreeable" efficiency suite for me, she promised, that included a small kitchen.

I had no experience with the specific technologies, equipment and applications that comprised GT. I knew I would need to cram a lot of background research into the next few days, focusing on graphene-based structural and thermal conductivity research, industrial mag-lev, as well as cutter heads for tunnel boring machines. Since the GT plan included construction of a train tunnel beneath the Atlantic that would lie over one hundred miles below the ocean floor at the mid-point, I suspected I may also have to explore technologies or approaches that could be applied to reduce human anxiety across much of the world.

On the flight that evening, my head was filled with fond memories of my prior work in biotechnology, but as we landed in New York, I accepted that, for the foreseeable future, my expected contribution to TFD would be all about creating, validating, marketing and monetizing certainty. I wondered if I would be asked to become another type of confidence man.

◊   ◊   ◊

While still deriving pleasure from the day-start pulsing of my salubrious waistband and wrist bands, I noticed on my smarts it was about twelve minutes past when I was scheduled to be awakened. I took a deep breath and pulled together the resolve to get out of bed.

I thought about Cadence as I showered and dressed. I wanted to see her, talk to her, be reassured by her. She would still be sleeping, calibrated to Pacific Standard Time, but I couldn't resist calling her just before leaving the suite, hoping she would be forgiving. "Cadence?" I pronounced with deliberate rising intonation in order to trigger the connect app in my smarts. After a moment her face appeared with a ghostly translucence in my field of view. I said "to mirror", transferring her image to the full-length mirror-screen on the wall near the closet. She appeared in the mirror wearing an old blue-green T-shirt that had been her favorite to sleep in, her long, black hair a bit disheveled. Her image now became sharper and more detailed, so that it seemed like she was actually standing there in front of me. She was standing barefoot on the hardwood floor of the bedroom, wearing her favorite loose-fitting flannel shorts imprinted with leaping reindeer.

"Oh my goodness! It's so early! But I'm glad you called." Cadence brushed her hair back with her hands and then wiped her eyes with her sleeve.

"Hi! Good morning!" I spoke softly, in a kind of stage-whisper, genuinely happy to hear her voice. "Sorry to wake you.

By the way, you look *great* without makeup!'"

"Still don't believe you. Are you off now for the big Q thing? ... the quarterly whatever?"

"Yes, the 'New Q.' I wish I'd thought of a good excuse to skip it." Cadence yawned as I spoke.

"What's wrong, honey?" she asked while completing her yawn.

"I don't know. I guess I'm feeling kind of disconnected." Cadence frowned as I continued, "I keep getting assignments that push me into ... that make me question things."

"For example ... ," Cadence prompted, folding her arms.

"I've been asked to transfer temporarily to a team in Waldon's area for that tunnel project. The Gravity Train. I've started looking into it. Besides being clearly dangerous at an overview level, there are some details that appear suspiciously obfuscated ... as if they are trying to hide something."

"They?" Cadence smiled, then in a monotone, robotic voice, added "indefinite pronoun reference".

"Well, the key execs, really, including Waldon and our new CEO, Svarog. And beyond that into the client realm. I mean, we've got to present our results to the French Ministry for Ecological and Agro-industrial Challenges, as well as our own federal agencies that deal with transportation and pipelines. I felt better about my job in Early Intention."

Cadence looked downward for a few seconds, then looked back up at me before she spoke. "I've noticed you often drop the 'human' out of Early Human Intention. You're not the only one, and I know it's just a way to shorten the name, but ... well, it's important to keep that human component in mind. Maybe at the meeting today, when you get to talk face-to-face with people there

… other people on your new team, maybe ... I think you'll feel more connected, you know? People connect better face-to-face. You may find a driving truth or greater purpose to feel good about."

"I know. I'll be okay. I shouldn't bother you with this kind of thing." I began to feel annoyed with myself for looking to Cadence to help me feel grounded that morning.

"Think of our lives as a story being told, and we get to write a chapter now and then, but ..."

"But maybe we don't get to write the whole story," I completed her sentence, then noticing it was getting late, added, "Yeah, that's it. You're right. I've got to try to rewrite or add or whatever ... to whatever I don't like about the story I'm seeing. I've got to run, Sweetie, but I'll call you tonight."

"Gotcha! I'm always with you, my love! I know you'll do great!" she reassured, coyly adding, "Perhaps I'll be wearing something more interesting when we talk tonight."

"Cadence, I'm shocked!" I exclaimed with mock disapproval.

"You feign shock admirably," she said dryly.

"Have a good day, Sweetie! I'll be thinking of you often."

"And I'll hope your worries soften." She smiled warmly as her image faded from the mirror.

Cadence and I had, inexplicably, gotten into the habit of end-rhyme on each other's sentences when we were alone together. It started when we first met in a coffee shop. She was better at it than I was. Her digital avatar mimicked that behavior fairly well. I'll never forget the days I spent describing her to the app, relating many stories about our experiences together, providing information on her education and professional background, her behavioral quirks, her favorite authors, movies, foods, drinks and so on. I provided pictures and videos of her, as well as recordings of her voice. It had been a bittersweet journey through nearly three years of memories of Cadence Ng, but the resulting personalized digital avatar became a glorious source of both companionship and solace to me since her sudden passing six months earlier.

Her death had been difficult for me to accept.

CHAPTER 2

Message from Mars

I left the suite. As I walked down the hall toward the elevator, a flashing text alert appeared on my smarts. I dubblinked it in case it had something to do with New Q. It turned out to be a message from Mars Janssen, who was a former TFD employee I knew only slightly. The text:

> *Hear urine town for nuke you. Watch for big pothole.*
> *You must kill wombat before it kills you. Let us please talk.*

I had worked with Mars on only one project a few years earlier. Our interactions had been difficult, with unexpected arguments about research conclusions and the trustworthiness of sources. I recalled he was a conspiracy theorist of sorts, but I couldn't recall any specific conspiracies. I wondered if the big

pothole Mars referred to was actually the Gravity Train project …
or the tunnel aspect of it. "Urine" and "nuke you" were not likely
voice-to-text errors, since the former would have required an
intentional override of in-context defaults, and the latter was a
common internal TFD form of textual humor … or perhaps dissent
… in referring to the New Q quarterlies. So "urine" was probably
supposed to be clever. As far as the need for me to kill a wombat,
albeit a predatory one, the metaphorical significance escaped me.
As the elevator doors opened, I stepped inside, certain there would
be no need to respond to Mars.

I went down to the breakfast area on the main floor, where I
grabbed a wrapped kale, leek and egg omelet sandwich and coffee,
while watching scrolling morning news headlines on my smarts
and staring blankly toward others as they stared blankly toward
me. Several people whom I did not recognize were tagged in my
smarts as TFD employees. Although most people in Manhattan
would likely have their tags blocked, at least until they reached
their workplaces where they would be less exposed to the general
public, here at the hotel it felt good to "where the badge" to enjoy a
sense of camaraderie, a sense of common purpose.

Most of the seats were high stools near counters around the
outer walls and along a circular counter in the middle of the room,
which surrounded a ring of courtesy screens mounted close to the
ceiling, showing news and sport highlights. There were several
small tables along a window wall, each seating two people. I
noticed one of those tables had an unoccupied seat. I would have
preferred a seat at a counter, but they were all taken. So, I
accepted that my next-best-action would be to move toward the
empty seat at the table by the window.

At that table sat a woman, her pullover top, slacks and shoes all black. She wore no obvious jewelry or make-up, and her dark brown hair was tied back in a simple ponytail. A puffy, black jacket was draped over the back of her chair. She appeared to be reading something on a notepad as I approached, suddenly slapping it down on the table and turning to look pensively out the window toward random pedestrian and vehicular traffic.

"May I join you?" I stood holding my plate and cup, my work bag slung over my shoulder, and I smiled as she turned toward me. Her tag was blocked, but she looked vaguely familiar, so I assumed we must have met at some previous quarterly.

"I'm just leaving," she said and slipped her notepad into her shoulder bag.

"I'm Connor Farrell, with Astrid's Early Intention group. You here in Manhattan for the TFD quarterly?" I tried to recall her name. "You look familiar. Katie, is it?"

"Melinda."

"Melinda. Right. Good to see you again. How are things?" I said, placing my work bag on the floor and sitting opposite her.

"You don't know me," she clarified.

"Oh, sorry. I ... uh ... your tag's blocked, so ...." Awkward. I had pretended to remember her in case she would be insulted if I didn't.

"I work in Waldon's group. Or *did* anyway."

I assumed she was expecting to be let go, since a couple of Waldon's projects were rumored to be losing funding shortly. "Oh, don't worry. That's going to turn around. Massive new potential for augmented reality," I said, politely projecting optimism.

"Just found out I'm being transferred to the tunnel project.

There's no way I can live with that." Melinda turned away again to gaze outside. Her face conveyed concern and frustration, and I recalled Cadence mentioning driving truth and greater purpose.

"You don't think you might find some redeeming value in it? Or maybe a greater purpose in applying your skills and experience to it?" I asked.

She turned back toward me. "The tunnel is an evil distraction. Sleight-of-hand on a global stage."

I hadn't expected to have the uneasiness I had just expressed to Cadence echoed by someone else before the New Q even started. I confessed to her that I had been assigned to the tunnel project too, although I did not mention my own trepidation about it. "We need to talk," I added.

"No point. I'm leaving TFD to look for *meaningful* work." Melinda turned again to look outside.

She should not leave, I thought. TFD needed her. I wanted her on our project team. It may have been because her suspicions matched my own. It may have been because she looked intelligent, unpretentious and confident. Had she really looked familiar to me earlier? Or did she look like someone I felt comfortable approaching? Since we had just met, I chose the most generic, impersonal argument I could think of to persuade her to reconsider.

"Vetting was rigorous for the tunnel team. Senior execs had to approve, so you have a solid rep. Good advancement potential if you stay," I said. Then I tried to be funny, adding "Hey, there's always light at the ..."

"End of the tunnel? Ha! And then I can return to *more* pointless things like augmented reality."

"AR is a positive for us ... you, me, everyone. Can trigger insight." I reassured her.

"Oh, please. Do you work in Sales? We've invested so much in trying to 'augment' reality. I've been drowning in that bullshit for nearly a year on Waldon's team. I've found I have no use for it. You want to see things differently? Use your imagination."

I realized that she would likely know more about AR than I did, given her time on Waldon's team. "Sounds like you'd prefer your reality be left unaltered."

"If you're going to augment reality, at least do something useful," she said.

"Ah! What would be useful for you?" I asked.

"Show me what the hell I should care about and why. Show me the insights ... the *epiphanies* that I keep missing. Anyway, if we could augment reality *that* way, then I would probably find it useful."

"I like that. What should we call it?"

"Wow. That's important," she said in a manner conveying that she felt naming the technology was, in fact, not important.

"The right name can sometimes energize the team or help them focus."

"Okay. How about *perspicacious* reality?" she offered. I nodded, wearing a pensive expression.

"Fortunately we have a marketing department to help with naming," I said.

"Oh dear. The time. Gotta go," she said, appearing to feign urgency.

"Please don't go. I was trying to be funny. My timing ..."

"Sucks."

"Right. If only there were someone like *you* on the tunnel team to expose it for what it is."

"Someone else can do that, I'm sure," she said while checking her pockets for something.

"Hey, other people might jump ship too. If everybody jumps ship, there will be no one to steer the boat toward the right dock ... the right goal."

"Oh, please." Melinda stood up and slung her bag over her shoulder.

"At least wait until after we've heard what the execs have to say about it this morning. And you should wait until we've met with the rest of the tunnel team today, face to face. That way you'll get a sense ... *we'll* get a sense ... of what's possible here. Melinda, there may be something very important we need to do ... something critical to work toward ... to apply ourselves to. I really think you should talk with the rest of the tunnel team before you decide. Maybe your greater purpose here is to reveal the evil distraction aspect to the world."

She paused, looking down at me with a blank expression, then took a breath and sedately said, "Very well. I will postpone my decision until the end of the day. If I do wind up deciding to stay with TFD on the tunnel team, it will only be to expose it for the unpardonable drain on humanity that it is."

"Good decision to stay," I said, reassuringly.

"*Postponing* decision," she corrected.

"Yes. Sorry. Postpone. Decision."

"And if I stay, my profile may help ensure we don't miss an epiphany on this one," she added.

Somehow I felt comfortable risking another attempt at humor.

"Your profile? With the ponytail? I don't think so."

"I meant my professional profile and experience as a research scientist and ... wait a minute ... are you deriding my physical appearance?"

"Now, Melinda, I'm sure you're aware that ponytails are considered 'retro' these days. And you're not wearing ... you're not following current fashion trends for someone your age."

"My age?"

At that point, I deeply regretted both my ponytail comment and saying the words "your age." Melinda appeared to me to be late thirties to early forties in terms of age. Not wanting to risk offending her, I went for the lower end.

"Like ... thirty ... something?" I offered, and she took a moment before responding.

"Accepted. Great impression of a deer in headlights, by the way."

"I *like* ponytails. I mean, I like *your* ponytail. I mean ... God, I'm an idiot."

"Okay. Nice meeting you," she said as she stood and slung her bag over her shoulder.

"Wait. New Q doesn't start for nearly an hour. More coffee?"

"Lonely, are we?"

"We could talk about our project objectives and methodology, in case you decide to stay."

"Sure. I'll just go gather the others condemned to our miserable team."

"If you leave now, no telling what evil agent of global distraction might sit down here before I've finished my omelet."

Melinda retrieved her coat and folded her arms around it,

pressing it to her chest. She stood with her head tilted slightly to one side, making eye-contact for a few seconds as though needing to contemplate before responding.

"As TFD's 'key pundit for next-best-action on leading-edge biomedical technology adoption', won't it embarrass you to be seen consorting with a retro?" Melinda said, adding continuous air quotes while she recited my punditry label oratorically. I recognized it from a recent article quoting me on a biomed topic.

"Interesting," I said, leaning back in my chair, slowly lifting my hands up behind my head, "So you're familiar with my work? My role? My consorting?"

"Oops. Well, now you're on to me. Yes, I've read a couple of your reports. Remarkably insightful, actually. I mean that."

"Thank you, Melinda. That means a lot to me." It really did mean a lot.

"Tell me, Connor, what does your insight point to right now for next-best-action?" Melinda inquired as she put on her coat.

"I would like to experience ponytail reality, please."

She smiled before responding. "So perspicacious," she said, "but I gotta go. Meeting someone at Gyre before the quarterly."

We gave each other a quick wave as she turned and walked toward the lobby door. As I watched her gracefully weaving between other people wandering through the breakfast area and lobby, I hoped I'd get to talk with her again later that day, either at the Gyre Ventures tower, where the TFD quarterly meeting would be held or, perhaps, later that evening at the company dinner.

As Melinda disappeared from my view, someone put their hand on the back of the vacant chair. I looked up to see a thin, intense, clean-shaven face, with arched eyebrows and mostly gray hair. It was an unhappy face, I thought ... the face of someone who must have spent years regretting something he had done, perhaps agonizing over that particularly unfortunate day he had used a pitchfork to ... well, at that point I realized it was the face of Mars Janssen.

CHAPTER 3

Wombat

"Ah! Mister Farrell. How fortunate. I am sure you recognize me," Mars said as he carefully seated himself in the chair Melinda had occupied, then continued, "Did you receive my text? We must talk about the tunnel project."

"Well, yes, but I'm afraid I can't talk about any proprietary ..."

"Please," Mars interrupted, tittering, "We are all connected, all twisted together in spite of each of us being self-absorbed. We are all paranoid. Each of us. No?"

I stared blankly at him for a moment, not sure where he was going with that.

"I did not come here to threaten you," he continued, "but if you will not speak with me, unfortunate things may happen to others whom you know."

"'Unfortunate things'? Gosh, nothing threatening about that.

What do you want from me?"

"As you may recall, I worked for TFD not so long ago. I left for other work in Europe. Now I find myself back in America, focusing attention on the Gravity Train."

Mars just sat quietly, looking at me for a few seconds as though waiting for a reaction. I obliged, saying, without enthusiasm, "Welcome back."

"So," he resumed, "you are now working for Waldon Perry. They must have pulled you in to gain more credibility. You have a reputation, it seems, for being objective. Apolitical."

"I report to someone else, but Waldon owns the tunnel project ... the Gravity Train project ... and I'll be team lead on that. Are you in Waldon's org?" I assumed Mars was back working for TFD.

"Waldon's organization? No, I am not working for TFD. The Gravity Train is just a 'wombat' ... a waste of money, brains and time." Mars took a look around at those who were standing or sitting nearby before continuing. "There will never be a New York to Paris tunnel. No one in a position to approve or fund such an operation is dull-witted enough to believe it is economically attractive, let alone safe ... or somehow immune to disaster. Disaster on a global scale would be the only possible result. No? Tell me, why would anyone consider such a thing? It is an interesting question, I think."

"And here you are in America, focusing your attention on the Gravity Train," I said, melodramatically. "Why would you come back here to work on something you think is a waste of money, brains and time?" I asked.

"The more interesting question, as I mentioned, is *why* it is being considered," Mars responded, sounding a bit irritated.

A man arrived at our table at that moment, wearing a beige raincoat over a business suit and tie. He stood with his raincoat pressing against the table's edge, clearly intending some interaction but not yet speaking, holding a partly eaten cheese pastry in one hand.

"Oh my goodness. Detective Burke. You were not expected," said Mars with polite formality.

"Thought I'd find you here," said Burke, stuffing the last lump of pastry into his mouth.

"Are you now ready to stop dithering and let me clarify my motives?" Mars said in a more familiar manner.

"First," Burke answered while wiping his face and hands with a paper napkin, "convince me you're not just trying to distract my team."

"If distraction is my objective, then have I not already achieved huge success?"

Burke snorted and look annoyed. "It won't be long, you know. Investigators on both sides of the Atlantic have practically ensured your indictment for grievous bodily harm on a massive scale."

"Investigators so eager to vilify me, I marvel at the political subversion of their principles on a massive scale," replied Mars.

"We'll see. We'll see," Burke replied, nodding. Then, after staring at me for a moment, he asked, "Don't I know you?"

"I don't think so," I said, anxiously.

"He is with TFD. Why don't you go to the TFD corporate meeting today, Detective? Perhaps you can round up all two or three hundred of them for questioning," Mars suggested, wryly, while Burke continued to stare at me.

Then Burke turned back toward Mars. "Might happen, smart-ass," he snapped, tossing his crumpled napkin onto the table and turning back to give me another look as he left.

"What the hell is going on?" I asked Mars.

"You should look away. Ignore it. Don't let this bother you," Mars deflected. "It has to do with some work I did while in Norway ... neural implant experiments."

I'd heard from someone that Mars had started working at a private research firm shortly after leaving TFD. "Must be that 'sub-atomic entanglement' team," I said.

"Yes. Very good," Mars began, slowly, smiling. "The idea comes from postulations by an interesting research team in Norway. Trondheim Forviklinger Fast they call themselves. TFF is the acronym. Only one letter different from our beloved TFD! They made analogies from sub-atomic particle entanglement to the broader world we can more easily experience, moving to interdependencies of components of nature ... weather, microbes, plants, animals, humans. We are all entangled, they say."

"Why are you being investigated?" I asked.

"There was a bad motive in the work at TFF. I did what I thought best."

"That guy mentioned 'grievous bodily harm'. What did you do?"

"It is a stretch of meaning at best," said Mars, "It will not result in indictment. If one does a bad thing ... an unlawful thing ... in order to prevent something much worse ... should we punish them?"

"I don't know what 'thing' you're talking about, but in any case, you're making a big assumption."

"And that is … ?"

"That you're capable of making an objective determination of which thing would be worse, as well as your apparent assumption that there was no *legal* pathway to stop that really bad thing you claim to have prevented."

"We must find some time later to talk," Mars said, standing abruptly.

"Wait! Explain your threat. What about those 'unfortunate things' …?"

"Later," Mars interrupted and quickly left the breakfast area.

CHAPTER 4

The News

For a few years on either side of the start of the new millennium, there was much predictive speculation on what changes we would see in the world in the 21st century, covering a wide and disparate range of themes: fewer wars; more wars; less hunger; more hunger; the end of the world; the saving of the world via miraculous technologies or deities; the Internet enabling the connection and cooperation between all humankind and cultures; the Internet reinforcing isolationism and legitimizing extreme enmity on a global scale; new technologies and global cooperation combining to ensure all of humanity has access to an adequate supply of clean water; clean water replacing oil as a driver of greed, international conflict and war.

Predictions continue, with increasing negativity, with increasing uncertainty. Yet most of us are still compelled to follow world events, and we seek out the latest predictions. After Mars left, I decided to check that morning's news before heading out to the New Q. I ignored an invitation appearing in the upper right of my smarts for a trial engagement of the *You Always Knew You Were Right! - Morning Edition* narrowcast. Instead I dubblinked while looking directly at the logo for *Know Doubt with Don Dander*, which was my go-to morning news and analysis source at the time.

The *Know Doubt* host, Don Dander, suddenly appeared as though seated at my table in the unoccupied chair. Don's simulated presence was a bit ridiculous, since the technology was not yet refined enough to make it reasonably realistic without the use of a mirror-screen. There was a way to override it and go with a flat, translucent image on the lenses, but it was too much trouble, requiring me to dubblink at several different target images in series. After a few seconds of background music while Don appeared to be shuffling and selecting views on several small screens on the table surface, his amiable, gray-haired image looked directly at me and spoke the usual greeting.

"Good morning, Connor! Thanks for engaging with me again. Always a pleasure."

The news items from Don included mention of a new vaccine showing promise toward providing immunity to the *Lapitunkeva* virus thawed from a melting iceberg in the Barents Sea, near Svalbard, a few years ago. While that particularly dreadful virus had not yet spread to a significant level in the population, the fact that it was nearly always fatal led to fast investment in related medical research.

Other news stories that morning covered such things as new

applications for molecular weaving, an imminent star collision that was detected occurring about eight thousand light-years away in our galaxy, and a warning about malfunctioning be-mod "wearies". The warning related to an unusual malfunction in someone's behavior-modification wearables that caused him to dance through the streets of London, violently shoving and slapping other pedestrians while singing in Italian. He stopped when police deactivated all his wearable devices. It was reported that the cause of that be-mod glitch is still being investigated.

Don Dander closed his morning overview by mentioning that, while scientists assured the star collision was beyond the range where we would need to worry about life on earth being wiped out by gamma-ray bursts, there were "those who point to *another* imminent threat to life on Earth." Don then held up a flat screen in front of his face to segue to a live broadcast from Liz Fedorova, a frequently referenced on-the-scene reporter in the area. Liz stood before a crowd of people who were chanting something unintelligible on the steps of a building, which I recognized as the entrance to the Gyre Ventures tower.

"Good morning, Don," she began, "as you can see, behind me is a good-size crowd … easily more than fifty people … protesting the proposed Gravity Train project that would link New York City with Paris via tunnel. One of the protesters explained to me a minute ago that they chose this location in front of the Gyre Ventures building because the TFD corporation will be holding an important meeting here today. TFD, a technology research and consulting firm previously known more widely as 'The Fifth Dentist', was recently added into a complex ecosystem of corporate and government entities working to make the Gravity Train …

more commonly known as 'the tunnel' ... a reality."

It was a shock to me to hear her say "TFD" and "The Fifth Dentist" in the context of reporting on a protest rally. I began to zone out a bit, staring at the caption on my smarts that read: *Elizaveta Fedorova – reporting LIVE from angry NYC tunnel protest.*

Angry. It was an *angry* protest scene, with signs visible in the background reading "Stop the Terrible Tunnel!"... "NO to further violation of our planet!" ... "WTFD?!?" ... and so forth. As I read the signs and observed the irate crowd, it occurred to me that I would have to walk through those protesters in a few minutes to get to the TFD New Q meeting.

The Gravity Train was initially treated by the mainstream media as an outrageous proposal to build a tunnel between two distant cities on the Earth, probably running under an ocean, at an inclination steep enough so that a train in the tunnel would, literally, *fall* from its starting city to its destination. In other words, the train would be gravity-powered. After a few weeks of news updates, op-ed analyses and comedic parodies of the concept, a group of scientists and engineers from several countries developed a proposal for what they deemed a plausible implementation of such a train. The idea was to build the tunnel under the Atlantic Ocean, connecting New York City to Paris. Some scientific and engineering references were cited to help build confidence that we could build such a tunnel ... over 100 miles below the ocean floor at the mid-point ... with "reasonable" safety for train passengers and, ideally, for everyone else on the planet. Diplomats in both the US and France began meeting on the topic, and the US Senate Committee on Environment and Public Works began working on a Gravity Train funding proposal. Now several of us at TFD, myself included, were about to begin work on assessing both the feasibility of the project and the associated risks.

"The issues behind the anger are numerous," Liz continued, "ranging from risk of catastrophic seismic disturbances resulting from tunneling that deeply into the earth, to the huge investment required for the tunnel's construction, placed for the most part on the shoulders of the taxpayers."

"Thank you, Liz, and we'll 'no doubt' have updates later in the day. I'm Don Dander, and thank you for choosing *Know Doubt*." Don, whom I'm certain was not an actual human but a digital avatar, thusly concluded the program.

Finally having an opportunity to finish breakfast and drink my coffee, I did so while pondering that news reporters were likely to focus on the plausibility that TFD … or any consultancy for that matter … could be completely objective when evaluating the Gravity Train's feasibility and safety. Many believed that artificial intelligence could enable certainty through complete objectivity of analysis, by removing the subjective human element from required mathematical and algorithmic rigor. Complete objectivity would, theoretically, enable much higher confidence levels for decisions, even taking mankind to the brink of absolute certainty about what the future held. Dozens of major studies had been performed by prestigious universities, think-tanks, government-funded research facilities and corporate development labs throughout the world, exemplified by the *Progressive Equitable Suasion* work published in late 2028.

Over the last few years, some ideas for purely objective algorithms surfaced at industry conferences. Perhaps there could be a consumer offering, like a brain implant enabled for mass distribution. It might be publicly positioned as "insight enhancing" or something similar. Potential marketing tag lines were tossed around, like "Acumen Assurance" and "Experience Perfect Discernment", which might also play into naming of offerings or promotional material. Along with all of that, I noticed what I believed to be increasing evidence of disturbing ulterior motives.

My apprehensions about TFD's integrity began to surface several months earlier when our own study of the feasibility of pure objectivity was proposed and commissioned by its founder, Ansell Beckmann, who was still our CEO at the time. Astrid, the senior executive leading the Early Human Intention division, asked me to lead the internal team and to present the results to her and the other senior executives prior to taking results to Beckmann.

The net conclusion of the study was that there existed no plausible path to "certainty" that ultimately relied upon a human core of logic. All assumptions, rules, processing logic, programming, mathematical deductive bases ... all of that is subject to human assumptions, sensory and knowledge limitations, personal memories and subconscious proclivities. Therefore nothing conceived, designed or built by humans could enable pure objectivity in answering a question or predicting an outcome, nor enable certainty in validating any decision. At least that was the conclusion of everyone on our team, who, being humans, could not be certain of anything.

One of the reviewing execs, Robert Svarog, then Senior VP of Cognitive Certainty, was not happy with the implications of the study.

"Fine. This goes nowhere else. Beckmann can't see this. Understood?" Svarog announced while sitting with his arms folded, glaring at me from across the conference table.

"Thank you, Connor," said Astrid, "good work by you and your team. Laudable analysis. I think Robert's point is that we don't want to defuse ... or veer from accepting ... some potentially valuable contracts now being considered by Ansell based on the COVEn prototype. We would be bringing a lot of new business into TFD, fueling expansion."

Turning and addressing the others in the room, Astrid continued, "We have just seen some good work presented. It was based upon the best available information and expertise, but it is not likely comprehensive enough to warrant avoidance of significant work along those lines. We stand a chance to learn much more from larger scale efforts. As far as taking this to Ansell goes, I'm afraid the timing is just not optimal."

"So, we won't ever show this to Ansell?" I asked, having trouble with their direction.

"Over my dead body!" was Svarog's response.

At that point, I resolved to get the analysis to Ansell Beckmann somehow.

I had the highest admiration for Astrid, but to hide or destroy the work felt like political manipulation and conspiracy. Early the next morning, I discreetly left a printed copy of our study on Ansell's desk before he arrived at the office. Ansell announced his retirement a few days later, and Svarog took over as CEO. The timing of Ansell's retirement roused a suspicion on my part that it had something to do with our study. Our conclusions may have diminished the potential for lucrative follow-on expansion based upon TFD's Cognitive Objectivity Validation Engine (COVEn) technology and related patents, I thought, or maybe there was some other reason Ansell left.

◊   ◊   ◊

After sucking all of my prior angst into the New Q event morning, I managed to summon the fortitude required on my part to begin the therapeutic exercises of standing up, sorting my wrappers, napkin, plate, utensils and empty coffee cup into appropriate containers ... and walking.

As I left the hotel, I resolved to walk at a quick pace and go directly to the auditorium where the main session would be starting. The Gyre Ventures building was only about four blocks away, and I hoped the walk would help me brace myself for whatever protest anger awaited. I assured myself everything would be okay.

CHAPTER 5

The Walk

Once outside, I turned right to walk northward along 3rd Avenue. "The shady side," I said to myself with intentional irony, since the overcast sky nullified notion of sun and shade. Thick with pedestrians, the wide sidewalk ahead was like a channel for flowing liquid, the humanoid fluid on the right-hand side moving generally in the direction I faced, while to my left the flow was mostly toward me, passing behind me after reaching the point of closest proximity. On another level, the approaching humans were like events in time, I thought, flowing from distant future to imminent, to now, to happening just a moment ago, to distant past. While events passed on the left, intentions progressed on the right. Immediate intentions nearest me, long-term goals out ahead, forgotten dreams were somewhere behind.

The tradition in American cities of tending toward the right when encountering traffic, vehicular or human, reduced the number of accidental collisions, and it allowed the comfort of being surrounded by those with similar logistical objectives. In this day and age, that tradition was especially valuable since nearly every person preferred to be insulated from the immediate, shared reality.

Now that advanced multi-sense technologies could be more easily obtained for personal use, their proliferation, particularly in metropolitan areas, was extensive. Indeed, most people I knew were using them regularly, although I had not yet joined the club. To me, the generation of sensations of touch, smell and taste represented a multi-sense distraction. Combined with visual and sonic distractions provided by more common smarts, the multi-sense extensions created a plethorization of insulating or distracting stimuli for each individual using them. Those people using multi-sense technologies were almost non-present wherever they actually were. They were not aware of where they were, in effect, but instead they experienced a personal sensory reality that was ... elsewhere.

Even without multi-sense tech, today's smarts could be quite isolating. For example, there was rarely any eye contact made between people passing each other on the sidewalk. While some will point out that eye contact between strangers was rare in the city, even well back into the previous century, that behavior had been strongly reinforced in recent years due to the widespread use of smart eyeglasses and smart contact lenses, now categorically referred to as smarts. Smart goggles were also used by some, typically young people. Nearly everyone on the street that morning was wearing smarts, I'm quite certain. As a result, each was experiencing a personal isolated reality.

Besides my trouble getting contact lenses on and off, in and out, I preferred eyeglasses since they made it easier to select an item from a presented menu of choices by staring at the item and dubblinking, which would register the wearer's choice via triangulation of the pupil or iris orientation on their eyeballs, simultaneous with detecting two rapid blinks of the eyelids ... a dubblink. The contact lens technology, not yet as refined, required visually swiping choices left or right as they were presented serially, or you could speak the choice aloud if you wore the optional nano-phone necklace or nose ring or whatever.

Pedestrians were completely absorbed in watching and listening to factional morning news shows, sports, music videos, reading financial reports and texts from friends, monitoring personal health data readouts from their devs, be they micro-devices, nano-devices or other wearables showing heart-rate, blood pressure, oxygen and cholesterol levels, skin temperature, breathing rate, step count and so forth, typically color-coded to indicate at a glance whether the metric was good (green), border-line (yellow) or potentially problematic (red). Those pedestrians were barely aware that there were other people near them, yet they still retained a basic sense of proximity that prevented most accidents. Some smart eyeglasses displayed warning lights or provided audible tones via microdevs in the temples of the frames in order to warn of approaching vehicles and other pedestrians who approached quickly on a "collision course."

As I scanned the crowd before me, I noticed everyone's tag was blocked, which was fairly normal for the city. In the city, people usually blocked tagging of themselves except for those people they had specifically allowed to see their tag ... typically their family and friends, sometimes co-workers. I recently heard that there were new apps about to be made available that could provide additional awareness functions. For example, an enhanced facial recognition capability could trigger a flashing red indicator or a warning vibration in one's wearables if the face of someone you did *not* want to encounter was detected. You need only load an image of that person and classify them as "avoid" in your personal contact list. Of course, that assumes the person was not significantly altering their appearance with ammu or pararen.

I saw many people that morning wearing active mood makeup ... "ammu"... that decorated or covered part of their faces and sometimes the skin on other parts of their bodies. Ammu, in my opinion, had evolved from use as a means of getting attention toward being used to *deflect* attention, perhaps toward disguising oneself. The idea, of course, is still to have the sparkling ammu paint applied in such a way that the active color changes or varying brightness or movement of the little sparkling grains in the ammu enhance attractive facial features or minimize less attractive ones. But when most or all of someone's face is covered by ammu, it seems to me that the wearer wants their identity to be hidden.

An adjunct to ammu is the use of the pararen fashion accessories or "dring" as they are more often called now. I observed many people walking by on the street that day who used ammu also wearing a pullover jacket or fleece with a dring print or rendering on their chests. Sometimes it was the face of an artist or entertainer, sometimes a political leader. Sometimes they wore a copyrighted "standard person" face on their chests, intended to represent their role in life or whom they wished to be ... an executive, a surgeon or a farmer for example … sometimes just a contented-looking person, sometimes an angry or dangerous-looking person. Dring faces typically had a repeating cycle, two or three seconds long, in which the facial expression would change slightly, then revert back to the base expression. On that day in Manhattan the pervasiveness of both ammu and dring was surprising to me. Clearly there had been a recent surge in usage.

As I walked along, I remembered that when I was a kid, my grandfather, a good-natured, thoughtful guy whom I called Pop-Pop, told me he thought some people had an "eyeglass personality". Those people would behave differently, according to Pop-Pop, when they wore their glasses. He said that sometimes they seemed to be more serious when they wore glasses, sometimes more focused (pun intended), sometimes more distant or less empathetic. That was, of course, back in the time before cybernetic enhancements had been built into eyeglasses, so the people Pop-Pop talked about were wearing glasses mainly to *improve their vision!* Some people still wear glasses for correcting their vision, but I assume that may end soon, given recent advances making laser surgery and intraocular lenses more effective and less expensive, as well as nano-technological progress in biological rejuvenation at a molecular level. Nowadays, I thought, it is impossible *not* to have an eyeglass personality. The information, entertainment and social interaction streaming in to people on their smarts led to extreme distraction and a kind of virtual isolation from the real world surrounding them.

My thoughts then drifted briefly to my mother. When I was a kid I noticed that my mother seemed to handle stress quite easily when she was wearing one of her mother's aprons. Grandma's aprons seemed to allow my mother to be much calmer than usual, so she had an "apron personality." I doubted many people wore aprons to feel calm.

As I approached the Bureau of Economic Certainty building, with its ostentatious, brass BEC logo just above the contrastingly austere, gray double-door entrance, I realized there was just another block to go. A young woman pushed open a door and quickly exited the BEC building without looking to her left. I may have been walking too closely to the granite steps just outside those doors, causing us to nearly collide, which caused her to fumble and drop her notepad just in front of me. We both bent down to retrieve it simultaneously, and our eyes met as we stood up. "Good morning! How are you?" I said cheerily, not expecting any response. The woman looked confused for a moment, but then, stepping further away from the door she said, "I'm doing good. I'm very content." She then proceeded to pass behind me and merge into the pedestrian flow heading southward.

The "very content" comment was familiar to me, as many people had begun using it as a means to convey that they sought no further interaction. Several weeks earlier, one of the popular morning "prep for the day" news narrowcasts suggested ways to avoid further conversation in random public encounters. One of those suggestions was to say that you were "doing good" and "very content" in response to "how are you?" or "what's good?" or "devs all green?" or any similar inquiry. The implication of being very content, theoretically, was that there would be no reason for anyone to think you might be seeking a new friendship or romantic experience. There was simply nothing anyone could offer you that you actually needed or wanted. That news segment ended with a close up of the host, smiling into the camera saying "I'm doing good. I'm very content." The response quickly took on an off-putting and hackneyed quality once the origin and probable intent became common knowledge. Walking on, I managed to continue not thinking about the protesters awaiting me.

After walking just another block, I found myself standing hesitantly, facing the imposing polished granite and glass-like polycarbonate entryway of the Gyre Ventures building on the corner of 52nd Street, trying to tap into the feeling of exciting potential that the TFD corporation's quarterly meetings had instilled in me in the past, but on that morning, it was only doubt, disillusionment and fear that I felt. I noticed a fair amount of traffic noise while crossing the 52nd Street intersection, although bicycles outnumbered cars about two to one. Fewer than half the cars had actual humans driving, which caused horn-honking to be sharply reduced over the levels heard a decade ago. The corner was busy with most people walking quickly, frequently nudging or brushing against someone else as they were distracted by their smarts and wearables. Many held a cup of coffee … artisanal, nitrogen-infused, cold-brewed, French-pressed, Turkish, Americano, classic, fika, or some other variant. No social interaction. People moved independently, silently, with no visible nods or gestures toward anyone else. Although some people may have been communicating via apps in their smarts, the overall observable ambiance felt solemn and funereal.

Then, of course, there were the protesters. As I surveyed them, I allowed myself to acknowledge my fear. I wanted to avoid physical or verbal contact with them at all cost. While there were other businesses in the Gyre Ventures tower, I assumed they might suspect I was with TFD, or perhaps they would harass me on the mere *possibility* that I was with TFD. I had nothing against the protesters, but I genuinely feared that any interaction with them would be difficult and unpleasant.

I had expected to be accosted by one or more people who would ask me if I worked for TFD. However, I had not foreseen being approached by a news reporter. As I stood sizing up possible approaches to the main entrance door, Liz Fedorova suddenly appeared right in front of me, holding her unnecessarily large microphone at her side like a weapon. It was just too much for me to handle. The realization that I was part of "the news" … part of live on-the-street coverage of civil disobedience … was numbingly overwhelming.

"Hey there! Devs green? Are you with TFD?" she confidently inquired.

After a few seconds of uncomfortable silence, I managed to say, meekly, with minimal active brain function, "I'm doing good. I'm very content."

"Ha! Good one! Okay, I have you as Connor Farrell. May I call you Connor?" Then, raising up the microphone, she said "sound check."

At that moment, I realized I had forgotten to block my tag. I sensed the entire universe bending, folding and withdrawing itself from any connection to my being. My world was coming to an end.

CHAPTER 6

The Lift

"So, Connor, you're with TFD, right?" At that moment I recalled my tag also identified me as a Research Consultant with TFD. Perfect, I thought, sarcastically. Liz peered at me with a curious expression, as though sensing that I had been sucked into some alternate dimension. I took a deep breath and resolved to forge ahead through the immediate horror.

"Yes," I admitted.

Liz seemed relieved and placed her hand on my shoulder, gently turning me to face around toward the camera, which was about the size and shape of a pint of whiskey and being held by a young man. His gray sweatshirt featured a dring standard-person variant called "Shocked Man," which continuously replayed a few seconds of a disturbing, horrified reaction on a young man's face. The camera was strapped to the man's hand and arm. Behind me, as I would later learn, was a clear view of the Gyre Ventures tower entrance and several picket signs. "Ready?" asked Liz. I nodded, and she began.

"Liz Fedorova here this morning at the Gyre Ventures tower with Connor Farrell, who is a Research Consultant with the TFD corporation, also known as The Fifth Dentist. Behind us you can see the protest rally triggered by TFD's involvement in the Gravity Train project. Connor, what can you tell us about TFD's role in this massive global project?"

I wanted to handle the interview well. I really did.

Apparently, noticing I had not responded, Liz gave me another prompt. "Are you personally involved with the Gravity Train work?"

"Not yet," I managed to say, "but I will be starting to work with that team tomorrow."

"Tell us, what will TFD be doing?"

"Well, TFD is about creating, validating, marketing and monetizing certainty," I began, drawing from TFD's new corporate mission statement.

"Help me here, Connor," Liz interrupted, "What does that really mean in the context of the Gravity Train?"

Part of my high school "career day" presentation popped into my head, and I just went with it. "What if there were a source for certainty on the best decision for you in choosing a school or a career or a job or a place to live ... or even a friend or life partner? What would it take for you to trust the source ...?" Detecting a look of confusion on Liz's face, I stopped at that point and tried to say something specific to the Gravity Train.

"So," I resumed, "TFD would help our government decide

whether or not to go ahead with the tunnel project. We'll evaluate all the concerns ... all the risk areas. That's what we focus on in TFD. Process and technology to move toward the highest confidence level in decisions, as well as quantifying the value of that improved confidence." I probably should not have mentioned risk areas.

"What about you, Connor? What's you're assigned role at TFD?"

"My role is usually that of ensuring an objective viewpoint. The idea is to explore or investigate things with no preconceived assumptions, no target conclusions, no politically right or wrong outcome. I just try to work with the team to bring the right information sources and experts together so we can objectively evaluate an idea, its feasibility and its potential value."

"A lot of people would argue that the Gravity Train project has been totally devoid of any objectivity up to this point. Many say it's all hype and political posturing." Liz then held the mike up to me for a reaction to her statement.

"I've seen or heard some of that in the news, yes. Again, we at TFD will be doing our best here to objectively offer our take on the Gravity Train's potential and, of course, the associated risks." I looked downward at that moment, regretting mentioning risks again.

"Let's talk about those risks. Anything that worries you? Keeps you up at night?" Liz tilted her head left and right. I began to worry that I was already saying too much, since I was not an official spokesperson for TFD on Gravity Train ... at least not yet.

"Well, I start on it tomorrow, like I said. So, I really can't comment on that. Right now, I only know what's been on the news. You know as much as I do today. Maybe more." I shrugged and took a small step back to suggest I wanted to leave.

"Connor, thank you and good luck with your work! Good luck getting into the building too!" Liz managed a little laugh that sounded genuine.

After giving her camera operator the usual disturbing "we're done" hand signal, as though a decision had just been made to behead someone, Liz grabbed my arm and asked if I would be willing to do another interview in a few days. I told her I needed to get permission from my boss. She handed me an old-fashioned, printed business card and asked me to call her.

I turned and faced the tower entrance. The Gyre Ventures tower itself looked different somehow. While I couldn't single out any particular detail that had changed since my last visit here three months ago, the tower, especially the approach and entryway, seemed eerily malevolent that morning. While contemplating that, I realized that not only was my tag not blocked from the protesters, but that they had also likely seen me interviewed just now by a reporter on the scene. My hope had been that I'd be able to sneak in around them, but that hope had now all but vanished. I tried to draw strength from a sense of convergence, a sense of common purpose, of camaraderie, of being part of the family of other TFD employees.

There in Manhattan, I felt none of that. Instead I felt scattered, isolated in crowds, rushed, vulnerable and naïve. I was forced to acknowledge the notion of logistical convenience for the aggregate. With TFD employees largely scattered across North America and Europe, the New York City area enabled extensive travel options. Although TFD did lease some office space at Gyre

Ventures, I couldn't help but wonder if it might be better to hold these quarterly meetings in a small town, perhaps upstate in Ithaca, home of their original corporate headquarters where they still maintained a small research team. In a small town, a company event drawing over 200 employees to the same place at the same time would have allowed co-workers to encounter each other as they approached the meeting site. That sense of common purpose would no doubt be energizing, I thought, and I had never been to Ithaca.

I realized I was avoiding the real issue. I had to walk through the protesters to the building entrance. I began moving forward with deliberate strides, calculated to display confidence, drawing upon some ballroom dance lessons I had taken with Cadence to add elements of smoothness and sophistication, convinced in the moment it was the sort of thing that would help me through the crowd. The protesters might simply step aside to clear a path for me. Yes, that should work, I thought.

"Hey! TFD guy!" A man in his mid-forties, a little taller and with broader shoulders than me, wearing a green knit hat, suddenly stepped in front of me, pressing his hand on my chest to stop my advance. "How do you live with yourself? How do you sleep at night when you're a part of this sham? This *bullshit*!"

"Look, I'm not promoting the Gravity Train or anything else," I told him, "I work for a company that does independent research to guide in prioritizing ..."

"Fuck you! 'Independent research'? Give me a fuckin' break. No such thing in this world."

"Wait. No. We really do focus on that. We have for years. We can provide insights and evidence for ..."

Another man who had moved over near me interrupted, "You're a puppet! You're a puppet! Can't you feel them pullin' your strings?"

"No, wait, …" I began to argue.

"Right! Who's payin' you? That's it! You do whatever they want! They're payin' you!" added the man with the green hat.

"No, wait," I began again, adding "we sell objectivity. We're being paid to be objective. We make the most money and get the most contracts by staying objective. That's what TFD does. So TFD will be *evaluating* things, not building or selling or promoting them. It seems like you would *want* us to do that, so that you'll have some analysis you can point to in case there are risks or other concerns that bubble up."

"Concerns that bubble up?" the man now seemed more agitated, "this thing is a deal between a bunch of self-absorbed maniacs tryin' to destroy the whole world! We already got concerns up the wazzoo! You guys should just refuse to even have anything to do with it! Take off your damn smarts and just *look* at it! See it for what it is and walk away! Walk away or do something to kill it!" The man poked my chest with his finger several times as he spoke, hard enough to cause some pain.

"Believe me, it's not my choice of something to work on," I said. "But it's our next assignment. We'll do our best to be objective. I'll promise you that, and that's about all I *can* promise right now. Please let me pass and go inside. Please let *all* the TFD people go inside so we can get to working on this. If *anyone* can give you something to use to support your cause, it's probably going to be us at TFD."

"Oh, so you're like the last resort for us, huh? You're gonna protect us all." said another man who was standing behind me at that point.

The man in the green hat, using a calmer voice, said "Convince me you're gonna do something good."

"Look, I lost the love of my life last August. She passed away a month before we were going to be married," I said. "I feel like she's still with me, everywhere, every day. My work now is all for her. What I do, I do to honor her memory. For something as important as the Gravity Train, it means more than life to me to be honest and ethical and thorough in evaluating the truthfulness of the evidence, the reliability of the science. Her memory ... my love for her drives me forward through the darkest and scariest pathways."

The man paused and just looked at me for a few moments. Then he nodded and held out his hand, introducing himself as Jake. As I shook his hand, he walked me a few steps toward the Gyre Ventures tower entrance, saying, "Sorry for your loss. Maybe she can drive you through that scary tunnel too. Hey, get in there! Do something good! Time to do something good!" Then, turning toward Gyre, Jake shouted, "Let this guy through! Let him go inside! He's gonna do good for us!"

I thanked Jake and propelled myself forward somehow, passing other protesters who politely let me by, carefully stepping over a few who were lying on the ground near the revolving entrance door, finally pushing on the door to get inside even though the door was self-powered and began turning as I approached. Once inside, I walked passed the security detail and crossed the opulent lobby, with its high, arched ceiling skylights and granite planters scattered around the perimeter, harboring shiny green shrubbery and a few clumps of orange and purple flowers. I walked straight ahead toward the bank of elevators, seeing no one familiar, all the while looking forward to the official wrap-up and dispersal at the end of the day.

All four elevators were elsewhere, moving around between other floors. One was moving downward but was currently at the 15th floor, based upon the indicator on the wall. While I waited, I started to think about the odd timing of these quarterlies. The TFD fiscal calendar did not line up to the calendar year, with the end of their fiscal year on January 31st, the financial results for that "4th quarter" being reported today in late February. New Year's Day for the TFD business was February 1st, owing to January being, typically, their strongest month of the year for revenue. When TFD was incorporated back in 2022, founder Ansell Beckmann and the leadership team set the fiscal year in order to "go out with a bang" with anticipated surging of new contracts in January. While their revenue assumptions turned out to be correct, it would have been better, I thought, to line up with solstices and equinoxes.

An elevator arrived, but was overly crowded after a few others waiting near me entered, so I opted to wait for another. Another elevator arrived within just a few seconds of the first one's departure, and it was unoccupied. I entered, comforted by the drone of the ventilation fan. I turned around in the customary fashion to face the open doorway, getting a "how you doin'?" from a man in workman's clothes as he entered and stood next to me, holding a toolbox at his side. As the doors closed, I saw a soft, vaporous reflection of myself on the satiny steel inner surface of the door. I pushed the button for the 35th floor. As the elevator slowly began to ascend, I imagined the image reflected to me was my spirit, my soul, drawn skyward with me through a vertical vacuity, cleared of all obstruction except for the building's roof. I imagined there was no roof. I imagined I could be lifted forever like this, as long as my spirit traveled with me, as long as the fan droned ....

"You're lookin' pretty calm!" the workman proclaimed, waking me out of my self-induced trance. I turned to see him looking at me with a broad, toothy smile. I was not sure how to respond.

He went on. "I saw youse out there with that lady. You know, that cute one on the news a lot. Which she was askin' you about the train tunnel an' all."

"Yeah," I said, reactivating myself, "Wasn't expecting that. Probably sounded like an idiot."

"No way! You did good, I swear. I stopped walkin' by so I could hear the whole thing. And then those other guys in your face *yellin'* after. Man! Tough mornin', heh? You're walkin' into a real mess, if you ask me."

"I expected the protesters to voice their concerns. Their anger caught me off-guard."

"If they started roughin' youse up, I would'a helped. Geez, I forgot to hit twenty-eight." He then found and pushed the button for the twenty-eighth floor on the elevator panel, while I got a mental image of him helping the protesters shove, punch and kick me. "I mean, I would'a stopped 'em. You know?" he clarified.

"Oh. Well, thank you." I checked our progress on the elevator location tracker above the door, noting our relatively slow pace as

54

we were only passing the fifth floor.

"Anyways, I'd still be shakin' from that. You live around here? One of the boroughs?"

"No. Just here for a couple weeks. Work stuff. I live on the west coast."

"No kiddin'. I was just there. Well, end of summer. Huntington Beach."

"Ah. Orange County. Nice area."

"My girlfriend got me to try surfin'." he said, shaking his head.

"Oh? How'd that go?"

"First couple days I could barely get up off my belly. Geez, I mean, I'm pretty strong, right? But it didn't help much. I took lessons. My girlfriend's brother lives out there, and he's real good. Gave me advice, you know? He said it took him years to get good at it. It takes years to get good at anything, he said. By the end of the second week, I was standin' or kneelin' on the whitewaters. I flipped over a lot. Swallowed, like, half the Pacific. Heh? But I had fun. It was beautiful like nothin' I ever seen. My girlfriend … she wants to live there."

There was a soft "ding" noise at that moment, and the elevator doors opened. The location tracker indicated we were at the twelfth floor.

"This you?" he asked.

"No. Going to thirty-five," I said, then noticing his anxious look, I asked him if he was okay.

"Doors opened and no one there," he said, as though that were a reason to be concerned.

"Happens," I said, shrugging my shoulders.

He took a deep breath, and as the elevator doors began to close, he spoke again. "Reminds me of this dream I keep havin' where I open a door, and it's supposed to be my girlfriend. Her name's Rita. But she's not there. There's nobody there, and I just feel so alone, so empty. Like my whole life is empty if she's not there. Rita, she's an angel. She says she loves me more than anything. I love her too, but ... I can't figure out if I'd be a good husband for her, you know? My father says I'd have to be a good one 'cause she deserves it. I guess I need to think about it some more."

At that moment, a memory popped into my head. Years ago, I had been describing to Pop-Pop all the pros and cons I had been contemplating in order to decide whether to move to California to start a new career there. After I'd spent quite a while explaining and rationalizing, he waved his hand at me and gave me a piece of advice. I decided it would be appropriate to share that with the man in the elevator.

"My grandfather told me something once," I began, "He said the really important decisions you make in life are made with your heart, not your brain. Don't go crazy trying to weigh all the options, because if it's really important to you, the answer is already in your heart."

The man looked at me, then looked down at the floor. After a few seconds, he looked up and said "My heart says I should be with her. My heart says maybe I open the door someday, and she won't be there. So I shouldn't wait. Like you found out. I mean, sorry for your loss. But the love of your life might not always be there in the flesh, right? Rita and me should be together. We should move together. Live together. I mean, why the hell not? I'm gonna ask her tonight! We'd be happy out there in California. I might not be the perfect husband on day one, but hey, it takes years to get good at anything, right?"

"Follow your heart." I felt that was a safe response for me to make.

"Yeah. Hey, thanks for sharin' what your grandfather said."

"You're welcome. Funny. I think you're the first person I ever shared that with." He was the first, to the best of my recollection.

"So, you live in California? Like around L.A.?"

"In California but further north. Near San Jose."

"They got surfin' up there? You ever done it?"

"I know people who go surfing around Santa Cruz. About an hour away from my condo. But, no, I've never done it myself."

There had been another "ding" noise as I spoke, and the elevator doors opened again. The progress indicator above the door showed we were at the twenty-eighth floor.

"You gotta try it," he said, "I mean, you live right there."

"Looks like your floor," I said, in case he hadn't noticed.

He took a step outside the elevator and turned back holding his toolbox against the door edge to keep it from closing. "Listen," he said, "while you're here, if you have any trouble with them guys out there, you can ask me, and I'll help you. My name's Wally Packer. I work the building, fixin' this and that."

As we shook hands, I said "I'm Connor Farrell. Appreciate your offer. Might just take you up on that."

"Hey, Connor, we both got stuff to do now. Heh? You gotta figure out the tunnel, and I gotta figure out how to be a married guy in L.A.. Geez, that might take a couple weeks."

"Wally, I wish you all the best," I said. I really liked Wally.

"Like the one guy outside yelled, *time to do somethin' good!*" Wally raised his fist as he quoted the protester, then switched to a wave as he turned to walk away down the hall.

As the doors closed, my reflected spirit returned. I hoped to be lifted even higher.

CHAPTER   7

Font

While only seven floors further up, the rest of the journey seemed longer to me, probably because there was no conversation to fill the time.   Upon arriving at the 35th floor, I walked across a spacious lounge area and started down the main hallway. I walked along glancing to the left and right, noting the familiar and unfamiliar: several private offices (including Waldon Perry's), several semi-private offices, two new conference rooms with seating for twelve or fourteen maybe, and a break-room exuding a pleasing coffee aroma. At the end of the main hallway was an intersecting hallway with an entrance into the lower end of the auditorium. There was also an entrance to the upper rows, but that was on the 36th floor.

As I entered I noticed a few people standing at the back of the auditorium, but it appeared there were a few single seats available.

Of the three possibilities that I noticed, two required me to turn left and head up an incline toward the back of the room. I decided to turn right and head downward toward the stage area in front, thinking that I would cross quickly to the opposite side where I could see an empty seat at the end of the third row. I crossed the front of the room, stepping awkwardly around some boxes, carry-on luggage, holographic projector hardware and a podium before reaching the far side of the auditorium, only to discover that the unoccupied seat had yellow tape across it with "RESERVED!" printed on the tape. It was the exclamation point in particular that convinced me to proceed upward, toward one of the other vacant seats about nine rows back. It was the fifth seat in from the aisle. Sliding in sideways, I caught my foot on a backpack strap, causing me to grab onto the shoulders of a man sitting in front of that row to keep from falling.

"Sorry," I whispered as the man turned around toward me, looking irritated. As I sat down, I heard a familiar woman's voice behind me say "nicely done". I turned to see that it was Melinda, sitting two rows behind me. I was about to say hello, but she turned away from me toward the podium as someone announced "Welcome! Welcome all!"

I turned to face forward and saw a man who looked vaguely familiar at the podium.

"Please be seated. Please be seated. Okay, I think we are short a few seats, so you may need to stand in the back for now. Sorry about that. We'll try to remedy that," the man spoke.

Two or three people called out that there were empty seats next to them and raised an arm to help those in the back find them.

"Welcome! Welcome all!" the man at the podium repeated,

"For those who don't know me, I am Robert Svarog's new Executive Assistant, Harper Golly." There was some polite applause from a scattered few in the audience, while Harper appeared to be working with a device held in his hand. At that moment the man seated to my right, who had been conversing with someone seated further up the row, leaned back in his seat and nudged me asking "are you Connor Farrell?" I turned and recognized the man as someone I had met at a project review in Fort Worth a few years earlier, though I couldn't recall his name. I nodded and offered my hand. As we shook hands, he politely reminded me that he was Randall Hewitt, and then he turned and pointed to Harper.

"Hell, *he* looks more like you 'an *you* do!" Randall exclaimed. I looked back toward the podium and finally realized that Harper Golly looked familiar because he looked surprisingly like me. I decided to put on my smart eyeglasses, realizing that the automated tagging of faces with names might be useful in this situation. As I put on my glasses, Harper began speaking again, "Done! Sorry, but we're ready now. I just had to activate the new CenterPeace engagement blocker to block all network dependent communications and data transfer in the auditorium during our sessions this morning."

After a few groans and other audible expressions of annoyance from the audience, Harper added, "Mr. Svarog wants to ensure your undistracted participation. We'll have a networking break in about two hours, but meanwhile, please sit back and enjoy our opening segment … an award-winning holographic video that Mr. Svarog requested, which I'm sure you'll enjoy."

Since there would be no tagging until the engagement blocker was deactivated, I removed my smarts, and as I did, the lights dimmed and the word *Font* appeared before us, as though formed by glowing gelatin suspended in space. A sound like the continuous ripping of fabric became just barely apparent, then increased in volume to an unsettling level, accompanied by low bass rumblings that shook the floor. The floating *Font* and sound effects faded and were replaced by a scene of a middle-aged man wearing glasses and carrying a black valise, shaking hands with a few young-looking men and women just outside a conference room door. All were dressed in business attire.

"Owen, Owen, Owen," a tall man with a condescending smile began to address the man with the valise, "we do appreciate, as always, hearing different points of view." Several others standing nearby reacted politely, chiming in with things like "oh absolutely", "preesh" and "food for thought".

"It's really all in how you communicate ..." the tall man continued, "the visuals and diagrams you show, the pictures you paint with your words, the words you speak, the words on your charts, the way the words on your charts convey the *special* messages and meanings ... those messages ... insights... those key points you want us to keep in our heads, those insights that we will take to heart and that will motivate us ... pull us ... toward a *new* point of view. Toward decision! Toward conviction! Toward action! A key factor is the font."

There was a pause. Owen twitched and looked confused. "The font?" he asked.

"The font, Owen. The font. The shape of the letters in the words, the style, the rendering, the embellishments ... the *personality* of the characters you employed to deliver your message ... the *history* that we can sense ... that we can *assimilate* ... from each alphabetical element. What were you using? Maybe Helvetica or Arial? Maybe Garamond used for some accent labeling? Too pedestrian! Think of meaning beyond the words and how you might convey that as an *artist*. Grow the faith! *Grow the faith! Reach through the font to touch our souls!*"

The tall man then reached to magnanimously grasp Owen's shoulders adding, in a perfunctory manner, "Our sincere thanks for your analysis and proposal. We'll let you know."

Owen nodded and waved shyly, perhaps a bit hesitantly, as he turned away from the rest and started walking down the hallway behind the others, away from the camera. Someone inquired in a whisper as to whether they should invite Owen to come with the group, but the tall man shook his head, grimacing in a funny way as if it were an absurd suggestion, directing the others the opposite way down the hallway toward the camera. The group passed behind the camera, leaving only Owen visible as he walked away. Then the camera began to follow Owen.

As Owen neared a men's lavatory, he paused and touched the left-hand side of his eye-glass frame, as though checking the time and his remaining schedule for the day. He then turned and entered the lavatory. The camera followed him inside, and the holographic effects provided the illusion that those of us in the auditorium had entered the lavatory with Owen as well. Owen put down his valise near a sink, then bypassed the more modern funnel-shaped urinals and made use of one shaped in the older basin style at the far end of the wall. Owen began talking to himself while standing before the urinal, his voice echoing strangely, beyond the quick expected echo from nearby tile walls, more like reverberation in a much larger space like a deserted museum or cathedral.

"So, it's all about the font, huh? Yeah! I spend two months ... *two months! ...* researching and integrating data and points-of-view, validating my conclusions! *Great* feedback! If only I had known twenty years ago that the *font* was so important, my whole life would be different now. Much more satisfying, I'm sure." Owen mused aloud, with an obvious sarcastic tone.

Upon completion of the task at hand, Owen then backed away to use a sink. As he did, the urinal flushed itself, with a lot of noise of water gushing forth, shortly followed by another noise like a high-pitched, oscillating siren. Owen turned around to see torrents of water overflowing from the urinal and quickly flooding the room. Now breathing heavily, looking confused and stressed, Owen grabbed the valise and was next shown stepping back out into the hallway. Owen looked down at the water, which was flowing out into the hallway from underneath the lavatory door at a surprisingly fast rate, and it was already up to his ankles. He ran back to the conference room, sloshing with each step for the length of the hallway, but the room was now dark and deserted. The entire floor of the building seemed deserted. Owen turned and looked out the windows across the hall, revealing a cloudy evening darkness outside. He appeared to notice and examine his own reflection in the glass, turning his head slightly one way and the other, touching his face here and there. Then Owen looked down, and the hologram view showed water flowing by, nearly reaching his knees.

"Connect to building maintenance!" he shouted to no one in particular, turning away from the window, and in a moment there was a calm, audible response, *"I'm sorry, but the local service is proprietary. Please say the access word now, if you know it."* Owen shouted "aaahh!", but that was not the access word, apparently. He started toward the elevator, splashing with each step, stopping momentarily to examine the room number plate on the wall by the lavatory door. The visual zoomed in on the room number so that those of us watching the video could see clearly the embossed characters "I33-II". Owen then ran toward the elevator about ten yards away, as quickly as he could manage, sloshing through several inches of water. At the elevator, Owen waited a moment for the doors to open, then rushed in shouting "lobby!". After a few seconds, the elevator doors still had not closed. Owen began frantically searching the complicated-looking array of buttons in the elevator, shouting "lobby!" imploringly a few more times, until he found the button in the elevator marked "LOBBY", which he then hit repeatedly with his fist.

While Owen pounded away, the camera's view moved out into the hallway, looking back toward the lavatory. Suddenly, the door to the lavatory flew off, cracking against the window panels across the hallway, a tremendous burst of water behind it. The surge of water caused a wave of maybe four or five feet in depth to move down the hallway toward the elevator with surprising speed. Owen poked his head outside the elevator, apparently curious about the noise, just in time to see a tidal wave of water approaching just a few feet away. Owen pulled back inside and leaned against the wall opposite the doors. "Oh my God! Oh my God!" he cried, his voice breaking pathetically, a close-up view of his face capturing his look of horror and disbelief.

The elevator doors began closing slowly, pausing several times, perhaps having difficulty moving against the large volume of water entering. By the time the doors closed completely, the water inside had risen above Owen's waist. In just a second or two, there was a violent jerking followed by what might have been close to a free-fall for a second, with many narrow columns of water briefly rising a few inches above the surface. Then there was another sharp jolt and another alarm began ringing. The doors opened quickly, dumping the water along with Owen about two feet down to the hallway floor. The elevator had not lined up properly with the floor, perhaps malfunctioning due to the weight of the water. The view shifted to show Owen pouring out onto the floor as though swept down a waterfall. He crawled to the wall opposite the elevator and used the wall for support as he slowly stood, while water continued to gush out of the elevator into the hallway, with some flowing back down into the shaft. While trying to wipe water off his face with his wet sleeve, Owen called "Emergency! Emergency!"

"How may I help you?" asked a synthetic-sounding voice coming from nowhere in particular. Owen, panting, blurted out "Help! Yes! It's flooded! I got flushed! Out of the elevator! It's flooded! It's flooding!".

"I'm sorry, I don't understand," the voice admitted, calmly and with an empathetic quality.

Owen appeared to be looking for something in his pockets as he tried to be more specific, saying "A leak! A leak in the men's room! So much water I can't even believe it! The whole *building* is flooding!"

"You are currently on the 31st floor of the Wavery Foundation building. Is the lavatory leak on that floor?"

"No! It was above this floor! The 33rd floor! Section I."

"Please say the room ID number now, if you know it."

"Yes. It was I33-II. Eye ... thirty-three ... eye ... eye", he repeated slowly to make sure he was understood, while putting on a pair of eyeglasses he had pulled from his pocket. The eyeglasses he wore earlier had apparently been swept away as he poured out of the elevator.

"I'm sorry. I show we have no room ... 'eye thirty-three eye eye'. Is it possible the room ID number is eye thirty-three eleven?"

"No!!!" Owen was now shouting and shaking. "I have a photographic memory! I can see the room ID clearly in my mind! Eye ... thirty-three ... eye ... eye!"

The view shifted upward and zoomed in on a close-up shot of a small video camera mounted in the ceiling, then the view shifted again, as if through that ceiling camera's lens, into a small room somewhere, dimly lit, with some sort of control panel and several screens with views of various rooms and hallways.

I now felt that I was in that room as well, noticing that Owen could be seen in one of the screens above the control panel, sitting on the floor, leaning against a wall, soaking wet. Owen's voice repeating "eye ... thirty-three ... eye ... eye" could be heard, faintly, in that room. Then the camera panned back to reveal a gray-haired man seated in front of the control panel, who began speaking in the same perfectly calm, synthetic-sounding voice that had been addressing Owen.

"Would it be possible for you to check the room ID number?"

"EYE!!! THIRTY-THREE!!! EYE!!! EYE!!!" Owen's face appeared red and contorted on the video screen, drops of water or sweat rolled down his temples and forehead, "EYE!!! THIRTY-

THREE!!! EYE!!! EYE!!!" he shouted again, his voice changing to a strange, gravelly roar. At that point, the man at the control panel looked sadly at Owen on the screen, blinking his eyes a few times. Then he reached over to the screen and touched Owen's face. As he traced a small cross on Owen's forehead with his finger, the screen lit up much brighter. At that moment, the hologram view in the conference room switched so that I felt I was back in the hallway with Owen. There was a thin, bright vertical band of bluish-white light in the wall in front of Owen. As he watched it, the band expanded into an oval shape, and within the oval there appeared an opening in the wall, large enough for a person to step through. Twinkling lights of the city outside began to appear through the hole. Traffic noises now could be heard, faintly.

Owen stood up, and a close-up view of his face showed him looking confused and apprehensive, his face reflecting the bluish-white glow of the opening. As he stood, the color of his face began to shift slowly toward a warm amber. The view shifted to reveal that the light around the opening had indeed changed to a bright golden outline, and the shape was changing from an oval to something more like a goblet or chalice. Water still flowed from the elevator onto the hallway floor, and it had started pouring down from several places in the ceiling as well.

Owen removed his eyeglasses and let them fall to the floor, his mouth slowly forming into a smile. The water accumulating in the hallway started to flow out of the chalice-shaped hole.

The view shifted to show the outside of the building, with a waterfall emanating from the glowing portal in the wall. Back inside, another close-up view of Owen's face revealed an emotional shift toward joy, toward elation, tears flowing down his cheeks, his breathing like heavy sighing. After a few seconds, he cried, "Mom! ... Dad! ... This is the best birthday ever!"

Owen calmly took a few steps forward, leaned through the goblet-shaped hole to be swept out by the gushing water. He fell, silently. The perspective moved outside the building through the opening, shifting downward, so that Owen could be seen falling within a sparkling stream of water until he apparently hit the sidewalk below.

At that moment, the auditorium went dark, and then the stage area filled with small floating headshots of the production crew and cast, tagged with their names and relevant certifications, randomly emphasized with a fluttering increase in brightness.

CHAPTER 8

The Agenda

"That's a keeper!" announced Harper from the podium, followed by a cha-ching sound like an old-fashioned cash register, probably intended to mimic micro-devs that make a similar noise whenever the wearer makes a purchase via their smarts.

"Hey, and I'll tell you where you can keep it," Randall said in a muted voice.

I sat there wondering why that video was chosen to kick off the New Q. Usually there was a guest speaker who would share a heartfelt, inspiring story from a personal perspective. Sometimes they would also show relevant slides or a short video.

I did not feel inspired by the *Font* video.

In fact, it was deeply disturbing to me, adding onto the already depressing dreariness outside. I was reminded of that dreariness as the opaque black roller blind that had been down for the holographic presentation was raised, briefly allowing us to see the view outside. It was sometimes an awe-inspiring view of modern city-scape with the East River and Roosevelt Island partially obscured behind a few tall buildings. On that New Q day, it was a dispiriting, hazy, gray rendering, adding onto the anxieties growing within me since the *Know Doubt* news report, since facing the building from outside with Liz Fedorova interrogating me, since the man called Jake asked me how I could sleep at night. Also, there was something about *Font* that reminded me of nightmares I had frequently as a child.

Fortunately, a white opaque roller screen was quickly lowered to cover the entire view. The day's agenda was then projected onto the roller screen:

10:00 AM – Welcome!

10:10 AM – Robert Svarog, CEO TFD Corporation

10:30 AM – Waldon Perry, SVP Cognitive Certainty

11:00 AM – Dr. Gotama Reddy, Director of Research

11:30 AM – Astrid Ekland, SVP Early Human Intention

12:00 PM – Networking break - (lunch and snacks will be available)

1:30 PM – New Ideas exercise

3:00 PM – Team presentations and discussion

4:30 PM – Closing remarks

4:45 PM – Networking break

6:00 PM – Dinner by Team / Division - (locations to be provided)

"Please offer up your full attention and welcome our esteemed

CEO, Mr. Robert Svarog!" Harper spoke with exaggerated gleefulness. I decided to put my smarts back on. Although there would be no name-tagging until the networking break (when I assumed the engagement blocker would be off), my smarts could still keep a record of what each speaker said, as well as all conversations I had in case there was some reason to reference them later.

Greeted by moderate applause, Svarog walked slowly from behind a partition near the stage to the podium, exuding confidence, wearing casual slacks and a shirt with rolled-up sleeves. Behind Svarog, there was a line graph displayed, showing a five-year history of TFD revenue and net profit with some numbers highlighted. However, the graph was not referenced immediately.

"Never again!" Svarog began to address the attendees from behind the sleek, black podium, "Never again! Never will the populace be mired in a quicksand of doubt as they struggle to make the right choice ... to choose the right direction for their flailing legs, to choose the right branch to grab hold of in order to move to safety ... to comfort ... to peace of mind once again. At last, we have established the TFD corporation ... established *ourselves* ... as the source of *certainty* for any significant action or policy contemplated by world powers!"

Svarog smiled and nodded as a round of applause spread throughout the room. After a few seconds, he raised his hands, inviting the attendees to respectfully restrain themselves. Svarog went on, first reaching back to the early days when TFD was led by its founder, Ansell Beckmann, then citing some recent TFD work in exploring linkages between emotion and cognition, announcing the formation of a new corporate strategy team reporting directly to him, finally stating … and *re*stating several times … our current business strategic focus on transformative technologies and businesses, with appropriate regional prioritization.

Svarog then spent about ten minutes going through the financial details typically covered in those New Q meetings. He wrapped that up with a declaration that TFD needs to explore new business potential, as well as new approaches to strengthening relationships with current clients as well as new prospects.

"What day is this?" he asked the audience. A few people called out "New Q".

"What day of the *week* is it?" he asked.

There were mixed responses to that. A larger number of people responded, first with a few "Tuesday" call-outs. Then at least two people called out "Monday", followed by a larger wave of people calling out "Tuesday!" loudly as a correction or scolding.

"Aha! More and more people are relying on their smarts to keep track of everything, including really basic things that you'd think we'd all be aware of," said Svarog.

"Not only that," he went on, "but most people tend to evaluate a situation or make a conclusion differently on a Monday than they do on a Tuesday. Or a Thursday. Or whatever. There's a 'day-of-the-week' cognitive framework. It's no joke! It's real! There are so many factors that affect how each of us perceive reality and draw conclusions from information, and each day is a bit different in weather, a bit further from some event that is affecting our thoughts, a bit closer to something that we look forward to. Or that we dread."

I had trouble accepting the idea that drawing conclusions from information would lead to a different result depending on which day of the week the analysis was performed, and I wondered where we were going with that.

A slide was then projected behind Svarog. It had the phrase "GROW THE FAITH" displayed throughout the screen area about a dozen times, each time in a different font style. Svarog then summarized by linking back to the *Font* video.

"Remember what that executive in the video tells poor Owen that he needs to do? Grow the Faith! Don't focus only on facts and accuracy and logic to get someone's interest or someone's buy-in. There's a nearly infinite realm of other means to help get a new client or keep an old one. In other words, the language or gestures we use, our facial expressions, how we dress when meeting clients, strategic use of humor or sarcasm ... all of that was just as important as logic or solid evidence in how well we perform in our jobs.

"Remember when Owen walks through that glowing opening. It's like a vagina! *A vagina!* He is reborn! All of us! All of us will be reborn as we learn to grow the faith!" Svarog shouted.

After leading the audience in chanting "grow the faith" a few times, he closed by introducing Waldon Perry.

Waldon walked to the podium and immediately began speaking with adrenalized speed. "Thank you, Robert! Thank you, team! Thanks to our focus on the tricky zone where ...." Waldon paused and took a breath, then resumed at a more relaxed pace. "Thanks to our focus on that tricky zone, where decisions that used to be made solely by human brains, individually or by consensus, with human logic and emotions, with human values, values that differed because of cultural mores, differed because of an individual's experience, values that were often built by religious doctrines and, ultimately, shaped by the circumstances and state-of-mind in the moment the decisions would be made ... thanks to our focus on applying new technologies to artificial intelligence ... thanks to our wise prioritization ... we have built unparalleled credibility in cognitive objectivity!"

As another round of applause began to fade, Waldon continued, "TFD's COVEn ... the Cognitive Objectivity Validation Engine ... is now the gold standard, worldwide, for certification, confirmation and assurance of correctness ... assurance of 'no regrets' ... for any significant decision or undertaking by a political regime ... or a large, private global enterprise which, of course, is just another kind of political regime." Waldon smiled and winked at no one in particular before continuing his presentation. He went through several Augmented Reality projects, offering thoughts on why some of them failed or were cancelled midstream, seeming somewhat distracted through that part of the overview. Finally, he moved to cover the Gravity Train.

"Just a decade ago, back in the mid '20s, the idea of a train or, really, any sort of transport device, being powered solely by gravity had been deemed ridiculous by the tech pundits and environmentalists. You can sled or ski down a hill, right? You can slide down a sliding board. You can just jump off a cliff, of course, and travel in a highly sustainable fashion to the ground," Waldon paused briefly to acknowledge or encourage some laughter, "but the *round* trip is the problem. Now, thanks to recent advances in carbon molecule-based structural technology, as well as expanded operational temperature range for industrial mag-lev, the door to gravity-powered travel has finally been opened."

A holographic image then appeared behind Waldon, taking up most of the stage, showing the Earth from space. It evolved toward showing just the top half of the sphere, then a flat slice so that the various interior layers ... crust, upper mantle, lower mantle, core, inner core ... were suggested by the color scheme. Finally, cute cartoon representations of the Statue of Liberty and the Eiffel Tower were added part-way up on either side of the semi-circle, and a thick, straight line was drawn, directly connecting the classic symbols of New York City and Paris through the interior of the Earth.

Waldon went on, "But a problem remained. In order to get enough acceleration from gravity, the downward slope of the tunnel had to reach a certain target inclination. In order to reach a train speed that made the project economically attractive, the middle portion of the tunnel would have to penetrate the Earth's mantel ... a feature of construction with which we had no previous experience. Many voices arose in protest ... you know who I mean ... citing dangerous and unpredictable consequences of tunneling that deeply through the Earth. If not for us here at TFD, this milestone project ... the Gravity Train ... would have been ignored or dismissed, if not expressly prohibited by law in both the United States and France.

"TFD met with scientists and industry leaders, and we were able to offer a preliminary opinion that feasibility is within the realm of the possible. That was just a small first step for us here at TFD, but it was a key step in that it gave government leaders what they needed to get their balls rolling on the project. Sorry. Sorry. Bad metaphor. We're talking about allocating funds for critical validation work, including a TFD project we're kicking off tomorrow. The project will examine the technologies, geological studies, potential side-effects, including side *benefits,* of having a functional Gravity Train. We'll also look into on-going maintenance costs, required subsidies, required regulatory revisions and other concerns.

"A new team is being formed in my area, which will include several key analysts and engineers from Cognitive Certainty and Research whom, I'm sure, will help TFD to achieve success on this project. Finally, to ensure objectivity, we're bringing Connor Farrell from the EHI division deeper into the fold to lead the project team. I think it is imperative that we have Connor's perspective ... essentially 'outside-in', yet still contained within the larger TFD family ... to help ensure complete objectivity in our final recommendation on the Gravity Train to government agencies here in the US and also in France. His previous assignments within TFD covered agricultural robotics and nanotechnologies, ADADA and other human behavioral and biomedical studies, in which he was essentially acting as a *human* 'cognitive objectivity validation engine' ... keeping us honest and ensuring the completeness of our work. Connor, please stand so the folks can see you. I don't think you've met a lot of the crew on my team yet."

Reluctantly, I stood, nodded quickly in a few random directions and sat down. Randall leaned over, saying "Hey, you'll be good on that! Ferret out good from bad. Let me know if you need another hired hand." Negative thoughts were spinning around in my head, but I managed to smile and thank Randall, whom I had already been thinking might be a good person to have on the team.

Waldon then spoke for a while about recent COVEn projects and new work he expected to see coming in involving Augmented Reality. Before he left the stage, Waldon introduced Dr. Gotama Reddy, TFD's Director of Research. Dr. Reddy took the podium to heartfelt applause from the audience, including a lot of whooping and shouting of things I couldn't quite make out. I assumed it all had to do with projects his research team was focused on currently.

Dr. Reddy talked about some curious research focus areas in different parts of the world. He mentioned thought-reading technologies, which would be a genuine bio-science capability to move us beyond the recent realm of "simulated" thought reading, which consisted of apps that would generate an assumed-to-be-probable thought stream for someone ... your lover or best friend or boss or mother, etc. ... based on whatever the app user just said to them in the current situation. From reviews I had seen, those thought-read apps were mainly used by people curious about what their date or lover might be thinking at some key moment. Even though the apps come with a disclaimer that the output is based only on probabilistic survey data, the users who reviewed it were very positive. People seemed to really enjoy seeing, clearly displayed on their smarts, the most likely thoughts their partner was thinking.

"Imagine if we could actually read each others true thoughts. What would that mean? Would it bring the world's people closer? Or maybe shock us into isolation?" Dr. Reddy paused for a few seconds, then added, "We don't really know. We'll have to wait and see."

Other new research areas highlighted related to use of micro-drones in mosquito control, pollenation and other environmental applications. Finally, Dr. Reddy brought up TFD's leading-edge research in correcting problems in early human brain growth and in multi-sensory reality augmentation. He mentioned an extension of some brain growth work into the realm of artificially "improving" a person's judgement or decision-making ability. "Of course," he said, "that assumes we would have any clue of good decision-making versus bad." The audience found that amusing.

Then, Dr. Reddy went down a path I wasn't expecting. He began to make some loose analogies to management of large data centers and large quantities of data, shifting that to cloud-computing, then shifting to what he referred to as the "hardening of technology". His closing point was that TFD should focus on the hardening of technology from human reasoning, through artificially intelligent algorithms, then through other application software and microcode, finally to implementation via manufactured micro- and nano-componentry. To the extent those micro-electronics can be biologically implanted, he said, we are moving toward "the next horizon, where the entire world will be functioning as a complex, integrated nano-bio-electronic cloud."

He then wrapped up his segment by introducing the Senior Vice President of the Early Human Intention division, Astrid Ekland, who stood up from her seat in the front row, turned and bowed slightly toward the audience before stepping up to the podium. I had worked in Astrid's EHI division for several years, and I had been promoted recently so as to report directly to her. My assignment on Waldon's project was temporary, I understood, so that officially I still reported to Astrid in the TFD hierarchy.

A thoughtful and much-admired leader, Astrid began by simply holding her hands out toward the audience as if she were about to give her eight-year-old niece a hug, saying "I can't tell you how happy I am to be here with you all today!"

"We love you!" a woman on the far side of the room shouted.

Astrid went on to summarize her team's accomplishments over the previous year, mentioning every person's name from every project. I think she specifically cited more than half the seventy-five or so people who reported to her in TFD, myself included. She did not appear to be using notes, although she may have had a name list available in her smarts. She spent a few minutes on our well-known ADADA software and associated medical implants. ADADA stood for Augmented Directed Autonomous Decision Acceptance, which was a marvelous set of technologies that were combined to provide a way to subsequently alter the brain formation that happens pre-birth and in the first two years of human life, in order to correct problems that can occur from bad or non-existent parenting, bad nutrition or severe physical abuse. ADADA changes the pre-wired thinking patterns of humans so as to minimize such things as anti-social behavior, paranoia, lack of empathy, as well as potentially dangerous psychotic tendencies. Astrid's segment ended with sustained, thunderous applause, after she declared it an exceptional honor to lead her team, adding "I'll now close with the words of our founder, Ansell Beckmann, as he ended his speech at our first quarterly meeting held here at Gyre Ventures some years ago. 'The way forward is best achieved through a pure space of sterling motives, resting upon a foundation of glorious deeds.'"

I had always been inspired by something in meetings with Astrid, in written memos from her, in articles written about her, even sometimes just getting a warm look from her as I passed her in hallways. There was just something about her that made me feel valued and made all problems seem like interesting challenges.

◊   ◊   ◊

As our networking break began, there was an announcement that our personal networking capabilities were being restored. There were tables set up in the lounge area near the elevators, offering various drinks, snacks and buffet sandwiches. Many of the TFD crew stopped by the lounge, as did I, for refreshment and casual conversation, but we were free to wander about elsewhere as well. I wasn't very hungry, so I selected a glass of lemonade and an "angry crab rangoon" wonton appetizer, those being fairly easy to handle while wandering around.

As I began casually strolling about, I heard someone behind me exclaim "Oh my God! It's Connor!" I turned around, expecting to see one of my co-workers waiting to exchange greetings and catch up on things. However, what I saw was Rob Greyson, a department manager I knew at TFD, apparently watching a video on his smarts. It took a moment, but then I began to suspect ... to dread ... what it might be. I dubblinked on an article heading which included the words "TFD employee", which caused a video of my earlier interview outside Gyre Ventures to be displayed. Behind me were two clearly visible signs held by the protesters, one said "Disagree with TFD!" and the other said "Certainty is Absurd" in quotes, with an unreadable scribble below it that was probably an attribution.

I verbalized the phrase "certainty is absurd?" to trigger a search, which turned up a quote from Voltaire: *Doubt is not a pleasant condition, but certainty is absurd.*

Greyson approached me and I held out my hand, which he took in a painful, bone-crushing grip while congratulating me on the interview. I'd forgotten about his handshake. Immediately afterward, and continuing for what felt like seven or eight concatenated eternities, I faced a continuous stream of people, many of whom I had not previously met, all of whom wanted to say hello and shake hands. Most made a polite effort to try to make me feel that the interview went well or, at least, not as bad as it could have gone. A few made suggestions for handling it better next time ... as if I would ever be doing another interview!

Waldon was one of the last to accost me. He congratulated me on "surviving" the interview, suggesting we should talk a bit before I make any more public statements. He then asked me to meet him in his office the next morning for a briefing on the Gravity Train and "another exciting project."

Toward the end of the break, as we began to move slowly back into the auditorium, Harper's voice came over the public address speakers announcing that we should be receiving individual instructions for the New Ideas exercise during the next minute. Sure enough, there was a message waiting for me on my smarts, directing me to go immediately to room B-30 on the same floor.

Another message was waiting as well, from Mars. I dubblinked it while walking quickly down the hall toward the "B" section of rooms. It read: *sorry for abrupt departure this morning ... Burke interruption most disturbing ... we must meet next week ... will text you time/place.*

CHAPTER 9

Fire, Water, Air and Synthesis

I made excellent progress to room B-30. I was first to arrive, grateful to be alone for the moment. I was especially grateful that the room had windows, affording an excellent and aesthetically appealing view of the city-scape with bits of the East River and the Queensboro bridge visible. The haze had cleared, and the sun was now adding warm highlights, which had a positive effect on my attitude. I had a few minutes to relax and enjoy the view while replaying that morning's conversation with Mars in my head, but I quickly switched over to recalling the encounter with Melinda, which was a more pleasing way to pass the time.

"Hey! What do you think?" Randall asked as he entered.

"I think we'll have some fun," I said, vacantly, as my daydreams faded.

The rest of our team then entered nearly simultaneously. Our New Idea team facilitator introduced himself as Trevor, and he turned to each of us to get an introduction. Besides Randall and myself, our team included Dr. Adora Coverdale, Dr. Vicki Esposito, Kenton Duckworth and Golden North. Except for Golden, I'd met all of them before. Adora had a doctorate in Earth Systems Science from Stanford University. Kenton was a young technical genius in the Research team who had also been assigned to the Gravity Train team. Randall was a former tech solution sales rep who moved into negotiating business alliance agreements. Vicki was Director of Developmental Research for EHI and formerly a clinical psychologist on the ADADA team. As she introduced herself, Randall leaned over near me and quietly commented, "Worked with that Vicki before. She's good." Golden mentioned that she was recently hired to be part of the new corporate strategy team reporting directly to Svarog.

Melinda was still very much in my thoughts, and I was disappointed that she was not a part of that "New Ideas" team, as it would have been a great way to get to get a sense of how she thinks creatively.

After introductions, Trevor explained that he would lead us through a process, the ultimate goal of which was to arrive at a single strategic objective for TFD which would be synthesized from each of our individual perspectives. We each took a seat at the table in the room as Trevor began to run through the guidelines for this team exercise. He stressed that we must try to suspend judgement, try to build onto ideas already suggested, try to connect or combine ideas when possible, choose our best idea to take forward and, finally, consider how best to describe it to the broader team back in the auditorium.

"Any questions before we begin?" Trevor asked and, hearing no questions, continued with "Brilliant! So, the first thing I'd like to do is have 'quiet time'. For the next two or three minutes, I'd like each of you, without talking, to think of from one to three possible new projects for TFD to undertake ... or to propose to our clients ... and to please just jot them down on the paper in front of you. You may want to think about this morning's presentations, especially Dr. Reddy's, if you find you are having difficulty thinking of new projects. Okay? Great! Let's go!"

While Trevor turned to quietly stare out the window, each of the rest of us quietly stared at the pencils and blank sheets of paper he had distributed around the table. Although it seemed strange for a team exercise, I was glad for the quiet time, and I used it to drift into some childhood memories.

I looped back to the memories of my mother's apron that popped into my head along the walk to Gyre Ventures. When I was four years old, I lived with my mother and grandfather. My mother, whose first name was Fiona, had suddenly and unexpectedly left my dad about a year earlier, taking me with her to live with her parents in their small row-house in Philadelphia. I called her parents G'ma and Pop-Pop, at their request, and my mother soon shifted to addressing them that way as well. G'ma passed away a few months after we moved in, due to heart issues. Pop-Pop behaved as though she were still there, sometimes turning to the empty chair that was G'ma's favorite place to sit asking things like "you hear about that plane crash?" or "anything you want me to do today?"

My mom had odd habits that caused some inconvenience and

occasional distress for the others in the household. For example, on two or three evenings each week the smoke alarm in the hallway outside the kitchen would start its ear-piercing, panic-inducing beeping, as a consequence of a fire in the kitchen. The first few times that occurred when I was at home indoors, I would run frantically to the kitchen to see mom stomping out a burning towel on the floor in front of the oven. "It's nothing," my mother would explain, calmly. Pop-Pop, who never seemed to move very fast, would arrive on the scene shortly afterward, offering cautious advice like "why don't you try using a potholder?" or "you know, it might be easier to just fry up those chicken breasts on the stove-top" … that sort of thing.

Mom would always use a hand towel to insert and remove baking trays, casserole dishes, stew pots, whatever, from our gas oven, in the way most people would use an insulated potholder or, perhaps, tongs. The towel often hung down into the flames below and ignited, leading to periodic beeping and stomping, as well as the charring of the ancient green and white linoleum floor tiles in the area in front of the oven. In the first few weeks of those frequent fires, I was very anxious about them and had nightmares about fires and alarms going off, about firefighters breaking down our front door and flushing the house with water from thick hoses, causing water levels in all the rooms to rise to my chin. I floated in the water as it lifted me up the stairs to the bedrooms, and for some reason, there was always an open window up there in my dreams. The water began to rise in the bedrooms until it swept me out of the open window. The *Font* video had brought all of that back into my head, including a genuine sense of fear and panic that I experienced as a child during those nightmares.

I would usually wake up at the point of being swept out of the bedroom window. In some dreams, before the firefighters arrived, my mother caught fire herself and dissolved in flames before anyone could figure out how to help her. In my dreams, neither Pop-Pop nor I thought of obvious things like pouring a bucket of water on her or suggesting to her that she try rolling around on the floor to smother the flames.

After the first few weeks of living in my grandparents' house with the gas stove, I began to accept the frequent kitchen fires as a part of life ... a part of *my* life, at least. The frequency of nightmares gradually lessened. My reaction to the alarms shifted to one of mere curiosity in seeing which towel it was, how long it took to stomp out the fire and which apron my mother was wearing. As my mother began to prepare dinner each day she would select an apron from several that had belonged to G'ma, still kept on hooks in the pantry. They were all ornate, frilly things, which tied in the back at the waist and had an upper part that looped over the head, covering the wearer's chest with busy flower patterns of various colors. Wearing the apron seemed to cause my mother to take on a new role or a new personality. She behaved differently while wearing one of G'ma's aprons, shedding her normal extremely anxious persona. Instead, she behaved calmly and consistently, ignoring Pop-Pop's advice and the cautionary alerts of the smoke alarm. She was never panic-stricken in the face of danger.

◊   ◊   ◊

"Okay, just another minute or so folks," Trevor announced.

"You should be jotting down things as they occur to you. Don't try to filter or prioritize yet." At that point in our Quiet Time session, I jotted down "calming clothing" as another apron-related memory popped into my head.

One morning in the summer before I started the 3rd grade at school, I found a box of cough drops on my mother's dresser. Although I didn't really have a sore throat at the time, I convinced myself that I might possibly be on the verge of having one, and I decided I had better suck on one of the triangular, cherry-flavored lozenges just in case. They tasted really good, I thought, and what possible harm could come of it? I suddenly felt absolutely wild, and I decided it might be fun to suck a lozenge out of the package. After opening the box and the inner paper wrapper, I put my mouth over the open end, inhaling quickly and deeply, sucking in exactly one cough drop which went, quite logically in retrospect, into my windpipe.

The lozenge managed to get stuck at the top of my windpipe at the back of my neck ... in the oropharyngeal region, I would later learn. I tried to "hawk" it out, as though trying to clear phlegm from my throat, but it remained defiantly in place. It tickled a bit, and I felt as though it might come loose at any time, dropping further down into my lungs. I was old enough to suspect that having a cough drop fall into a lung was a potentially dangerous thing to have happen. So I ran to my mother for help. She was in the kitchen, wearing one of her aprons which somehow enabled her, as usual, to react calmly. I pointed to the cough drop box in my hand and then pointed to my throat, while the frightened look on my face would have served to convey urgency were it not for her apron.

"Oh, poor sweetie! Open your mouth so I can see." I opened my mouth as requested, but my mother was not able to see the cough drop. "Did you swallow it?" she asked casually, "I don't see anything back there. You must have swallowed it."

"Huawch ... feel it ... huawch ... stuck ... huawch." I hawked.

"Well, then let's go see Mr. Zedner. He'll know what to do." Fiona, sounding calm and reassuring, led me by the hand outside and toward the house up the street where Mr. Zedner, a retired pharmacist, lived with his old dog Duke, who began his usual barking when the doorbell rang. After a minute or two of barking, Mr. Zedner answered the door, and Fiona explained the situation. "He thinks he has a cough drop stuck in his throat. Can you please check?"

"Huawch," I added.

Mr. Zedner, looking confused and irritated, ordered me to "open wide" so he could properly assess the situation. "I don't see anything. Was it one of those that are kind of rough on the edges at first? You know, a little scratchy?" he asked.

I nodded, reluctantly, as I began to suspect what he might conclude.

"Well then, my guess is you swallowed it, and it scratched your throat on the way down. Maybe try gargling with salt water or maybe just swallow a spoonful or two of honey. Yeah, that's the best thing ... honey." My suspicion was confirmed. Mr. Zedner then patted me on the head and nodded toward my mother, as though to say "we're done", and he stepped back inside and closed the door.

"Alright then! Let's go! I think we have some honey at home." Mom sounded a bit annoyed as she took my hand again, pulling me along back home. I tugged at her arm and shook my head to indicate I did not think this was a good plan.

"Let's try the honey, Honey!" she smiled down at me, having added a musical lilt to her speech.

"Huawch!" I complained.

"Stop making that noise!" The apron was beginning to lose its power.

As soon as we arrived back at Pop-Pop's house, my mom went into the kitchen to look for a jar of honey, while I ran to the bathroom and leaned over into the bathtub. On the walk home, I had concluded that I must, somehow, save myself from possibly choking to death. Once over the tub, with my head lowered and face downward, I began to slap the back of my neck as hard as I could while repeating the hawking noise, hoping it would bring the cough drop up from the depths of wherever it was. After three or four slaps accompanied by hawking, with no result, I heard my mother shouting from the kitchen. "What are you doing? Stop that noise! I found the honey!"

But I persevered, and as I resumed slapping, something clicked against the back of my upper front teeth. I spat it out and was quite relieved to see it was the cough drop. The tickling in my throat stopped as my mother arrived on the scene.

"What's that?" she pointed to the slimy-looking, triangular red blob in the tub.

"A cough drop."

"Where was it?"

"In my throat."

"*There was a cough drop in your throat*?!?" exclaimed my mother, incredulously.

Later that evening, I used the Internet to look up diagrams of human neck and esophageal regions with detailed labeling of the various internal components, which helped me settle into the conclusion that the cough drop had gotten stuck to the back wall of my pharynx, just behind where my tongue curved down into my throat. I listened several times to short audio recordings, embedded in an on-line dictionary, of the correct pronunciations of "pharynx" and "oropharyngeal." I even practiced saying those words aloud a few times. Being able to name its location was strangely comforting to me, and it provided a sense of closure to the day's adventure. I also concluded that any future attempt to suck a solid object into my mouth would be a very bad idea.

◊   ◊   ◊

Trevor then announced the end of our quiet time and that we would begin sharing ideas. I looked down at my "calming clothing" scribble and decided that it needed something. As Trevor called upon Golden to share her best idea, I added "confidence-inducing wearables" to my note sheet.

Golden began to speak, at first talking about various qualifying factors and analogies, about how so many people struggle with so many decisions, eventually getting to the idea that we should start a consumer division for certainty assurance. "People want to be certain about things they buy for themselves and whom to date. They ask their friends if that dring shirt is right for them. They ask their friends 'should I marry that guy or gal?'" Golden offered as examples of typical decisions that would be assisted by such a TFD offering. It reminded me of my Career Day speech.

"Great!" Trevor sounded happy and encouraging as he typed something on his notepad and shared his screen so we could see it on the wall screen. The top line read: *Start a consumer division for certainty offerings.*

"Thank you, Goldie!" Trevor exclaimed. "Let's hear more! Kenton ... ?"

Kenton shrugged, then offered "I think we should hold an invention event ... 'eVention' we can call it ... let our research team bring out whatever stuff they work on in their spare time. We can all look at it, poke at it, wear it and play with it. Maybe check out relevant artifacts. Whatever. Got to be something in all that worth a scrum, I guess"

"Great! Great! We'll let Marketing handle the naming part, but let's get that down on our list!" Trevor then added a bullet reading: *Research team presents their ideas at TFD internal showcase.*

"That's not what I nnnh ... said," said Kenton, putting the back of his hand to his mouth and appeared to be choking on something. I couldn't help but think it might be a cough drop.

"Sorry?" Trevor asked. "Are you alright?"

Kenton waived his hand dismissively.

"I'm just trying to net these things out." Trevor explained.

I suggested perhaps we change the bullet to "employee eVention emersion" or "e-cubed," adding that we need to emphasize the hands-on exploration aspect. Kenton, still covering his mouth, nodded in acceptance.

"Brilliant. Vicki?" Trevor spoke with somewhat less enthusiasm, and gave me a withering look as he typed changes to Kenton's bullet.

Vicki shared a warm smile with the rest of us, then offered her suggestion, "I think TFD should really dive into developmental disabilities in young children."

"Wonderful!" Trevor exclaimed, seeming to have recharged a bit.

We then moved along to complete our list of ideas for consideration. I suggested, of course, that we do an investigation of the potential for calming or confidence-inducing clothing or wearables. Adora suggested we develop a new global strategy for human nutrition in the long term. Randall eloquently proposed an investigation of unconscious behaviorism to explore the potential to defuse subliminal interference in rational thinking. Trevor posted the full list on the big screen:

1 > Start a consumer division for certainty offerings

2 > Do hands-on employee eVention emersion: e³

3 > Dive into developmental disabilities in young children

4 > Investigate calming or confidence-inducing wearables

5 > Develop long-term global strategy for human nutrition

6 > Explore unconscious behaviorism; e.g. can we defuse subliminal reshaping of rational thought?

… any others?

Trevor then asked us to ponder the list, as a team, and consider any other ideas we ought to add. "You can even add one of your own ideas that you didn't rate as your best." After a minute or so of silence, Golden said she also had thought of new research into developmental disabilities in young children, in response to which Trevor announced he would add it.

"We already got that one. Number three." Randall broke in.

"No, it's fine! Remember, no judgement!" admonished Trevor.

"But it's same damn thing!" Randall complained.

"Let's just add it, Randy." Trevor resolved as he displayed the modified list, then announced we would now move on to the next step wherein we would build a proposal from our ideas.

"You can call me Randall or Hewitt," Randall Hewitt declared.

"Certainly," said Trevor as he put our revised idea list on the screen:

1 > Start a consumer division for certainty offerings

2 > Do hands-on employee eVention emersion: e^3

3 > Dive into developmental disabilities in young children

4 > Investigate calming or confidence-inducing wearables

5 > Develop long-term global strategy for human nutrition

6 > Explore unconscious behaviorism; e.g. can we defuse subliminal reshaping of rational thought?

7 > Dive into developmental disabilities in young children

We all stared at the list on the screen. "So now, do we vote on these?" Vicki asked.

"Not yet. First, I'd like us all to play a little game. We're going to build one sentence using all of these words," said Trevor as he put a list of words on the screen: consumer, certainty, research, invention, developmental, disabilities, mood-altering, wearables, human, nutrition, unconscious, behavior, subliminal, rational, children.

All of us noticed quickly that those were prominent words from our own ideas list. Upon pointing that out to Trevor, he said we could skip building the sentence, but instead we should move ahead to build an idea proposal, as a team, that combines or blends elements of several ideas from our list.

After a long, painfully awkward, recursive round-table discussion that was mainly intended to be inclusive of all of our individual ideas, we arrived at a long, painfully awkward, recursive proposal. Trevor put it on the screen while we sat and stared at it. On the screen:

Investigate association of unconscious behaviorism with developmental disabilities, for consumer market potential in terms of nutritional components and/or wearable technologies sourced partly from TFD hands-on employee eVention emersion process, with validation of certainty level of investigative approach and derived associations, while diffusing subliminal reshaping of rational thought.

At that point, Randall, who had been adjusting his position in his seat and sighing for about the last ten minutes, suddenly spoke up.

"I feel like we're on the bus here." Randall announced, to no one in particular.

"The bus?" inquired Vicki.

"Nothin'. Never mind." Randall folded his arms and slipped further down into his chair.

"Well, here's a thought," Vicki began after a moment, "We are all probably thinking that the *point* of mentioning nutrition and wearables is that they might be of value to those afflicted ... to the patients." Vicki spoke with some authority, "Normally, the 'magic elixir' is intended to diagnose the problem, or cure it, or treat it to

mitigate symptoms, or maybe prevent it from afflicting others."
Vicki paused and looked around, noting our consensual nods.
Randall pointed his finger at her with a dramatic flair. "So if we
agree," she continued, "let's add something about diagnostic,
curative, treatment and preventive potential, and maybe try cutting
the last half of it."

"I love it!" said Trevor.

"Hey!" Randall snapped, "Quit bein' so damn judgmental!"

Eventually, we arrived at:

*Investigate association of unconscious behaviorism with
developmental disabilities, including diagnostic, curative,
treatment and preventive potential via nutritional components
and/or wearable technologies.*

"Well, I guess the potential value of it would be more obvious."
Adora contemplated.

"You think?" Randall asked, rhetorically.

"Yes, I *do* think that," Adora pleasantly smiled back.

"We should say something about e-cubed or eVention when we
present it," Kenton urged.

"I agree," Vicki and I reinforced simultaneously.

"Goldie?" prompted Trevor.

"Okay, um, it's actually Golden, if you don't mind." Trevor
raised a hand as though to say *mea culpa*, as Golden continued,
"I'm fine with it. I mean, the consumer part isn't spelled out, but I
guess it's okay as long as it isn't specifically excluded."

"So ... Randall, what do *you* think now?" Trevor asked.

Randall shrugged. "Ain't *too* shabby, I guess," he allowed.

"Randall, that is the highest praise I have ever heard you lavish upon anything!" extolled Vicki, managing to extract a snort from Randall.

We all agreed to take it forward. Since Vicki was key in getting us to the final proposal, Trevor suggested she should be the one to present it to the larger TFD team. However Vicki appeared reluctant to take that on in spite of Trevor's urging, and she suggested Adora handle it. Adora agreed, and we were set.

◊   ◊   ◊

Back in the main auditorium, people sat more or less where they sat earlier in the day. We sat through five or six presentations from other teams, some scripted in detail, some delivered more casually but with emphasis on the key idea. Harper then called for whomever was presenting from our team, and Adora rose to travel down to the podium at the front of the room. She introduced herself and introduced the concept of having a strategy for global human nutrition. Adora stressed the importance of that concept, as well as the importance of TFD taking a leadership position there. Then she moved to our proposal, with subtle implication that the intent of the proposal is mainly to secure TFD's role in the global human nutrition strategy realm.

I thought her confident, heart-felt delivery was perfect, and her launching of our proposal on the heels of the global nutrition issue was reasonable given the current political climate, although our team had not explicitly discussed our motivation for the proposal. Just before Adora left the podium, she called out to her sister, Availa, who sat near the front of the room on the side opposite

Randall and me, welcoming her as one of this year's TFD new hires who had been a former college intern.

Other proposals were concerned with such things as artificial nano-snakes that would eat insect eggs normally killed by freezing temperatures in northern regions affected by climate change, fabrication of synthetic nutritional proteins from crude oil, quantum cryptography extensions and genetic modification toward producing human babies with improved decision-making potential.

Harper then took the stage to announce we were officially adjourning for the day. At the same time, we each received notification via our smarts on which dinner destination we had been assigned. I was to dine at the Snegurochka pub, which was a recently remodeled restaurant and bar located close to my hotel. I decided to walk back to the hotel and freshen up a bit before going to the pub, which caused me to be one of the last to arrive.

CHAPTER 10

The Pub

As I entered the Snegurochka pub, the hostess near the door stepped in front of me, wearing a silvery-blue, glittering, fairy-like dress, a snowflake-shaped crown and white boots made of thick felt. She wore ammu on the left side of her face in the shape of a lily with sparkles that drifted upward along the stem, seemingly causing the pink flower to pulse with light. I was genuinely impressed with how carefully and artistically the lily had been rendered, and I couldn't help but comment, saying "I love your ammu. It's really beautiful." Her kind and nurturing face compelled me to add something about flowers thriving well on a face that can inspire poetry, which may have sounded both stilted and flirtatious. After a few moments with no reaction from the hostess as she seemed to be looking at something in the distance, I introduced myself and said I was with the TFD party.

"TFD? Okay, we've had a few technical glitches," the hostess began distractedly, "but the menus should be working in a minute. Just got the message on that!" I assumed the message was displayed on her smart lenses, which likely caused her, mercifully, to miss my awkward compliment. But then she added, "You are so sweet, by the way! Poetry!" lightly tapping the back of my hand as she made eye contact. "I need you," she continued, pointing directly at my nose, "to follow me." The hostess then flipped her shoulder-length, curly hair and led me through a narrow, dimly lit passage. She held open the dark opaque curtain at the far end.

"Sorry, we're remodeling and expanding," she said. Then, with a dramatic, graceful sweep of her arm to indicate tables along a wall of windows, she added "TFD at all tables by the windows! Please enjoy!"

As I turned to her to offer a thank-you nod, she winked her left eye, revealing more ammu on the eyelid, sparkling with a greenish light, indicating, as was the acceptable social practice, that she would welcome further interaction. I politely raised my eyebrows as though intrigued, becoming immediately anxious that I may have overstepped the bounds of etiquette as I turned away to enter the room behind the curtain. It was, after all, a company-sponsored business team dinner, so flirtatious, rude and lewd behaviors had to be avoided in order that TFD's corporate image not be tarnished.

Snegurochka's main dining area was a fairly large space. There were many micro-drones and nano-drones with blinking lights, some stationary, some moving like fireflies against the dark ceiling, above suspended light fixtures. On the far right was a bar, a door to the kitchen and an entry into an alcove with restrooms. To the left was the TFD section, which contained several rectangular tables, each seating eight or nine people.

A few people I didn't recognize sat at the table closest to me. I put on my smarts to scan the TFD attendees, and the recognition app began framing faces of co-workers, adding tags with their names and other key profile information. It appeared the TFD people there were mostly part of Waldon Perry's organization. Those facing away from me would also be tagged within a few seconds, based on whatever personal data could be pulled from their smarts and wearables.

"Connor!" came a deep voice from behind. I turned to see Rob Greyson extending his hand. Based upon my experience during the networking break, I tensed the muscles in my right hand before clasping Greyson's, and it proved to be good preparation for the unnecessary firmness with which he gripped.

"Ah! Karate man! Solid grip, my friend! Please join us at our table." Greyson gestured to the farthest table along the windows. I followed and stood behind the only available chair at the head of the table, smiling and glancing across the faces to see whom I would be attempting to socialize with for the next couple of hours. On the left side, Greyson sat closest, with two young men in the next two seats who were not yet tagged in my smarts. By the window on the left was Brendan McCarron, a man in his late fifties whom I had worked with on several projects in the past. He had been assigned to the Gravity Train team as well. I considered Brendan a friend as well as a co-worker.

On the right-hand side, sitting closest to me was Nilima Patel, whom I had met before. Kenton, the lead technician who was on my New Ideas team earlier in the day, sat between Nilima and a young women tagged in my smarts as Availa Coverdale, whom had been introduced in the auditorium earlier by her sister Adora. Next to Availa, by the window, sat Melinda. She was looking outside, her hair still tied back in a simple ponytail, wearing no makeup or jewelry except for a small earring adorning her left ear.

"Good evening," I said cordially, "may I join you?"

"Please, sir, we are honored!" Greyson bellowed with a grand gesture. I sat while exchanging nods with Brendan and glancing at Melinda, although she continued to gaze outside.

"I think you know most of us here. But perhaps not Garren and Deepak, former interns now graduated and employed here at TFD on my team," said Greyson, gesturing to the two men beside him.

"Welcome to TFD, gentlemen." I said, addressing the interns, then turning to the rest, "Brendan, good to see you again in person!"

"Mr. Farrell! It's been too long!" declared Brendan.

"How are you, Kenton? Nilima, how are you?", I continued.

"I am good! Good to see you again, Connor!" Nilima said warmly.

"And, Availa, is it?" I asked, "Are you part of the tunnel project? Sorry, I mean the Gravity Train."

"He means the *gravy* train!" Greyson added.

"Hi Connor!" said Availa, "Yes, I'm Availa, but no, I'm on another project starting up. I joined TFD about a month ago. Great to be here! Still learning, though. Still learning."

"Great! Welcome to the team. And uh ... it's good to uh ..." I began to address Melinda.

"Yep. Me again. Sitting by a window so I can look outside for inspiration," she said, looking outside.

"Nice to see you again, Melinda," I said, mentioning her name so she would not think I'd forgotten it. Her tag still blocked, she turned toward me making eye contact for a moment.

"I'll look forward to getting to know you better this evening," I said. Then, feeling there might have been something inappropriate about that, I added "I mean ... more about your prior work at TFD ... key projects and so forth."

Before Melinda could respond, Availa jumped in with "Oh! She's helping me! She's my mentor! She knows all about this project I'm on. It's based on the COVEn thing, and it can help people be better people, you know, so that there will be fewer people with violent tendencies or other mental issues. We're looking to see how Augmented Reality can be used to help with those mental issues."

"Might that be the extension to the ADADA work?" I asked, " I didn't realize it was based on COVEn."

"It's not," replied Melinda, looking out the window. Then, turning toward me, she added, "we're *making use* of COVEn to help us make sense of *decades* of largely ignored research on the topic, including *why* it was ignored, but the technology is completely unrelated. Well, *largely* unrelated. Hard to prove anything is *completely* unrelated to something else."

"Ah, so the research wasn't *completely* ignored then," I said, trying to be funny. Watching Melinda carefully for a reaction, I noticed her shifting her lips over toward the left side of her face as she turned away to look out the window again. I felt as though I were being pulled toward her.

Outside the window there were streetlights visible, as well as lights from buildings across the street. There was a fair amount of traffic, both vehicular and pedestrian. It was already dark out, so translucent reflections of the Snegurochka interior features could be seen as well as phantom images of people inside the pub. As I observed Melinda's reflected face in the glass, she turned back suddenly and looked directly at me, as though she noticed me looking at her and found that annoying.

"Well, okay, so sorry" Availa apologized, "like I said, I'm still learning. But it really is an exciting project. And I'm so lucky that Melinda agreed to keep on mentoring me even though she got moved to the Gravity Train work."

"We're *all* still learning." Greyson assured, "I'd really like to hear some inside scoop on the Gravity Train." Then, looking at Kenton, he added "Perhaps the Kenster has something he can share."

I was hoping for some off-the-cuff comments from Kenton that evening myself.

"Nnnh ... the train," said Kenton, gasping as he did at the New Idea session, as though having some difficulty speaking, which caused others at the table to look at him curiously.

"He's improving himself, aren't you Kenton?" Brendan interjected, then further explained, "Kenton is wearing a be-mod dev that stops him from saying a certain offensive word that he used to use quite a bit."

"Wait. That would be 'fuck', right?" Deepak asked, appearing to feign innocence. "I'm just guessing," he went on, "because I heard you say it so often when I was an intern. Wow, I mean, I'll bet there are a lot of times you wish you could still say it. A *lot* of times."

Kenton stared blankly at Deepak as Brendan admonished, "Now, now. Let's not make it any harder on our dear Kenton. He's doing the right thing. Makin' his mum happy."

"Well, I think it's very noble of you, Kenton," said Availa.

I had read about that behavior modification technology which had a range of potential applications. For f-word issues, for example, a microdev implanted in an earring, headband, fedora … whatever … would sense specific target activity signals in the orbitofrontal cortex, then conjointly detect nerve impulses that would cause muscles around the lips to contract to form an "F" sound. Upon identifying the immediacy of intended utterance of the banned word or sound, with a predetermined target level of confidence, an undergarment worn by the patient would administer a brief electrical shock. When be-mod wearables were first introduced, references to such microdevs bifurcated into "wearies" … wearables that were intended to encourage or prevent a certain behavior ... while those that benignly monitored and collected data about our personal health were mostly still referred to as "wearables." I started to imagine what the electrical shock from a weary might feel like, just as a pair of hands pressed down on my shoulders, causing me to stiffen suddenly, as though I had been actually shocked.

"Oooh, someone could use a nice, relaxing massage!" came a vaguely familiar voice, and I tilted my head upward to see, looking down at me, the face of the hostess who gave me the glitter wink earlier. Her face was attractively framed by her light brown curls, highlighted by a yellow-orange glow now emanating from the table surface.

"You are all so very welcome here!" the hostess continued,

"My name is Pru, and I will be your hostess this evening. My apologies for technical difficulties earlier, but our menus are now working, so feel free to explore on the table top or on your smarts. As a reminder, some of our entrees can be ordered non-synth for an additional charge. I'll stop back in a minute in case you have any questions, or you can just tap the table menu with your finger three times."

She squeezed my shoulders at the utterance of her name and again as she turned to leave. In between squeezes, her thumbs gently traced little circles over my trapezius muscles.

"So, Connor, will you be tapping the table to inquire about that 'nice, relaxing massage'?" Brendan teased after a moment.

"Probably not," I answered, feigning a slight chuckle.

"I'm glad you said *probably* not, since *definitely* not would be hard to believe," said Melinda, looking at me and wearing a serious expression. As she turned to look out the window again, Brendan turned toward me, raising his eyebrows and silently mouthing an "ooo" sound. I had a strange feeling in that moment … something like jealousy … but I couldn't place it because it didn't make sense.

Just then, the table surface shifted to a cooler greenish-blue glow, and a wave-like movement began as if to simulate looking down upon the surface of water into a clear pool. Melinda and Brendan touched the table at their place and made the usual circular motion with a finger to request the menu. The simulated water surface reacted as if stirred. I decided to follow suit and use the table surface, while the rest at our table chose to use their smarts. Categories of food and drink were revealed to me as holographic icons, floating just above the surface of the "water".

As I explored the menu, it was somehow comforting to me to observe Melinda gracefully reaching into the space before her, grasping or swiping various offerings. Similar activity started at the table next to us, as Pru completed her welcome greeting for that group.

"Always the same," Brendan remarked, "everywhere you go these days, the 'lamb' is some kind of crap made of crushed bugs. And no non-synth for it either."

"For profit's sake old man, who eats lamb these days anyway?" Greyson inquired, rhetorically.

Pru returned to our table, making a noise as though clearing her throat, holding the neck of a wine bottle in each hand, the bottles slung over her shoulders like baseball bats.

"I've got a nice Pinot Noir here that was biodynamically produced in New Zealand and a Pouilly-Fuissé from the Burgundy region in France," she said. "Shall I open both for your table to get you started? I'll check later to see how you're doing, but just let me know if there is something else you'd prefer."

"Got any snappers of your own? Any kids?" Brendan directed his question at Pru.

"Uh ... well ... no. Not so far, anyway." Pru responded, looking quizzically at Brendan.

"Is that how you plan to hold your first-born child?" Brendan asked, pointing toward the bottles.

"Ha!" Pru responded, "when I have my first born, I certainly won't hold it like this!"

"Well, let's assume the wine deserves better than your giving it, and we'll have both opened," said Brendan, looking around the table for signs of agreement and getting a few nods. Then he added, "as for myself, I could murder a pint of the black stuff."

"Excellent choices!" Pru said, affectedly, and began opening the bottles, adding, "we have blueprints for almost anything, so if you have special dietary needs, let me know and we can probably print it up for you ... and we even get the *flavor* right sometimes! Just kidding! It's all yummy! I swear!"

Pru answered a few questions on available teas, draft beers and stouts while she poured a taste of each wine into two glasses near Greyson and me. "I'll leave you gentlemen in charge of tasting notes and distribution," said Pru as she turned to leave.

"She's weird. Don't you think she's weird?" Availa pondered aloud, "I mean, kinda goofy."

When people get together in business meetings or in social situations with their co-workers, they often seem to be playing a part. For those business-linked gatherings, the same role-playing occurs whether in an office building or "remotely" from a home office or coffee shop. Over the years, I've noticed that some people play a different character in front of their co-workers in a setting like Snegurochka's compared to their day-to-day behavior at work. Each appeared to become whom they thought they were *supposed* to be in order to improve their standing in the corporate talent pool. A couple of years earlier, I realized that I was doing the same thing, deliberately acting more thoughtful, collaborative and non-judgmental toward the goal of projecting good consultative qualities, even moving now and then into an ostentatious level that may have irritated some people.

More recently, in spite of my efforts to monitor and minimize such behavior on my part, I still noticed that I was one of the players, often pragmatically justifying it to myself as normal for a human. It's like theater, really, with "real people" becoming actors, following a mostly improvised script. It's not completely improvised because sometimes we pick up on cues where something we just read in a news article or financial report might be the best comment to make at that time. Anxious introverts like myself can sometimes perform quite convincingly as a confident extrovert in such situations. In thinking back to the discussions at our table that evening, it is actually easier for me to recall it as scenes in a play. To ensure accurate dialog, I'm using the conversation as recorded on my smarts. That night I played a thirty-something, well-meaning, pedantic consultant named Connor.

CHAPTER 11

THE PUB

Scene 1

(The group has begun to explore the pub's menus by interacting with the table surface. Some are using menus available on their smart lenses, which they access by rolling their eyes and double-blinking. Several conversations start with some overlapping and distractions. Unless otherwise specified in the stage directions, no one looks directly at anyone else as they speak.)

GARREN.
(Turning to watch PRU as she exits toward the bar.)
I like her.

AVAILA.
(Interacting with the menu.)

Goofy.   Hey, *this* looks good.

GARREN.
(Glancing around room.)
So many choices.   So little time.

NILIMA.
Oh yes! The menu is very good. Very complete!

DEEPAK.
Yawn. *(Not actually yawning but says the word 'yawn'.)*

GARREN.
I wasn't talking about the menu.

GREYSON.
So … Connor ….

NILIMA.
So, Connor, what is going on with you?   I mean, Waldon said something about bringing you "deeper into the fold". Is that just the Gravity Train or other projects too?

DEEPAK.
Yeah, really. So do we have to share files with you and invite you to Knapsync calls and whatever?

GARREN.
(Oratorically.)

No! We just have to *grow the faith!*

NILIMA.

I'm just curious. I want my team to properly focus on the most important work.

CONNOR.
(Looking like a deer in headlights.)

Well, don't worry about inviting me to anything for now. Waldon asked me to look at some key projects and weigh in on feasibility, potential extensions, partner ecosystem expansion ... *(Taking a breath and shifting to a confident look and decisive tone of voice.)* ... new ways to monetize value out of whatever the end result or benefit is.

DEEPAK.

What I don't get is so many of the TFD projects I read about, evaluating proposals over the past few years, they were failures.

GARREN.

Failures? No way!

DEEPAK.

At least one out of every three failed. Why do we think we're so good at being certain when we fail so much?

AVAILA.

I think some of those were just TFD saying they thought the *proposal* would fail if someone actually tried to do it. So if we say someone else's idea is no good, that doesn't mean we failed ... right?

CONNOR.

(Taking a sip of wine and appearing to ignore both DEEPAK and AVAILA.)

Monetizing value across ecosystem constituents, as you know, has been getting trickier over the years. Most of us assumed it would gradually get easier to set up complex ecosystems of businesses and government agencies ...

GREYSON.

Ah! Government agencies!

CONNOR.

... all connected into a particular solution or business process ...

GREYSON.

Nothing ever gets easier.

CONNOR.

... but the technology linkages keep growing like tangled vines.

BRENDAN.

Yes, for example, Connor and I talked recently about the efficacies of mass deployment of new agri-bots throughout central and southern Africa, wherever we can get governments to agree to finance it … how we could manage all that … all the parties involved … impact to the locals … good things and bad things.

AVAILA.
(Turning to look at CONNOR.)

My sister, Adora, whom I think you know … her research work at Stanford included something to do with new carbon capture technologies, but I think everything they looked at had worse side-effects than just reducing the carbon level in the environment. So the side-effects turned out to be the more important thing.

CONNOR.

Yes, that's exactly the kind of thing I'll be looking at, with a focus on two key projects.

NILIMA.

And what are those?

CONNOR.

ADADA and the tunnel. Well, more properly, the Gravity Train.

GREYSON.

Gravy train.

CONNOR.

Right. Although I think it's okay to call it "the tunnel", since most of what I suspect needs review is the tunnel part of it. So, Melinda, Brendan and Kenton are also on the tunnel team, and we may ask others to help. One or more of you here, possibly.

NILIMA.

I would love to help.

CONNOR.

We would love to have you!

BRENDAN.

Absolutely, we would!

NILIMA.

Are any other nations worried about the tunnel?

CONNOR.

Other European nations are asking about the possibilities for insurance, which is raising a lot of interest ... and new concerns.

GREYSON.

Which nations?

CONNOR.

Germany and the UK, so far. France too, but they're mostly interested in liability insurance.

GREYSON.

Liability?

CONNOR.

For spearheading the joint initiative. The thinking is that both the US and France would share liability for any consequences.

MELINDA.

I can't imagine anyone crazy enough to take on that kind of risk.

BRENDAN.
(Looking at MELINDA.)
One in your hair. A nano. A blinker. *(Points toward the top of her head.)*

MELINDA.

(Looks at BRENDAN and begins feeling around in her hair.)

KENTON.

Yeah, minor consequences. Like destroying the whole nnnh … planet.

GREYSON.

(As he speaks, MELINDA plucks a blinking nano-drone out of her hair and squashes it like a bug on the table surface using her thumbnail.)
How fast does that thing go anyway? I mean, is it faster than flying?

BRENDAN.
(Looking at MELINDA.)
Drones to drobes, eh?

CONNOR.

Well, it could be much faster than commercial aircraft. The actual speed will depend on several factors, like friction. Even with mag-lev there's air-drag and other things that can introduce friction, the steepness and straightness of the tunnel, how the train is held in place at the station ... and a few other things I can't recall at the moment. One idealized calculation I saw ... which did not factor in air-drag ... estimated the trip taking about 42 minutes, not including boarding and disembarking.

AVAILA.

That's like 5,000 miles an hour!

CONNOR.

Yes, in that ballpark, as an *average* speed for the trip. But the special appeal of the gravity train, of course, is that it travels by gravity alone ... no other energy source is needed. It continuously accelerates by gravity until the middle of the journey, then continuously decelerates, also by gravity, for the second half of the trip. At the middle ... where it reaches its top speed ... it would be traveling around 10,000 miles per hour, or about 16,000 kilometers per hour, ignoring air drag. *(He pauses and looks around a bit, as though worried that he is revealing too much proprietary information at this social gathering in a public restaurant.)* So, I guess, not quite as fast as some early news articles incorrectly claimed. I mean it won't be expressed as some fraction of the speed of light, most likely, but the top speed itself will still be very fast. It will be quite a novelty.

GARREN.

Whoa! No way! We should say it's a fraction of the speed of light anyway. I mean, you know you're going gruesomely fast when people measure your speed as some fraction of the speed of light!

KENTON.

Right! Like this morning, I rode my bike to work at over one billionth the speed of light! It was nnnh … orgasmic!

AVAILA.
(Sounding shocked.)

Oh, my God!

GREYSON.

Well, ten thousand miles an hour, that's still pretty damn fast. Like twice the speed of the fastest military jets. Aren't there some ways to eliminate the air drag?

CONNOR.

There are a few things being looked at to reduce air drag. Not realistic to think we can eliminate it entirely though.

AVAILA.
(Looking up toward the ceiling.)

New York to Paris. Will it still be a romantic journey for some, even when it's only a 42 minute trip? *(Turns toward CONNOR.)* Do you know why that route was chosen?

CONNOR.

Limits of technology, mainly. They wanted it to connect two major cities. Traveling under an ocean was kind of "icing on the cake" for marketing purposes. The distance between New York and Paris around the surface of the globe leads to a maximum depth at the mid-point of an ideal, perfectly straight tunnel of about 140 miles ... about 220 kilometers ... which is about as far below sea level the experts think any part of the tunnel could be built.

NILIMA.

Wait! So, now, that's down below the Earth's crust ... into the upper mantle, isn't it? How is that possible?

AVAILA.

Right! That's how it looked on Waldon Perry's chart this morning.

KENTON.

New graphene-based structural shell and other reinforcing componentry, you know, like molecular weaving and stuff. It can withstand astronomical stresses, so they say, and it can even warp or bend a little if it needs to. The mag-lev rails bend too.

CONNOR.

Right, and that 140 mile depth assumes the "optimal" tunnel, which would be a perfect straight-line tunnel between the two cities.

BRENDAN.

Have they decided yet? On going straight-line?

CONNOR.

That's still being looked at. They may decide to go with an arc-shaped tunnel that wouldn't need to be quite so deep in the middle, although it would slow the train down a bit. Our work at TFD may affect that decision. One thing we'll look at in the next few days is the proposed tunnel boring technology and possible reuse of materials unearthed. The biggest problem may be in the transitional zones between layers, where there may be more shifting ... more stresses. *(Pauses and turns toward KENTON.)* By the way, *(Gesturing with air quotes.)* "astronomical stresses" is more of a marketing term here. *(PRU arrives at the table holding a tea cup and mug of stout.)* The stress might be better described as planetary or geologic.

PRU.

(Placing a tea cup in front of NILIMA, then stretching to hand a mug to BRENDAN.)

Oh! I have totally had planetary stress before. Believe me! Both of these drinks can help.

NILIMA.

Oh good! Thank you, miss!

BRENDAN.

(Reaching across the table for the mug.)

Thank you, luv.

(PRU exits.)

GARREN.

Do governments do marketing?

BRENDAN.

Ah! Don't get me started on *that* one! *(He takes a swig of stout.)*

NILIMA.

But how can we know ... or at least be confident ... that we are doing a reasonable thing? Is it *healthy* for the earth if we build that tunnel?

GARREN.

Well, we're all about certainty here at good old TFD!

CONNOR.

Well, indeed, how can we know? There may be a way to be nearly certain of the level of safety, and, well, that's why we're here.

MELINDA.

Nearly certain. Great. What could possibly go wrong?

CONNOR.

I mean, that's why TFD is involved. To try to get everyone to a more comfortable level of confidence.

MELINDA.

(Looking out the window.)

Unless, of course, it begins to appear that we would be crazy or delusional to be confident about a project that ….

BRENDAN.

(Interrupting.) Ah! Right! A lot of people are fired up about this, one way or the other.

CONNOR.

(Looking at MELINDA.)

Melinda, I know there is a lot to investigate here. Not only the geologic concerns but biologic ones too. I'm thinking extremophiles, for example, microorganisms that can survive nearly indefinitely in the most extreme conditions. We could inadvertently release some eight million year old germ or fungus or something. Our job is to make sure all that comes out and present our concerns to the key agencies in the US and France.

MELINDA.

And we need to make it public too.

NILIMA.

That's why we need Connor here! *(Puts her hand on CONNOR's shoulder, then turns toward him.)* You are great at getting trust. People trust you because you are honest and objective always. You are a person of quality. I have to ask you something though. I think Availa mentioned bad side-effects earlier. I think I get the side-effect concerns for the Gravity Train tunnel. What would be side-effects for ADADA?

GREYSON.

Great question! Seriously.

CONNOR.

Well, I haven't started looking into that one yet. Might be something that requires a longitudinal study ... a long-term behavior tracking experiment. I really don't know yet. We ... uh ... we may find some side-effects worthy of concern.

MELINDA.
(Looking at CONNOR.)
We need to talk. Seriously.

KENTON.
(Nodding and gasping.)
Nnnh.

(Fade to Black.)

CHAPTER 12

THE PUB

Scene 2

(It is now nearly two hours later. The meal has been served and consumed, including dessert. Several at the table have a coffee or tea cup in front of them. Most have a wine glass, some still containing wine. BRENDAN has a mug with an inch or two of stout left. AVAILA has a plate with some fragments of chocolate cake left. Conversation continues but has gradually drifted away from work topics. Everyone now mostly looks at others at the table as they speak.)

GARREN.

Have you seen the new AR app?

BRENDAN.

Oh, Jesus! More augmented reality.

DEEPAK.

Which app?

MELINDA.

Let's not.

GARREN.

(Removing his eyeglasses and handing them to DEEPAK.)
This one! It's one of those "why wait" apps.

AVAILA.

(Looking up suddenly.)
Hey! Don't point that at me!

KENTON.

(Reaching for the eyeglasses.)
Yeah! Hey! Knock it off you guys!

DEEPAK.

(Leaning back to prevent KENTON from taking the eyeglasses.)
Chillax. Shut down. *(Looks at AVAILA through GARREN's glasses.)* These don't show your actual naked self, you know. They just try to make me think I have x-ray vision. It's just a trick. Just a game.

GARREN.

This one's different because it shows you the virtual nudity the way you prefer. Like it knows what your preferences are, right?

And it makes people look as much like that as possible. I mean, as much like it as would be ... credible.

KENTON.

I said knock it off! You're embarrassing Availa. You should be embarrassed *yourselves* for using that kind of AR app.

MELINDA.

We should be embarrassed to use *any* kind of AR crap.

BRENDAN.

(Reaching to position his hand between the eyeglasses and AVAILA.)

Fellows, this is not appropriate here. Let's put that away.

GARREN.

(Taking the eyeglasses back from DEEPAK and putting them in his shirt pocket.)

Sorry. Sorry, Availa.

DEEPAK.

(Genuinely apologetic.)

Me too. I am sorry.

GARREN.

One cool thing about that new app is that you can set it to turn you off. Like, if you really don't like someone, you can set it to make them look really kind of ... well ... unappealing, every time you look at them.

AVAILA.

Oh! That is so one forty-four! *(Looks first at BRENDAN, then at KENTON.)* Thank you, gentlemen, for coming to my rescue.

KENTON.

(Speaking softly, while looking at the table surface.) My pleasure. Anytime, Availa.

GARREN.

Yeah. One forty-four. But the *really* cool thing is that you can set it to decide for itself how to make women ... or men ... people ... *more* attractive to you, based on what it knows you prefer. It does it by basically looking through all available data of who your friends are, what videos and pictures you've looked at online, what ads and news articles you tend to look at, where you buy your clothes, what devs you wear, stuff it can scrape off on-line dating sites. You know, like, *everything*, really.

MELINDA.

Well, here's where I have to get up on the soapbox, I suppose. *(GARREN looks at DEEPAK with an exaggerated look of puzzlement, mouthing the word "soapbox".)* We, as a society, as a community, as a species ... as a bunch of pathetic, misguided organisms trying to figure out how in hell we are going to survive in spite of ourselves ... we spend so much time ... so much "nnnh ..." *(Imitating KENTON's behavior modification shock reaction and gasping.)* time ... working on augmented reality. Collecting every conceivable kind of data to understand people better so we can more easily manipulate them! So much human genius, human endeavor and technological marvelousness is channeled *(Pointing at GARREN's shirt pocket.)* into that bullshit! I have no use for it. I have no use for augmented reality, as I prefer to see things as they are. *(She begins shouting.)* You want to see things differently? Use your fucking imagination! What would be useful for me? *(She stands and continues shouting.)* I'd like *perspicacious* reality! Augment reality so that all the important stuff is clearly highlighted! Clearly tagged! There is so much crap and distraction in life! Show me what I should actually care about and focus on! Show us what is truly important to us as individuals! As a community! As a *species*, for God's sake! I want to trade *smart* lenses for *wise* lenses! I want to look through those lenses and see ... oh my God ... see! Finally! *(Gesturing about the pub and the scene outside the window.)* What all of this means! Why am I here? What are the key "take-aways" for me? For *us*? What are the problems we need to focus on and fix before it's too late? What are the *epiphanies* out there? Right in front of us! That we keep ignoring! That we keep missing! Missing! Every! Fucking! Day! *(Pausing to take a breath, then continuing calmly without shouting.)* I, personally, would like perspicacious reality, please. Thank you for your attention.

BRENDAN.

(Raising his mug as MELINDA sits back down.)

Here! Here!

WALDON.

*(He has just walked over, apparently unnoticed, from a

different table.)

I'll summon Pru. I'm sure they can print it up for you. Maybe add a non-synth side of ...

MELINDA.
(Interrupting.)

Was I too loud?

GREYSON.

Mr. Perry!

CONNOR.
(Standing and indicating his seat.)

Waldon, have a seat.

WALDON.

(Speaking to CONNOR.) I'm good. Need to leave in a minute. *(Looking toward others at the table.)* Just wanted to thank all of you for your on-going commitment to TFD, and I do hope you enjoyed our little get-together.

VARIOUS AT TABLE.

It was so very nice! Oh thank you! You're the greatest! Thanks Mr. Perry! Loved it! Absolutely!

WALDON.

(Turning to BRENDAN and cocking his head to one side.)

Brendan, I hardly ever see you anymore. If you're around tomorrow, stop by my office around 9 AM, if you're free. Okay?

BRENDAN.

I will do that. Certainly.

WALDON.

(Patting CONNOR firmly on the shoulder.)

You too, Connor, like we planned. I need to give you both some further direction.

CONNOR.

I'll be there.

WALDON.

Melinda, … *(Pausing.)*

MELINDA.

I'll be out of town for a few days.

WALDON.

(Making a brief chuckling noise before speaking.)

I knew that. Just wanted to ask how your Dad was doing.

MELINDA.

Ah! Well, he's still that guy, you know, contemplating, re-thinking, reworking. He still seems to be enjoying life in his pastoral fantasy.

WALDON.

(Smiling at MELINDA.)

I wish I'd gotten to know him better before he retired. Only worked with him for a few months. Hey everyone, you may not know this but ...

MELINDA.
(Raising her hand to get WALDON's attention and speaking in stage-whisper.)
Please, no!

WALDON.
(Speaking loudly.)
Melinda here ... is the daughter of our esteemed founder, Ansell Beckmann.

AVAILA.
Hello! You told me you weren't related!

WALDON.
(Noticing the withering look he is getting from MELINDA.)
Okay, sorry, but it's something you ought to be proud of. Forgive me. *(Waving as he walks away.)* Good night all!

GREYSON.
That's awesome. Wow. I mean, I knew your name was Beckmann, but it never occurred to me ... for some reason ....

NILIMA.
(Leaning forward and facing MELINDA.)
I didn't know either, but I think it is wonderful! Truly, you

should be proud!

                          KENTON.
                          (Nodding.)

Perspicacious.

                          (Blackout.)

CHAPTER 13

Leaving Snegurochka

Suddenly, there appeared spinning groups of sparkling lights, as if blown by swirling winds, at each of the TFD tables. They were nano-drones, previously hovering like twinkling stars near the ceiling, now looking more like glimmering snowflakes in moonlight. Two hologram heads appeared above our table, a man and a woman, probably the pub's owners. Their voices could be heard, speaking in unison, thanking everyone for visiting the pub and wishing all a good evening. As they finished their well-wishing and faded away, Pru stepped up to the table.

"Well, I'm sure those holo-heads made you feel extra special! Ahem," Pru again pretended to clear her throat, "but, I just wanted to say thanks again personally, as well as mention that, because of our recent expansion, we temporarily don't have curbside. So … "

"Oh, my God," said Availa, expressing mild annoyance.

"Right, sorry," Pru continued, "so, you'll have to tell your cars or rides to pick you up at the tram stop there," gesturing out the window, "or you could just stand outside anywhere, and they usually can find you that way."

"But it's raining ... " Availa complained.

"Yeah, and there's dihydrogen monoxide in the rain here," Kenton snorted.

"Ew! One forty-four!" Availa exclaimed, looking at Kenton and smiling.

"There's a canopy," offered Pru.

"It's not so bad, Availa. We'll be good" Nilima assured.

"Thank you. I think we're good" I said politely to Pru.

"I hope so," said Pru, smiling at me coyly as she turned to warn the other tables that they may be inconvenienced by their autonomous cars arriving to pick them up on the wrong side of the building, due to the recent remodeling and expansion not yet reflected in the local zone digital traffic blueprints, GPS annotations and autonomous curbside pick-up guide maps.

At that moment, nearly everyone suddenly stopped talking and stared forward as though looking at something in the distance. I glanced around and noticed that all around the room, the other patrons, the bartender, Pru and another hostess, were frozen in their gaze, most likely getting a "community service" message on their smart lenses. Melinda had turned to look out the window, her reflected face appearing saddened and drained. I didn't see the message, as I had removed my smarts. I assumed that Melinda was not wearing smart lenses.

Community service alerts were beginning to feel strange to me. Of course, we'd been getting emergency alerts on our smart devices for well more than a decade, warning of approaching tornadoes and flash-flood conditions, asking for help in finding abducted children ... and so forth. The scope of community service alerts had slowly expanded, especially over the last three years, to include warnings of possible upcoming shortages of various food staples, like corn or orange juice, and "warnings" about upcoming events in the recipient's metro area. For example, while in Palo Alto two weeks prior, I got a community service alert that traffic and parking in San Francisco the upcoming weekend would be adversely affected by the Roodoo Blaine Mog concert, punctuated by an "end of message" line with an embedded symbol you could dubblink to purchase tickets to the concert. Another embedded symbol linked you to a parking space reservation service. There was no boundary between civic responsibility and product promotion.

As others at the table began to rise to collect their coats from the racks, I stood and took a couple of steps back to make room for others to get around me. I bid Nilima and Kenton good-night, then nodded and waved to Greyson and the interns as Brendan and Melinda slid along the benches to extract themselves.

"C'mere young man!" Brendan smiled at me and grasped my shoulders, "good to see you! Looking forward to working with you again." Then, leaning in and whispering in my ear, "Hey, that Pru's a fine thing, eh? Maybe you ought to say 'good night'." Brendan gestured with his head toward the bar where Pru was standing. She was leaning back on it with both elbows, looking down at her boots.

"Brendan, it was good to see you too," I replied, "guess we'll get some 'further direction' in the morning. On the other thing, uh

... not sure I'm ready to explore new relationships yet."

"Losing that sweet girl of yours had to be bloody brutal. But hey, it's been a couple, right? You can always just inquire about a massage, right?" Brendan winked and gently poked my stomach with his fist.

I smiled and nodded politely, trying not to think about Cadence. Brendan then turned to say good night to Melinda, who had walked up behind him. As Brendan moved away toward another table, Melinda stepped up to me. "Nice meeting you today," she said, "sorry for my outburst. I think I repeated myself a bit from our breakfast meeting. Guess two glasses of wine should be my limit."

"Oh. No, please don't apologize. What you said was very important ... and very sober!" I meant to sound supportive, but I thought it may have sounded like I was just assuring her she didn't sound drunk, so I added "I mean, I agree we could do ... *should* do ... a better job ... *prioritizing* which problems we invest ourselves in ... in *fixing*. Sometimes it takes a *hero* to fight for doing what makes sense, I mean, with the *tools* we have." God, I'm an idiot, I thought.

Then I recalled a strong cathartic feeling I had while Melinda was standing and delivering her condemnation of augmented reality. She must have felt something like that too, I thought.

"Hey, I bet it felt pretty satisfying to deliver that message to us tonight," I said.

Melinda, expressionless, regarded me carefully for a moment, then said, "So, I'm gone for a few days, but we should touch base when I'm back. It may be worthwhile for us to meet and talk in person on ADADA and the tunnel, if you're still around."

"Absolutely!" I exclaimed, realizing that she had chosen to stay with TFD, but then I felt I may have sounded too eager, so I toned down my energy level and added, "I'm staying here in town for two weeks. Maybe longer. Depends on how the work goes. Hey, I'm really glad you decided to stay and work on our team."

Melinda shrugged. "Well, I almost decided to leave this morning with that asshole Svarog shrieking 'vagina! vagina!' during his pitch. But then I thought that, if I stay, maybe I'll get to be a public spokesperson for a worthy cause."

"Redeeming value. You can influence whether the tunnel goes forward. You're very compelling, I mean, like with your critique of AR." I tried to reinforce the correctness of her decision to stay.

As I took Melinda's extended hand, she clasped my hand in both of hers, extending two fingers gently under the cuff of my shirt sleeve, lightly pressing the inside of my wrist, saying "I think the world needs more heroes." In that moment, as we gazed into each other's eyes, as I felt the soft coolness of her fingers on my wrist, I realized that her eyes and her mouth were, quite possibly, the most beautiful facial features I had ever been privileged to see.

She turned and walked quickly toward the exit as I stood there for a bit, wondering what I was supposed to be doing. Then I remembered I needed to get my coat and walk to the hotel. I felt relief in acknowledging that we had finally reached the official wrap-up and dispersal at the end of the day. I was delighted that Melinda decided to stay and work on the Gravity Train project.

As I was about to walk out the pub entrance to the street, I heard Pru say "Hey!" I turned back to see her walking toward the reception desk. "I hope you'll stop in again if you're in town for a while," she said.

"I will," I said, although I wasn't actually sure if I would or not. "Thank you, Snow Maiden," I added. Pru smiled and waved as I left the pub.

My head was full of Melinda.

CHAPTER 14

Night and Day

I found myself in my hotel room, with a vague sense of having walked the several blocks from Snegurochka, moving with other pedestrians in an animate mass while crossing streets, not noticing traffic signals or traffic, relying on the awareness and self-preserving instinct of those breathing around me to ensure my own safe transit, occasionally smiling in gratitude, to no one in particular, for the multitude of late-night strollers in the late-night city, enabling the crowd-sourcing of next-best-action at each curb and crossing. Along the way I had been comforted by white-noise from rain on the hood and shoulders of my coat, as well as from nearby splattering on sidewalk and street surfaces ... a trance-inducing reverie.

A lamp in the room switched on, sensing my presence, but I had not moved from the entryway yet. I stood without a plan, feeling a rain droplet ... a dihydrogen monoxide droplet ... gently caressing my cheek as it moved downward, powered by gravity alone, leaping from my chin to merge with the general wetness of the front of my coat.

I removed my dripping wet coat and draped it over the shower curtain rod in the nearby bathroom. I then proceeded to remove my shoes, socks and trousers, since they were all fairly wet. I grabbed a large white towel from a rack and began drying my face and hair as I walked to the bed. On reaching the bed, I spread the towel out over the bedspread and laid myself down upon it. There I reclined, staring up at the ceiling, as the day began to replay itself in my head.

The replay began with hearing Melinda's voice say "nicely done," over and over, each time with a slightly different inflection, varying breathiness and volume, tone changing from sweet to harsh and back again.

I recalled my first sight of her face as I surveyed the breakfast area in the hotel that morning. We made eye contact momentarily before she turned away. I began to adjust my recollection of that first look, seeing in Melinda's face more of the appealing qualities I discerned as we said good-bye at the pub less than an hour ago.

It occurred to me that she may have found out about her transfer to the tunnel project only moments before I walked up to her table. The way she slapped down her notepad and turned to look outside ... it might have been her initial reaction to her reassignment. Somehow I missed that earlier, probably due to preoccupation with my own doubts and concerns about that project. I recalled Melinda saying "remarkably insightful" about my bio-tech reports, and how sincere her face appeared in that moment.

My thoughts then drifted to *Know Doubt with Don Dander* that morning, the anxiety build-up as I approached the Gyre Ventures tower, the unexpected news interview, the tension build-up and release portrayed in the *Font* video, the TFD New Q event and dinner at Snegurochka, finally zeroing in on one particular moment when I first arrived at the pub. I regretted telling Pru her face inspired poetry, as it seemed excessively flirtatious in retrospect. I wondered if that's what prompted her to wink at me and rub my shoulders.

I considered Melinda's parting handshake that evening as a significant moment, certainly worth further examination on my part, especially the sensation of her fingers on my wrist. I tried to re-experience it by very lightly touching my right wrist, gently stroking with two fingers from the base of the palm up two or three inches onto the wrist. As gently as I was able to do that, it did not measure up to the cool smoothness of Melinda's fingers, nor the soft, feather-like quality of her parting touch.

Maybe Brendan was right about me needing to explore new relationships.

◊ ◊ ◊

After a while I called Cadence and transferred her image to the mirror.

"Connor! So nice to hear from you! So? How did things go today?" Cadence wore a lovely silk robe with multicolored butterflies and flowers imprinted on a deep blue background. She was sitting with her legs crossed, on an antique wooden chest we had placed by the footboard of our bed.

"Cadence, my love," I began, but I stopped there. I tried to say something else … anything else, but I stood silently in front of the mirror-screen. I dearly loved Cadence when we were together, and her avatar had been such a comfort to me, engaging in conversation, cheering me when I felt sad, helping me make decisions. My mouth was open, but I was just breathing through it. Still no words for Cadence. Perhaps it was time to let her go, I thought.

Projecting genuine concern, Cadence asked me what was wrong as I quiesced the DA app that drove her avatar.

◊   ◊   ◊

Cadence and I both had been fond of hiking, and the Big Basin Redwoods state park and several Open Space Preserves in the Bay Area provided attractive venues. We gradually developed a habit of hiking every weekend, usually on mountain trails, working our way up to our fifteen mile target hike length in about two months.

We had moved in together about a year into our relationship. One Saturday morning we chatted and enjoyed our coffee while lounging on the deck outside the kitchen of our 2nd floor condo. On that morning, as we gazed at the flowers and shrubbery in the enclosed courtyard below, Cadence suggested we go camping that weekend.

I was not a big fan of camping and hadn't done it since my teenage years. Cadence had never camped, never slept in the outdoors. I looked at Cadence with a deliberately baffled expression, which elicited a response, "I don't know. It just popped into my head, but can we? Please?"

So we did. We spent a couple of hours figuring out what we would need to bring ... how much water, food for snacks, food for dinner, first aid supplies and so forth. We brought an old sleeping bag of mine, big enough for the two of us, which could be rolled up and attached to my backpack. Cadence suggested we bring marshmallows to roast, adding that she assumed that's what everyone did while camping. Cadence then suggested I bring my old acoustic guitar, but I declined since it would have been too cumbersome to lug it around for miles in the woods.

"We can always just sing *a cappella*," I offered.

"I fancy harmonizing with my fella!" she rhymed.

We went on our camping hike that weekend. We built a campfire. We sang and harmonized. We roasted marshmallows. Just a few minutes after Cadence had eaten her first marshmallow, while she roasted another one, she began to feel strange. What seemed like a mild allergy at first, causing her to sniffle, sneeze and clear her throat a few times, moved into clear trouble breathing and then frantic gasping for breath. She clutched her stomach, turned to the side and vomited. Then she collapsed on her back, panting. I stroked her forehead and held her wrist, noting that her pulse seemed very weak.

I made an emergency call from my smarts. The man who answered identified himself as Adam and asked a few questions. He said Cadence appeared to be having an allergic reaction. Possibly she was in anaphylactic shock caused by something she encountered in the woods or by something she had eaten. After getting my statement of acceptance of responsibility to administer emergency medication via injection, Adam dispatched a med-drone to my location, as best as could be determined by enhanced GPS, which would carry a hypodermic injection of epinephrine which I was to administer as soon as it arrived. Adam also said an EMS team would be coming to transport Cadence via helicopter to a hospital for further evaluation and treatment.

While we waited for the drone, her breathing stopped. I frantically applied CPR, looking up now and then to catch sight of the drone. It arrived after a couple of minutes, circling us once and then setting down a few feet away. I rushed to it, pulling the hypodermic needle out of a white pouch with a red cross on it, and I quickly injected its contents into Cadence.

There was no reaction to the epinephrine. I went back to doing CPR, but I was already fearing the worst. As I knelt there, panting, my heart racing, my face wet with tears, I heard the faint sound of a helicopter rotor getting louder with each passing second.

I accompanied Cadence on the rescue helicopter. It was later determined that the likely cause of her death was a severe allergic reaction to the gelatin used in producing the marshmallows.

It was sunny the next morning as I walked on the shady side of 3rd Avenue toward the Gyre Ventures tower. Once again, people appeared to be talking to themselves, but more likely they were voicing commands to start apps or stop a video display. People appeared to be staring blankly into space without purpose, but more likely they were following news feeds or getting updates on the weather forecast or reading text messages from co-workers or checking the readouts from their personal health monitor devs ... and so forth. Once inside the tower, I went directly to Waldon's office. Finding the door open, I stood outside and surveyed the view for a moment.

I recognized the back of Waldon's head. He was sitting behind his desk, facing away from the door, looking out the window at an impressive view of the city skyline against a hazy blue background, tall buildings splendidly illuminated by the morning sun. What a wonderful workspace, I thought, before revealing my presence with "Good morning, Waldon."

Waldon spun around, "Ah! Connor! Have a seat."

I sat down in one of four excessively padded chairs surrounding Waldon's desk, noticing several pictures of Waldon taken at various business meetings and award presentations on the wall to the right.

"Get a good rest?" asked Waldon. "I hope so," he continued, "since we've got a lot to talk about."

There seemed something dark and disturbing about Waldon's voice at that moment.

"Brendan may be a bit late, but we should get started," Waldon continued as he stood up to walk behind me and close his office door. Then he slowly, contemplatively, moved back to his desk chair and sat down. "Since it's just you and me, I want to mention that Robert knows someone shared your 'poo-poo on the path to certainty' research results with Ansell a few months back, after we all agreed, I believe, not to."

I knew, of course, that someone had done that, but I tried to appear surprised.

"Now, I don't know who. I don't *want* to know. But Robert

told me the other day that he suspects it was you."

That *did* surprise me, although it probably shouldn't have. The only person in the room who might have appeared concerned about withholding the results from Ansell was me.

"Don't worry," Waldon went on, "He has no proof, but in situations like that ... you know, where a key business exec or government leader suspects you of disloyalty ... it's usually a good idea to keep a low profile. You know what I mean. Hey, I'll tell you, good choice letting Adora do your team idea pitch! I would have felt a bit uneasy if *you* had delivered it with Robert sitting right there in front of the podium! Ha! Just kidding Connor! It's gonna be okay!" As I tried to absorb it all, Waldon sedately added, "Just be careful."

Being careful and keeping a low profile while leading a fairly high-profile validation analysis on the Gravity Train was going to be tricky. I thought I might talk with Brendan about it later ... maybe Randall too. It occurred to me Melinda might agree to take the lead on presentations to Svarog and the executive team. Maybe she could be our public spokesperson as well.

"Now, hey, back up to the surface, right?" Waldon laughed as he seemed to be trying to lighten things up, "I want to ask you a question. What are the key issues facing mankind ... humankind ... as a whole?" Waldon's expression suddenly turned dour.

Still processing his earlier remarks, I attempted to buy a few seconds of time to reflect. "Do you mean right now and for the next few years coming up? ... or longer term? ... worldwide or US-centric?" A few unpleasant seconds ticked by with no response or reaction from Waldon. Then he raised his hands as if to say "whatever," and I began to share my thoughts.

"So ... ah ... I think the key issues are linked to our understanding of the effects of civilization on human life. Industrialization of everything, application of advanced technologies, bio-chemicals, genetic modifications, neuropharmacology, be-mod, nanoscopic engines used for so many things ... used even inside of people. All of that is pushing hard, but there is a sense that we may be inadvertently hurting ourselves. From what I've read, including recent research we've done here at TFD, there appears to be growing anxiety about the *speed* of change, the *risk* of change. There is also an emerging viewpoint ... coming from just a few scattered voices in the aether ... that people are being subconsciously manipulated."

Waldon turned to the side and gave a loud snort. "Manipulated by whom?" he asked.

"That's a matter of conjecture, I think." I replied, "While specific persons and entities have been named, there appears to be no consensus yet in any public discussion I've found."

"Manipulated toward what end?"

"Nothing manifest. Some innuendo toward manipulation ... or tuning ... of how people see their basic needs in life, personal goals, maybe even belief systems."

"Belief systems? Like religious beliefs?"

"More like how we see reality. How we make sense of the world in our minds, so that we're not in a constant state of bewilderment. In general, I think it forms the basis for how readily we accept something as true or normal or even possible. It would certainly include religious beliefs, I think, but it's more than that. There are drugs and diet supplements now being advertised as 'insight enhancing'." I paused and wondered if this was in any way the sort of thing Waldon expected to hear. Just then came a knock on the door. "Come in!" Waldon invited.

"Mr. Perry. Sorry to be late." Brendan apologized as he walked in, pulling a large knapsack off his shoulder as he sat in the chair next to me.

"We're good," Waldon said, smiling broadly. "Connor just shared his views on key issues facing mankind these days. Before we go any further though, I'd like to hear *your* thoughts on that."

"Key issues? Facing mankind?" Brendan asked, looking somewhat puzzled. "Well, hey, ah … I'll tell you. Well, the first thing comes to mind is food. You know, like …"

"Not time for lunch yet," Waldon quipped, looking over at me, as I managed to fake a small chuckle.

Brendan continued, "Right. Ha! What I'm thinking though, is that food is a very comprehensive area, with many problems … potential problems … ranging from producing enough to feed the world, to sustainability of whatever the practices are … like genetic modifications and all that … what we take out of the soil, what we put *into* the soil … where the cattle graze … that sort. I think a lot of people worry that we're taking too many risks in doing things that may have long-term consequences we didn't see coming."

"Even though we've made a lot of progress in those areas?" asked Waldon, turning to look out the window behind him.

"Progress? You mean how we got through the famine of '29?" Brendan sounded incredulous and looked over at me before continuing, "That was mostly luck, really. Mostly …."

"I agree," I interrupted. "The progress we've made can be viewed through more than one lens. For example, the long-awaited global approval of geo-engineering techniques for solar radiation management. Like SRM2 with sulfate aerosols, while reducing the effect of rising greenhouse gas levels, appears to be causing a need for fortification of organic matter and other moisture retainers in soil, to counteract regional reduction of precipitation. And the shift to less meat in human diets, while a good idea in some ways, had the unexpected consequence of what amounted to a global trade and economic crisis."

"Bang on!" Brendan jumped back in. "We made progress in the mid-twenties with shifting away from meat ... mostly beef ... but we didn't get the strategy right for long term management of cattle populations, goat populations, protein balance in food production, dealing with issues in global synchronization of ....""

Waldon turned back to face us, cutting in on Brendan, "Gentlemen, I appreciate hearing your views. I think you're both on the same page in that you both view the big human problems from the perspective of the *humans* ... I mean, the populace in general. What you need to understand is that the big problems ... the big issues facing mankind ... are problems faced by the *enablers* of life itself. The big issues must be viewed from the perspective of the enablers."

Waldon paused there, shifting his gaze between Brendan and myself, but neither of us displayed any reaction of which I was aware. I puzzled over what he meant by "enablers of life" but could not bring myself to ask.

"As we move toward the middle of this century," Waldon resumed, "the equation of life ... how it continues to be possible for the human race to *exist* ... will increasingly depend on *acceptance*. Yesterday, Svarog went on a lot about certainty and 'choosing the right direction' and crap about comfort and peace of mind. He has to say all that crap. I do too, when I'm in front of a large crowd or talking outside TFD. But you two are part of the trusted team, and we've involved you both in a lot of really important and confidential work in the past. You've both been rewarded for your excellent service. Of course, you'll be rewarded again for your work on this new project. Trust me."

"Not sure I follow you. Acceptance ...?" Brendan folded his arms and cocked his head to one side.

Waldon leaned back in his chair, placing his hands behind his head before continuing. "Most people don't need to be *certain* of anything in order to live and be happy, but they do need to *accept*. They need to accept that whatever their *leaders* appear to be certain about ... in terms of strategic vision, laws, regulations, taxes, how we farm, how we manufacture, in terms of how we make electricity, how we raise our kids and educate them, what is considered noteworthy in art and entertainment, how long of a life-span is reasonable for a human ... in terms of many, many things ... all of that needs to be accepted as being in their best interest. Otherwise, literally trillions of dollars a year are lost across global economies as the leaders of central governments, corporate CEOs and chief executives of regulatory agencies have to contend with all the expense of changing practices and policies ... or somehow proving that we're *already* on the right course ... or even just demonstrating that there is no acceptable alternative."

I began to feel as though I were possibly asleep and having a nightmare ... or maybe I was an unwitting subject in a psychology experiment that TFD was conducting ... either way, I could not accept that acceptance was the key issue of the world. "Waldon," I began, slowly, "sorry, I thought this meeting was about the Gravity Train, and I'm having a little trouble getting my ..."

"It *is* about the Gravity Train!" Waldon interrupted, then after a moment he continued calmly. "Well, at least partly. Mostly it is contained within the expanded ADADA project, which I've also asked you to validate."

"Expanded?" Brendan pondered aloud. "I mean, I know 'acceptance' is there in the acronym, but I thought it was referring to helping a badly developed or damaged brain to shift toward better decision making ... better self-awareness and self-control. It meant the brain's acceptance of some internal new growth or rewiring, so to speak."

"It does." Waldon sat up straight and looked down, fiddling with his tie. "Augmented Directed Autonomous Decision Acceptance was the project name, as well as the name we've given to the set of technologies behind it, but there are two phases to the project." Waldon continued, now looking at me, "The second phase, which I am now disclosing to you both, under the usual information handling restrictions of course ... the second phase expands the scope of 'acceptance'. It's not just concerned with having your brain accept corrective brain growth in support of reducing violent tendencies and all that stuff ADADA-certified engines provide. We're moving further into assurance of acceptance of decisions made by world leaders ... by the enablers of life ... for the greater good of mankind."

I attempted to settle into the concept with some rephrasing. "So the ADADA engine could be used ... *would* be used ... to ensure acceptance by the populace of some key decision or initiative or new law or ... I mean, it will become a kind of delivery mechanism ... for propaganda?" I paused, worried that I may have misunderstood and had, possibly, offended Waldon.

Waldon raised both hands, speaking calmly and reassuringly. "Let's not use that word. Don't say 'propaganda'. There's a lot of *good* here. In phase one, we did studies showing ADADA's value in helping those who were mistreated or neglected in their early years. Just as we can help those individuals find a way to comfortably fit in with their families, their co-workers, society ... in phase two of ADADA we are helping *all* individuals. We're helping them to live in a world of less conflict, less volatility, less *anxiety*. Seriously, what's better than that? What could be more valuable or more important?"

"How about *trust*?" Brendan asked, "I mean, don't you need people to *trust* the source first, and then that leads to acceptance of what they're being told?"

"Right, trust has been enabling and driving acceptance for centuries," I added, "when humans have had leaders who have *earned* that trust."

"We're doing more than that!" Waldon barked, then pulled back to a more heartening tone. "We are not just going to certify 'trust-ability' of something or someone. We will be *obviating the need for trust*." Waldon paused at that point, projecting a sense of satisfaction that he had somehow, perhaps with the mere sound of the words he had just spoken, secured the commitment of myself and Brendan to the new project. "Now, gentlemen," he continued, "you each have a package of documents waiting for you on the TFD server. Some are Gravity Train related. Most relate to ADADA phase two. I want the both of you to start diving in on the new research related to acceptance. Pull in whatever other supporting sources or experts you need to help you define and describe validation studies for the ADADA phase two pilot. Delegate and coordinate. Keep Melinda and Kenton busy here too. Let's talk again toward the end of next week. You can show me what you have so far, and then you can tweak it and be ready to present to Robert at his staff meeting the following Tuesday. We're all counting on you!"

Waldon then stood, signaling that he wanted the meeting to end at that point. Brendan and I rose to shake Waldon's hand, mumble a 'thank you' and exit to the hallway.

"I need to sit down," Brendan said, turning to walk toward a couch against the wall a short distance away. I followed, hoping that I could maintain my work persona of the thirty-something, well-meaning, pedantic consultant.

"Sorry. I was feeling a bit light-headed for a moment." Brendan began, "I feel like I'm struggling here. There's no good that would come of something like that ... like what Perry was describing. Not sure I want to be here right now. You know what I mean?"

I was concerned and disheartened about the apparent direction being explored for the ADADA technologies, yet I focused on projecting a calm demeanor and suggested to Brendan that we look further into it, objectively. "I hear you, Brendan. But you know what? Let's go through all the research he's sent us and look for other sources too. Let's talk to a few experts. Let's try to look at it as calmly and rationally as we can. If we think we see potential danger in applying technology to control people that way, then ...."

"*If we see danger*?!? Are you *joking*?" Brendan interrupted,

"Sorry to lose the rag here, but it's *got* to be dangerous! It's immoral! It's against all life and time!"

"But we can best make the case against it by approaching it with normal, objective, thorough analysis," I responded assertively, "so, upon seeing evidence of potential for danger or malfeasance, we would include something in our validation study proposal designed to bring that out. You know, a 'responding variable' of some type that would strongly indicate danger of unpredictable results in any real-life application, for example."

"This is such a huge pile of crap! How long's a 'reasonable' life-span?!? Sorry, but I'm having trouble with this!" Brendan leaned back, staring upward, breathing heavily.

My thoughts raced around, trying to identify some possibility of a partial solution ... maybe some way to apply part of the ADADA phase two work as a treatment for some other serious mental disorder, but not a tool to influence the general population. Waldon's remark that 'it *is* about the Gravity Train' flashed into my head. Did he mean that acceptance directed by the 'enablers' would be used to get that project approved?

"I know," I empathized with Brendan, "I'm having trouble with it too, but if we argue viscerally, our comments will be ignored. We have to present a compelling logical argument, if we can, that shows this new application for ADADA is doomed to failure."

"What if it's not 'doomed to failure' for those buggers who want to use it?"

"In our information gathering, our research, our analysis ... in all of that ... we must try to take the perspective of those 'enablers of life' Waldon mentioned, so that our results will be meaningful and actionable from their perspective."

Brendan stared at me imploringly and asked "What if it's not possible for us to take that perspective?"

CHAPTER 15

Pruven

I had no answer for Brendan as to whether we really could adopt the perspective of those striving to obviate the need for trust. Later that day I met with the rest of the Gravity Train team, except for Melinda, who was officially on vacation. I had expected only Brendan and Kenton to be there, but Kenton arrived with Omari Tinibu and Availa Coverdale. Omari worked with Kenton in the Research group, and it seemed logical to me for him to join our team. Since Availa was focused on ADADA and follow-on work, it surprised me that Kenton asked her to join that day.

Availa was convinced that we shouldn't treat her work as separate from the Gravity Train. She postulated that the tunnel construction, if it were to be approved, might require brain adjustments for anxiety reduction.

"The work crew on the tunnel will definitely need that, and

maybe everyone on the planet. I talked with my sister about that last night, and she totally convinced me," Availa explained.

I made a mental note that both Availa and Adora should be pulled into any meetings where we might want to explore that connection.

The rest of our meeting merely consisted of apportioning out different document sources and sub-segments of related research to review and assess. We had a little over a week before we would have to present our findings and preliminary conclusions to Waldon in preparation for a final review with Svarog and, probably, the senior executive team. In general, the team's spirit was positive and relaxed. Even Brendan seemed a lot more settled than he was just after the meeting with Waldon a few hours earlier.

◊　　◊　　◊

As I walked alone back to the hotel at the end of the day, I decided there were two more people I should talk to about the conversation that morning with Waldon: Melinda and Mars.

After finishing the quick-pick dinner sandwich offered in the lobby, I spent a couple of hours reading and planning for how I would get more people involved from TFD who were experts in various related fields. Should I meet with them one-on-one? ... as a group? ... in person? There were advantages and disadvantages to each approach.

I felt discombobulated. I'd heard Pop-Pop and some of my grade school teachers say "discombobulated" when I was a kid, and I had assumed it was just a made-up word. As a teenager, I heard someone use it, and I was surprised to find it in several on-line dictionaries and learned that it had been in use for well over a hundred years. A good word, it nicely conveys the intertwining of confusion and frustration by both its definition and its sound when spoken.

I was definitely discombobulated. So much so, that it occurred to me I should get out and do something to clear my head. Recently, my choice would have been to talk with Cadence, but the idea that popped into my head was to head to Snegurochka's. I could just sit at the bar on my own. That would be fine.

The Snegurochka pub was only a couple of blocks away, but I enjoyed walking outside at night, so I took a longer route which took me nearly an hour to get there. I hesitated at the pub door, suddenly feeling anxious at the possibility that Pru might be the greeter tonight. Would she remember me? Should I call her by name?

As I entered, I noticed Pru behind the hostess desk and admitted to myself that she was the driving force behind my desire to visit that pub again, as well as my choosing a convoluted route to delay arrival.

"Good evening. Welcome to Snegurochka's," Pru said, somewhat wistfully. Then, before I could speak, her face shifted to pleasant surprise, "Hey! I know you from the TFD thing. You're Connor, right?"

"Yes. Hi Pru. How are you doing?" I was surprised she recalled my name. My tag was blocked.

After a minute or so of chit chat about the weather and our recollections of previous weather, I pointed toward the bar and asked if she would join me for a drink if she got off work soon. Pru said she'd be wrapping up in about ten minutes, but she preferred to meet for a drink elsewhere.

"I really like Lacey's up the street. Do you know where I mean?"

"Yes, I do. I'll go over and get us a table. Thank you!" I said and waved as I left.

◊   ◊   ◊

Lacey's was a charming little cafe, connected to a hotel lobby but not exclusively for use by the hotel guests. I sat at a small table and ordered a glass of wine. Pru arrived shortly and ordered one of the same for herself. We talked about local restaurants and pubs until her drink arrived, at which point we toasted to variety and adventure.

"So, Connor, what is it you do exactly? For a living?" she asked.

"I study this planet and its inhabitants," I said. That was, actually, what I did. However, it sounded odd when I put it that way, and I liked that it sounded odd.

"Oh. My my. I guess you're … an 'extraterrestrial being' of some kind?" Pru seemed a bit put-off, perhaps re-evaluating her decision to meet me there.

I pushed it a bit further. "Interesting. Your pre-wired assumption is that anyone who'd bother studying the Earth or its indigenous creatures must be from another planet. I'll make a note of that."

"Ha! Do you plan to include me in your study?" Pru gave me a coy look, then added "I suppose you want to know all about me."

"I want to know about people *like* you. I'm not interested in people as individuals. Only people in statistically aggregated clumps." I began to feel more comfortable.

"Clumps? Wow. Well, I'm afraid I can only speak for myself." Pru took another sip from her glass while shifting her eyes to look outside.

"No problem. I'll just map you into the clump of the population you represent with your buying and engagement preferences, credit-worthiness, health issues, sexual habits ... and so forth." I realized that mentioning "sexual habits" was a bit risky, and I worried that I crossed a line while she stared at me expressionlessly for a few seconds before responding.

"There aren't many like me. I'm a fairy, you see," she spoke while looking down into her lap, as though embarrassed to admit being a fairy.

"Fairy? As in the magical being featured in the clump of human literature called 'fairy tales'?"

"I'll warn you, some tales about fairies are not completely true."

"Well, then at least they are *partly* true. That will have to do, I suppose. So, tell me, the sexual habits ..."

"Of fairies?" Pru interrupted. "Well, it's a wide range of things to try to describe, from chasing each other through trees while trying to sing in harmony, to 'tushy-twos' ... where two of us agree to fly around naked together with our bottoms touching."

"Fascinating. It would benefit my research if I had a deep understanding of those behaviors."

"And fairies can sense each others' thoughts. Our thoughts blend."

"Risky. Entanglements like that can strengthen or they can confuse."

"Helps fairies agree on what to do when we're together," said Pru, shrugging her shoulders.

"When you're with someone like me, what do you like to do?"

Pru took a sip of wine, then began sliding her glass around on the table. "I like tracing curlicues with a wine glass on the flecked surface of these tables. See what it does?"

"The lens-like base of the glass magnifies the flecks ... seems to pull them up closer, lending the table an appearance of having a watery constitution. As the glass moves on, the sparkling flecks return to their previous locations in the solid table surface."

"Right! The flecks indulge me for a moment, then return to reality."

"You make the glass dance gracefully. Like movement in ballet. Like movement of celestial objects. Light bends both in their gravity and through your glass," I said.

"Ooo. I feel so close to far away stars and planets right now. Connected to them," said Pru.

"Far away things feel closer when you focus on them ... when you think about them," I said, then changed my voice to sound stern and professorial, "Okay, survey question. Select the best response. Do creatures disposed to sensuality gain more insight from observation? ... from analysis? ...from analogy? ... or the touch of someone's hand?"

Pru stared at me with a puzzled look for a moment, then she asked, "Connor, what's going on here? What are you trying to figure out?"

I became aware that I was drifting in thought but unable to reign myself in, so I continued, "The wider the landscape, the narrower our personal perspective. The more insight we think we gain, the less reliable our comprehension of the big picture."

"Are you stressed out by your job? I saw your news interview. I thought you handled it very well. I mean, you came across as knowledgeable and confident." Pru seemed to be trying to bring me back to Earth.

"Thank you for saying that," I said, realizing my meeting Pru that night may have been ill-timed.

"I mean it. Will you be doing another interview soon? Are you worried about it? Because, if you're worried, you really shouldn't be."

"No. I mean, no, I'm not worried about that, but it is possible I might be interviewed again. About the Gravity Train work. Sorry, I'm feeling a bit random tonight. Too many things spinning around in my head."

"You poor thing! I don't think I could handle doing live interviews for the news, especially on such a controversial topic. I admire you, Connor. I hope it gets easier and that you can relax a bit soon." As she spoke, Pru appeared to be collecting herself as though about to leave.

"Yes, thank you. Pru, I'm sorry. I think I should have waited till work was a bit less stressful before trying to get to know you better. I appreciate your meeting me for a drink."

"It's completely fine. I'm a little tired though. Maybe we can try this again another time?"

"Sure. So ... Pru is short for Prudence, I guess? That right?" I wanted to get a little more personal with her, but that was all I could think of asking.

"Nope," she said, standing up, "it's actually short for Pruven." Then she spelled it for me.

"Wow! That's so cool! Pruven! I like that!"

"But I'd prefer if you'd just keep calling me Pru," she said with a smile, "and for me on the insight thing, by the way, it's the touch of someone's hand." She then touched my hand as she began to step away from the table, adding, "Thanks for the drink. Let's do this again soon ... maybe after your work heebie-jeebies subside a bit. Good night."

"Thank you, Pru," was all I managed to say.

CHAPTER 16

Studying Earth

For the next few days I remained in Manhattan, studying hundreds of pages of research results and theoretical pontifications related to the concept of deeply tunneling into the earth. I worked through the weekend, streaming content while reclining in a comfortable chair in my midtown suite, texting twice a day with Brendan to share updates on our progress.

There was definitely no shortage of material to read, with the bulk of it having been produced within the previous five years. While some earlier work warned of extreme pressure in the upper mantle ... as well as in the Moho transitional layer, the existence of which had been first postulated in the early 20th century, using data on the speed with which earthquake vibrations traveled at various depths ... recent studies focused more on "theoretical testing" or mathematical modeling of various technological approaches for deep tunneling into the earth, using computer simulation of the material properties and the expected stresses and temperatures.

Funding for deep tunneling or deep drilling projects like those had been impossible to secure, mainly because the potential benefits of obtaining samples of the mantle's mineral composition did not appear to be worth the billions of dollars required to retrieve them. Even though some recent studies made fairly convincing arguments supporting the idea that advanced technologies could minimize (though not completely eliminate) the potential for disastrous setbacks in such an endeavor, the gain of scientific knowledge was not seen as worth the investment or the risk by those who could supply the funds ... mainly the central governments of the largest economies and a few large global corporations.

News reports on the Gravity Train or "GT" proposal, while first treated as a joke by the mainstream press and eliciting salacious commentary on social media, gradually evolved toward seriously composed editorials and analysis of the long-term investment potential. Opinion pieces danced around the appeal of the GT for both business-related and personal travel, as well as the energy efficiency theme. Reflecting on comments made by Svarog and Waldon earlier in the week, I metaphorically mused that it was TFD's mission to "choreograph the dance" of appealing factors, perhaps adding a musical score inspiring confidence and exaltation in human achievement. The world's audience should leave the GT proposal "theater" with feelings of closure on the decision and excitement in the way forward. They should want to meet friends for a drink afterward and share their experiences, how they were emotionally moved, how TFD's analysis had helped to grow their faith, what visions formed in their heads as they saw the economic components pirouetting into perfect formation on the stage. They could try to recollect at what point the underlying orchestral chord-play reached, for them, its intense crescendo of finality and acceptance.

On Monday, after spending way too much time amusing myself by pondering various ridiculous advertisement campaigns for the Gravity Train, I decided to walk to Gyre Ventures and sign out for a temporary office in the part of the building leased by TFD. I told myself that the more formal office ambiance would help me focus on my work. Brendan would likely be there too, so I voiced him that perhaps we could meet later in the day. I wasn't sure if Melinda would be back yet.

As I walked, I thought about what might lie ahead. I thought about the unsettling meeting with Waldon the previous week. The expressions he used ... like "enablers of life" and "obviating the need for trust" ... increasingly haunted my mental processing of all the tunnel-related background knowledge and hypotheses. I worried about my own future. I had been truly satisfied with my career at TFD up to that point, but I worried that we were shifting away from objectivity toward a role that was almost certainly political. If that were really happening, then I didn't want to be a part of that transformation. Perhaps potential career changes should be explored? Perhaps my mind was just running a little wild ... jumping to conclusions. Perhaps I needed more information.

I arrived in the tower lobby and took an elevator to the 35th floor, reserving an office for the day via my smarts while ascending. Soon I would meet with Brendan to compare progress and postulate on what remained to be explored before pooling our analyses for presentation to Waldon. We had decided to start our Gravity Train focus on the technical feasibility aspect, postponing research on potential dangers as long as we could.

I had been contemplating the other day, while in my discombobulated state, how to best pull in the perspectives of others and allow some cross-pollenation between their fields of expertise. It was time to decide how to approach that, I thought. I reached my assigned office and sat down at the desk, thinking about blending many areas of expertise, shifting focus from here to there as people converged to interact, wondering how that could be organized or led ... or choreographed. All of a sudden, I remembered Pru swirling her glass around on the table that night at Lacey's.

It made me think of moving a lens around to focus on some "flecks" ... some people ... in a larger group. The conference room could be the lens, and the flow of time during the day could be the equivalent of moving the lens. Poetic, I thought. I sent out an invitation to what I called a "vortex of brainstorms." I reserved a conference room in the TFD office area for Wednesday for the brainstorming. All the invitees were welcome to stop in any time during the day, as often as they liked, for as long as they liked, to talk about the Gravity Train or ADADA or both, sharing their insights, hopes and concerns.

Shortly after sending out the invitations to the vortex meeting, I heard a knock and turned to see Melinda standing in the doorway. "Hey there! May I interrupt?" she asked. She wore a bright magenta, off-the-shoulder top with lace sleeves, black pants and moccasins.

"Hi! How was your trip?" I was genuinely happy to see her.

"Fine. Fill you in later. Listen, I'm busy all day, including dinner. Wondering if we could meet after dinner tonight. There's a coffee shop near my apartment in Brooklyn, where it's usually easy to have a work-related discussion without people overhearing all your secret, proprietary bullshit. You free? Like around seven-thirty? I have a car service, so you can just meet me in the lobby downstairs. Okay?"

"Uh ... yeah. Yeah that works." I replied. The possibility that she would want to meet after work had not occurred to me.

"Great! See you in the lobby."

"I'll be there."

Melinda turned with a quick wave and walked away down the hall. She was definitely more cheerful than she was that night at the pub before her trip. I didn't know where she had gone, but wherever it was, it must have provided some positive energy. As I thought about her more light-hearted temperament, I received a message from Brendan. He would stop by in a few minutes so we could touch base on our progress.

While waiting for Brendan I pulled the vortex meeting invitee list up on my notepad:

Melinda Beckmann – Principal Scientist, Cognitive Certainty

Dr. Adora Coverdale – Principal Scientist, Early Human Intention

Availa Coverdale – Technician, Cognitive Certainty

Kenton Duckworth – Master Inventor, Research

Dr. Victoria Esposito – Director of Developmental Research,

Early Human Intention

Connor Farrell (moderator) – Principal Consultant, Early Human Intention

Randall Hewitt – Alliance Manager, Cognitive Certainty

Brendan McCarron – Applied Technology Consultant, Research

Golden North – New Market Developer, CHQ Strategy

Nilima Patel – Senior Engineer, Cognitive Certainty

Dr. Gotama Reddy – Director of Research

Omari Tinibu – Research Engineer, Research

Dr. Reddy had been TFD's Research director for about two years. I'd noticed he was quick to assimilate new technology areas, offering interesting perspectives on their potential application. I also felt strongly that Dr. Reddy's point of view on the concepts of pervasive thought-reading and alteration of the human decision process would make him a valuable participant in the vortex meeting.

While skimming through TFD employee bios, I noticed Omari had done some previous work in mathematical modeling of canal and flood-wall construction design, which might be useful from a tunnel feasibility viewpoint. In addition, Kenton and Omari agreed their research focus should be on carbon molecule structural experiments, relieving the rest of the team from that headache-inducing technological realm.

Adora and Availa would, I hoped, provide some insight around the application of ADADA to protect the health of workers who would build the GT tunnel. My previous work with Vicki, Randall and Nilima gave me a strong sense of their value in hypothetical realms, especially in connecting to solid practical adjacencies.

Although new to TFD, Golden's focus on consumer decision certainty would be interesting, I thought, to bring into the vortex. I also thought it might be prudent to invite someone from Svarog's new strategy team. I copied both Waldon and Astrid on the invitation but did not explicitly invite them.

◊   ◊   ◊

Brendan arrived, and our mutual empathy soon helped improve my outlook. We shared status on our research, briefly touching on the points each of us assessed as important so far. Then we agreed on two topics for more in-depth discussion. One was the mathematical modeling of the earth's interior composition to be drilled, and the other was the proposed tunnel boring machine and related equipment.

My concern was mainly about the modeling. While I had worked on many projects in the past that relied on theoretical testing or mathematical modeling, all of those projects had relied on modeling actual, scientifically verified properties of the materials involved. For example, with recent resurgence of plans to add nuclear fast breeder reactors to the power generation base in some countries, there is much interest in predicting what would happen if, say, a nuclear reactor's cooling system suddenly failed. Once the structural plans for a specific breeder reactor become available, you can mathematically model the extreme conditions created by such a failure. For example, the resilience of the liquid sodium pipelines at a specific point in the cooling structure can be tested by using the *measured* physical properties of liquid sodium and the actual construction materials and techniques used. By mapping a mesh of many discrete points or "elements" into the structure, the finite element method (FEM) could be applied to model how the entire structure would be affected by various stressing scenarios. Modeling the design or material specifications was much preferred, of course, over building a nuclear reactor and breaking the cooling system just to see what happens.

For the Gravity Train's tunnel construction, the modeling was entirely based upon the *assumed* physical properties of the earth's mantel at various depths. Until we actually dug into the mantel, we could not be certain of its precise composition and properties. So, while FEM could provide a very high level of confidence in the safety of a breeder reactor, the confidence level attached to safety of the Gravity Train tunnel was entirely dependent upon the accuracy of assumptions the scientists made about the mantle composition. In the studies I read, there were many footnotes with qualifiers and postulations about the possible effect on confidence level and implications for reliability of those studies, but my own opinion was that none of it formed the basis for evidence that such a tunnel would be safe. Several studies postulated that there could be a layer of diamonds near or within the mantel transition zone. Billions of tons of diamonds. More recent studies, however, suggested other structural formations in the mantle that could mimic the characteristics of diamonds by their observed seismic wave conduction properties. So maybe there are a trillion diamonds there ... or maybe none.

A related concern was the issue of temperature. Temperature will keep increasing with depth, reaching perhaps to 1200°C or about 2200°F at the tunnel's deepest point, which would be about

225 kilometers or 140 miles below the ocean's surface. The melting points of most construction steels in use were not much higher than that … only 150°C to 250°C higher … which could lead to stressing or deformation concerns about any steel structure at that depth.

Theoretically, higher melting points could be achieved through application of super-hard carbon structures like carbon nano-tubes, fullerene or graphene, but from technical evaluations we found it appeared we were still at least a decade away from being able to scale those structures up to the size of a train tunnel cross-section.

Even if some alloy with a higher melting point were used, there is still the issue of how to deal with the heat being generated along most of the tunnel. There were numerous safety concerns linked to the heat level. If the train became inoperable at or near its maximum depth, there did not appear to be a way to preserve the lives of the passengers beyond an hour or two.

Brendan's concern was mainly about the new type of tunnel boring machine (TBM) being proposed. Engineering work was not yet complete, but there were diagrams, 3D visual models and lengthy descriptions of component material properties. There were explanations of how the "spoil" … essentially whatever dirt and rubble the TBM loosens as it drills … would be used to help form the tunnel walls so that not all of it would have to be removed from the tunnel.

"They think they can make some kind of adhesive slurry out of all that muck and push it out to the edges of the tunnel as they go," Brendan said with an incredulous look, "but let's talk about the drilling end."

Brendan showed me a diagram labeled "cutter head" on his

notepad. It was a large dome-like structure which had two concentric rings of smaller cutting disks attached which, according to notes on the diagram, could also spin independently. It reminded me of old drawings I'd seen of the solar system as described by Ptolemy back in the 2nd century AD. Ptolemy was an astronomer who had come up with an elaborate view of how the Earth moved relative to the Sun, moon and the other known planets. Basically, the Earth was seen as the center of the universe, and each of the other celestial bodies orbited around Earth in a circular path. The trick was to be able to explain irregularities observed in the movement of those other celestial bodies, which he accomplished by asserting they each moved on yet another smaller circular path, the center of which followed along their larger orbit circle.

"It reminds me of the old solar system models of circles upon circles," I couldn't resist saying, "with the sparkling points of the rough, super-hard grinding surfaces representing distant stars in the background."

"Right," Brendan said, dismissively, "So, it *could* work ... at least the cutter part ... assuming we aren't too far off in modeling the composition way down there, but what worries me most are the articulation jacks."

"Articulation? You mean for the drilling angle?"

"Right. So, it can go off course a little, and you want to adjust the aim or the direction it's going. But the hydraulic system to reorient the cutter head is pretty standard stuff. I mean it's today's state-of-the-art, which is pretty good, but I'm not sure it can handle what it needs to. Especially when we don't even know what it needs to handle."

"They're planning to have one TBM starting at each end of the tunnel," I reminded Brendan, "so articulation adjustment will be extremely critical."

"Right. So I thought that should be highlighted as a problem. Potentially."

"What about the spoil conversion for tunnel wall construction?"

"From all I've seen, they have a sweet goal of reusing 80% or more to minimize what they have to truck out on the muck train. So far, the prototypes tested only reuse about 30%. That leaves an awful lot of crap to take back up to the surface. And then what in bloody hell do you do with it?"

I wanted to try to maintain some optimism. "Well, there was some speculation that further processing at the back-end … up on the earth's surface … could allow us to reuse or recycle most of that for other tunnel construction materials," I began, "Did you happen to read any of those interviews?"

"I did read them, but you still have to get all that stuff back down hundreds … thousands of miles to where you're working in the tunnel, right? Between that and just maintenance, you know, replacing things that wear out or break … well it's a big deal, I mean, for the cost and the time it takes."

"Right," I was forced to agree, "and the estimate they're comfortable with now of drilling 15,000 feet per day is *very* optimistic, I think. Even with that, we're talking about three and a half years to build the tunnel, assuming they drill seven days a week. Two years, maybe, if you start a TBM at each end and stay on top of the course adjustment issue."

"But add in the maintenance and all that. You'll double the time." Brendan opined.

"And if they don't hit that 15,000 feet per day target or if they have weekends off ... well, we could be looking at a ten year project, maybe more." I decided we had enough on the feasibility concerns, so I suggested we shift focus to undesirable side effects or dangers of the project. "Brendan, thanks so much for talking about this today. Could you send me a short write-up of your findings and concerns so far? In the next two days, we should probably focus on the 'do no harm' aspect ... the possible dangers. Then we should be ready to go back to Waldon on this."

"What about the new ADADA phase? Don't we owe him something on that? Maybe I should switch over ... ?"

"Good idea! I'll focus on tunnel dangers for maybe another day or so, then switch to ADADA as well. That vortex of brainstorms thing we're having Wednesday includes ADADA in its scope."

"No need to remind me," Brendan assured. "I'm looking forward to that, by the way. Okay if I hang out there with you for the lot of it?"

"Absolutely! And feel free to do other work while you're in the conference room. I certainly plan to," I said, and then we agreed to meet again soon to compare notes.

I spent the rest of the day looking into potential dangerous side effects of the tunnel, which covered a wide range of possible catastrophes. One in particular stood out for me as a reason for the project to be cancelled, and that had to do with convection currents in the upper mantle, which were responsible for continental drift. Beneath the ocean floor of the Atlantic, the mid-section of the tunnel would be close to the fault line between the North American and Eurasian continental plates. Those plates were continually drifting apart and shifting position relative to each other. A couple of the Research team folks would likely have some useful thoughts on that tomorrow.

It became clear to me, as I pasted links to research related to mantle convection into my notes for the day, that there was really no point in going any further on the Gravity Train assessment. There would be four or five key summary bullets to show Waldon, but the mantle convection bullet which, given its dramatic potential, would logically be the last summary point to cover, providing a clear, convincing argument for TFD to give the project a thumbs-down.

Just before I had planned to leave for dinner, Mars messaged me asking if we could meet for a drink at a nearby bar. He had "other plans" for dinner and would only have maybe 15 minutes to meet. Perfect, I thought.

CHAPTER 17

Exploring Mars

It was a little after 6PM. I didn't see Mars in the tower lobby, so I walked to the bar alone, thinking that a 15 minute "hard-stop" on a meeting with Mars would mean my endurance would not be tested. Upon entering the bar, I noticed Mars sitting at a small table and sat down across from him. His face alternately conveyed rancor and sincerity as he spoke.

"So, you are now working for Perry," Mars began as he did when we last met in the hotel breakfast area. "Have you had a chance to think about what I asked you? The question of why the Gravity Train is being considered as a reasonable investment?"

During my research over the past several days, wherein the foundation of rationale for the safety of the Gravity Train consisted mainly of computer simulations based on incomplete knowledge of the earth's composition deep in the mantle, I had been wondering how the project managed to stay active for so many months. I was very curious about Mars' view on that point, and so I went directly there in my response. "Yes, why *are* we still looking at this project? I mean, a lot of people have been poking into it since August. Given the tenuous simulations and modeling work done to placate concerns, the risks of the tunnel should have driven the proposal into the recycle bin months ago. So, why are we here now talking about it? What is *your* opinion?"

"Yes, it has been quite a distraction." Mars leaned back, turning toward the window and resting his arm along the top of the faux leather bench seat. Outside played the scene of a typical busy evening in the city: streams of pedestrian traffic, rivers of cars with a few larger vans and mini-buses appearing to float like debris on the car river. Now and then a small VTOL craft could be seen, whose owner was able to afford the overwhelming permit fees allowing vertical take-off and landing within the city limits. "Perhaps it is serving its purpose. No?"

Just then a server bot arrived at our table with a tray containing two mugs of a dark brew. "Ah! Here, Connor, you should try this porter," Mars suggested as he took both mugs, placing one in front of me on the table, "I hope you don't mind my ordering for you. My treat, of course."

It annoyed me that he would order for me. I was not a porter fan, but I tasted it and found it surprisingly satisfying.

"An unusual craft brew. More complex than other porters," Mars reflected after sampling his own.

"This is pretty good, thanks," I said, raising my mug toward Mars, and he gave it a salutatory clink with his own.

"You will not like what I am about to say, but …." Mars began.

I'd heard him use that phrase before in presentations and during project review meetings. Typically, that was the phrase he had used in the past just before dropping another conspiracy bomb at TFD. "I left TFD," he continued, "because it became clear that certain people were subverting our principles. Ansell left, I think, for the same reason. I believe all of TFD ... all of its employees ... will soon be used for unfortunate purposes."

Mars placed his fingers on his temples, staring at me as though demonstrating a mind-reading or divination trick of some kind. "Tell me, are you by chance also looking into the ADADA phase two work? You are not allowed to tell me if you are, I know. So I will assume you are looking at phase two, since that would make the most sense for Perry to do."

"Have you unearthed a dark motivation for such a project?" I asked, wondering if Mars knew more about it than I did.

"Let me tell you a story," he continued, placing his hands around his drink. "When we realized that stem cells, other special cell transplants, microsurgery and electrical stimulation of cells in the orbitofrontal cortex ... such things could enable new brain growth ... 'purposeful growth' they called it ... the vast field of possibilities began to open. There was a lot of speculation on where it might be useful. The initial intent, of course, was a benign application ... healing damage to human brains caused by neglect or abuse in their infancy. Fixing that kind of unfortunate condition ... what do they call it? Failure to thrive? But there was so much more ... so many ideas began to emerge from those clever people who studied it. Clever people. Things were discussed ... ideas like enhancing a sense of having been nurtured ... or of humanity's nurturing of humanity ... which was supposed to reduce conflict in the world. Ah yes! Not so different from the old talk of 'brain washing' when you think about it. Changing perception of reality? Even if we pretend it is for a noble purpose, it is still scary. No? Trust me. Even more frightening things were presented."

"Such as … ?" I prompted.

"One scientist introduced the idea of altering the inner sense of caring … the inner sense or memory a person has of their early days in this world … the sense of what a mother is … of *who* their *own* mother is. So that a person would tend to honor, protect … or *love*, in a sense … an assigned individual, like a president or king or other government leader. They could be made to love, honor, trust, defend and obey that leader … in a manner such as to defy reason. We … our kind of people … thought of things like that. University professors, research scientists, medical professionals, TFD technicians … fathers, mothers, sisters, brothers … people like us. What prompted them, do you think? Are we programmed to evolve in that direction? Perhaps we are already being manipulated somehow … directed toward the secret ambitions of a very few people who control life on this planet."

A year ago, his narrative would have crossed into the realm of conspiracy theory for me, but the "people who control life" phrase was eerily similar to Waldon's "enablers of life." Yet, my own brain was preconditioned to dismiss anything as outlandish as thought-control on a global scale. Helping individuals better adjust to the world, especially after early development problems, seemed both feasible and beneficial. However, a group of respected professionals postulating the mass programming of humans to behave irrationally in order to serve the selfish interests of a select few individuals seemed unlikely. Struggling with it, I stared at Mars without answering.

"Tell me, Connor, has anyone spoken to you recently about the 'enablers of life'?" Mars asked while casually gazing out the window.

My breathing stopped as I continued to stare across at Mars, who then turned back toward me. My mouth had opened as though about to form words, although I had not yet formulated any. Mars raised his palms toward me as he spoke.

"Ah! No need to respond. I can see that someone has. Perry, I assume, yes? No matter. The key is that you are now aware of the thinking ... the diabolical scheming ... behind the phase two work. Does it bother you that the TFD mission appears to be shifting ... secretly shifting away from enabling certainty toward coercion ... subliminal coercion of acceptance?"

I took a long breath and began to replay the meeting with Waldon in my head. The idea of obviating the need for trust lurked in the shadows of my mind. Finally, I asked Mars what motivated him to seek me out.

"Interesting. I came back to New York because someone on Astrid's team contacted me about the re-purposing of ADADA," Mars revealed. "It was so offensive to me that I decided to see if there was some way I could stop it. So, I'm here to expose it. Perhaps to neutralize it. Perhaps to bury it."

"Do you think ADADA is linked somehow to the Gravity Train?"

"Astrid is a smart person. Smart." Mars took a swig from his mug of porter, and then, seeming to sense what I was pondering, he continued. "When that venomous creature Svarog took over from Beckmann a lot changed around TFD. Have you had direct contact with Svarog?"

While Svarog came across as reasonably benevolent in front of large groups and on video interviews meant to be widely circulated, I had seen him behave quite differently with small teams in his office, including the day I presented our feasibility assessment of true certainty. His behavior under those more private circumstances leaned more toward self-glorification and heartless bullying. That wasn't only my opinion; it was reinforced by comments I'd heard from co-workers. Mars had been subjected to a lot of direct contact with Svarog for over a year.

"Not much," I replied.

"Well, you have heard stories. Stories of horror. No?"

I thought about Svarog using his 'over my dead body' threat with me in reviewing work on feasibility of certainty.

"Okay, so let's talk about ADADA phase two," I spoke slowly as I tried to stop thinking about Svarog's unprofessional behavior, "I've started looking through the research papers."

"Some is political crap. Funding for the right conclusions, if you know what I mean. It still happens, of course, even today. The studies from Harvard Medical School are pretty good though, as are a few others, maybe some work from UCSF and Johns Hopkins."

"I read those." I was annoyed that Mars seemed to assume a certain naivete on my part about the range of drivers for research projects. "Have you seen work from that new alliance group, Synthlicit Universal?" I asked, in order to make the point that I was looking at non-traditional sources as well. "They're beginning to explore ways to counteract acceptance," I said, "on the assumption that artificially-induced acceptance ... or a similar kind of mind-control of the population ... may become technically or medically feasible soon."

"Ah! Interesting that you found that one. Yes," said Mars, "that work is underway. I was involved in it before coming back here. The idea comes from postulations by the research team at TFF in Norway. Someone made analogies from sub-atomic particle entanglement to the broader world we can more easily experience, moving to interdependencies of components of nature ... weather, microbes, plants, animals, humans ... so, we are all entangled, they say."

"How did you connect with TFF?" I asked.

"Adora. She worked for them in Trondheim before joining TFD." Mars suddenly changed his expression as though recalling something important. "Are you familiar with acatalepsy?" he asked pointedly. I struggled to think what it might be.

"Some sort of condition resulting from brain injury?" I guessed.

Mars smiled broadly and briefly chuckled. "No. Not the usual case, at least. It comes from an ancient philosophical doctrine postulating that humans are incapable of knowing anything with certainty. Not only is there no true certainty but no true knowledge. No true perception either."

As Mars continued to speak, the look on his face shifted to serious concern. "The idea that surfaced is that, since the human brain requires outside control or manipulation ... reprogramming ... or 'purposeful new growth' in the context of the ADADA bullshit ... in order to get to that state of complete certainty, then there must be a way to deactivate or disable the ADADA-induced certainty, using similar means. The idea of a way that some people are toying with is via EMP … Electromagnetic Pulse."

"Wait. I'm familiar with EMP and related electromagnetic wave generation. I thought that stuff doesn't really affect human brains though, other than negligible amounts. It affects electronics, communication networks, power grids, some wearables …," as I spoke, something popped into my head related to a study I reviewed several years earlier.

"Wait. Are you talking about an extension of TMS? Transcranial Magnetic Stimulation?" I asked.

"The material … stuff … is new," Mars said, "New stuff. Yes, some may consider it an extension or an augmentation of TMS."

"TMS … that's been used for years to treat depression. Are we re-purposing it?"

"Of course. Everything can be re-purposed."

"Right. Even humans," I said.

"Ah! Very good Mr. Farrell! Once you accept that, more hidden things will become apparent. The TMS extension was recently used in a study focused on altering the capabilities of those experimental brain implants that were supposed to enable thought-reading or thought-transmission. Another wombat, yes? But a very strange and unexpected thing happened in early experiments with the device. Ah! The device! Yes. They call it the ACE. It produces the special kind of electromagnetic pulse needed to apply the new type of TMS over a fairly wide area. They discovered that ACE affects *everyone*. No one expected that. Yes! It turns out the pulse it generates also works on people who have *not* had the ADADA implant! So now we are faced with a question, yes?"

Mars seemed to be waiting for me to respond, but I chose to

wait for him to continue. He turned away, scratching his chin, then turned back and took a deep breath. "We ... especially you and others at TFD ... we must prepare for mass deployment of the ACE pulse device. The key is how to do that when trust is an issue. The only path I know of is through NIRC."

I recognized the acronym NIRC, for the National Institute for Resolve and Confidence, the new federal agency established to help connect and coordinate research related to human decision confidence. NIRC was ostensibly created to help the United States be more competitive in that area with certain research organizations in Europe, Japan and China. What confused me at first is why NIRC would help anyone to proliferate a device that could undermine human confidence in general. I asked Mars what might motivate NIRC to help.

"NIRC itself, as an agency, as a concept, as a documented mission statement, is of no use," he began, "but NIRC as a collection of *humans* can be useful. I worked with some of them briefly in the past. One of the humans in NIRC will help us, if we enter the ACE device into their national competition."

"National competition?"

"Yes," he replied, "They are calling it the 'National Innovation Challenge' or something like that. They will be looking at prototype inventions as well as theoretical propositions that relate, as one would assume, to resolve and confidence." Mars finished the last of his porter, then said, "Time for me to go, but I will ask you one question first."

"Yes?"

"What is the Gravity Train?" Mars asked, speaking slowly with his eyebrows raised.

I knew what he was going for in that moment. "Merely a distraction," I answered.

"Excellent! We will talk more at another time."

"Wait, I have one question for *you*," I said. "Whom, if I may ask, is the specific 'human' at NIRC we're counting on?"

"Ansell Beckmann," replied Mars as he rose to leave.

CHAPTER 18

Muffins and Metaphors

I stayed behind at the bar, obsessively checking the time while finishing dinner. It was only a five minute walk back to Gyre, but I wanted to be a few minutes early. Given what I had just learned from Mars, I decided it would be best to have a face-to-face meeting with Ansell Beckmann as soon as possible, and I planned to ask Melinda for her help in arranging that.

At precisely 7:22, I found myself back in the lobby of the Gyre Ventures tower. There were a few people here and there chatting amongst themselves or via their smarts to someone elsewhere. No sign of Melinda yet, so I strolled about, enjoying the calming effect of the flowers and greenery spread about the space. From a corner, looking back across the lobby, the overall effect was pleasing. The ceiling was about fifteen feet high around the perimeter and nearly twice that height at its "cathedral" peak in the front portion of the lobby. Bright lights trimmed the skylight frames inside so that, even after sunset, there was a soothing glow emanating from parts of the ceiling. A nurturing ambiance, I thought.

"Connor! You ready?" I heard Melinda calling. She was standing just inside the revolving door, looking somewhat stressed.

"Hi! Yes, I'm ready!" I walked toward her as she started back out through the door. Switching to a jog, I was just quick enough to step into the moving door section with Melinda.

"Everything okay?" I asked as we exited and approached the car.

"Oh yeah. I'm fine, thanks. Just didn't want to hog the spot," she explained as we got into the car, adding, "and I really hate that lobby."

Before I could ask why she hated the lobby, she voiced some directions for the autonomous car to follow, then turned to me. "Thanks so much for meeting me tonight," she began, "We're going to my favorite local hangout, a coffee house called Clementina's down near Prospect Park. It'll only take twenty minutes to get there. Way faster than on the subway. I never take the subway. We can start talking as we ride, if that's okay. My main concern is you mentioning ADADA side-effects the other night at the pub. Are you already looking at something in particular? Or are you broadly searching to see if anything has been reported so far that looks suspiciously like a side-effect of ADADA treatment?"

"Well, uh," my head was spinning a bit as the car suddenly accelerated to close the gap ahead to the next car, "We have to be careful exactly what we say in the car, since we're monitored and maybe even recorded. Can we wait on that till we get to the coffee house?"

"Okay. No need to jump into that. Why don't we get better acquainted while we ride? We had a nice interaction in the breakfast area when we first met, but my impression at the pub the other night was that you were a little too formal. You didn't relax in that setting, for some reason. You came across as very reserved and professorial."

"Well, I won't disagree, but in all fairness, a business dinner like that ... well, to *me* anyway ... is not the right venue to be completely relaxed or completely transparent. I felt like I still needed to represent TFD in a way."

We rode silently for a little while, then Melinda said "Let me tell you about me." She then began to go through a number of highlights of her life, starting with her growing up in the Ithaca area in upstate New York. Melinda liked the quiet surroundings of their rural neighborhood, but it did hamper friendships with other children. There were no other girls her age for about a two mile radius, so getting together to hang out always required some advance planning and kids being shuttled back and forth by their parents. Melinda's parents were so busy they were hardly ever available for shuttling. There were surprisingly few extracurricular activities that would have enabled Melinda and her friends to stay late at school.

"As a kid," she said, "my biggest dream was to live in a city where I'd have a lot of friends to play with and hang out with who lived within a block or two of my house, where I could walk to school, walk to the grocery store, walk to a park ... everything nearby."

Melinda's dad, Ansell, had been a professor of Operations

Research and Engineering at Cornell University. Melinda's mother was also a professor at Cornell, teaching courses in Global and Public Health Sciences. They met while teaching at Cornell, married a few years later, and Melinda was born about a year after that.

While Melinda was in her senior year in high school, Ansell convinced her to apply to Cornell for admission as a Biological Engineering major. She was accepted and enrolled in Cornell's program, with a particular focus on nanobiotechnology.

She said her first and (so far) only romance lasting more than three months started in her junior year at Cornell. The young man, Cooper, was also a student there, studying statistics with the goal of a career as an actuarial analyst for an insurance company. They were quite close and happy for a while, but they broke up just before graduating.

When Melinda was in her mid-20's, her mother died in a car accident. Shortly after that, her dad left Cornell to become an independent consultant, soon incorporating himself under the name "The Fifth Dentist". Within a year, Ansell had two other consultants working for him. Within three years, The Fifth Dentist had grown dramatically in both revenue and number of employees, and Ansell began to spend more and more time in New York City.

Melinda had made some friends at Cornell whom she would hang out with, especially when her dad was out of town, but she did not like coming home to their "empty house in the middle of effing nowhere." She had found only temporary or part time employment in Ithaca, including some volunteer work, and so she decided it was time to fulfill her childhood dream of living in a big city. On her 28th birthday, she found a job in Manhattan with a pharmaceutical company that was expanding into the realm of surgically implanted biotechnology. She found a tiny, relatively cheap apartment in lower Manhattan.

She was disappointed with the job for reasons she did not really go into. After a few years, she accepted a long-standing offer from her dad for a position at The Fifth Dentist. The higher salary enabled her to afford a nicer apartment in Brooklyn, where she still lived.

I thanked her for the background story and provided a narrative about my own life. I told her I grew up in Philadelphia, on the edge of an area called Frankford, a few blocks from a large city bus terminal. It was mostly row houses and a few apartment buildings in my neighborhood. I lived in a row house that belonged to my grandparents.

I told her about my parents splitting up when I was three years old and my mom taking me with her to live with her parents. I told her that G'ma died a few months later, so it was just Pop-Pop, my mom and me living in the narrow two bedroom house. My dad disappeared, and about two years later my mom told me he died. Mom frequently reminded me how poor we were and fretted over every expenditure.

I went to a public elementary school about eight blocks away. There were no school buses, so I just walked. My mom walked me the first day, and then I was on my own. There were two boys in my class that year who became my friends, and they were basically my only friends until I started sixth grade. They both lived on the other side of the school, so when we got together to play, we mostly met in the school yard.

On my street and right around it there were older boys who

looked for kids my age to tease or bully. They were good at finding me, especially on my way home from school.

I told Melinda that my childhood fantasy was much like hers in that I wanted to live somewhere else, but it was the reverse in the sense that I wanted to get *out* of the city and live in the suburbs or on a farm or in a log cabin way up in the mountains … anywhere else but the city. That pretty much shaped my personal journey until I got to middle school where things got a little better.

I made a couple of new friends, my mother got a steady job so we could stop worrying about having money for food, and I starting thinking a lot about what the future might be like for me. I was able to attend college only because I managed to get a full scholarship for the first year. After graduation, my first full-time job was in software engineering for a company in Cupertino, California. Living in a small apartment in the Cupertino area, while not exactly matching my childhood fantasy of living in the suburbs, was much more comforting than where I grew up. I was happy at work, at home and in my personal life. I felt like I had been reborn.

I told Melinda all of that, and I told her that I applied for a job at TFD because I was intrigued by an article I read about her dad and the company he'd founded. I felt fortunate to become a part of it. Astrid, who was my first-line manager at the time, had no problem with my working from home in the Bay Area, as long as I could come to New York a few times a year for the New Qs and other key meetings.

I wrapped up my life summary by recounting how I met Cadence, which became my first major romantic relationship. "But unfortunately, that ended a couple of years later," I obfuscated, preferring at that moment to avoid mentioning our investing in a condo together or our plans to marry or her death.

"Thank you, Connor. I feel like I know you a lot better," Melinda said, smiling at me as the car pulled up to Clementina's.

As we entered the coffee house, I noticed a little area had been cleared to the immediate left, with a black metal music stand placed as though someone would be performing there. A large "retro" studio microphone dangled from a cable slung over the stand.

Melinda took my hand, leading me through a labyrinthine arrangement of little tables and chairs toward the far corner on the right. "I like it back here. More privacy," she remarked as we sat down together at a little table with two chairs by the back wall. Clementina's was fairly crowded, with more than twenty patrons and two servers working a counter at another corner of the room. A screen above the counter continually showed views of the various things available ... mainly a variety of coffees and teas and several kinds of muffins.

"You know, I just realized it's poetry night here." Melinda sounded frustrated as she pointed toward the music stand, "so it may not be as conducive to talking as it normally is. There's probably 'open mike' time too. Sorry, I think I goofed."

I assured her that it was perfectly fine. "Melinda, don't apologize. This is great! I haven't been at a poetry reading or any kind of 'open mike' night in a long time. And those blueberry muffins look truly irresistible in the digital rendering over the counter. Let's stay and relax."

"Well, I'd like that as long as you're okay with it. Thanks for being flexible."

We ordered different teas: chai latte for her, lapsang souchong for me. I also ordered a blueberry muffin. After taking just one bite, I concluded it was the best tasting muffin I had ever eaten in my life. When I openly shared my muffin assessment with Melinda, she looked at me as though she suspected I may have lost my mind. "No, it really is yummy! *Very* yummy!" I insisted. She reached over, pulling off a little morsel from the top to sample it. At first, her face expressed complete conviction that I was correct in my assessment; then she wore an expression of intense, desperate craving. I held the muffin near to her mouth, turning the unbitten side toward her, and she took a large bite out of it while gently holding my wrist. She attempted to say "thank you" while chewing, managing to say something like "ankle" and to catch a large crumb in her hand that fell out of her mouth. We both laughed.

Just then, the hostess took the microphone, told us her name was Jillian, welcomed everyone and mentioned that all the readings were posted on the coffee house website. Before she sat down, she announced there were two local poets scheduled to read and introduced the first poet, Cora Nakamura. "So good to have you here again!" the hostess remarked, as a forty-something woman with black, curly hair approached the microphone. Cora then began to read from a notepad she held.

Cubicular Entanglement

Once in a dream we carried sabers,
heels of our palms against carved roses,
you and I, ready to parry.

In those days, our perfunctory banter grew
to stave off death as we performed,
making aria out of the evidence of solitude.

Later, our voices pianissimo,
swathed in woven murmur
across the cubicular terrain, as though
long-stemmed roses, painting a patina
of each other's presence on the skin of our backs,
as though bows, causing us to quiver,
barely caressing our strings to invite chords.

Here, now, layering our flesh to the sound of the sea,
discerned as from atop a cliff overlooking the shore,
our souls, on the edge of that cliff, sensing a history
from the smoothly curving, sand-colored,
foam-licked forms beneath, are afraid to fall.

Will we dissolve in a warmer song,
fading to silence? ... fading to nothing?
Or will an ancient melody sung by weathered seafarers,
inlaid with rime, form the coda? ... cue the exit?

We will attend the partitions between our lives,
awaiting notes resigned to harmony.

Cora thanked the audience as she searched through her notepad for something. Melinda leaned over to me, asking "What do you think?"

"That struck a nerve for me, because I think it was getting at how disconnected we can feel in the midst of so many ways we think we're connected. You know what I mean? And the music undercurrent there … I'm not saying I understood it all," I admitted, "but it affected me anyway."

"I know. I'm going to read it later on their website. That's how I react to most poetry. I get a feeling … a sense of what the key message is. Then I go back and read it again. On that second read, a lot of things become more obvious to me. Sometimes I get an insight about something in my life that relates only in a metaphorical way."

"Did you get a sense of someone dealing with unrequited love?" I asked.

"Definitely, and that 'here now' part with the layering of flesh … it could be 'here now' in reality or maybe just in the narrator's imagination. You know?"

"Right. And the aria coming out of solitude. I loved that."

"To me, the 'cubicular' thing was like the way some work areas are still set up, with those half-wall partitions around small work areas. But it seemed more symbolic of how our lives are lived … some things private or partly concealed, some things thumb-tacked to the walls for all to see."

"Right! How can we be sure we're really connecting to someone else around all the partitions."

"Imagined or presumed connections can be powerful," Melinda said as she turned back to face Cora, who had begun to read another poem. At that moment, I wondered if poetry … symbols, metaphors, unexpected comparisons … could somehow be harnessed to provide more insightful augmented reality.

Cora read a few more poems, and we exchanged a few thoughts on each one. The hostess then stood and returned to the microphone, introduced the next reader, Eamon Penfield. A thin, gray-haired man, wearing what appeared to be a mortar-board cap and gown, stood up from his seat and walked to the music stand. He carried a few sheets of paper, appearing to have hand-written notes on them. Eamon stood behind the music stand, placing his notes on the stand and adjusting its height. He then read aloud with an eloquent, "cultured American" voice, with dramatic inflections and gripping timbre.

Tarantula

As the sword Excaliber incised on the solar plexus of a czar a scar, so, too, the tarantula tattoo, between a puma and an anaconda ... or a cougar and a cobra ... left Laura's likeness like a penumbra or an aqua bandana, left an anathema of filthy char upon the skin of an avatar.

Avatarantula! And we have voice via vox humana through miasmal rattan, an avalanchula of propaganchula, which makes of vicar-capitular dogma impromptu apocrypha.

Apocrypha!
"What shall we do?" they ask. What shall we do?
The answer? On pagan totem mount a man,
For the sake of God!

Insert parenthetical dramatic pause: a parentharantula.

I climbed a hill, steep and pebbled with tell-tale stones. "Rock candy", I mused, with the sound of each step an ad hoc, ticktock, rock-knock outcropping of dropped terra-cotta pottery. I felt the breakage and the noise that was the wind. I squinted into the wind and stepped on something soft: a squirrel, crushed and bloodied on the stones. Blown from a tree, I supposed. How many nuts had it buried? How many would it have been able to find again? Had it ever paused, somewhere on that hill, wondering why it was on that hill? ... wondering when it would all end? The wind, now breathing through breathless trees near the path, gained volume. Where did it come from? What was the source?

The wind courted articulation. What was its tale? What was its moral?

From benumbing clamor, it transmuted to question in a smothered human wailing.

My mouth began to move as though words assembled. Was I answering? ... or failing?

As I walked on, the outside air was loud and damp and stuffy, filled with emissions of carbon-based energy and carbon-based life forms with carbon-based guilt and carbon-based sorrow ... like a tumbledown subway station in a big city ... like a sonically lanced miasmaranchula.

Finally. at the end of my journey, I arrived at a shop displaying religious gifts ... "Saint Teresa's". I stood at the storefront, the window filled with an echelon of mass cards, crucifixes, shining

ciboria and plastic Jesi ... suitable for dashboard ornamentantula.
I saw my self-concept genu-reflected in the glass, in the brass and
in the massively vast cast centerpiece bust of our Savior at last.

But beyond the transmogrified light, there seemed a shadow,
crawling over the top of our Savior's head, toward His face.
Slowly, shaggily, it crossed His forehead to rest directly over one
eye.

The spider on His eye allowed only an eclipse of the world to
be seen around it, only a corona of human dilemma, lycosa
tarantula vox barbara, a tarantist dance of light between its
shifting legs, nano-bent around nano-hair, tubularly invaginated
within nano-follicles.

And in that twisted light it all changes, you know,
And sadness looks like apathy,
And pain becomes reluctance,
And anger shows through more clearly than resolve,
And, finally, our loneliness is our peace.

That, sweet Savior, is the Why.
As big as the spider on Your eye.

Eamon took a deep breath and nodded.   Then, just before
stepping off the platform, as the cafe audience began to applaud,
he pulled up his gown to extract a palm-sized tarantula from his
trouser pocket, the creature glistening as though fried in oil or
sugar-glazed.   He raised it to his mouth, biting off a good size

chunk of it, and he chewed it with a satisfied look on his face.

Melinda leaned into me whispering, "I loved that!"

"What a great voice!" I responded. "He could read the average corporate financial report and make it sound profound." I then instantly regretted saying that, as upon hearing myself say it, I thought it trivialized the content. Sure enough, after a moment Melinda reacted.

"Voice of God," she began, looking not at me but straight ahead, "but I try not to get too caught up in theatrics. I prefer to focus on what the meaning is ... or what the words make me think of. Anyway, I think it was adequately affecting, even without his voice helping."

"But don't you think that *how* something is said can change its meaning? ... or at least drive it home into your brain ... or your heart ... you know, make it more meaningful through the experience? I really thought his delivery *added* a lot." I attempted to repair any damage.

"You know, you're right," said Melinda, turning to me and smiling, "his voice did help to pull me in and focus my attention. Sent a chill up my spine now and then. His voice did add a lot."

Nice recovery, I thought.

"Nice recovery," Melinda said, and as I turned toward her, she winked at me.

Just then Jillian the hostess announced that it was "open mike" time and invited anyone else who wanted to read their work to raise a hand.

Over the next hour, several people took turns reading a few of their own poems at the mike. I enjoyed getting a sense of their comfort level with words, and I envied those who seemed to be very comfortable in expressing themselves. Melinda and I quietly exchanged comments now and then on our impressions of the poems.

"You ever do any writing?" Melinda asked, after the last of the open mike readers finished.

"Not creative writing. Not fiction or poetry or anything like that." I couldn't help but think of countless reports I had written over the years, none of which would have ever made anyone feel anything in particular, except possibly frustrated or less confident about a few applied technology proposals.

"You should try it. I think you'd enjoy it, based on some of your comments tonight. Try writing under a pseudonym if it feels hard to get out of your own way." Melinda said, rubbing my shoulder.

At that point the hostess took the mike, thanked everyone for coming and announced "last call" for ordering tea or other drinks that evening, since they would be closing in 15 minutes.

"Sorry, I forgot they usually close up around ten o'clock here," Melinda remarked, "We haven't gotten to talk much about ADADA side-effects. Also sorry, again, that I forgot it was poetry night."

"Oh, it was fine. It was fun. Maybe we can meet at work later in the week? I'm doing that 'vortex' thing on Wednesday in the conference room near Waldon's office, so we could maybe talk there." I was trying to be helpful and sound optimistic.

"Well, my apartment is just a couple blocks away. If it's okay with you, we can just walk over there when they shoo us out. We can talk on the way, and you're welcome to use my car service to get back to your hotel in mid-town."

"Sounds good." It would be fun to walk around a bit in the neighborhood, I thought, and I was curious to see where she lived. It was a clear, calm night ... not windy or bone-chillingly cold. Along the way, Melinda did not bring up any concerns about ADADA, nor any other work-related topic. Instead, she walked silently, occasionally gesturing or pointing toward something she wanted me to notice. I merely made a brief comment, like "that's so beautiful!" or "very nice!" in reaction to whatever she brought to my attention.

She first pointed out the relief sculpture of knights on horseback in a row of stone blocks along the front of a building across the street. Then she invited me to notice elegant carvings of birds featured on the handsome wooden double-door entrance to a four-story residential building. The streets we walked on were tree-lined, and Melinda would point to this tree or that tree as we walked, indicating her admiration for that particular oak or maple or magnolia. She pointed out, with an "Oh! I love that!" expression on her face, several building fronts that had a low stone wall around the entryway, some with plants or shrubs visible above the wall, most were lit with little spotlights to allow greater appreciation of the botanical ornamentation. I remember thinking at the time that Melinda was not trying to impress me by pointing out things I might like, but she was sharing with me those things she personally found most endearing and most welcoming about her neighborhood.

Upon reaching the front door of her building, Melinda walked to the bottom step between two ornate Corinthian columns and turned to face me. I planned to simply say thank you and good-night, possibly kissing her on the cheek as well. Before I could say anything, Melinda took my hand in both of hers, unexpectedly sliding her fingers up inside my shirt sleeve as she did at Snegurochka's.

"Want to come up?" she asked.

CHAPTER 19

Entanglement

Once inside, Melinda indicated the basic layout of her 3rd floor apartment, then invited me to explore while she straightened up the kitchen alcove and made some tea. I first turned to the shelves in the main living area, hoping to learn something about her interests or her past from the books and framed pictures. In terms of books, she had quite a few ... more than most people kept nowadays, anyway, outside of digital books to be read on notepads and smarts. There were four shelves of books, mounted on a wall of exposed brick that ran behind a comfortable-looking, burgundy-colored couch.

On the top shelf, most of the books were exquisitely bound in expensive-looking leather with gold-inlaid printing for the titles, author's name and publisher. They were different sizes and with different styles of decoration and printing on the spines, so they were not a "set" of books. I reached up and gently pulled one out to examine ... Hawthorne's *The Scarlet Letter* ... which featured a pattern of flowery decorations in red, black and gold, ornamenting a cover of green cloth. It was a beautiful old volume, with the top edge of the pages painted gold. There were some intriguing sketches embedded into the pages of printed text. I noticed in the first couple of pages that the book had been printed in 1892.

At that point, fearing that I may have already somehow damaged or decreased the value of a bibliophile's coveted treasure, I replaced it as carefully as possible on the shelf where I found it. As though sensing my apprehension, Melinda again invited me to poke around, "You can check them out. They won't crumble to dust, I swear. Top shelf is all stuff from my dad, including the book safes."

"Book safes?" I selected one volume with no title on the spine, just ornate gold trim. It looked quite real, like a normal book, albeit overly ostentatious. I opened it to discover it was not a book but a small hiding place for money or jewels or secret papers or whatever one wanted to keep hidden. It was admirably made, with a plush, padded velvet interior and opulent leather cover. It was empty. "So are there secret things hidden in a book safe here somewhere?"

"They're all empty, as far as I can recall. They're all hand-made in Italy by some artisan. I like how they look and feel, but I wish dad would just stop giving me those. I don't use them."

Sure enough, I discovered similar book safes on the other shelves, along with actual books: several art books showing paintings by Renoir and Cezanne; novels, including some by authors whose works I enjoyed. A surprising coincidence, I thought.

"We appear to have some common interests," I remarked as Melinda brought in a little tea service tray and set it on the coffee table in front of the sofa.

"Oh my goodness! Are *you* into book safes *too*?!?" she exclaimed, staring at me wide-eyed.

"You feign shock admirably," I responded, in the way Cadence used to do with me.

"I made *tea*! *Why?* *Why* did I make more *tea*?" Melinda asked, melodramatically.

We sat side-by-side on the comfortable burgundy couch and, after giggling for a while, compared our interest in books, in music, in art. We shared funny stories about people we worked with and people we knew in college. We laughed uncontrollably at times. She leaned on my shoulder and began to grab my hand now and then to emphasize a point. After a while, she shifted closer so that that I could feel the warmth of her thigh against mine. I began to feel radiantly happy. We talked a bit more and then quietly looked at each other for a minute.

"You know, I could really use a nice, relaxing back-rub," Melinda suddenly pondered aloud, adding with theatrical wistfulness, "if only that hostess from Snegurochka were here. What was her name?"

"Pru," I instantly regretted saying.

"Oh, you *remember* her!" Melinda teased, "Do you think of her often?"

"Let's focus on *your* immediate needs," I deflected, "Perhaps I could be of some assistance … ?" I stood, bowed and gestured grandly.

Melinda stood and led me into the bedroom, turning on a small, old-fashioned lamp on the night-stand. She then turned to face me, looking rather serious and concerned. She explained that this was only going to work if I respected her wishes and dutifully followed her instructions. She then went through the specific restrictions on my behavior.

"So the deal is, then, that you must not remove any clothing ... mine or yours ... and you absolutely must not touch me anywhere else but on my back. You must not touch me below the waist ... at all .... and you must not reach around to my breasts or belly."

"Your 'belly'?"

"You know what I mean."

Perhaps noticing that I was smiling, she added "I'm serious! I'm trusting you here, so don't violate that trust. It's very important to me."

I was annoyed that she seemed to think I possessed only a teenager's level of self-control. Certainly, I thought, I could give her a simple little back rub without transgressing into orgiastic revelry. Her intensity led me to wonder if it would be best to excuse myself, but after a moment, recalling how good it felt to spend time with her on the couch, I decided to forge ahead. "Of course you can trust me," I assured, "This will be good. It will help you relax."

"Great," she said, "and it may help *you* relax too. We can even talk about work-related crap if you want, but first ..." she paused, pulling her lace-sleeved top over her head and handing it to me, "please find a place for this in the closet ... in one of the cubbies maybe."

Given her resolute restrictions, I wasn't expecting her to remove any clothing. While carefully maintaining eye contact until turning toward the closet, I did manage to notice that, above the waist, she was now wearing only a beige, strapless bra. As I stepped into the closet, several micro lights lit, revealing little shelves and cubbyholes along the back wall, holding mostly sweaters, sweatshirts, T-shirts and some other items not immediately identifiable. None of the cubbies were empty. The closet measured about six feet by eight feet ... surprisingly large given her small bedroom.

"You know what?" Melinda's voice called from somewhere near the night-stand, "Just put it on a hanger, please, for now. I'll check it later and decide whether I need to launder it or press it or whatever. Oh, and there should be some empty hangers over on the right side. No, wait, I think it's the left side. Thanks!"

I hung it up as carefully as I could and came back into the bedroom fairly quickly, finding Melinda lying on her stomach along the edge of the bed, her head resting on its side upon her crossed arms on the pillow. She was completely naked. I was amazed by how quickly she had been able to remove her remaining clothing. I lingered in the closet doorway, appreciating her beauty in the soft, warm light of the night-stand lamp.

"I'm over here," Melinda deadpanned.

"Ah! Over *there*! Okay, I see you now," I replied, trying too hard to be funny as I moved to stand, awkwardly, at the side of the bed near her head. Her eyes were closed, and her ponytail flowed along the pillow to touch her right shoulder. She was quite alluring, lying there like that.

"So, I thought we agreed we wouldn't remove any clothing," I said.

"No, my dear, we agreed that *you* would not remove any clothing. No restrictions on me were discussed as I recall," she said dryly, adding, "but I don't plan to remove any of *yours* this evening."

After a moment, she opened her eyes and tilted her face toward me. "What are you afraid of?", she asked, "Do I look scary? Really, Connor, earlier you seemed ready to bravely face the hidden dangers that will confront you when a bunch of rapacious executives and self-serving politicians are told that their train tunnel fantasy should remain no more than a fantasy. In contrast, I'm sympathetic to you, share your interests and values, am naked … and in a fairly submissive posture, actually. No sexual nuance intended, of course. Rather non-threatening, I would think. So, relax and help me feel good, staying within the constraints I've articulated. You should try to enjoy it too. Seriously, let your mind go wherever it wants to go. I mean, you don't think I can read minds, do you?"

I collected myself and began to gently touch her shoulders and back, not massaging so much as softly caressing. Melinda reacting by smiling and breathing deeply. "If you still want to experience 'ponytail reality' you can pull off my hair band," she offered. I did want that, and I gently freed her hair from its sole constraint. Then I slowly smoothed her hair off of her shoulders and began running my fingers lightly all over her back, carefully complying with all restrictions on where I might touch her. As I admired the particularly attractive hourglass shape of her torso, I found it increasingly challenging to resist touching below her waist. I resolved to maintain my integrity and trustworthiness.

I began to knead her flesh a bit, adding some pressure from my palms now and then, pressing my fingers in between her ribs, pressing my thumbs down on either side of her spinal column near her waist and gliding them up to her neck, whereupon I would grip and squeeze her shoulders. It was during those more vigorous motions that Melinda whispered "oh my goodness" now and then, which were the only words spoken by either of us for quite some time. After a few minutes, I shifted to running my hands from the sides of her waist, with gentle pressure, upward until my fingers pressed into her armpits. I wanted to touch every inch of her body's many curvatures.

As the temptation to touch her outside the permitted zone grew, as my heart rate increased, I noticed her swallow and start breathing a bit faster. I focused carefully on her face and noticed sporadic eyebrow movement up and down, another swallow and an occasional pause in her breathing. I wondered if, like me, she was having erotic thoughts. Melinda moved her arms upward on the bed, reaching above the pillow so that her head no longer rested on her arms but on the pillow directly. On the next run of my hands up from her waist, I moved my hands beyond her shoulders, along her arms to her wrists, which I gently squeezed before trailing my fingers lightly back to her shoulders and then back to her waist.

After several repetitions of that motion, Melinda suddenly stiffened and whispered "Stop" as she held one arm straight out off the side of the bed. I stood up, not sure what to do or say next. Melinda looked up at me and softly spoke, "Don't go away. Hold my hand."

I sat on the edge of the bed while she continued lying prone, squeezing my hand. After a minute, she began to lift herself up off the mattress. She stood, pulling the pillow up to her chest and holding it in place with her arms as though to retain modesty.

"Well, it was nice to spend time with you, Connor." She spoke with unexpected formality as she held the pillow in place with her left arm, extending her right hand toward me.

I took her hand in mine, kissing it while gazing into her eyes. After a moment, Melinda tossed the pillow aside and wrapped her arms around my neck. She stood up on her toes as we kissed and held each other gently for a few seconds. Then she slowly pulled back and touched my cheeks with her fingers, saying, "Okay, my dear. Time for you to go."

At that moment I realized I had forgotten to ask about meeting her father, Ansell. As she stood there facing me, still naked, I felt it would be highly incongruous to bring up either work or her father, let alone both, but I went for it anyway.

"Melinda," I began.

"Yes?" she inquired cautiously, raising an eyebrow.

"I'd like to talk to your father. There's something I want to ask him."

"For my hand in marriage? Seriously? I mean, we kind of just met."

"Oh ... uh no ... sorry ...."

"And I'll be thirty-nine next month, so you really wouldn't need his blessing anyway."

"No. Right. I mean, I want to ask him for his views on what we're assessing now at TFD. New potential for ADADA applications. That sort of thing."

"Ah, good! You made me a little nervous there," Melinda feigned wiping sweat off her brow, then put her hands on her hips, "Just kidding. Figured it was work-related. I'm going upstate to

Cornell this weekend, and that's right near my dad. I'll be staying at his place."

"Could I come with you?" I asked, completely bypassing a lot of internal checkpoints and filters.

"Yes, absolutely, but I'll have to tell him you're my new boyfriend," she warned, adding air-quotes around the word boyfriend, "cause there's no way he'll allow you to visit if he thinks it's work related, but he'll be fine if he thinks we're romantically involved. Don't start asking about anything related to TFD projects right away though. I'll let you know when it's safe."

"Thank you," I said, stepping out into the hallway. I turned back to see Melinda slowly closing the door as she smiled and mouthed a kiss.

When I reached the landing between the second and third floors, I heard the click of a door latch behind me. I turned to see Melinda's head and one shoulder poking out of her doorway.

"Hi Melinda!" I called, trying to be funny, adding, "I was just passing through the neighborhood and thought I'd stop by." Melinda stared at me for a second, as though assessing something.

"So. I knew it was poetry night this morning when I asked you to meet me," she admitted, "and I've had, like, eight million of those blueberry muffins, so I knew they were fabulously delish."

They were quite unexpected revelations, yet I managed a comeback in the same tone of mock disapproval I had often used with Cadence, "Melinda, I'm shocked!"

"Me too," she said softly, adding, "you feign shock admirably, by the way."

With that, she stepped back inside and closed the door.

CHAPTER 20

Review and Analysis

The following morning, while day-start was being personally reinforced by my wearables, I considered that perhaps I could work in the suite that day. It would be mainly to prep for the vortex meeting the next day, deciding which key issues I would advance, ensuring I had all my references organized and so forth. I wouldn't need a full day for that, I thought, so I took some time to reflect on recent events. In my head played a comprehensive, uncensored documentary about my time with Melinda the night before.

It began with a montage of scenes from our time in Clementina's and our walk to Melinda's residence. Then it shifted to an in-depth, annotated depiction of our time together in her apartment, climaxing with the back rub sequence, which I replayed in my head several times to make sure I noticed and understood all of the nuances and possible hidden meanings. My head was full of

Melinda, and it was an exquisitely satisfying recollection.

After a while, I concluded that it might be more productive to work in the TFD offices that day. There might be a need for our GT team to meet to discuss something prior to the vortex. Waldon might want to talk to me in person about some concern he had. Melinda might be looking for me.

I spent most of the day at Gyre reviewing my previous notes on GT and phase two of ADADA. I called an impromptu GT team meeting mid-afternoon just to touch base with the core team of Melinda and the others. There were surprisingly few issues, and most comments were along the lines of "well, I guess we'll see what comes up tomorrow." Melinda's behavior gave not the slightest indication that anything had happened between us the night before, but that is exactly how she should have behaved. It would be best, I thought, if neither of us revealed any signs that we had a personal relationship. My conclusion at the end of the day was that I should have stayed in the suite.

C H A P T E R   2 1

Vortex

At 8:22 Wednesday morning, I arrived at the Gyre tower and made my way to the 35th floor to a conference room I had reserved for the vortex meeting. I also reserved an old-style whiteboard with markers and erasers, so that we could draw or write things to focus upon without the use of any electronics. I had read studies that linked the physical handling of pencils, chalk or dry-erase markers with stimulating parts of the brain that might expand perspectives on problem solving. Coffee, tea, water, doughnuts and other snacks I pre-ordered had already been set out on a side table, opposite the whiteboard.

Brendan arrived a few minutes later as I was catching up on news with Don Dander on my smarts. We bid each other good day and began to share what we anticipated would likely happen in the vortex.

"If you ask me, there's no way the Gravity Train can go forward. We've got too many safety issues, and the temperature thing … I mean, there's no way to deal with that with anything we've got. There's just no remedy," Brendan declared.

"I agree, but we should try to maintain an 'openness' in our attitude. Let's see how many others have already reached the same conclusion," I said.

"And if they haven't?"

"If they haven't, then we need to poke at it. We need to see what logic or evidence they're bringing to bear to dismiss any concern." I thought it would be useful to know what argument, if any, they might present to Waldon or Svarog to counter any recommendation we made.

"Alright. Got it." Brendan clapped his hands, then asked, "What about ADADA?"

"Again, let's try to get others to talk. While there are fewer feasibility concerns, there are other issues. Moral issues. Humanitarian issues. Let's see if anyone seems to have heard rumors about secret intentions behind the technology."

"Alright. I think we're good. Let's make sure the doughnuts are too," said Brendan, standing and making his way over to the snack table. He asked, "What time do we start?"

"Officially, my invitation read we start at 9:00am and end at 4:00pm, but everyone can come and go as they please. Including you, Brendan."

"Well, thank you, but I'll likely stay the duration. Might work on my own a bit during the boring parts. And I don't mean tunnel boring," Brendan said with a wink.

We helped ourselves to coffee and doughnuts, and we relaxed a bit, gazing out the window. Within a few minutes Dr. Reddy arrived.

"Good morning, Dr. Reddy," I said.

"Am I too early?" he asked before stepping through the doorway.

"Not at all. We're ready," said Brendan.

"Okay, so you are ready," said Dr. Reddy to Brendan, then turning toward me he asked, "but are *you* ready?"

"Absolutely!" I said, gesturing toward the table.

"No, no. Wait! *I* am Reddy!" Dr. Reddy said, holding his palms to his chest. He then moved to the whiteboard and began drawing circles as he spoke.

"Okay, so for Gravity Train we have the Mid-Atlantic Ridge," he began, writing "MAR" in one of the circles, "small volcanoes and small earthquakes," he went on, writing "v/e" in another circle. Then he wrote " $^{\circ}C$ " in yet another circle, pointed to it and said "Hot!"

Reddy was quite knowledgeable about the challenges and dangers of the tunnel construction and on-going use and maintenance. He began talking about new iron alloys being developed that could get us to a 1700°C melting point, about 3100°F, which he thought would be enough for the 140 miles maximum tunnel depth planned. Even so, he still had concerns for ongoing use, especially since the mantle temperature at that depth might be as high as 1100°C or 1200°C.

"On the positive side," Reddy said, "I am aware of some recent progress on graphene layering and carbon nano-tubes ... most of it not yet publicized ... that could raise the melting point of the tunnel structure to nearly 6000°C or more in the critical region of maximum depth."

"But that stuff ... playing with the carbon atom structures ... they haven't been able to scale it sufficiently to build a decent steak knife out of it. Forget a train tunnel or track," Brendan complained.

"There is new work that has made some big leaps. I don't know the details myself," said Reddy, "but in briefings where some highlights were disclosed to me and other research executives, I got the impression that we were very close to having the capability to produce architectural structural components."

"Structural components. Might be just nuts and bolts," said Brendan.

"No, no. More than that. Graphene layering combined with other engineering approaches," said Reddy, "so I think we are talking larger components. Kenton and Omari will be here later today, and they can tell you a bit more."

"What about the Mid-Atlantic Ridge? You drew a circle for it. Do you have any specific concern?" I asked.

"Well," Reddy began, "we don't have a good way to model potential effects of shifting of continental plates, hydrothermal abnormalities or volcanic activity along the ridge. The plate shift concern is probably the most worrisome. But, if we can't get to a comfort level with the newer graphene structure potential, then we could propose having the tunnel go no deeper than, say, seventy or eighty miles. That should minimize the geologic stresses mentioned in some recent news reports."

"So you're saying that instead of expressing a concern, we should just offer them suggestions of ways to avoid risk," I tried to confirm his position.

"We are suggesting it *because* of our concern," Reddy explained.

"Even if it means changing the GT concept itself?" Brendan asked.

"No. No. It's still a GT ... still a Gravity Train that uses gravity as its power source. But the trip would take longer to make. Shallower depth in the middle will reduce acceleration," said Reddy.

"What about thermal conductivity? Any new news there?" I asked.

"Oh, yes, yes. If we can use the new carbon-based tunnel structure, it should have much greater thermal conductivity than steel alloys. Perhaps a thousand times more," said Reddy.

Brendan jumped in. "What about all the heat inside the tunnel during construction? You know, when they've got machinery in there to handle the spoil and so on."

"That is a very good point," said Reddy, "and I must confess, I have not looked into the materials reuse or disposal aspect of it. Definitely you should check on what they are planning to do about the machinery. Even the drill itself. Check the boring machine's cutting face. How will they test it?"

Brendan and I went through what we had learned about the planned TBM. For the most part, our concerns were about engine cooling approaches and the potential cutter-head articulation deficiencies.

After a while we moved on to ADADA phase two, and Reddy asserted his view that the new phase was "genuine bio-science" and that any promising path toward direct mind connection should be aggressively explored. He said that even a "partial mind connection" ... very limited thought reading, for example ... was a step forward for humanity that we should not dismiss as inadequate or flawed. Brendan and I both expressed concern about potential misuse of phase two as a means to control independent thinking or to trick someone's brain into accepting falsehoods as true or as unavoidable aspects of reality.

It surprised me that Dr. Reddy had no particular concern on the potential misuse of the technology, nor did he appear to believe that TFD would have any responsibility for preventing misuse. "Everything that exists can be misused," he summed up his viewpoint, "and what are we supposed to do about that?"

"But as systems get more complex, it's harder to tell if someone's misusing them," said Brendan.

"Yes," Dr. Reddy responded, "but the problem of managing and securing widely dispersed heterogeneity and interoperability can be addressed ... ironically, perhaps ... by increasingly heterogeneous and inter-operable managing automatons. Think of nano-bio-technology. All of that must, of course, evolve cooperatively with the biology of our planet, including human evolution."

As Brendan and I looked at each other, weighing the implications of converged human and bio-tech evolution, Dr. Reddy explained he had to leave for a meeting with Svarog.

Less than a minute after he left, Drs. Esposito and Coverdale walked in together.

"Good morning Dr. Esposito, Dr. Cov ...," I said before Vicki interrupted.

"Stop! She's Adora. I'm Vicki. Let's be informal," said Vicki.

Vicki and Adora each poured themselves a cup of coffee and

sat down. Vicki asked for an update on what we had learned during the past week or so on ADADA and the tunnel. Brendan and I spent about twenty minutes going through highlights of recent relevant studies and on-going work. Vicki thanked us and said they would focus on ADADA in sharing their insights and perspectives.

From Adora's perspective, ADADA phase two was merely an extension of the original technologies and their applications, which included treating anti-social behaviors. It could be used to create a strong sense of empathy for others in the mind of someone who previously felt no connection to other human beings, not even their own family. It was precisely the empathy aspect, which enabled the vicarious experience of another's feelings, that Adora believed could be adjusted or extended toward acceptance of something as true or reasonable.

Vicki agreed, but added, "Anxiety is another aspect we can address. By a mechanism similar to synaptic development toward increasing empathy, we can allow the brain to release anxieties related to a person's uncertainty about the future or about the correctness of any decision they have made or will need to make in the near future."

"But I feel like we're saying having less anxiety is worth giving up independent thought ... free choice ... at least some of the time," said Brendan.

"I've struggled with that," Vicki began, "and I try to think of it as a compromise. With independent thought comes independent decision-making and independent responsibility. With responsibility comes a sense of liability, guilt for failure to do what was expected, anxiety about potential failures or misconduct, anxiety because they might be wrong in their convictions. It may sound like an oversimplification … and I suppose it may be … but the fact is, well, if limiting the scope of independent thinking can significantly reduce anxiety and guilt … or even eliminate it … such a compromise is worth considering, in my opinion."

"As long as some independent thinking is still allowed," Adora added, "for personal choices."

"Good point Adora," said Vicki, "and I think that should work."

"How can we ensure that compromise you mentioned will not be subverted or abused?" I asked.

"Get some folks on your cyber tech team in here!" Vicki said with a laugh.

"Yes. Kenton and Omari will be stopping by later today. There are many things that can be done, you know, but we can never really be certain of integrity," I said.

"No more than we are today," added Brendan.

"What about things that could be done to help the tunnel work crews deal with anxiety about potential for accident during construction?" I asked.

"Ah! Yes, Connor," Adora spoke up, "I recalled your suggestion about calming wearables from our strange little team exercise at New Q, and I looked into it. There are already two options available by prescription, and they are used for situations where an emergency rescue team may be facing very stressful, scary stuff on a particular mission."

"Anything we can leverage there?" I asked.

"Probably," said Adora, "and I've asked Availa to look into it a bit further. I do think there is good potential for use of existing offerings to help there."

"Excellent! Thank you, Adora," I said, "and I'll check with Availa later to see if she's got any news on that."

After they left, Brendan and I spent some time reviewing our notes and sharing our own concerns about the two projects being assessed.

"This limiting of our independent thought ... they make it sound like some bloody health benefit!" said Brendan at one point. "Who's going to believe that?" he added.

I recall thinking that Brendan's question was intended to be rhetorical, but the odd twist was that everyone exposed to the thought control technology could be *made* to believe ... to accept ... that having their thoughts manipulated was to their benefit. They would likely accept that they should feel grateful to the "enablers of life."

Although our vortex meeting was less than half over, we began to toss around ideas on how we would be summing up our position and recommendations. Brendan suggested after a while that we take an early lunch break, but just as he did, Golden North arrived.

"Good morning!" Golden said brightly as she entered, adding "Oh! I thought there'd be more people."

"Good morning, Golden," I said.

"We've had a few visit for a bit," said Brendan.

"And I'm sure there'll be a few more this afternoon," I added.

"Great! May I ... ?" Golden asked as both she and I gestured toward the snack table.

Golden began by talking about her experiences in recent discussions with Svarog and the Strategy team. She noticed that Svarog often fell into a rage when there was dissension in the room.

"One thing that Svarog kept bringing up about the Gravity Train was the cost of the project. He saw some recent estimates of costs exceeding 500 billion US dollars. Early on, I think the estimates were not much more than a tenth of that," Golden said, and then she asked if we had looked into cost.

Brendan and I gave her the rundown on what we saw as reasonable cost. We pointed out that some early estimates assumed certain "expected technologies" would become available in time to sharply reduce costs. Those technologies did not yet appear to offer viable construction options, and we reminded her of the importance of contingency planning, since there were many things that could cause delays or unforeseen damages.

"So, Golden, what we have settled on is an estimate of just over 200 billion US dollars for the basic tunnel construction," I said, "which includes processing and reuse of some spoil. It does not include cooling of the work area, or the train rails or the trains themselves. Nor does it include those contingencies we mentioned."

"So we could be looking at a half-trillion easily ... maybe more," added Brendan.

"Well, gentlemen," Golden began, crossing her arms, "I think you're in for a world of pain if you go to Svarog with that."

"Shootin' the messenger, are we?" Brendan remarked.

"All I'm saying is that ... well, maybe you can put up an expected *range* of cost. You know? Like have a low-end view with a little asterisk that lists all the stuff not included. Maybe in really tiny print on a slide," Golden suggested, quite seriously and sincerely.

If I had said that, I would have been trying to be funny. Brendan gave me an "is she kidding?" look.

"You know, that's not a bad idea," I said, looking at Brendan, "let's make sure we do it as a range."

"Ha! Bloody hell!" he responded.

"And I think it may work, even if we *don't* try to hide all those contingency costs," I said.

"Risky, I think, if you don't hide them," said Golden.

◊   ◊   ◊

After Golden left, Brendan and I decided to stay in the conference room and have a "snack lunch." That gave us an opportunity to compare notes and think about how we might change our summary for Waldon and Svarog. It was a little after 1:00 PM when Kenton and Omari arrived.

They had both been involved in advancing and prototyping new carbon nano-structural patterns, which were relevant to the heat issue of the Gravity Train tunnel. They also participated in investigation of structural and bio-chemical aspects of pre-birth human brain development, including radial neuronal migration variants, which were closely related to the ADADA work.

They talked about their previous work in detail, pointing out potential connections to our vortex project focus, both the Gravity Train and ADADA follow-on work. They did not seem aware of the potential for ADADA Phase 2 being applied to limit independent thought, so Brendan and I recounted some of the day's earlier discussion. Both Kenton and Omari reacted with puzzled expressions, even shock now and then. I asked for their reaction.

"Well, I'm properly turbed," Kenton began, "I mean, once you start ... *messing* ... with somebody's brain, I mean, it's not contained, it's ..."

"Vascular," Omari interjected.

"Right! You said it," Kenton confirmed.

"Good use of non-offensive terms, Mr. Duckworth," said Brendan.

"You have a technology that looks like it is virtually unlimited in what it does. So how do you limit how it is used? Make rules? Make laws? People will break them," said Omari.

"Cybersecurity will become the answer. So, it all gets put on the shoulders of techies like Omari and me. We'll be responsible if something goes wrong," Kenton complained.

"We'll get shleepokked!" Omari articulated.

"And then we'll get ... you know ... a word that begins with 'F'!" Kenton added.

"Fired?" I asked, trying to be funny.

"Availa?" Kenton asked, triggering his smarts to message her. After a moment he said, "Hey, could you pop over to the conference room on thirty-five? The one in Reddy's aisle. Minute or two. Cybersecurity thing with ADADA. Solemn gratitude."

"Is Availa looking into security on ADADA?" Brendan asked.

"Not specifically," said Kenton, "but she's a total savant on cyber threat stuff. Knows a lot more than I do."

"A thousand times more than me," said Omari.

"Yeah, and Omari knows a thousand times more than I do," Kenton said, "so I'm, like, infinitesimal by comparison."

Availa arrived in less than a minute, sat down quickly and asked, eagerly, "How can I help?"

I gave her some background on our intent and topic scope, then mentioned the security concern on ADADA phase two. Availa looked at me and frowned.

"The weird thing is," she said, "there's no security component to the phase two plans. I got to take a peek at them a few days ago, and there's no mention of it at all."

"Right. Well, what should they be mentioning?" asked Brendan.

"For ADADA ... really anything that effects brain growth or emotional shifts ... I would think there should be all the standard stuff to security of devices someone would need to interact with to hack into the system. So, maybe a mix of biometrics. But, when the trick to get into somebody else's head is to have a special implant in your own brain, then we need to guard against the control implant being used by the wrong person. By a villain, so to speak," Availa said.

"But how do you stop them?" asked Kenton.

"The structure of each person's brain is unique, so I've heard, and with magnetic resonance equipment, you could check a brain's structure and be, like, nearly a hundred percent accurate in knowing whose it was," Availa said.

"I don't see how we could apply that here," Brendan said, "how could we use that?"

"My thought," said Availa, "it that we should have an ADADA feature designed to build some kind of brain structure verification technology into any implant made, as well as safeguarding the application at the system level with other new technologies that are already tested and ready."

"Build mag-res into a bloody implant? Think it through, miss," said Brendan.

"Wait. No. I didn't say the implant would have mag-resolution," Availa explained, "but there could be other ways for it to verify some particular features of the brain's structure … the anatomy of it. I'm not a neuroscientist, but look how far we've come in the last decade. In the last two or three years even."

"She's right! We're not that far off, really," said Kenton, smiling as Availa turned toward him.

"You know, Availa," I began, "we brought the security point up earlier today when your sister Adora and Vicki were here, and they referred us to Kenton and the tech crew."

"Whoa. I'll talk to Adora. If they don't feel like *they* can jump on that, they probably know someone who could help," said Availa.

"Thank you," I said.

"Yeah, hey, and thanks for answering my call," Kenton said, smiling at Availa.

"Anytime," she responded, returning the smile.

"Sorry for being thick, miss. You have a good idea. We just need the right subject matter expert to figure out what technologies we might need. And if they exist," said Brendan.

"Oh, and Adora warned me you would ask about the wearables," said Availa, "and I think we're in pretty good shape there with available technologies and offerings."

"Are they suited to our purpose?" Brendan asked.

"Very close, I think," said Availa, "and they're also easy to modify to shift the mix of nerve and brain points being stimulated or suppressed. So I think, working with scientists and medical professionals, we could adjust the wearables to be more effective for the tunnel hazards."

I thanked Availa, Kenton and Omari for their time.

◊   ◊   ◊

Later in the day, Nilima and Randall joined us, and they brought up additional cost components for the Gravity Train proposal.

"So we looked at the cost of using the new graphene layering for the middle of the tunnel. First of all, we think they have underestimated the length of tunnel that would need the graphene structure," Nilima said.

"Yeah. Slightly off. Early estimates were for five to seven miles," said Randall, "but looking at temperature at depth estimates and the geometry of it all, well, we might need over three hundred miles of the tunnel to have those graphene properties."

"That's got to be pretty expensive. Did you estimate the cost?" I asked.

"We did, and we found ..." Nilima began.

"Assuming it can actually be built, that is," Randall interrupted.

"Yes," Nilima continued, " assuming it can actually be built, we found that the cost of the structural shell for that tunnel section likely would be between $330 billion and $480 billion."

"U. S. dollars," Randall added.

"Hey! We're pushin' up to a trillion now!" Brendan declared.

"More than that," Nilima said, "because there is also the cost ... many costs ... of accelerated global warming."

"We really don't have a good estimate on that," Randall said, "because it depends on what the goals are and whether current global warming projections are correct."

"What's making global warming speed up?" Brendan asked.

"The heat released to the surface from the tunnel, mostly from the part of the tunnel below the lithosphere. Mainly from that section of graphene-based structure," Nilima explained.

"What's your guess on the cost?" I asked.

"I'll send you the spreadsheet of forty-eight individual cost factors," said Randall, "each one estimated as a range. You add the top of all those ranges together, you get over a trillion dollars."

Melinda entered at that point. My head was already as full of Melinda as it could possibly be, while still having a few brain cells and synapses available to more-or-less process our vortex discussions. When I saw her walk in, I felt that my head might actually explode.

"Hello!" she said, melodically, as she walked to the nearest available seat.

"Hey, Melinda," Randall said, "we just went through some cost points on the tunnel. So, could be like $400 billion or so extra for a graphene-based layered structure for the tunnel down where it needs it … in the high temp zone. Then another $100 billion up to maybe a trillion for costs related to moving heat from the mantle up to the surface and into the atmosphere. The latter is just a side-effect of the tunnel, but it might just be the most costly part of it."

"And what did you and Brendan come up with?" Melinda asked me. Her voice was delicious.

"Also a range. Most likely between two hundred and five hundred billion," I managed to say.

"So total cost then could approach two trillion dollars. Two trillion! Why is anyone considering going forward with the

Gravity Train?" Melinda asked, incredulously.

"Good question," I said, "as is the question of who needs it? Were people asking for this? Is it addressing some critical need for travel? Business travel? Is there anyone who wants to sponsor it for promotional purposes?"

"Hey, Connor," Randall spoke up, "on that sponsor thing … usually there's a bunch of folks looking to hook up with a big venture like GT. You know, suppliers of materials or manufacturers, and even more so the consumer discretionary types … like breweries, auto brands, banks, hotel chains … you know the drill, I think."

"We should look into that. Would you mind taking the lead on that, Randall?" I asked.

"Already did," Randall said.

"So? Any takers?" Brendan asked.

"Not a one! Kinda weird. I talked with marketing and sales execs across more than two dozen corporations, and *nobody* wanted anything to do with the Gravity Train. Hell, I even tried teasin' them with free advertising and cross-promotional stuff! *Free* now, you understand. Nobody'll touch it! I mean, what the hell?" Randall was definitely discombobulated.

"Well, we should highlight that with Svarog," Melinda suggested.

"Absolutely," I confirmed.

◊   ◊   ◊

The discussion drifted into some personal complaints about the work and the attitude of some of our executives. There were a few ideas on how best to bring up the key points with Waldon on Friday. Nilima and Randall both had some other work they needed to switch their focus too, they said, but they invited me to let them know if they could be of further assistance on the work.

When Nilima and Randall left, it was nearly four o'clock, and Melinda was still there with Brendan and me. We had each poured a bit more coffee into our cups, and we split the last doughnut three ways. After we unwound a bit, Melinda downed the last of her coffee and moved to sit next to me.

"Well, Connor, I think we're set for you to meet my dad this weekend."

"Great! Thank you for arranging that. Shall I get us a car?" I offered.

"Nope. I'm driving. If you could come to my place early Saturday morning, that would help."

"No problem, Melinda. How long of a drive is it to your dad's house?"

"About four hours or so. Depends. By the way, I'll be gone for a few hours Sunday afternoon. Meeting some old college friends of mine for a luncheon, but I'll be back to give you a ride home. To your hotel suite, I mean."

"Sounds good! Just let me know what time I should arrive at your place Saturday."

"Probably around nine should be good. Okay, see you Connor! See you Brendan!" With that, she waved and bounded out the door.

"Good day, miss!" called Brendan, who had been sitting at the far end of the table writing on a notepad. He then looked over at me. "Well," he said, "sorry if I wasn't supposed to hear that, but hey ... sounds like you'll be hanging out with Ansell Beckmann this weekend!"

"That's the plan. Melinda said he'd have nothing to do with me if it were work-related. So we're pretending I'm her new boyfriend. It'll just seem to him like a social thing, but I do plan to run some of our stuff by him. Get his thoughts."

"Just pretending, are you?" Brendan asked.

Before I could respond, there was a knock on the door frame. To my surprise, it was Waldon.

"Gentlemen," Waldon began, "I assume Golden was already here. Did she bring up the concern about cost estimates?"

"Yes, she did. We had a good discussion," I said.

"Excellent. Look I have about ten minutes. Could we just do our little pre-Robert review now? Let's just focus on Gravity Train, since that's likely all we'll cover with Robert next week. Is that okay?" Waldon asked as he sat down at the far end of the table.

"I think we're good to do that," I said, getting a nod of agreement from Brendan.

We shared with Waldon the key points that we thought we should raise at the Svarog review, along with a brief commentary on each. Brendan wrote them on the white board while he and I commented on each one:

□   Extreme heat (safety, construction materials, global warming)

□   Difficulty modeling due to lack of data at required depth

□   TBM articulation uncertainty

□   Mantle convection / continental plate shift may limit safe tunnel depth

- ☐   No potential sponsors or likely commercial investment
- ☐   Cost approaching $2,000,000,000,000

"Gentlemen," Waldon began to respond, "first of all, my thanks to you for your diligence on this and for bringing in folks from other TFD areas to talk about all this today. So, the next-to-last bullet on potential sponsors ... you can just drop that one. That's more of an operational revenue source point that we're not focusing on right now. The key here is *feasibility* of the Gravity Train, but I am willing to acknowledge that cost could be a factor in whether the GT realistically has any potential. It certainly won't be feasible if the global economy can't support building it."

"But we're fine to include cost as an issue," I hoped to verify.

"Yes and no," said Waldon, folding his arms. The room was silent for a few seconds, then he resumed.

"Yes, you can include a bullet on cost. You can even list the drivers you mentioned, like the graphene materials thing, but no quantification of those. No quantification of cost," said Waldon.

"But Waldon, ..." I started to say, but he interrupted.

"No quantification. Look, the early estimate we had is the one Svarog and other people have been repeating with they meet with government agency people. That was $3,300 per foot, so about $60 billion for construction, without contingencies. Let's put *those* numbers on the board, but all those other cost increase issues should be listed without quantification, unless Svarog specifically asks for it at the review meeting," Waldon directed, then asked if we had any other questions.

I looked over at Brendan, who only shrugged his shoulders.

"I think we're good. Thank you for the feedback," I said to Waldon.

CHAPTER 22

Scrutiny

That evening, Brendan suggested we have dinner at a pub he liked in lower Manhattan. I happily agreed, hoping we might find some things to talk about other than vortex or Waldon's feedback. Brendan insisted that I try a draft stout that he said was particularly good there. It was surprisingly good. I went with Brendan's recommendations for dinner as well, and both the potato soup appetizer and the fish and chips entree were delicious.

Our conversation never strayed into the realm of TFD, with the exception of Brendan asking about my plans to visit TFD's founder that weekend. My motivation was hard to articulate, since I didn't want to get into the things Mars had mentioned. So I said I felt the need to get Ansell Beckmann's perspective on our new projects, and I hoped he would have some insight as to possible benefits. If he saw no benefits, then perhaps he could suggest a way to pull the plug on those projects.

◊   ◊   ◊

The next day, Thursday, I decided to work from the suite. Most of the day I spent re-reading the key reports related to Gravity Train technologies and geological factors, although I'm not sure why. Melinda messaged me around mid-morning, and we conversed on our smarts for a while. She mainly wanted to know what happened with Waldon the day before. After my dinner with Brendan, I had messaged Melinda that Waldon came in asking for a preview of what we planned to highlight for Svarog on the tunnel project.

Melinda seemed upset about Waldon asking us not to bring up the commercial partnership point that Randall raised, as well as Waldon's directive that we not quantify the cost of the tunnel. I mentioned that we could still list all of the factors that could possibly raise the cost above the earlier accepted estimate of $60 billion, and we could add some further detail as we discussed it in the review meeting. She was clearly disappointed in me, and she told me I should have fought harder to get focus on the facts. She was right, of course, and I could not explain to her why I had not made a stronger argument. I didn't understand it myself.

Melinda explained she already had "other commitments" when I offered we could get together that evening or perhaps Friday evening. She did confirm that we were still on for the trip to her dad's house on Saturday, reminding me to be at her apartment around 9:00 AM.

◊   ◊   ◊

That afternoon, following nearly an hour of obsessing over how I could have done a better job on the preview with Waldon, I decided to call Cadence. It had been over a week since I last invoked her avatar. During that week, I briefly entertained the notion that it might be time to let her go … that it might be time to erase her avatar definition data from my smarts.

I did not go through with it. It felt as though we needed to have a parting conversation. I recall thinking that this might turn out to be that conversation, but I also wanted to talk to her about my immediate personal turmoil. Cadence might have some insight.

"Cadence?" I invited her to join me. She appeared, and I transferred her to the mirror.

"Connor! How are you? Is everything okay? You must be really busy!" she said, apparently in reference to the long gap in time since our last conversation. This time she was wearing a short skirt and an embroidered, tie-front top that was a favorite of mine.

"Cadence, good to see you! Yes, I'm sorry, it's been a bit crazy here. And that's actually something you may be able to help me with," I said.

I explained the current situation with our team evaluation of the tunnel project, as well as the dilemma we faced on how to handle the Svarog review. While I spoke, Cadence appeared to walk over to the couch in our living room, sat upon it and reclined, propping her head up on her arm, her elbow resting on the arm of the couch.

"That's terrible!" she said, "Why in the world would they assign you guys to look into it if they don't want to know what you found out?"

"I guess they expect ... or Waldon thinks they expect ... to have confirmation of the brilliance of the Gravity Train concept and plans," I mused. Cadence appeared to be looking up at the ceiling as she continued to recline without speaking for a while. Either her avatar was intending to project some deep thought around what she would say next or, perhaps, her response delay was due to searching through reference files I had provided of our previous conversations and correspondence.

"Is it just Svarog at that review meeting?" she asked, unexpectedly.

"Well, no, actually," I said, "it includes most of the exec team. Besides Svarog and Waldon, I expect we'll have Astrid and a few others. Dr. Reddy the Director of Research, for example. Possibly other execs from Marketing, Sales and Finance."

"Connor, I doubt that they're all subservient minions," she said while stretching.

"Yeah, but Svarog can be so nasty ... shouting, swearing, threatening," I said, without thinking too deeply about what she said.

"Can you meet with them ... or maybe a couple of them ... before going to Svarog? Let them scrutinize your findings. If they poke holes in any of it, you'll have time to adjust before the big review," Cadence suggested.

"Hmm, yes, that might help us to have a more convincing presentation for Svarog."

"Besides that, you'll get a sense for how much you can rely on those other execs to fight for you at the Svarog review. You may have a couple of good allies you can count on to back you up."

While the suggestion made sense in general, in light of the review with Waldon I did not feel comfortable previewing it with others on the exec team.

"Thanks," I said, "I'll definitely ponder doing that."

"Feel better yet?" Cadence asked, smiling sweetly as she continued to relax on the couch.

CHAPTER 23

Founder's Home – Day One

Via deliberate and focused manipulation of the steering wheel and pedals on the floor, causing the car to change direction or slow down or accelerate as required, based upon visual information received merely by looking ahead, sensing the reasonableness of our speed around curves using biological input from her muscles and joints and, too, from within her vestibular system, Melinda drove us up a mild ascent on a winding road through the woods toward her father's house.

I was unfamiliar with the Ithaca area, near the southern point of Cayuga Lake in the Finger Lakes region in upstate New York. I was fascinated by the alternating landscape of dense woods and open fields. A few inches of snow had fallen overnight, and the snow clung to the branches of evergreens, so that they were assemblages of white and green materials. The fields were completely white, but the roads had been cleared very well. I noticed the slight rising and falling of small hills, the occasional signs of habitation such as a house, its roof covered with snow. Now and then I saw a house with a barn nearby. The houses were mostly traditional colonial style, but I also saw a few that were very different, of a more modern architecture with dramatically tall front windows. One house appeared to be V-shaped. I tried to imagine what Ansell Beckmann's house would be like, assuming he had sufficient funds to build the house of his dreams. What did he dream about?

"We're pretty close. About another ten minutes to go," said Melinda.

"So, your dad's house …" I began.

"It's better if you see it without preparation," Melinda interrupted, "I'm curious to hear your first impressions."

I sat back and decided not to press further on the house, allowing myself to enjoy the tunnel-like enclosure formed by trees along the stretch of road we were driving through at that moment, particulate sunlight filtering and reflecting throughout leaves and branches. Melinda appeared to be enjoying it too, her face radiating an inner calm. I felt truly happy to be traveling with her.

We approached a driveway entrance flanked by stone gargoyles, each the same height of about five feet but otherwise completely different in attitude and pose, as appropriate for gargoyles. Melinda steered us between them, and we drove through a densely wooded stretch, finally emerging into a nicely landscaped area with a few trees, flower gardens and a large pond lined with trees on its far side. After taking in the ambiance of the grounds, I turned my attention to the stone house which was styled to resemble a castle with a tower on one side.

I was intrigued by a drawbridge-like structure at the foot of the front entrance, including heavy chains that ran from the near edge of the drawbridge into two holes in the stone wall above the front door. I assumed it was a facade, but as Melinda pulled up near the drawbridge, it began to rise. I then noticed there was an actual moat filled with water, perhaps seven or eight feet wide, running around the exterior of the house.

"Oh, for goodness sake!" Melinda complained as she opened the car door and emerged, placing her hands on her hips.

"Guess we're not welcome," I said, trying to be funny.

"No, it's more likely he meant it to be raised up when we arrived so that he could lower it with some drama and fanfare. We're a little early," said Melinda as she walked toward the edge of the moat. As I joined her, I could see some koi swimming about, most with red spots on otherwise whitish skin.

"Who be you? What do you seek?" came a low bellow from somewhere above our heads. I looked at Melinda expectantly, but she rolled her eyes and gestured for me to respond. After a moment, I shouted toward the house, "Good sir, I have been conveyed here by your brilliant and charming daughter in order to make your acquaintance." Upon hearing no reply, I continued, "We hope you will grant us passage over the dangerous waters that surround your domicile." After another few seconds, the drawbridge began to lower.

"He's a package, but don't worry," Melinda assured, "this is going to be fine."

After the drawbridge lowered completely, we began crossing it toward the door. When we were only halfway across, the double doors at the entrance opened by themselves, revealing only darkness inside. There was no sign of Ansell. Melinda then led me inside across the dark foyer, opening another set of double doors into a large, well-lit room with a stone fireplace in the wall on the left. Near the fireplace sat a man appearing to be in his late sixties, with gray hair and beard, holding a book in his lap. The man looked up, smiled at the two of us in the doorway and stood, declaring, "My 'brilliant and charming' daughter!" Melinda and her father approached each other and shared a hug. "And he whom she has conveyed," Ansell continued, turning toward me and extending a hand, "good to meet you Connor."

"Good to meet you, sir." I said as we shook hands. Ansell seemed genuinely welcoming as our gaze met for a few seconds. I wondered if he recognized either my name or my face from his TFD days, but if so, he did not reveal it, nor did I ask.

I took a moment to look around. Except for the wall around the fireplace, which was all stone in several shades of gray, the rest of the walls were covered with dark wood panelling upon which various ornate bronze or copper-colored sculptures were hung. Some of those sculptures resembled dragons, some with wings, others were of medieval knights and horses. The beamed ceiling was vaulted upward slightly toward a wall of tall windows, providing a view of a well-maintained garden area surrounded by dense woods.

"Melinda, I am truly happy to see you!" Ansell proclaimed.

"Good to see you too, Dad," said Melinda.

"I love your house and the yard around it too," I said, "almost like living in a fairy tale."

"Beautiful out there, isn't it? Even this time of year. You both should stroll around the grounds a bit. But first, let's have some food and drink," Ansell gestured toward a table at the far end of the room upon which were laid plates and serving trays with various *hors d'oeuvre*. A variety of libations were displayed on a counter against the wall behind the table.

"I'm up for it!" said Melinda as she quickly made her way to the table.

Ansell and his daughter spent some time catching up on each others activities and projects. Melinda seemed especially superficial in commenting on her current work assignments, and I just assumed that was normal for her. When Ansell asked her how Svarog was working out as CEO, for example, Melinda's response was, "he's not as inspiring as you, so we have to look elsewhere for inspiration."

Ansell apologized for having to work that weekend. He said he was working on a paper he would be presenting on Monday, and he would need some time to himself that weekend to finish it. Melinda reminded him that she, too, had other obligations and would be gone Sunday afternoon. She also assured her dad that I would have some work to do too, so that I wouldn't bother him. I nodded as though acknowledging that, although I didn't know what she meant.

"Melinda, I am truly happy to see you!" Ansell said again, as we tidied up after our lunch.

"You already said that," Melinda scolded playfully, "but thank you."

"'A double blessing is a double grace.'" Ansell replied. Then, turning to me, he added, "Shakespeare."

"Very well, my lord," said Melinda, as she and I left the room.

◊   ◊   ◊

Melinda and I sat in a couch-like window seat in the breakfast table area, leaning over the top cushion, looking out over the pond. Little lumps of snow dropped from the tree branches into the pond, causing ripples on the surface of the water which emanated in growing circles from where each snow lump landed. The sunlight reaching through the trees to the water surface added a somewhat hypnotic sparkling effect. As we watched, the frequency of snow lump dropping increased, and the density of ripples increased, so that many circles and interference patterns appeared on the pond surface.

A single leaf, ellipsoidal in shape, blew gently into view near the window. It appeared to pivot or flutter about its principal axis, while at the same time moving along a corkscrew path downward along an angle, so that it crossed in front of Melinda and me. The leaf suggested analogous movements, both in ballet and in the rotations and revolutions of celestial objects. How odd, I thought, that I had not connected dancing with the orbits and rotations of planets and moons before. How odd, I thought, that something as small as that leaf could suggest human performance as well as something on a planetary scale. I then shifted focus back to watching snow melting off of the tree branches, silently falling into the pond. I would have been content to do that for the rest of the afternoon, but Melinda broke the silence.

"To me it's a perfect metaphor for how things should be," she began. "This is what it was supposed to be like. Augmented life. When all the personal connectivity and social media stuff was first introduced around the turn of the century, it was all so promising. The more we improved it, the more accessible it all was ... the more accessible each of us was to each other. There was so much potential there. Each of those little snow bits melting down into the pond is like a post or a tweet ... something any of us can share with others, anywhere in the world. And the ripples are how they reach others through a network of networks. Now there are so many snow bits that the ripples are all running into each other, combining into new patterns. And it's all so beautiful in the pond!"

"But not so beautiful in our human interactions," I surmised.

"Well, think about waves in physics, as I'm sure you'd be orgasmically delighted to do. Depending on how they line up ... the phases and frequencies ... they can reinforce and add energy to each other, or ...."

"Interfere with each other," I interrupted, "or even completely cancel each other out."

"Right! They can strengthen effectiveness or they can corrupt the message ... corrupt the purpose. The more we communicate today, the less we understand each other. The more often we connect, the less we cooperate. The more we think we learn, the less we really know. The bigger the window, the narrower our personal perspectives. The more insights we think we gain, the more convoluted and the less reliable our comprehension of the big picture becomes." Melinda's expression seemed increasingly despairing as she spoke.

"Yes," I said, "I sometimes get information that's hard to fit or reconcile with what I've already accepted as the truth. That wave interference thing. If only there were a way to clear away interference, interconnection, entanglement."

"Some entanglements are good, I think," said Melinda, softly, looking toward the tree tops.

I noticed Melinda's eyes seemed to be welling up a little with tears, and so I asked her if she was thinking about a specific entanglement just then.

"I may have mentioned working at a pharmaceutical company before joining TFD. They were expanding into neural implants," she began cautiously, "and I volunteered ... I was involved in that work."

"Did you volunteer to do some testing for them?" I asked.

"Yes, I did."

"Did you get a neural implant?" I asked, though it seemed extremely unlikely.

"Yes," she said, "they were working with TFF and another outfit in Europe. I got myself implanted, although there were some problems. Things didn't go exactly as planned."

"That's too bad. I'm sorry to hear that."

"The study was supposed to be about sharing feelings ... experiencing the feelings of others who also had implants. Directly sharing actual memories from one person to another. But the study was sabotaged. Someone tampered with the implant devices before they were surgically inserted into the test subjects, including myself."

"So what happened? Did the implants not work at all?" I asked.

"They worked pretty well, actually, but there were false memories installed into our brains. Mine was of having a son who died when he was only three years old. He died because of negligence on my part. It was all my fault. His death ...." Melinda stopped there and silently stared out the window.

I took hold of her hand.

"His death was my fault!" she cried.

"What sort of monster would put that kind of memory in someone's head?" As soon as I asked that question, I realized it might have been Mars Janssen. I couldn't bring myself to tell her in that moment about my conversation with Mars and the issue of bodily harm, but I resolved to tell her later that weekend.

"They're still investigating," she said.

"How are you dealing with it? I mean, is there anything I can do to help?" I asked.

"I loved him. I still love him. His name was Jason. I love him, and I miss him," said Melinda as she leaned toward me, resting her head on my shoulder.

◊   ◊   ◊

After a while I looked back outside and noticed at the far end of the pond, partially obscured by shrubbery, a smoothly curved white, dome-like shape resting near the edge of the water. I pointed it out to Melinda and asked if she knew what it was. She responded with laughter, wiping her eyes, patting my shoulder.

"That's my dad's boat! You didn't know he was a crusty, seafaring sea dog, did you?" Melinda continued to laugh and cry.

"Seriously?" I asked.

"Oh absolutely! There's a fountain that runs in the center of the pond. It can't be there in the winter because the water freezes sometimes and causes the fountainhead to crack. Twice a year,

Dad rows that little boat to the middle of the pond to detach or reattach the fountainhead, depending on the season. He wears a ship captain's hat and uniform jacket!" Melinda began laughing so hard she had trouble catching her breath.

"Fascinating! Sounds like quite an adventure, and he's called to it by the change of seasons. Powerful drama. Powerful metaphors too," I said, as Melinda's laughter began to wind down a bit.

"Ayn Rand wrote a novel about it," Melinda said, recovering her composure, then turning and giving me what I'm sure was the most serious look she could manage at that moment.

"No kidding," I said, feigning intrigue.

◊ ◊ ◊

While continuing to look out at the view of the pond, which I twice proclaimed to be a "winter wonderland", we spent another hour or so conversing about seasonal patterns of insects, birds and animals, as well as seasonal callings that we and other people we knew experienced. We shared our perspectives on recent technology application news, including a forthcoming smarts enhancement that could determine the "approachability" rating of a stranger you encounter by somehow intercepting and evaluating readings from their wearables. From there we moved to a discussion about potential for humans to read each others thoughts or feelings by direct brain to brain communication, *without* implanted devices. A memory about Cadence popped into my head, and I decided to share it.

"Cadence and I had spent the day hanging out in Los Gatos, a delightful little town with lots of little shops and eateries, with a hiking trail accessible from the center of town near where the local grower's market vendors assemble on Saturday mornings. The trail runs along a creek at first, then climbs up to a pleasant view on a hillside. You'd like it," I told Melinda.

"I think I would," she said.

"After dinner, we walked around a bit and saw a pretty fountain in a courtyard. A stone wall half-circled the fountain area. We decide to sit on the wall and enjoy the peaceful surroundings. On the other side of the fountain was a grass field with a few small, recently planted trees. There was a wooden bench on the near edge of that grass field, upon which sat a man and woman in their late twenties, casually dressed, apparently together although not engaged in conversation at that moment.

"At one point, Cadence put her hand up near my mouth as though to indicate I should be quiet. She appeared to be straining to hear something. After a bit, she explained she heard a bird make a sound like 'Tierney-Tierney', which, coincidentally, is my middle name."

"Your middle name is Tierney-Tierney?" Melinda asked, eyebrows raised.

"Just Tierney, actually," I assured her, then resumed my story.

"Cadence held my hand, and we sat quietly for a while, listening for that bird. Every time I thought I heard it, Cadence gave my hand a little squeeze, so I knew she was hearing it too. My breathing slowed as I closed my eyes and began to visualize a glowing energy being released from my body through my limbs. It was an energy that was connected to anxieties. I listened to the soothing noise the fountain made. My anxieties were dissipating as we sat on that wall, mostly through my legs, with my feet dangling a few inches above the ground. At least, that's how it felt. After a dozen or so waves of anxious energy moved out of me, I opened my eyes again, the fountain's cascading water in view, a slight breeze now teasing the leaves of the trees beyond the fountain, the couple on the bench still sitting quietly.

"Just then, Cadence gripped my hand fiercely and gasped. It was as though she experienced a sharp pain of some kind, without warning. I held her hand in both of mine and asked, in a whisper, what was wrong.

"'Something's about to happen,' she said, barely audibly, intently watching the couple on the bench. I looked toward the bench. The couple were still sitting close to each other, silently, turned away from each other. In a few seconds, the man slapped his hand angrily on the bench as he rose, and he walked away from the bench, away from the woman, without looking back, without a word. The woman didn't react at first, didn't turn, didn't speak, but after another moment or two she leaned her head down despairingly into her hands in her lap, shaking and sobbing.

"Cadence moved off the wall and stood facing me, her face expressing concern. 'Come with me,' she said, pulling on my wrist. We walked together up the street into an area of townhouses with large trees along the sidewalks, their thick foliage providing both ample shade and softly soothing rustling from leaves caressed by the breeze. I wanted to know what just happened. What had Cadence experienced?

"'Let me show you something,' she said, turning and facing me after we had walked a bit further into the shade. She told me to close my eyes and relax. She asked me if I was feeling anything unusual. Then she giggled while suggesting that perhaps it was *not* unusual for me.

"After standing there for a few seconds, I did begin to feel something. It began as a slight pulling sensation on the right side of my head, as though the hairs on that side were lifted up by some static electricity charge. Then it got a bit stronger, as though someone was gently pulling on my hair.

"'You're pulling on my hair,' I announced, with the inflated confidence of a child having solved some kind of puzzle game at a friend's birthday party. Cadence instructed me to open my eyes, and when I did, I saw Cadence leaning over to the right, her hands behind her back, her head tilted nearly 90 degrees to the vertical, her long hair hanging straight down toward the sidewalk. The pulling sensation I felt continued for a moment until she straightened her head. Cadence just stood there, smiling at me.

"'Well, it felt like something was pulling my hair,' I finally managed to say, while pointing to the right side of my head.

"'Funny! That's just what *I* was feeling,' she said to me. Her eyes were sparkling. It was just the weight of her own hair hanging down, but somehow I felt it. Somehow she had made me feel it.

"I shook my head and rationalized that it was a stronger pull than that. It was more than just the weight of her hair. My argument was, of course, ridiculous, since the key thing was that the young lady had somehow managed to make me feel that my hair was being pulled without anything actually pulling it. Cadence invited me to lift her hair to feel its weight. As I did, I was surprised to find that it was heavier than I had imagined. I had felt the pull of gravity on Cadence's hair, as though it were something pulling on my own hair."

I stopped there, becoming somewhat overwhelmed by other memories of Cadence at that moment. Melinda leaned over and gently touched my cheeks.

"What happened? What happened with you and Cadence?" she asked.

"She died. Allergic reaction. Anaphylactic shock." As I spoke, it felt as though a vise handle was being turned to release its grip, relieve its pressure.

Melinda pulled me toward her and wrapped her arms around me. Pressing her cheek against mine, she whispered, "I'm so sorry, Connor. I'm so sorry."

That evening, Ansell took us out to dinner at a nice Italian restaurant in Ithaca, where we were met by a faculty member in Cornell's Bioengineering department. Ansell introduced her as his good friend, Dr. Velasco, and she immediately asked us to please call her Amelia. As Ansell stood and helped Amelia with her chair, Melinda leaned over to me and whispered "girlfriend."

We talked about many things that evening. The most interesting topic from my perspective was the extension of Internet of Things technologies to new areas. One of the new IoT areas was humanity itself. In other words, adding humans to the list of possible "things" that were being monitored, classified and studied via data aggregation … and controlled. Wearables already enabled some human data to be collected and monitored, and to a limited extent, personal enforcement wearables could be activated remotely in order to wake someone from sleep or serve as a reminder to behave a certain way, along the lines of Kenton's be-mod for avoiding bad language.

Several research facilities in the Nordic region, where the national governments of Norway, Finland and Sweden had supplied funding to subsidize and encourage investment in new technologies, had already begun experimentation into embedded devices that would have a broader range of monitoring and controlling capabilities. TFF, where Mars had worked after leaving TFD, was one of those companies.

Ansell explained his recent decision to work remotely with the TFF team. He began by musing about the human brain, evolution, and the potential need for adjustments to how the human brain was evolving. He expressed disappointment that we were not evolving in a way supportive of human priorities. He used terms like "synaptic adjustments" to suggest ways we might alter typical categorical thinking by humans … the way we tend to impose categories … to somehow make it easier for us to recognize connections or similarities between categories. Ultimately, he explained, his personal goal was to push IoT toward enabling collective thinking by many humans, along with collective agreement and acceptance of decisions.

"In my view," Ansell said as he leaned back and stretched a bit, "IoT is still all about e-Commerce and management of utilities and supply chains and mechanized equipment."

"But you mentioned human priorities," said Amelia, "how do we determine what those are? Does every human have a voice? Do they get to choose priorities?"

"As much as possible," Ansell replied.

"We might have billions of priorities. We need a way to limit those to just a few," said Melinda.

Amelia crossed her arms and fixed her gaze on Melinda. "I just worry that the few overarching priorities will be those of leaders of nations, those in power, which in most cases will be politically motivated or, worse yet, selfishly or criminally motivated for personal gain."

"But they're the 'enablers of life' according to certain people running TFD now," I said, feigning innocence.

There were a few seconds of silence, and then Amelia burst out laughing.

"Melinda's correct that we need to have just a few priorities for IoT extensions," Ansell began, "but we need to focus on building in ... designing in ... safeguards to prevent abuse."

Amelia leaned forward with her elbows on the table and addressed Ansell directly. "But if those 'enablers of life' are funding everything, won't it be difficult to allocate money toward safeguards?"

Ansell nodded, then replied, "no worries my dear, there are those who will always be working to keep things in check ... to combat evil intentions."

◊   ◊   ◊

Back at her father's house, Ansell excused himself to return to his study and work. Melinda took me by the hand and led me upstairs, giving me a quick tour of the layout ... bedrooms, bathrooms and a little sitting room with a window near the staircase. "We can see the moon and stars from here," said Melinda, and she assured me the daytime view included rolling green hills, trees and lots of birds.

She took me back to one room on the opposite side of the house from her dad's room.

"We can share this room tonight. Comfy queen-size bed, which we can also share. My dad won't come anywhere near us, so don't worry about that. He has no rules for my behavior anymore," she assured me, then added, "however, I have a special rule about first nights together."

"Let me guess. I have to be naked while you're fully clothed?"

"No, my dear, but I'll keep that in mind for future diversions."

"Hmm. You really love rules. Fine. What is it?"

"This will be our first night sleeping together, and I believe that first nights together should be just that ... sleeping."

"Okay. Wait, are you saying ..."

"No roll in the hay tonight," she interrupted.

CHAPTER 24

Founder's Home – Day Two

I awoke to the sound of a bird outside the window, tweeting sharply and forcefully what sounded like: Tierney-Tierney! ... Tierney-Tierney! The tweeting stopped immediately as I opened my eyes, so it's possible I only dreamed hearing the bird. It was the first time I had heard any bird make that sound since the day in Los Gatos when Cadence revealed her special abilities. I propped myself up on my elbow to gaze upon Melinda, still sleeping tranquilly at my side, facing me. Her face, more beautiful than ever, provoked me to imagine where Melinda was just then. Where might she be in her dreams? What adventure might she be having? With whom was she facing some challenge or delight?

Sunlight began to enter the room, finding its way through imperfectly closed curtains and reflections into the bedroom from the mirror and skylight in the adjoining bathroom. I spent a few minutes admiring the softly luminescent highlights added, gradually, to Melinda's face and form. The effect reminded me of paintings by Edgar Degas and Mary Cassatt. Although I could certainly have enjoyed the beauty of that view for hours, I decided it was time to awaken her. I gently stroked her hair a few times, which, although her breathing changed rhythm a bit, did not appear to draw her out of her sleep. Next I tried tapping my finger lightly upon her hip. That too, apparently, was insufficient prompting.

I became emboldened enough to place a gentle kiss on her forehead, then another on her cheek, then another on her nose, as Melinda finally began to move a little and smiled. She reached and caressed my face, still with her eyes closed. I placed a kiss on the palm of her hand, then another on her wrist. Then I slowly leaned in to kiss her on the mouth, but just as I was about to make contact with her lips, she opened her eyes which caused me to pull back a bit. "Nice … waking up to that … to you." she said.

"Mmm. Same here," I replied, lightly touching her cheek, neck and shoulder.

As we reposed on the bed, shifting closer, Melinda wrapped one of her legs around me, and we pressed together, caressing each other's backs. After a while, I couldn't resist going further. I reached under the sheet and began to lift her camisole up from her waist. Melinda moved to enable and assist me to pull it off her completely.

"Wait!" she protested, suddenly grabbing the cami as I moved to fling it aside, "Remember you agreed that we wouldn't, you know, have a 'roll in the hay' on our first night sleeping together."

"Yes, I did agree. A very reasonable policy. But, it's the next day now," I said, matter-of-factly.

"Oh," Melinda replied, as she tossed the cami behind her.

◊   ◊   ◊

It was so very fortunate, I thought, as Melinda and I descended the back staircase to the kitchen, that Melinda wasn't planning to leave until around noon. We had had a leisurely morning, satisfying on many levels, and Melinda was still able to shower, dress and finish packing before 11 AM without having to rush. As we entered the kitchen, we saw Ansell sitting out on the deck beyond a sliding screen door. "Hey Dad!" Melinda offered her greeting as she opened the refrigerator.

"Coffee and croissants on the counter," her dad called from outside, "grab some and come sit with me out here."

We did just that. It was comfortably warm out on the deck, which was partially enclosed with an electric heater running. We relaxed and chatted for a little while before Melinda announced that she had to get going to her "alumni meeting" at Cornell.

As I walked Melinda back through the kitchen toward the front door of the house, she reminded me of her plan for the day and gave me a specific assignment.

"Okay, so I'll be meeting my old friends for lunch in Ithaca, then we'll be hanging out on campus … reminiscing, regretting, regrouping, recovering … all that kind of stuff. It's healthy, I think."

"I hope you have fun reconnecting and feel great. I'll look forward to hearing about it," I said.

"Wait. Hearing about it? Not sure there'll be anything I can share," Melinda said, projecting an air of mystery.

"Well, I will certainly share with you whatever I wind up doing this afternoon."

"You should try a little creative writing while I'm gone. Seriously. Write some poems or a short story," she said.

"Well, I've only written reports and analysis summaries. Not sure I could do fiction. I mean, forget poetry. But I'm not sure I could write a story either." Her suggestion took me off guard.

"Sometimes people get in their own way. Try being someone else ... stepping outside yourself."

"You mean, like pretend I'm someone else? Back at Clementina's I think you suggested I write under a pseudonym."

"Yes, I did, and I'm suggesting it again. I'm giving you an assignment. Try writing a story for me. I hereby request a short story with something to do with seasonal drives or urges."

"What sort of urges?" I asked.

"It'll come to you. Write something about entanglement and alignment. Something about reality being augmented *without* advanced technology. Something about penetrating the mantle and the core. Something about *physics*!"

"Whoa! Hold on there. This is getting too complicated," I protested.

"It's just all the stuff we're looking at and talking about every day. Connecting them in a little story may help you get your head around them ... or feel more at ease about them," Melinda smiled, then she added, "One more thing. It absolutely has to have 'layered flesh' in it."

"'Layered flesh'? Oh my God! I cannot satisfy such a request," I said, melodramatically.

"Be someone else. Be ... Mr. Wonderland, I think."

"Seriously?" My head was spinning.

"No! Mr. *Winter*wonderland! Walter! Walter Winterwonderland!" Melinda seemed ecstatic.

"I can try, Melinda, but I just don't know ..."

"If you get stuck, just 'walk away from it now and then'. Dad told me that, like, a billion times during my college years." Then, while shaking her finger at me, she added, "and, you must not ask my father about any TFD-related stuff until you finish the story."

I reluctantly agreed to her terms. My only concern was that I wouldn't finish it in time to ask Ansell my questions before we had to leave. Shortly afterward, Melinda gave her father and I each a hug and a kiss on the cheek as she left to meet with her former classmates.

As I walked her out to the car, I was mildly anxious that Ansell would raise the drawbridge before I could walk back. Melinda explained that, although she'd be back in time for dinner, she preferred that we leave right away, stopping somewhere on the way home to eat. She explained, adding appropriate air quotes, that her dad had already planned a private dinner with his "good friend" Dr. Velasco.

"So ... your implant," I said, awkwardly, as we reached her car, "Can it connect to other people's thoughts if they *don't* have the implant?"

"You're wondering about that night in my apartment?"

"Well, yes, I mean ...."

"Yes, I could sense your feelings and thoughts that night. Mostly feelings, I guess."

"What kind of feelings were you sensing?"

"Well, you ... you had some very intense desires, you know?

Desires that would have required you to break my rules. And you were really struggling with that. I admired your self-control, since I could feel how difficult it was for you that night," Melinda turned and opened the car door, adding, "Kind of hard to talk about this."

"Sorry. It just seemed to me like your feelings may have been combining with mine ... intensifying my own feelings. It was kind of that way this morning too, I think. Does your implant somehow do that?" I asked.

"Not sure. It wasn't supposed to have that capability. Although it wasn't supposed to let me read thoughts from someone who didn't have an implant either. But I think we *were* in each other's heads that night. And this morning too. I'm sure of it. I'm a little jealous of Cadence by the way. Sounds like she may have been able to do more that I can, even *without* an implant."

Melinda then waved and, as she began to drive away, she called out her lowered window. "It reinforces what I've suspected for a while. There's a new phase of human evolution beginning!"

As I walked back to the house, I wondered which of us had really been naked that night in her apartment after our date at Clementina's.

Ansell offered me the study with the fireplace as a work area, saying he wanted to work in his library that day. The study was quiet and somehow helped me to stop thinking about work commitments and focus on creative composition. Fairly quickly, I got the idea that the story would be based on my first meeting with Cadence. I decided to change the circumstances. Instead of meeting her while living in Cupertino, I thought of the possibility that I was living in New York. Instead of seasonal trips to New York for New Qs, I seasonally visited the area around San Francisco and San Jose. So, in the story, I met Cadence on one of those seasonal trips, and we only got together seasonally when I was in California. I changed her name to Taylor for the story.

At first it was a slow and frustrating exercise, but after the first hour or so, it started going along more smoothly. I felt I was making good progress and was surprised by how much I enjoyed the writing process. I took a couple of short breaks but spent nearly four hours working to complete a first draft. As I read through my story draft, noting changes and adjustments I felt it needed, Ansell entered the study carrying a bottle of wine and two glasses.

"Hoping you'll have a drink with me before dinner," he said, then, observing me closing my notebook, added "no need to close up shop."

"I'd rather finish it later. It helps to 'walk away from it now and then', I hear."

"Hmm. Where'd you hear *that* bullshit?" Ansell asked with a grin, as he poured a glass for me, adding "as if any of us can truly walk away from anything! It's a *Barbera d'Alba* region red. Not my go-to, but I like it now and then."

As we sipped the wine, Ansell asked me how the story was coming along. Melinda had told her dad about the assignment she gave me.

"Surprisingly good," I said, "at least from the standpoint of my enjoying writing it."

"But not from the standpoint of it being a good piece of work?"

Ansell probed.

"I'm not the best judge, I think," was my response.

"What kinds of things did the writing process make you think about?" he asked.

At that point, I tried to describe my focus during the afternoon. There were times when I segued into thoughts about how some unexpected events in one's life feel like they were preordained, predestined. My first encounter with Cadence, for example, felt like that to me. It felt so perfect and unavoidable that it had to have been arranged by powers beyond those of mere mortals. I thought about the idea of preordained purpose. Perhaps each of us is predestined to play a specific role in some little particle of drama in the vast universe of commotion and spectacle. I wondered if, in fact, I had some preordained purpose to fulfill. Was I on the right path to fulfill it?

There were a few parts of my writing activity that afternoon that I had especially enjoyed, parts that employed the use of the sounds of words ... the "sonics" of a paragraph. I flipped though my draft and read a sentence aloud to Ansell as an example:

Suddenly, the music's tempo quickens: wire strings now playfully plucked with carved goat femurs, new sounds emerging like sleigh-bells sewn on leather strips rhythmically bludgeoned and trampled.

"What about you? Do you enjoy writing? Do you enjoy the creative process?" I asked.

"I write academic papers," Ansell said, "and while I do get some satisfaction out of that, it's not my main source of satisfaction in terms of the creative process."

"So what is?"

"Let me show you," Ansell said, standing and gesturing for me to follow.

He led me upstairs to the room farthest from the stairway. It did not appear to be used for anything but storage. There were several large wardrobe boxes and stacks of books on the floor. There were two mattresses leaning against a wall and parts of a bedframe on the floor near them. He walked to the closet at the far side of the room, opened the door and said, "Here we go!"

On one side of the closet was a sliding partition which opened to reveal a staircase leading upward. Ansell started up the steps and I followed. Lights came on has we climbed into a large loft. There was a peaked ceiling and a window on each of two walls. There were paintings placed randomly around on the floor, leaning against the walls. An easel stood near the middle of the space near two tables of various little jars and tubes. On the easel was a painting of a pastoral scene.

"As you may have already surmised, I like to paint," said Ansell.

"These are really good," I said, "I've tried painting, but I couldn't get the hang of it. Not too bad with charcoal sketching though, but it's been a while since I've tried any of that."

"Well, there may come a time when you decide to try it again. It may surprise you. You might just find it very satisfying," Ansell said.

"So, this one you're working on," I said, pointing to the easel, "it looks like a view of your property here." The painting was impressionistic in style, showing two wooden chairs placed together, turned slightly toward each other. Behind the chairs could be seen part of the pond with some trees further in the background. The chairs were also partly shaded by branches from a nearby tree.

"Hmm," Ansell reacted, "well, it's actually a portrait of my wife Barbara and I."

"Oh?" I said, looking back at the painting in case I missed something, but the only things in the painting besides the pond, trees and grass were the two wooden chairs.

"That setting. The placement of the chairs. The way they are turned to facilitate two people enjoying the setting, the pond, the trees. Turned to make it easy to see each other's face, have a quiet conversation, enjoy each other's presence, sense each other's feelings and memories," Ansell said, "Barbara and I are in the painting. In every brush stroke."

"I see what you mean. That's really beautiful," I said, "and there could be something more to it, in the form of analogies ... or metaphors, if you will ... in how well a person's brain can see the connection of one thing to another. Even if the connection is not obviously logical. Not sure I'm making sense, but I'm thinking along the lines of how some augmented reality apps introduce odd associations, like metaphorical connections between apparently unrelated things. Visual poetry. Like a kind of entanglement ... has Melinda talked to you about that?"

"Yes, she has. Speaking of metaphors and Melinda. She seems to genuinely trust you," Ansell said, "and I think you might be a good person for her to have in her life. By the way, I wouldn't mention to her that I said that, since she often does the opposite of what I'd like her to do. On purpose, I suspect."

Ansell then led me back down to the study, sharing some of his thoughts on Melinda's past along the way.

"Some time ago, just after her mother died, Melinda and I had a falling-out, and we had very little contact for several years. She moved out of this area to the city, where she'd gotten a job with a pharmaceutical research outfit. She led me to believe, through a few emails she sent over the next year or so, that she was helping some bio-chemists with mathematical modeling and 3D visualization tools." He paused to take another sip of wine, then went on, his voice sounding angry.

"And maybe she was doing that, but she was also a guinea pig. A paid volunteer for a neuroscience test program. I got some detail after we reconciled and started to spend more time together. She says she can't tell me everything because she signed a legal non-disclosure agreement, but I think she actually can't recall a lot of what happened. They surgically implanted microdevices into her brain."

"She told me about that," I said as we entered the study, "and she seems very sensitive to the intrusion of technology into our lives. Surprising she would allow it to be embedded inside her."

"She was clinically depressed at the time, Connor, I'm fairly sure, although she did not seek counseling or treatment. Sometimes that can make you change your priorities on what's important in your life. Even personal integrity and safety can wind up moved to the back burner for a while, I suppose. I should tell you that the trial microdevices were geared toward brain growth, neural connections, memory erasure and creation of synthetic memories. The idea was to apply the learning toward potential treatment for those individuals who had bad experiences in the first couple of years of life, including time in the womb, because of abuse or neglect. That's when all the key programming of the human brain happens, and it's impossible to change it later on. At least, it was thought to be impossible until recently."

"The ADADA project!" I suddenly realized that Melinda's connection to ADADA may have preceded the work at TFD. "It's all about exploring and trying to change that early programming in the human brain."

"Melinda has memories of having a son. She recalls giving birth to a baby boy and raising him until he was nearly four years old. His name was Jason," Ansell said.

"She mentioned that to me yesterday ... the memory of having had a son."

"Her memory is very real. A lot of detail over time with Jason as a baby, a toddler, a little boy. Detailed memory on her relationship with Jason, the feelings she had for him. But no physical evidence of any kind. No photographs. No corroborating recollections by any friends or relatives. So, yes, Jason appears to have been created by implanted memories," Ansell explained.

"And those were implanted by someone hacking the project, right?"

"Yes, it appears the project was hacked, Connor. Not sure by whom or why, but some of the participants had unusual memory changes and behavioral changes that were not on the agenda, so to speak, for what was supposed to have been introduced into their brains. In the end, it was deemed a failed study, with the failure being one of cybersecurity, as opposed to bad hypotheses or sampling issues."

"Did they ever figure out exactly how that happened?"

"No, but whoever hacked it would have had to be very close to the project. There was no publicity about it until months after it ended. And then there's the question of motivation. The hacker's intent is a puzzle, since it was not just random destruction of data, nor was it a theft of good data. I suspect there was some purpose behind the tampering, but I've stared at the evidence for a hundred hours or more, and I can't figure out what the purpose was. I can't find a pattern.

"You mentioned memory erasure as a part of the study. Was there anything erased from Melinda's memory?"

"Not that I've noticed ... other than, as I mentioned, possibly some details of the project itself being erased. Melinda hasn't noticed either, although she would have to encounter some evidence of something that happened to her that she would not have been likely to forget. That hasn't happened, so we're thinking the hacker did not do erasures. The microdevices were theoretically capable of causing erasures, and the erase function had been tested successfully with rats and crows. That first human study, however, did not include erasures. They were saving that for a follow-on, which never got funding due to the problems with the first study. There's another thing about Melinda ...." Ansell gestured for me to follow him out of the study and into a large room at the end of the hallway.

"My library and work area," he announced as we entered the room. I looked about to see that the ceiling was very high ... nearly twenty feet, perhaps, where it met the walls ... and the center of the ceiling arched up a few feet higher. Two of the walls were lined, floor to ceiling, with books on shelves. The shelves on the 2nd story of the room were accessible by a ladder in the corner where the bookshelf-walls met. There was a narrow metal grid platform along the walls about nine feet up that enabled access to books on the higher shelves by using a movable ladder attached to a rail near the ceiling. The rest of the room was nicely furnished with leather lounge chairs, a large oriental carpet and an ornate roll-top desk in the corner near one of the tall windows on the far wall.

"This room. She avoids it," said Ansell, "Never comes in here, really. The ceiling is too high."

He paused, drawing a puzzled look from me, then continued, "Melinda is altocelarophobic. Meaning she has a fear of high ceilings. So .... places like museums, train terminals, concert halls ... and this room ... have the effect of causing her extreme anxiety."

"I've heard of that, I think. It's very rare, isn't it?" I asked, recalling her comment about hating the Gyre Ventures building lobby. I wondered if the high ceiling at the Snegurochka pub caused her some anxiety at the TFD dinner as well.

"It used to be very rare, but I've seen some numbers recently showing that the portion of the population affected by altocelarophobia has grown by an estimated factor of five hundred over the last decade. Puzzling, to say the least."

"I have acrophobia, so climbing up to those books on the highest shelves would stress me out, but high ceilings don't bother me at all. When did you learn of her fear?" I asked, wondering why he would have built a house with a twenty foot ceiling if his daughter would be troubled by it.

"It appears to have been a side effect of the implant work ... or maybe the hacking of it. She had never exhibited that affliction before.   She used to love hanging out in the library when she visited here, but ever since the implant work ....."

"So, if that affliction was caused by brain augmentation, perhaps it could be corrected by it as well," I postulated, "also, what if the rapid increase in ... what was it?"

"Altocelarophobia."

"Altocelarophobia," I repeated slowly, "What if it were caused artificially, intentionally, by subversive parties testing the effectiveness of fear tampering or phobia cultivation?"

"Most of the trouble in the world is caused by human behavior," said Ansell, "serial killings, arson, sexual abuse ... most of that can be traced back to problems in early cognitive development.   Even wars are fundamentally triggered by human thought, human ideals that were likely malformed by some early brain development problem.   What is still not understood is whether we can fix that retroactively somehow.   The ADADA project was all about that.   It was Melinda's idea to use cognitive objectivity validation capabilities of COVEn to analyze all relevant previous research, as well as reactions to the research from government agencies, politicians, corporations, news media and the general public.

"Looking back, there is an enormous incongruity ... a huge disconnect ... between what we learned about early brain development and the focus and resources applied to helping kids who were neglected or abused in their infancy.   Melinda is acutely aware of that, and that's why she's pressing hard on the cognitive objectivity angle, to help us understand why the brain development issue had been largely ignored for so long.   She may do well to connect with some folks I met recently in Norway, just after I took on the role of Chief Science Officer at NIRC, the National Institute for Resolve and Confidence."

"Really! Are you leading any special projects in your CSO role?"

"Acataleptic conjunctures" Ansell said, matter-of-factly, as though it should be obvious to me what he meant. As Ansell glanced over at me, I made a welcoming gesture in an attempt to indicate he should continue. I recalled Mars mentioning acatalepsy.

"Let me explain," Ansell continued while walking over to a window and gesturing toward the trees outside. "You work for a firm whose business model is based on certainty. Do you think it is possible for anyone ... any person on this planet ... to be certain about anything? By the way, I assume you, as team leader for that certainty project at TFD, are the source of the hardcopy report left on my desk in my last days at the helm of TFD."

"Yes, I was the source," I admitted.

"You did good, and I thank you. So, you're still wrapped up in certainty, I suppose," said Ansell.

"Well, I used to work in the Early Human Intention group, and *that* I could get my head around and believe in, but since I switched over to Cognitive Certainty ... well, let's just say the focus on certainty has made me less certain about how close we can be to it, without ulterior motives getting in the way."

"Ulterior motives?"

"Yes. Like someone or some entity ... you know, a government agency or big corporation ... manipulating people in a sophisticated way, so that they would feel certain about something ... or at least accept that something was true and believe in it. And in doing so, they would somehow be helping the cause of the government or some profit-making engine in the private sector."

Ansell then nodded and refilled our glasses. "You know the story of the company name 'The Fifth Dentist', right?" Without waiting for an answer, Ansell went on. "When I was a young lad, my father used to joke with me about the 'four out of five' phenomenon. A bunch of companies were advertising their products, trying to convince people that there was some proven value to whatever it was. They were running ads on TV that included the phrase 'four out of five doctors' ... or scientists or auto-mechanics or diabetics or seniors or whatever ... the ads said that four out of five of them used the product or recommended it. My dad used to say 'it seems like you can get four out of five people to agree with anything! If only you could get that fifth person! I want to know what the *fifth* guy thinks!' There were a couple of toothpaste brands, I think, running ads saying four out of five dentists used or recommended their toothpaste. Dad said he always wondered what that fifth dentist used. So when I founded what is now TFD, I never used the acronym. I always said or wrote 'The Fifth Dentist', and it was kind of a tribute to my dad."

"And your early marketing connected to that, right?"

"We started out positioning on revealing the alternative ... four out of five customers bought Brand X, but what did the fifth consumer buy? *Why* did they buy it? That sort of thing. But it quickly evolved toward a point on confidence. All about 'getting the fifth dentist on board.' We would help our clients get to the point where all of their buyers or partners or citizens were in agreement on the issue. Of course, it's tough to make that happen in any scenario, but our credo was geared toward helping our clients feel more confident in their options and decisions."

"So, what you mentioned earlier," I said, "acatalepsy … acataleptic … the conjunctures … ?"

"Right. Acataleptic conjunctures. What that refers to is connections or linkages between things that our brains are not wired to make. Normally those connections are incomprehensible to us humans, but the hypothesis is that our brains may be capable of resisting thought control … *if* they are led to connections that we could not conceive of otherwise. To enable those connections, we conceived of a device. We call it the Acataleptic Conjuncture Enabler, or the ACE. It uses a type of electromagnetic pulse to enables brains to make those unusual or unlikely connections."

I then told Ansell about Waldon and the "obviating the need for trust" speech. I told him I'd met Mars, who suggested the ACE device as a potential protective shield against the implants designed to ensure acceptance of decisions and policies of world leaders … the enablers of life.

"Can you help us get hold of the ACE device?" I asked.

"You already have it," said Ansell, and he went on to explain. "There are teams in Norway and the US working on prototypes that will have the required signal range. They are collaborating but also taking some different approaches, different tactics on circumventing some apparent technology limitations. The US team now has a prototype that seems to be working as designed … or nearly so. I think it should be close enough to serve as a shield to the acceptance scheme."

"Where is it? Who has it?" I asked.

"It's right there in the TFD lab area at Gyre Ventures," said Ansell, "your contact person is Kenton Duckworth. Just before I retired, I authorized Kenton to spend up to half his time working on it. I told him it was top secret, so not surprising you didn't know that was happening. I'm sure Svarog doesn't know, or he would certainly have either stopped it or taken control of the project."

"And with your role in NIRC, could you help us to copy it and distribute it to wherever it's needed?" I asked.

"Yes, I think I can. You just need to get the device and enter it into NIRC's international competition in the next couple of days. I'll give Melinda the details."

"Thank you so much! Did I hear you say *international* competition? I thought NIRC was going to focus on national research efforts."

"They were, but I convinced them to shift somewhat into international cooperation, since there is so much interesting work going on outside the US at this point. We need to 'prime the pump', so to speak, in getting some new efforts off the ground here," Ansell explained.

"Sorry, but are we looking to hand ACE over to foreign agents?" I grappled with what I felt was a treasonous tone to the plan.

Ansell replied, "We have to consider the world in its entirety … without political boundaries. Besides, Norway is very close to getting it working in their own labs."

"Okay, I'll have to deal with that. One more thing, when you said ACE could enable 'unlikely connections', would that include metaphorical things?" I asked, having spent most of the day pondering metaphors for my writing assignment. I was still confused at that point, not comfortable that I had a real understanding of the work he was doing at NIRC, nor what Kenton had been working on secretly.

"Could be. I mean, there's a reason why metaphor can inspire people or help them process emotions," he said, "but let me give you an example from my own life. I moved here just after my wife's death. Some of our old neighbors were asking why I killed her ... as if I could ever have killed Barbara. That was hard to take, so I needed to get away from them."

"I understand. Well, actually, I'm not sure I do." Since Melinda had been somewhat vague regarding her mother's death, Ansell's statement raised some anxiety for me.

"Some neighbors kept asking why I killed her," he said flatly.

I prompted for more, "But why would they ... I mean ... you didn't actually ... ?"

"Kill her? No!" Ansell interrupted, but after a pause, he added, "Well, I'm not sure, really. Maybe I did." Then he began to wander around the room as he told me the story of her death.

"I left for work early one morning. Had an 8AM class to do and wanted to get there early to draw some diagrams on the board before it started. Barbara didn't need to be at Cornell until 11, so she told me she'd enjoy a couple extra hours of sleep and drive herself separately later. We each had our own car, obviously, and we parked them side by side in our two-car garage. After my first class, I began to have an uneasy feeling that I left the stove on ... a tea kettle on one of the burners. I tried connecting to Barbara to ask her to check it, since she likely hadn't left yet, but got no response. Not unusual. She sometimes turned off her phone. Drove me crazy sometimes doing that."

Ansell topped off each of our glasses as he continued.

"Melinda was off doing a shift of volunteer work at a nearby hospice center. I decided not to bother her. I drove home and dashed into the kitchen to check. All was well. The stove was off and the kettle was on a metal rack by the sink. I called for Barbara but got no response, so I assumed she was already on her way to Cornell. I left then to drive back there myself, but when I was in the driveway about to get into my car, I felt compelled to look in our garage. I pushed the remote switch on my visor and walked to the door as it opened. Barbara's car was in there idling, and I got hit with an intense, choking cloud of exhaust fumes.

"I covered my nose and mouth with my hand and ran squinting through the fumes. All the car windows were open. At the driver's door I found Barbara, leaning back into the seat, her head turned toward the open driver door window." Ansell looked incredulous for a moment, as though reliving the shock, then he continued.

"Sometimes when I remember all that, I say to myself, 'That was on *you*, Ansell. You left the tea kettle unattended and didn't hear the whistle.'"

◊   ◊   ◊

When Melinda arrived, she and I quickly loaded our suitcases and thanked her dad for hosting us for the weekend and treating us to dinner the night before.

"Well, now we've got to go save the world," Melinda said, nonchalantly.

"'Be wary, then; best safety lies in fear.' Shakespeare." Those were her dad's parting words.

We set out for New York City, stopping at a fast food place

near Binghamton for a quick dinner.

While driving, Melinda talked about her afternoon at Cornell, which she had enjoyed. Later she asked if I'd gotten any good information from her dad.

"Yes, I did, and he's agreed to help through NIRC if we need to get something to one of the research teams in Norway," I said and shared the details from my conversation with her dad.

Then I told her about the conversation I had with Mars, wherein he talked about his choosing to sabotage a study at TFF in Norway. I also told her about Detective Burke saying Mars was under investigation and might be indicted for "grievous bodily harm on a massive scale."

Melinda drove silently for a while, then asked, "Did you write your story, Walter?"

"Yes I did, although I think it still needs some editing and revision."

"And did you enjoy writing, my dear?" she asked.

"It was very satisfying," I said, "and I'll even let you read it, if you agree to be interviewed on the news about the Gravity Train."

Melinda agreed.

CHAPTER 25

Melinda's Interview

I set my day-start to 10:00 AM for the morning after we returned from Ithaca, which was prudent, since I don't think I fell asleep until past 3:00 AM. Before leaving for Gyre Ventures, I sent Melinda a digital image of Liz Fedorova's business card, convinced she would do a better job than me relating our progress on the Gravity Train. While at Gyre, I got a message around noon from Melinda that she would be doing an interview with Liz in a few minutes, so I monitored Don Dander's channel on my smarts while doing other work.

A news update started at 12:30 PM, and I transferred it to a flat-screen on my desk just as Brendan poked his head into the doorway. Melinda had messaged him too, and I waved him in to watch it in my office. Don Dander was the news update host, and he began by showing a brief video clip of a spokesperson for the

U.S. Department of Transportation, who announced that "excellent progress" had been made on the Gravity Train project. Afterward, Don announced they were going "live to Liz in mid-town, outside the Gyre Ventures tower." The screen view then switched to a view of Liz Fedorova standing next to Melinda with the Gyre entrance in the background.

"Hello Don," Liz began, "I'm here with Principal Scientist, Melinda Beckmann, who is part of a special team at TFD, working high up in the Gyre Ventures tower behind us to arrive at some conclusion about the feasibility and safety of the proposed Gravity Train. Can you give us an update, Ms. Beckmann?"

Liz then held the microphone near Melinda's chin.

"Hi Liz. Thanks for having me on," said Melinda. "First of all, we're reviewing our analysis with our CEO, Robert Svarog, tomorrow. So, we're nearly done. Making a few last minute adjustments today. You know, crossing eyes and dotting cheese."

"'Dotting cheese?' Has she gone daft?" Brendan complained.

Liz appeared more confused than amused as she asked, "But what can you tell us about progress in terms of major concerns? Dangers? Risks?"

"Sorry. We do have some concerns about the durability and resilience of construction materials, as well as the overall cost estimates. We'll review all of that tomorrow with the TFD executive team and, within a few weeks, with government agencies here and in France"

"So tell me, you mentioned durability and resilience concerns. What kind of dangers are lurking around those issues?" Liz asked.

Melinda did not respond. Instead she turned back toward the Gyre building.

"Any examples you can share?" Liz prompted.

"Maybe you should've done this one," Brendan said to me.

"No, she'll be okay," I assured him, wondering if she would be okay.

Melinda turned back to face the camera.

"Maybe just one?" Liz prompted again.

"Well," Melinda began, pausing for several seconds before continuing, "the extreme heat down ... down at the depths we're targeting. That's the main issue behind resilience and safety concerns. That and shifting continental plates at the depth ... if ... if we go too deep."

"The depth and heat concerns have come up before in public discussions," Liz pointed out, "but is there anything new? Anything you have uncovered that hasn't already surfaced?"

Melinda looked as though she were struggling to remember something. Brendan complained to the flat-screen, suggesting Melinda bring up drill articulation.

"Here's one," Melinda responded after taking a big breath, "we, the public, are being manipulated into thinking that this Gravity Train crap is actually some kind of beneficial endeavor coming from compassionate, benevolent international cooperation. Think about it. If there were no dangers, no chance of human lives being lost, no ecological damage ... even if it were a completely and obviously safe project, why the hell would anyone want to do it? Beyond novelty, there's nothing there! No benefits! No human needs are being addressed for the population of the world. It's just a carefully orchestrated distraction. I mean, it's ... it's ... *disgraceful*! Think about all the things we *should* be putting all that money and human resource into!"

Liz interrupted, "it's a distraction, you say. So why are we doing it?"

Melinda shouted into the microphone. "To get everybody focused on the wrong thing! To get everybody to look down when there's something happening above their heads! Something that they ought to know about!"

"What's happening, Ms. Beckmann? What's happening above our heads?" Liz asked.

"We're about to become flesh robots! Flesh avatars! A few heartless, unfeeling villains who think the world owes them something will play games with the rest of us. It will be a new kind of augmented reality. A virtual reality made of all the real things in the world. All the real people who aren't working the controls. We'll just do and say and think whatever the fuck they want us to! And we'll be made to feel like it all makes sense! I'm talking about *mind* control of *millions*! *Billions* of people!"

With that, Melinda abruptly turned away and walked toward the Gyre entrance as Liz called after her a few times in vain.

Brendan and I continued to watch as Liz turned back toward the camera, saying "I think that's it for now. Back to you, Don."

"Christ, *that* went well. Pure class," said Brendan.

CHAPTER 26

"Entanglement"

by Walter Winterwonderland

A seasonal phenomenon, our meetings persist ... not with politely persistent, short-term-recallable, tip-of-the-tongue amicability, nor rosy flirtation. They are more like desperate migratory appointments of fish or fowl, more like debauchery of winter rains, sweeping bastions, seeping through hard-packed puddle walls surrounding each of our dry years and, too, like sledge-hammer blows to a spike, deliberate and focused, driving further toward the mantle, toward the core.

Our meetings are cyclic and, though it is only Taylor and me, large, scaled to the earth's orbit, held in equinoxic lock-step within an illusory celestial order of a trillion spheres teased by a rationalized Ptolemaic extravagance of circles, centered upon the edges of other circles, which navigate the edges of yet other circles, distancing us from those on solid ground, from the builders of belfries and sluices, who shift their bodies about in the accepted sun-centric scheme, shaping clay.

We sit, this night in February, at a table for two in Café Dégagé, *by a rain-wrinkled window. Rays of light from accent spotlights just outside ... electromagnetic waves ... impart an unlikely patina of golden aridity to nearby arboreal vibrancy, while refracting passively through droplets and rivulets on the pane, entering* Dégagé *to apply phantom cat-whiskers to Taylor's face, alternately sparkling and spookily shadowing her deep blue eyes, refusing to illuminate her with even a modicum of decorum.*

It is here that I first met Taylor, several years ago. I recall entering the cafe for the first time that evening, feeling hesitant, tentative and awkward. A young woman sat alone by a window, reading a book. Her vibrant floral print dress seized my attention with its fertile, regenerative, botanical exuberance. She seemed too elegant for the setting, wearing old-fashioned jeweled bracelets and a necklace, with sparkling flat skimmers on her feet. Fairy-like, I thought, magical. I paused on my way to the counter, staring at her. After a moment she sensed my presence and looked up at me. Before I could turn and walk away ... hesitantly, tentatively, awkwardly ... she smiled and told me, "The chai is delightful! You should try it!" I thanked her and inevitably ordered chai at the counter.

While waiting to be served, turning around to see that woman, Taylor, sitting with perfect posture, her back toward me, I wondered if I could muster the courage to casually walk by her table with my drink as I looked for a place to sit, making eye-

contact and, depending on how confident I felt in that moment, possibly asking if I might join her. I had spent the day in business meetings assessing strategic investment alternatives, connecting with new ecosystem partners and finalizing my own project commitments for the next few months. I had come to Café Dégagé *alone in order to relax and clear my head, but the complication of potential interaction with the woman in the flowery dress by the window was, by far, the most challenging and anxiety-inducing hurdle I had faced all day.*

Carefully conveying my mug of chai, I navigated around other tables and chairs to move into her vicinity. While speech was beyond my capabilities at that moment, I did manage to make eye contact and gesture inquisitively toward the other chair at her table. "Oh! Of course! Please join me!" she said sweetly with an effervescent quality. I sat down, and at first we merely smiled at each other, Taylor giggling a bit now and then. I didn't know what made her giggle, nor did I ever quite understand why simply smiling felt so correct and appropriate at the time. She looked at me, leaning forward on her elbows, hands crossed over her book holding it flat on the table.

"Oh, you can keep reading if you like," I said.

"Don't be silly! Let's talk," she said as she closed her book and moved it to the window sill.

It was as if it had been pre-ordained that we would be drawn together, that we would sit together, that our life paths were already entangled somehow, that we had been given the opportunity ... or perhaps the responsibility ... to explore and understand why it was so. We began to exchange some basic information: our names, birthplaces, fields of study and avocational interests. We then moved into the realms of our careers, favorite books, beaches and hiking trails. During all that, we began the odd behavior of rhyming the ends of each other's sentences occasionally as we talked.

After an hour or so, she began to sway in her seat in time to the background sitar music, and then she stood, taking my hand, leading me a few steps away from our table. She led me through dance steps I could never reproduce on my own, adding little ballet-like flourishes for herself which she somehow managed to execute without bumping furniture or other patrons. Then she took hold of my hands and placed them on her hips, enabling her to begin graceful, evocative movement of her arms as we navigated the labyrinthine space. There were a few other patrons scattered about in the cafe, but I don't know if any of them watched us dance. My attention was focused solely on Taylor.

We danced to the counter, ordered more chai and returned to our table. At Taylor's prompting, we began trading stories of odd things we recalled from our childhoods. We didn't notice the time passing and were a bit surprised when one of the staff approached and apologetically informed us the cafe was closing, as it was nearly 1:00 AM, and he had to lock up in five minutes.

I offered to walk her home. She appeared to decline at first, saying it was only a few blocks and was perfectly safe, but after a moment she added that she would love the company. As we turned the corner around Café Dégagé, we were both startled by the night sky: a crescent moon directly in front of us and about half-way up toward the top of the sparkling bowl of the heavens, with two bright, non-twinkling, star-like points, planets other than our own but within our solar system, aligned perfectly with the moon. "It *must be a time of alignment," I said. "Or maybe entanglement," she countered.*

On parting later that night, we held hands outside her small, charming house for a moment. We kissed, and she asked me to let her know whenever I was back in the area so we could meet "for chai or whatever."

For a dozen seasons we've met here, coinciding with industry conferences and quarterly meetings I attend in San Jose and Cupertino, me traveling from New York, she walking from her house near the beach here in Santa Cruz, the cafe maintaining charm and gaining clutter. Growing clientele led to more tables, less space, louder background music. Table density now precludes all dancing save side-gliding moonwalk steps required for mere circulation.

"You need that or narrow hips."

"Whispers work if you read lips."

Now as we sit, this night in February, at a table for two in Café Dégagé, *piped-in music begins to assert itself ... African, maybe Kenyan ... a sound requiring wire strings of a pre-historic and accidental metallurgy, stretched across bamboo, a sound suggesting not a hunt along the Zambezi but an ox-drawn cart in Bohemia, a sound containing convocations of barefoot peasant women dancing with movements evocative of planting, harvest and copulation, their hands lifting their breasts, now their hands in the air, now lifting their long skirts, now throwing themselves upon the ground, those dancing women, rolling and rising again.*

Taylor pushes toward me the glass of wine we are sharing, with a twitch of her body, as if reacting to the unexpected ring of an old telephone in a quiet room. The glass contains a paraboloid section of wine, two inches along its principal axis, held within and mimicking the shape of the glass due to the electrical forces around the involved molecules and gravity, both of which can be relied upon nearly always, I muse. Suddenly, the music's tempo quickens: wire strings now playfully plucked with carved goat femurs, new sounds emerging like sleigh-bells sewn on leather strips rhythmically bludgeoned and trampled. We find it impossible to resist. We begin to sway in time, Taylor rocking her hips in her seat, but there is no room to dance here, here in winter, here in Santa Cruz, at 9:00 PM.

In my mind I see the women again, throwing themselves upon the ground, upon the music, the rhythm, an earthly dance between them and their own withering shadows, throwing themselves upon their own memories, their deeds, their doubts, their desires. The music begins to soften and soothe, and those women in my head now fall upon beds of straw, wearing only beads, baubles and cinnibarbarous body-paint, rolling and rising again, in the protocol of rain.

I close my eyes now and envision Taylor dancing in an open field of poppies. In that splendid place, she dances as though the world had been peeled of concealments, revealed in poetry and dreamed away, leaving no substance to enlist resistance, as though gravity pulls neither upon her limbs nor her soul. I open my eyes and look into hers. I feel she has only just arrived at the table from somewhere millions of light-years away, as she has done again and again, in lock-step with each earthly season, deliberate and focused, to share herself with me for a little while.

Several times we have passed the glass, and now, encouraged by a slight nod from Taylor, I consume the last of its contents and then slide its base on the table, slowly tracing curlicues on the flecked surface. The lens-like base of the glass magnifies the particulate features beneath, lending the table an appearance of having a watery constitution as the glass moves, sparkling flecks returning to their previous appointments in space and time.

"In solid mass."

"In the wake of the glass."

I look at Taylor and I say, "I see people dancing. What do you see?" She does not speak but places her hand on mine, so that we now both hold the glass with our layered flesh. Under her relaxed and confident direction, Taylor's impossibly delicate fingers lead me in moving the glass along the semi-smooth surface of synthetic stone, infused with fish-scale flecks, making a noise like a small bell, five yards away, brushed, quivering, against stucco. Together we experience the optical and auditory illusions, together manipulating marble, defying laws of physics, finding secret passage through walls of cold, solid stone.

CHAPTER 27

Svarog

"Sorry, but this whole thing is so disturbing to me. I feel like I spend all my time on it ... that I have to. I have no other choice. But I so desperately want to be done with it so I can think of ... I don't know. Something else! Anything else!" Melinda appeared distraught as she stood by the window in her office at Gyre, her clenched fists convulsing in front of her as though pounding on a locked door.

Brendan and I sat in guest chairs in the office. We had just listened to Melinda reliving her interview with Liz. I felt that I needed to respond to her, but I wasn't sure what to say. I felt responsible in encouraging her to stay with TFD. Brendan beat me to it. He slapped his knee and rose from his chair before speaking.

"Ah, listen," he began, "none of us here ... no one wants to be in this position. Right? But hey, if we walk away, what then?

You'd regret it. We'd all regret it, don't you see?"

"I already regret everything," Melinda said, "I regret looking into this in the first place. I regret staying here after they assigned me to the fucking tunnel." Then she began to gather up her work portfolio and coffee, clearly signalling she was about to leave our little meeting.

Just then came a knock, immediately followed by Waldon Perry opening the door and peering inside. "There you are! I was looking for you folks. Thought I'd walk you over to Robert's conference room upstairs for the staff meeting. You can tell him all the good news we have!" Waldon spoke with an odd tone that lacked the appropriate level of irony. Melinda had frozen in an awkward position, looking as though she were about to demonstrate the proper way to pour coffee over a leather portfolio. Brendan turned to look me in the eye, wearing an expression of mild disbelief. I decided to ignore Waldon's "good news" comment.

"Thank you. I think we're ready," I said, and I gave Melinda a pleading look to encourage her to come to the Svarog review as planned. It seemed to me that she was not just preparing to leave her office but preparing to leave TFD permanently.

"Just follow me!" Waldon smiled and gestured out into the hallway. Melinda joined. As we walked along, Brendan asked what we should expect, but Waldon ignored the question, instead asking Melinda if she had seen her father recently. Melinda only shook her head to indicate a negative response. Waldon then said to Melinda, "Oh, by the way, several of us on the exec team talked Robert out of firing you for the public interview you gave yesterday. He was pretty upset. I'll handle future public statements and interviews for TFD on the Gravity Train and ADADA until further notice."

◊   ◊   ◊

Svarog was pacing back and forth at the far end of the conference room as we entered. "Waldon! Finally! Now we can get started," he bellowed in our direction. Svarog then stared at me with a look of puzzlement. "So, you're *not* at the dentist this morning?" he asked me, "I thought you weren't coming in till noon."

"Robert, this is Connor Farrell, our Gravity Train team lead," Waldon announced, placing his hand on my shoulder, "and also from the GT team, we have Brendan McCarron, and I think you've met Melinda."

Svarog apparently thought I was his assistant, Harper. Amazing that even Svarog would confuse us, since he spent a lot of time in close proximity with his assistant on work days, even being accompanied by Harper on most business trips. After introducing us, Waldon took his seat. Svarog stared at me for a few more seconds, then nodded and began to go through the meeting agenda with the group.

"Okay, so we're all here. I'm short on time, so we'll skip Gravity Train stuff this morning and reschedule it. I want to talk about ADADA phase 2 today, and we have issues with cash flow and research spending that we'll get to. ADADA first, and then we can excuse the team standing in the back. Okay?" Svarog then sat down near the far end of the conference table. Melinda, Brendan and I were the "team standing in the back", since there were no other available seats. One man in the back corner politely offered his seat to Melinda, who politely declined.

"So, Julian, what was your concern?" Svarog asked while looking down at his own hands which were pressing, palms-down, against the dark wooden table surface. Then he added, "You started to say something before Waldon came back."

A man sitting across the table began speaking, whom I recognized as Julian Valdivieso, TFD's VP of Inbound Marketing. Julian talked for a while, carefully posturing around concerns he had that TFD was straying into what he called a "disputable area", finally summarizing his position more adamantly by saying, insofar as ADADA phase 2 was concerned, that "our intent may be misunderstood, so that we will be seen as potentially hurting … manipulating … deceiving … nearly all of humanity itself."

"Well, I certainly hope you can handle your responsibilities in ensuring that doesn't happen," Svarog responded, sounding somewhat annoyed.

"It's not just a matter of spin, Robert," Julian protested.

Svarog raised his hands in a gesture of surrender. "Then we need a new marketing strategy," he announced dismissively, then redirected his remarks to those of us standing. "Let's move on. ADADA phase 2 needs some validation of its operational security and integrity. Melinda … you guys in the back … how fast can we ensure phase 2 can be secure against sabotage? I really need something by mid-March. Some government guys are whining about how somebody might fuck with phase 2. Alter the intent. You know what I mean."

"Could the cyber-security team address that?" Melinda asked. It seemed a reasonable question, given that none of us standing in the back had much experience with security of systems.

Svarog did not answer Melinda. Instead he turned to Waldon and snapped, "I thought you briefed those guys!"

"Only on validating the feasibility of the concept. We didn't get into security." Waldon explained.

"Well, it isn't feasible if it can't be secured!" Svarog bellowed back at Waldon, then he continued, looking back and forth between Melinda and me. "Cyber-security is in its little box, and they are also looking into this. I want you guys to look into it as a part of your validation research. Right? I want the security question looked at outside the traditional parameters, since this project is far from traditional. Okay? You guys have reputations of being able to handle new stuff. Tricky stuff. I need this as fast as you can do it. Any questions? If not, you are excused."

Melinda and Brendan deferred to me. "One question, Robert," I began, "looping back to Julian's point ..."

"No thank you! We've covered it," Svarog interrupted.

"Please, Robert, there is another related concern," I said and paused for some indication that I might be allowed to continue.

"Robert, let's hear the question, for goodness sake," said Astrid.

"Alright. So?" Svarog looked at me and shrugged.

"Besides the security issue and the misunderstanding of our intent," I began, "there is also the issue around the planned ADADA phase two work and the actual intent behind it. It's pretty straightforward, and for those who understand it ... which would be a large portion of the world's population ... no amount of marketing spin is going to reduce their objections to it. No amount of distraction will be enough to keep them from knowing what ADADA phase two is or reducing the potential for global scale protest and activism."

"Okay. You done? Don't think I heard a question," Svarog glanced over at Waldon.

"The question is whether we should consider a scenario where the ADADA phase two implants are *elective* ... a choice to be made by each person in participating countries," I explained.

"Interesting," said Svarog, "see if you can get an accurate sizing of that portion of the world's population that would be objecting or protesting or whatever. Then find what type of content or messaging would encourage them to *elect* to have the phase two implant. If you can, then we'll talk. For now, I think we need to move onto other topics on our agenda. Waldon ...?"

"Yes. Thank you Connor, Melinda, Brendan. We'll circle back later," said Waldon.

"Thank you," I said as the three of us made our exit.

CHAPTER 28

Intervention

After the meeting with Svarog and the TFD executive team, Brendan and I accompanied Melinda back to her office. None of us spoke until we were inside with the door closed. After we took turns venting our frustration over the GT review being unexpectedly postponed, we lamented that TFD was being run by a CEO with such vile, contentious, arrogant behavior. It was then that I realized why Melinda spoke so passively to her dad about Svarog as CEO. If Ansell knew what it was really like here at TFD now, I thought, he would agonize over it being all his fault ... that he left the tea kettle unattended again and didn't hear the whistle. Eventually, we began to talk about Svarog's request regarding the possibility of elective implants for ADADA phase two.

We agreed there were three main follow-up activities, and that we would each take the lead on one. Melinda would talk with ADADA phase two developers and force the issue of the lack of a security component. Brendan would loop back to Availa and do whatever he could to help get either Adora or some other expert to help with brain identity scanning or an equivalent implant usage authorization technology. I agreed to take the lead on the elective implant topic.

◊   ◊   ◊

Back in my office, I was having some trouble focusing. The previous evening I had sent Melinda the short story I wrote at her father's house, as an attachment to an email. In the email, I mentioned how her suggestion of writing as Walter Winterwonderland helped me unlock new ways to express my thoughts. I did not mention her interview with Liz.

I had a dream that night, similar to my childhood nightmares about being swept out a window as my house filled with water from firefighter's hoses. I hadn't had a dream like that since I was a teenager. The key difference in the new version was that the setting shifted from my childhood home to the TFD offices at Gyre Ventures. I was swept out of the window in room B-30 on the 35th floor, where we had our "New Ideas exercise" session.

The water came from sprinklers in the ceiling at first, but then the pipes in the ceiling burst and ridiculous amounts of water came pouring into the room. I was panicking. Over the public address system, a voice resembling our team facilitator Trevor's kept telling us to remain calm and that the door to the room had been "sealed for our safety."

A young woman slightly resembling Golden North grabbed my arm as I lost my grip on the window sill, but she was unable to hold me. I had awakened at that point, just as Randall Hewitt's voice came from further back in the room shouting, "Damn it, Connor! Grow the faith!"

Yes, I was having trouble focusing, flipping back and forth between wondering what Melinda would think of my story and wondering if I would be forever haunted by the Font-ish nightmare.

◊   ◊   ◊

I decided to try to clear my head by going for a walk around mid-town, maybe heading up to Central Park. I left the Gyre tower around noon. The level of protesting outside Gyre had not decreased much since the day of the New Q, when I was accosted outside the building by Jake and others. Typically, the number of protesters peaked around lunchtime. The day of the Svarog meeting was no different, and I noticed at least thirty people with signs standing around outside as I exited Gyre.

I'd walked about half the thirty feet or so to the corner when I thought I heard someone behind me call my name. I turned around but didn't recognize anyone in the immediate vicinity, so I started back toward the building in case someone I knew was there but obscured by the crowd. Suddenly, two men with signs blocked my path.

First, they dropped their signs on the pavement. Then they grabbed my arms near the shoulders and began half-lifting, half-pushing me toward a corner of the building. As they moved me along, one shouted, "No tunnel! No tunnel!"

"Connor!" I heard my name called again. The voice sounded closer. The men shoved me hard against the concrete wall of the Gyre tower, and one of them quickly pulled out of his coat what looked like a curved saw blade. Panicking, I lurched and twisted to try to get away, but then I felt something metallic pressing on my neck, followed by an electric shock that caused me to stiffen like a mannequin. The man holding the blade looked me in the eye and smiled for a second, just before he lifted the blade ... clearly about to plunge it into my neck or chest.

Just then, someone grabbed both of the protesters by their collars, yanking them backwards. I saw that it was Wally, the building maintenance man I had met in the elevator. One of the men let go of me and took a swing at Wally, hitting him in the face. Wally took the blow and returned the punch to the side of the attacker's jaw, knocking him to the ground. Then the other attacker who was holding the blade let go of me and quickly leaned into Wally, who screamed in pain, backing up several steps before falling to the ground.

"Hold it! Police! Put your hands in the air!" An officer shouted from the curb.

Both attackers then ran, shoving others out of the way as they went, knocking several people to the ground.

"Hold it right there! Police!" an officer shouted in the direction the attackers fled. The police may have followed them, but I'm not sure. My view of the surroundings had become an oozing blur that flickered with the rhythm of my heart, which was pounding faster than I thought possible. I was unable to move or speak. A ringing sound filled my head.

The next thing I recall was lying on the pavement with a stinging sensation in my nose. An EMT who was bending over me, asked me if I could hear him and whether I was in any pain. He then explained that I had fainted and asked if I was prone to fainting. I told him I was fine, and he helped me to my feet.

I could see Wally on the ground just ahead of me. There was quite a lot of blood on his chest and hands, as well as on the pavement. He had been stabbed through or very near his heart. A gurney had been placed next to him. One of the EMTs wore a uniform that looked more like a police officer's, and I assumed he was a paramedic. The paramedic examined Wally's head and chest, moving rapidly, grabbing things out of a pouch he had brought. From my viewpoint, I couldn't tell exactly what was happening to Wally.

"Do you know that man?" an officer asked me.

"Yes. Yes, I do. He's the maintenance guy for the tower. Gyre Ventures," I said.

I took a few steps toward Wally, and he appeared to be breathing. "You'll be okay. You'll get help. Everything's gonna be okay," I told him.

"I did somethin' good, didn't I?" Wally asked in a whisper.

"You saved my life! You saved my life, Wally."

Just then, an officer standing behind me shouted, "Stay back, miss!"

"No! No! No!" I heard a woman shrieking.

"Please, miss!" said the officer, but she managed to get by him and dropped down on her knees at Wally's side.

"Wally! What happened? Oh my God!" she threw herself on top of him, kissing his face over and over. Wally did not respond.

The woman appeared to be about Wally's age, with short, dark curly hair, and I assumed she was Rita, whom he had told me about in the elevator.

"This your husband, Miss?" the paramedic asked.

"He's my fiancé. Please help him," she managed to say, and she moved off of Wally.

"These guys know what they're doing. He'll be okay," I called out, intending to reassure her.

The woman turned toward me with a look on her face that seemed a blend of exasperation, incredulity and shock, covering her ears with her hands. I read it as a sign that I should shut up.

"We're good to go," the paramedic said. Then he and the EMTs moved Wally onto the gurney.

They lifted the gurney and extended the set of wheels underneath.

"Miss, we're ready to transport your fiancé. Would you like to come along in the ambulance?" asked one of the EMTs. The woman nodded in response and began to walk alongside the gurney.

As they moved toward the ambulance, Wally managed to slowly raise his arm enough to touch her cheek. The moment he did, she took his hand in both of hers and kissed it.

The paramedic stood by his car with lights still flashing, speaking loudly and clearly into a hand-held device. I recorded what he said on my smarts:

Paramedic Laraway. At scene. 52nd and 3rd Avenue. Northeast corner. Victim a Caucasian male, early thirties. Penetration wound passing near heart. Apparent cardiac tamponade due to possible laceration of right ventricle. Exit wound not determined.

Severe trauma. Performed emergency pericardiocentesis. Patient in gurney. Pericardial catheter in place. Apparent facial contusion, some blood in mouth, laceration of tongue. Transporting to Presby. Upper East. Accompanied by fiancée. Readiness for arrival confirmed.

CHAPTER 29

Fear of Influence

I went back into the TFD offices and told Melinda what happened outside in front of Gyre Ventures.

"Connor, I'm so glad you're still here! Still alive!" she said.

"And Wally seemed okay when they loaded him into the ambulance," I said, "and I really hope for the best for him. He's a real hero."

"I just can't believe someone was trying to kill you," Melinda said, "that they singled you out. You specifically."

"They were shouting 'No tunnel!' I assume they were protesters who saw me in that interview the other day," I said.

"But there's been no violence from the protesters before now."

"Well, I guess that can happen as these things drag on," I said.

"Oh God!" Melinda said suddenly, "I hope it wasn't because of what I said yesterday! My stupid interview!"

"No! Don't blame yourself. You said what needed to be said," I tried to reassure her.

"Why are we in the middle of this? I don't want to be!" Melinda complained while pacing.

"I hear you, Melinda. But you know what? Let's look at it as calmly and rationally as we can," I said. For some reason, I was playing the thirty-something, well-meaning, pedantic consultant again. As I performed my next line, which began, "If we see potential danger in applying technology to control people that way, then ...," Melinda interrupted.

"Stop acting like you can stay dispassionate in the middle of this. Some guy just got stabbed in front of the building! To protect *you*, for God's sake!"

"But we can best make the case against it by approaching it with objective, rational analysis," I responded. Thinking back to it, I may have been trying to avoid thinking about the violence outside the building and Wally's injury.

"And what the hell do you plan to do with that analysis?" Melinda asked with her arms folded.

I began to feel that I might not be able to stay in character.

"Well, look, uh ... finding evidence of potential for, uh ... malfeasance, we could include something in validation work designed to bring that out. Right? I mean, a responding variable that would ... uh ..., " I managed to say before Melinda mercifully interrupted again.

"They don't care about 'responding variables' or objectivity. They're planning to take over the world! Control humanity!"

"I just can't help but think we have to present a compelling logical argument."

"Connor, from the perspective of those bastards, logic is a plague. Seriously, are you about to suggest something about taking their perspective?" Melinda asked, then, looking absurdly bright-eyed and joyful, she added, "Hey Melinda, let's just take the perspective of a bunch of deranged demigods."

Something shifted for me at that point, I think, because the incident outside at noon began to replay itself in my head.

"Alright then. What should we do?" I asked, feeling like I could accept reality again.

"Connor, what's happening here is outside the realm of reason. We need to step outside that realm ourselves to stop it."

"If you mean using that ACE device for sabotage, count me out," I said. My brain filled with flashbacks of my conversation with Mars the morning of New Q. I was not comfortable with the idea of tampering with people's brains or thoughts in order to prevent someone else from attempting to tamper with people's brains or thoughts. "What if we wound up doing more harm than good?" I asked.

Melinda sat up on a low file cabinet in front of the window and turned her head to look outside. As I watched her, I thought about our relaxed and cheerful connections at the coffee house, having tea in her apartment, looking out over the pond at her father's house, and I couldn't help but wonder when ... or if ... we would laugh together again, hold each other again. Melinda turned back toward me.

"I know you have courage and compassion. Where are you hiding it all?" she asked.

"We'd be destroying potential to heal widespread anxiety disorders, probably including post-traumatic stress and OCD. Can we live with that? How do we feel good about it?"

"Your pal Mars can tell you how to do it, I'm sure," she snapped.

"He isn't my 'pal'," I objected.

"Right. Sorry. He's your BFF. Your bestie. Your mentor. Your guru," Melinda said while moving her arms and hands as though catching those verbal labels out of the sky.

"I'm only using him to learn what's behind the tunnel … and the ADADA work," I said.

"Which is exactly what he wants you to do," Melinda said, with decisive tone. I took a moment to process that. Before I could respond, Melinda added, "Mars is a villain. Mars is the villain behind the brain implant hacking. Behavioral anomalies. Thought control. My own false memories of Jason, for God's sake."

"He's a villain because he sabotaged the implant experiment," I said.

"Thank you for acknowledging that!" Melinda said, looking up at the ceiling.

"But you're asking me to do the same thing here. Aren't you? Sabotage?" I was distraught. I couldn't help but think that using the ACE to subvert new brain growth technology was going to do a lot of harm. It would stymie efforts to address a broader spectrum of mental and psychological ailments through implants and neuronal migration adjustments. Dr. Reddy's comment from the vortex meeting popped into my head, and I felt I had to say it.

"Everything that exists can be misused, and what are we supposed to do about that?" I asked.

"Okay, Connor. I talked with people at Trondheim who worked with Mars on the implant project. That's where I was on my little secret trip after New Q. They know exactly what went wrong and why. I like them. I've decided to leave TFD to work with them at their lab."

"Wait. You were in Norway? You're going *back* to Norway? To the Trondheim team?" I was not ready for that. It felt wrong somehow for Melinda to leave at this point in the GT project or in our personal relationship.

"Right, and like my dad told you, if you can get the ACE device to NIRC today ... to the fucking National Institute for Resolve and Confidence ... they'll help to derail everything Waldon and Svarog are trying to facilitate," she said.

"Listen, Melinda. I'm thinking Trondheim may also be able to erase your false memories. It's worth exploring while you're over there. Don't you think?"

"No. I want to keep it all," Melinda spoke without hesitation.

"Why? Christ, Melinda. Someone tampered with your brain, your memories, your thoughts. You *know* that now. Why not fix it?"

"I can't. I want Jason. The memories," she said, looking down at the floor.

I put my arms around her. "I think I understand. He's real to you. He's your son."

"I love him," she said, "and I'm not going to let him die twice."

"What would you say to Jason if he were somehow able to come back and ask what life would have been like growing up with you?" I asked.

"I don't know," Melinda said, "but that's a fair question. I want to think about it. Meanwhile, Connor, please take this." She put a small, folded piece of paper in my hand. I unfolded it and read it aloud, "'We will attend the partitions between our lives, awaiting notes resigned to harmony.'"

"Sound familiar?" she asked.

"Yes. It's from a poem that night in Brooklyn. At Clementina's."

"I am so glad you remember where you heard it. That means a lot to me," said Melinda, smiling. "It just seemed like such a good parting message. I'm hoping we'll be together again. I think we have good potential, my dear," she said while pulling a few items from her desk drawers and placing them in a canvas bag.

"I'm not sure what to do next," I admitted.

"My dad arranged for someone to fly you to NIRC from the heliport on the roof of this building," said Melinda, adding, "and you leave in half an hour. If you decide to go, that is."

"What's the rush?" I asked, hoping to have more time to decide.

"NIRC entries have to be there by 5PM sharp today. To qualify for entry in their Innovation Challenge competition. It has to be officially entered so the international judging team can have access to it."

"Can't we just use an autonomous droner?" My only other experience in a helicopter was riding along with Cadence the day she died.

"Droners are a bad idea right now," she explained, "because they can be hacked. You need a human pilot. Kenton has the ACE prototype ready. Go get it from him quickly, and get up to the roof."

"Wait. Why can't someone else take it? How about Brendan or …."

"I already checked around," she interrupted, "Brendan said he's too old for this crap. Kenton was horrified at the thought of being physically transported through the atmosphere. Omari just laughed and said 'no way'. And please forgive me but, as I said, I need to be done with this. I'm leaving."

"We should do it only if there's no other way. As a last resort," I said, imploringly.

"Choose your poison. I have to go. This is *my* last resort."

"But Melinda, there must be another way. Let's talk. Let's …."

"Good-bye, Connor," she said and briefly embraced me before exiting her office.

I stood there alone, still not sure what I would do next. After a minute I noticed I was still holding that paper with her parting message. I read the line again a few times to myself. Then I read the last part aloud, although there was no one else to hear it.

"Awaiting notes resigned to harmony."

I was curious about the poet's choice of the word "resigned" and repeated that word aloud.

CHAPTER 30

Sphere of Flying

Brendan, Omari and Availa were in the lab area with Kenton when I arrived. Kenton explained that the ACE was ready to transport and fit nicely into a backpack. It weighed nearly forty pounds, which made it somewhat less convenient to transport than I had imagined. I was puzzled by the need to physically transport it to the NIRC headquarters, so I asked, "why can't we just upload the software to their private network?"

"Because there really is no software to upload. It's all microcircuitry ... nano-circuitry ... this physical prototype is all there is, really," Kenton responded, sounding apologetic.

"But there would have to be records of how the circuits were designed, for chrissake! It would have to be reproducible!" Brendan was a bit more agitated than I'd ever seen him.

"It *is* reproducible, but it would take days ... maybe weeks ...

to do it. You need a combination of 3D printing and some other special processes for things down at the molecular level. Then you need to do component verification and system tests. I don't think we have that kind of time," Kenton now sounded annoyed, perhaps recalling his own frustrations with the technology development process.

"And they don't have the right equipment at NIRC to reproduce it. I checked," said Availa.

"Besides, I'm pretty sure the contest requires the actual device to be entered, if it is a physical device," said Omari.

"Got it! We have to take it to NIRC in DC right away. No time to lose!" I spoke emphatically, mostly to convince myself that it was time to take action ... the next best action.

My smarts showed an icon for an incoming call from Ansell Beckmann, which I dubblinked immediately.

"Connor, my friend," Ansell began, "did Melinda talk to you about the heller?"

"Yes sir. I will take the ACE to NIRC. We have it here in the lab, ready to go. In a backpack." I'm not sure why I mentioned the backpack.

"Okay, great! There's a two-seater heller that's parked on the Gyre roof a lot. I know the owner, and he's agreed to let us borrow it. I found you a pilot, and he'll take you to Washington. He's on the roof now and thinks he can get you to National Airport by 4:30. NIRC is only a 10 or 15 minute car ride from the airport. One thing though ..." Ansell paused for a breath, "... you'll have to take off in 10 minutes to be reasonably sure to make the 4:30 target."

"Get that bloody thing on your back now, and run to the

elevator!" Brendan suggested.

"Right. Leaving now. Message you when I get there, Mr. Beckmann," I said.

"No need. I'll get notified. Safe travels!" Ansell said and disconnected.

◊   ◊   ◊

With the ACE backpack slung over my shoulder, I ran down the hallway to the elevators. I pushed the separate call button for the one elevator that had a baseball-sized diagram of a helicopter on each of its doors. It arrived quickly. I stepped in and pressed the button labeled "Heliport."

As the doors began to close, someone's hand blocked one door which caused them to reopen. It was Melinda.

"Mind if I join you?" she asked.

"Please, come in," I said, "but, unfortunately, there's only room for one of us on the heller."

"Oh, I'm only joining for the elevator ride."

We stood facing the door. She held my hand as we were drawn skyward, and this time not even the roof would stop me. I was so happy to see her, to hear her voice, to hold her hand.

"Thanks for sending me your 'Entanglement' story, Walter," she said, "I enjoyed it, but I do have one complaint."

"Oh? What's that?" I asked.

"Your 'layered flesh' part. I was hoping for more extensive layering than just one hand on top of another," she explained.

"Hmm. I see. Sorry," I said.

"One other thing," said Melinda, "nothing changes. They keep meeting over, what, a few years? But there's no progress, no big changes, no decisions, no moving forward, no walking away."

I stood there for a moment realizing that she was right. Most stories have some event or transition in them to make a point, show character building, create a dramatic climax. Why didn't *my* story?

"It's more of an homage to pleasant highlights of a relationship that keep being re-enacted. Lots of movement with planets and dancing and wine glasses. Metaphorical movement, maybe, and I liked the alignment thing. But no actual progress in either of their lives," Melinda added.

The elevator doors then opened, revealing a small lobby area with a closed door. On the door were two metal signs. One said "HELIPORT ACCESS & OBSERVATION ROOM", and the other had thirty or so lines of fine print … probably important safety warnings I should have read.

"Okay, let's go!" I stepped out, turning back to Melinda, pulling her hand gently.

"Connor, I just came back to give you a nicer good-bye. Let's do that here, now," she said, taking my hand in both of hers and, once again, sliding her fingers up my wrist. We moved closer, held each other and kissed in the elevator doorway. It was a long kiss. I recall the elevator doors clicked three times while we embraced, trying to close while Melinda blocked one door with her foot.

"Courage and compassion, my dear," said Melinda as we parted.

◊　　◊　　◊

The Observation Room had large windows along the wall opposite the door, through which I could see a small, bubble canopy helicopter in the launch area of the building's roof. Looking to the left, I saw a man wearing a baseball cap and flight jacket, his back toward me. He was looking at gauges mounted on the wall and appeared to be making notes on a clipboard.

"Hi. I'm Connor. I'm here for ... ah ... someone was supposed to give me a ride to the Navy Yard in DC. To the airport, I mean. Uh ... Randall?" He had turned toward me on "Navy Yard", and I realized it was Randall Hewitt ... or someone who looked more like Randall than Randall did.

"Hey Connor! I'm your guy! Used to be a pilot. Beckman called and said you had a kind of emergency. I've owed him a favor for years. Long story."

"Alright, so ...," my head was spinning.

"Ought to mention," Randall interrupted, "since we're not a scheduled flight, we'll be subject to ..."

"Wait. Please, let me explain. I've got a device in the backpack ... a prototype ... that I have to get over to NIRC, the federal agency, no later than 5PM."

"And NIRC's in the Navy Yard. That right?" Randall asked.

"Right. NIRC is new and they're using an old building there for now. Assuming I decide to go, could you just drop me at the Navy Yard?"

"Beckmann said you'd need a ride to Ronald Reagan Washington National Airport, which I think is about as close to the Navy Yard as I can get you without gettin' us shot at."

"Okay. I'll get a car at the airport. Thought maybe we could save time landing in the Navy Yard."

"Did you say you haven't decided if you're goin' yet?" Randall asked, then tossed the clipboard onto a table where it landed with a loud splat.

"Too many things going on. Too many things to consider about my own future."

"Well, you gotta think about your career, I guess."

"It's a career ending move for me, I think, whether I do it or not."

"Could be more than one career for you. You know?" Randall pulled a cigar out of his shirt pocket and passed it under his nose before continuing. "Before I joined TFD, I worked a horse an' pony ranch ... that's when I got into flyin' hellers. Before that I was deputy sheriff in Parker county, Texas."

"Really? Wait. I know. I mean ... sorry," my head was spinning, "I need to focus."

"Been there. Both times I made the big switch? It was because I decided I couldn't live with myself anymore if I didn't. No time to explain right now. Speakin' of time, we may not have a lot. So, if you decide to go, your deadline is ... what'd you say? ... 5PM? And why the hell can't you decide if you're goin'? If you don't mind my askin'."

"Yes, 5PM deadline. They have a hard deadline for that competition we're entering. They do that, I think, when the entrants will compete for federal funding. One minute late and they won't accept it."

"Roger. So we need that money?"

"No. We don't need the money, but we need the device to be accepted into the competition."

"So we don't need the money. Is that why you're not sure if

you're goin'?"

"No. It's because ... if I take this thing to NIRC, I think I may be unraveling safety ... or sanity ... for a lot of people. No time to explain."

"Got it. If you go, you gotta be at NIRC by 5PM exact. Life or death. So, we gotta land at Ron Reagan no later than 4:30, on account of you'll need at least 30 minutes to run to the car line, grab a car and get through traffic to the ol' Navy Yard. Trust me. So, let's see ... well, looks like you got about two minutes to decide," Randall said, as though two minutes should have been plenty of time.

"Two minutes? That's it?" It seemed insufficient to me at that moment.

"Well, we're lookin' at one-ten to one-twenty in miles-per-hour for most of the trip. Now, the vector I normally would use ..."

"Please. I just need a minute to think."

"Hell, you got nearly *two* minutes to pick somethin'. So you're good. No worries. Just don't get on the bus, like they say."

"The bus?"

"Yeah. Well, when I was a young 'un, Gramma used to say that to my mom and pop at dinner ... when they got into suggestin' things to do together as a family ... places we could go and such? Anyway ...," Randall suddenly switched to a different voice, as though imitating someone else, "kind'a means all y'all don't really wanna do nothin' ... don't really wanna go no-whar ... but all y'all so damn bored, you just peck some dumb thang to do just to be done peckin' it."

Returning to his normal voice, Randall continued, "Ha! That there's how my gramma 'splained it to me once. 'Bus to Abilene' she called it! Well, you still got *one* minute. Sorry." Randall put the cigar back in his pocket, then gestured as though locking his mouth with a key.

"There's a plot to manipulate people, to control humanity. I have to admit, that does seem like where it's going. They're experimenting now. They're making ... I don't know. The prototype in my bag here may be able to prevent that. I don't know. Melinda is leaving for Norway. Should I go after her? I don't know. If I take this thing to NIRC, I may wind up getting killed," I said, frenetically.

"You kiddin' me? You think somebody's gonna kill you?" Randall appeared incredulous.

"They tried earlier today. I was just lucky. They may try again no matter what I do." I mused aloud with a sudden, bizarre level of calm detachment.

"Damn it, son! I'd get the hell outta here if I was you! Go find that gal in Norway!" Randall advised.

"Wonder if I could live with myself if I *don't* take this thing to NIRC. Melinda told me to use whatever courage and compassion I could draw upon. Guess she thinks I still have some."

Randall took a step toward me and, speaking more calmly, said, "See? Ever'body's gotta find that place. That place somewhere inside you where you know ... you just *know* deep down what's right."

I had a strange sense that Pop-Pop was communicating to me through Randall. The ACE device had to get to NIRC, and I was the person to take it. I knew that was right because I felt it in my heart.

"Okay. I know what I have to do. Let's go!" I declared and

gestured out toward the heller.

"Roger," Randall said as he began to gather up some small items on a table near the wall behind him. "By the way," he went on, "I think Beckmann said you was afraid of heights? Make sure you don't look down when you're in the chopper ... on account of the floor bein' mostly clear polycarb. Well, 'cept for the center brace part of the sub-floor an' all."

"Fuck." I was beginning to realize the flight itself might be torturous.

"I mean, you can see right through it ... all them little buildings and roads and such ... way, way down below ... way ..."

"Oh my God! Stop! Please!" I held my hands up toward his face.

"Got it. Take a breath or two, Connor. She's all cocked out there. I'll just go start 'er up. Come on out when you're ready. Just keep your head down, you know, on account of the rotor." Randall then gestured as though signaling a beheading or the end of an on-the-scene news interview.

"I'm ready. Jesus. God."

Randall went out to the heller and climbed into the pilot seat. After taking a few deep breaths, I pulled the ACE backpack off my shoulder and, carrying it under my arm, stepped outside onto the roof.

The heller's engine started with a loud rumbling and the large blades of the propeller on top of the craft began to move slowly. As I got closer to the blade path, I could see Randall inside the heller, waving his arms and gesturing downward. I stopped to think what he might be warning me about, and then he repeated the beheading gesture.

How could I have forgotten to keep my head down? I waved back as though to say "yeah, I know, I know," and I bent over as a precaution against being hit by the blades. I climbed in through the clear plastic door. The noise level inside seemed even louder than outside, which I found surprising. Randall immediately handed me a headset consisting of large, padded headphones with a microphone attached in front on a movable stem.

"Can you hear me?" I heard as I got the padded cups over my ears, and I nodded dramatically to convey that I was able to hear him.

"You can just talk, and I'll hear you through the mike," Randall said, pointing out what should have been obvious to me, then added, "Hey! I'm your pilot!"

"Good," I said, not sure what else to say.

"Okay! I'll try to keep us up there near one-twenty in miles per hour as much as I can. No weather issues. Full gas tank. I'll have you down at National Airport by 4:30. Absolutely no worries."

While at TFD, I had traveled to twenty cities across several states in the US, plus a few other cities in Canada and Europe. All of that travel had been via plane or train, and I somehow managed my anxiety, even on two particularly unnerving flights on small, 8 passenger corporate jets where cross-winds caused the craft to dance exuberantly like a kite flying over the sands of the Jersey shore on a windy morning. That happy simile about the dancing kite really does not reflect the horror of the actual experience, but it is the way I prefer to remember it.

Be wary, then; best safety lies in fear. Ansell's quote from Shakespeare played in my head. If fear would actually help keep me safe, then I would certainly be protected on this mission, I thought. Unfortunately, I was still not adequately prepared for the next two hours.

◊   ◊   ◊

Immediately after we took off from the heliport, I felt that my life hung by a thread. Cruising only a hundred feet or so over the tops of skyscrapers in Manhattan, I had a strong sense of how precarious such an activity was. The distance to the ground was made excruciatingly obvious, even without looking down. Just seeing the landscape of building roofs, peaks and antennae triggered alarms in my head, reminding me of how easily one could fall to their death while foolishly believing they could fly at high altitudes in a motorized plastic sphere.

As we gradually moved out of the New York City metropolitan area, I began to feel less anxious. I even looked downward now and then, noticing that the landscape appeared increasingly more snow-covered, less populated, more serene. Even though, logically, I knew we had increased our altitude since take-off, I felt in my heart that we were closer to the Earth. My fear of heights magically vanished as it always did while traveling on airplanes, once we got more than a few hundred feet off the ground.

I spent the next hour or so relatively relaxed, in spite of the noise level of the heller motor. I half-listened to brief interactions between Randall and two different Air Traffic Control people on my headphones, not really following what they said. It all sounded orderly and calm to me, reassuring me that all was well. I noticed the landscape below gradually becoming greener or browner, with less snow covering grass or shrubs or harvested fields. I enjoyed the mostly pastoral views from our vantage point while reassuring myself that I was doing the right thing. Taking ACE to NIRC was my next-best-action.

"Miner four-niner, contact KDCA approach on one-one-eight-point-niner," said a voice on the intercom as we were about ten minutes away from National Airport.

"Going to one-one-eight-point-niner, miner four-niner," said Randall, at which point he pressed several keys on a keypad to the right of the main control joystick.

"KDCA approach, miner four-niner, level two thousand," said Randall. There was no immediate response. Randall waited a few seconds and repeated his call.

"KDCA approach, miner four-niner, level two thousand," Randall announced again.

"Miner four-niner, KDCA approach. You are vectored toward US Capital building," said a voice on the intercom before asking, "how many souls on board?"

"KDCA, miner-four-niner. Two souls. We are heading to Ronald Reagan Washington National Airport, dropping off one soul who is delivering a package to the Department of the Navy," replied Randall, speaking slowly and distinctly.

"A package? Okay, miner-four-niner. You need to listen carefully here. Threat alert received ten minutes ago. We are on full alert for imminent terrorist attack on the US Capital by aircraft or drone. You are not a scheduled flight. You may not continue on your current flight path. Repeat, miner four-niner, you may not continue on your current flight path. You must follow instructions I give you to approach alternate landing site. KDCA approach."

Looking around, I then noticed two small quad-copter style

craft, most likely drones, one just ahead and one just behind our heller on the right-hand side. Turning toward Randall, I could see another one of those drones on his side ahead of us. There was likely a fourth drone covering the other corner, but I couldn't see it from where I sat.

"KDCA. Miner four-niner. Roger. My passenger's got to get his package delivered by 5PM though, so ...." I then heard background static as Randall released the transmit button, allowing Air Traffic Control to respond.

"Miner four-niner," said the voice on the intercom, "turn left to heading one-one-zero. Descend immediately and maintain three hundred."

After a pause, Randall responded, "KDCA. Miner four-niner. Say again?"

"Miner four-niner! Turn left immediately to heading one-one-zero! Descend and maintain three hundred! If you do not comply within thirty seconds, you become a target! *You will be shot down! This is not a drill!*"

A jolt of horror and disbelief surged though me. I felt it throughout my brain and my body. My heart raced, thumping wildly, as I panted for oxygen, my hands shaking. I turned to face Randall, and I am sure he noticed my look of panic.

"KDCA. Miner four-niner. Roger! Wilco! We're on it! Turning left to heading one-one-zero. Descending to three hundred." Randall responded, changing his grip on the joystick and tilting it to one side, causing our aircraft to tilt and swerve, suddenly dropping in altitude as well. I noticed a marble-sized metal ball held in a slightly U-shaped tube on the front panel rolled quickly to one end of the tube.

"Are they really serious? They're ready to shoot us down?" I shouted into the headset microphone. Randall did not audibly respond. Instead, he turned toward me, managing to smile while waving his hand dismissively, as though to say "ah, don't worry about this."

But I continued to worry about it. I especially worried when, in the next moment, Randall leaned forward and flipped a lever that caused my headphones to switch off. I turned toward him and slapped my headphones in case he was not aware that they were no longer working, but Randall merely nodded and patted my knee a couple of times, then pointed forward dramatically as if to say "we need to do this" or "I got this" or "onward Christian soldiers" or something intended to inspire acceptance on my part. Acceptance. At least, that's how I read it. Perhaps he spared me some additional anxiety that might have been caused by my listening to more of his conversation with KDCA approach.

For the next few minutes, we traced a wild path, swerving left and right as though continually readjusting our course, rising and falling as though sledding over waves of snow, all the while gradually descending. Finally, as we flew close to the treetops in an area of thick woods, I could see we were approaching a clearing in the middle of those woods. Once over the clearing, we slowed down our pace and circled, while descending, over the grassy area that was completely surrounded by dense trees and undergrowth. Randall then started a straight descent, landing in roughly the middle of the clearing. He did not stop the engine but slowed the rotors and then switched my headset back on.

"Hey Connor! Well, we made it! Listen. They told me you need to step out and wait for them to come get you. Gotta take off again. They'll come for you! Don't worry! Hope you make your delivery on time!"

As I awkwardly unfastened and extracted myself from my seat harness, I asked where we were and who was coming for me.

"Ah ... well ... you're a couple miles from National Airport. Don't worry, they'll transport you where you need to go."

"Who are '*they*'?!?" The frenzied quality of my voice surprised me at that moment.

"Military. I got to go friend. Sorry about all this. Take care." Randall worked some controls causing the rotors to sound different and speed up. I managed to remove my headset and grab the ACE knapsack before unlatching the door and half-falling out onto the grass. I stood up as far as I dared under the blades and waved a "thank you" as I shut the door. Randall wasted no time in taking off, waiting only until I cleared the immediate area under the rotors, leaving me standing alone in the field, watching the heller grow smaller as it turned and headed off over the treetops. The droners, which had been hovering above us, now started off over the trees as though following Randall, except for one. One droner stayed and hovered directly above me about a hundred feet above the ground, monitoring me on video, I assumed.

After a minute, the noise of Randall's heller had faded to nothing. The droner above was surprisingly quiet, so I was left in near-silence in that odd place. I turned and looked around the full 360 degrees of my private little field of grass. It measured between one and two acres, by my rough estimate, and it featured nothing other than the same view of dense trees and shrubbery along its border no matter which way I looked. My smarts showed the time was 4:32PM. If we had landed at National Airport, I was pretty sure I could have reached NIRC by 5:00PM, but not knowing exactly where I was nor when "they" would retrieve me, if indeed they ever did, all bets were off on whether ACE would be accepted into the NIRC competition and deployed as a shield against the ADADA phase two conspiracy. Unfortunately, we had no fall-back plan for getting the ACE device to the right people.

Then there was a faint noise that sounded like a racing car revving up in the distance. As it grew louder, I was able to determine the direction it came from, and I stood facing directly toward the source. The sound evolved to something more like a motorcycle engine, struggling with off-road conditions, growing louder with each passing second. Suddenly, there were lurching movements of low-hanging branches where I had been staring, followed by the abrupt emergence of a van, flattening the shrubs in its path and breaking a few branches as it entered the clearing. It did not slow down but continued to approach me, causing me to consider running away from it. As it drove nearer, I could hear the engine decelerating, and so I just stood there, waiting for whatever would happen next.

The van pulled up so that I was standing directly in front of a sliding door on its side, and I noticed that it was painted to be camouflaged in the woods. It also had some actual leaves and branches caught on it here and there, adding to its ability to blend into the local vegetation. The door slid open in one quick movement, and a young, uniformed man stood at the opening.

"You got a package for the Navy?" he inquired.

I nodded affirmatively, and the young man gestured for me to enter. I stepped up on the running board, taking a seat on a padded bench on the opposite wall, facing the sliding door. The man slammed the door shut and sat down on a small bench seat opposite me, just to my left of the door. A dim light in the ceiling was the only light in the van, as there were no windows and a gray, opaque partition separated us from the driver. Although it was not clear to me what branch of the armed forces he represented, the man's uniform was definitely of a military nature, so I thought of him as a soldier.

The soldier then knocked his fist twice against the gray partition, and the van began to move. We began moving fairly slowly, and soon I could hear bumps and scrapes along the sides of the van, supporting the notion that we were heading off-road, through the woods. The time was 4:40PM, and I finally recovered enough to verbally interact.

"Hi," I began, "this thing in my knapsack ... I have to get it to the NIRC headquarters by 5. It's in the Navy Yard. I assume that's where we're heading. Will we make it by 5?" I held out a small piece of note paper. "The address is on this, if you need it."

"Our orders are to take you to the Ronald Reagan National Airport," the soldier responded in a flat automaton-like fashion.

"Ah, well, yes, that's where the helicopter was going, but I was going to get a ride from the airport to NIRC. And, since we're a little late ... with all the ... I mean ..."

"Our orders are to take you to the Ronald Reagan National Airport," the soldier repeated with a vocal delivery remarkably identical to his previous utterance of those words.

I concluded that he would not respond differently to any other question.

Based on changing outside sounds and a smoother ride, I assumed the van merged onto a busy highway toward the Ronald

Reagan National Airport, as ordered. I sat for what seemed like forever, bracing myself now and then with my arms and legs, when required, to counter forces due to turning and braking. There were no seat belts or hand-holds in the van.

I tried to focus on what I should say when I reached NIRC. What argument could I make to get them to accept the ACE technology entry if the deadline had passed? There appeared to be no network access from within the van, so I couldn't check with Ansell or anybody else for ideas until we arrived at the airport. *Of course, they may not have any good ideas, so I really need to come up with some plan. Would they have sympathy for me because I was incorrectly suspected of being a terrorist? Would it be a good idea to tell them I was a suspected terrorist? So hard to know what to do in a situation like this.*

That's what I was thinking.

The van suddenly stopped, and there came two loud knocks from the driver side of the partition. The soldier bolted up from his bench, violently threw the sliding door open and jumped out of the van.

"Let's go!" he shouted, waving me to stand up, which I did. The next moment I stood outside next to the soldier, my eyes having some difficulty adjusting to the light outside, even though it was still cloudy. I looked around and could see we were near a long line of people with luggage waiting to get the next available car. The time was displayed on my smarts as 4:48PM, and the fastest route time estimate to NIRC was thirteen minutes.

"Listen," I pleaded, "my name is Connor. I've got an emergency here. I have twelve minutes to get to NIRC. Can you guys please just drop me there instead?"

"No!" came a sharp and definitive-sounding response, but then the soldier took a breath and said, "but you get the next car!" He then walked confidently to the next car in the approach lane, just as a man with a rolling carry-on bag opened the door to get in. The soldier put up his hands, waving them at the man with the carry-on in a way that typically signaled some sort of problem.

"Excuse me, sir! Sorry, but we are under a security alert, and we've got this car now for an emergency response team action. Please remain calm. You'll have to take the next car over there. We regret any inconvenience." The man gave an "okay, no problem" wave and walked to the next car. The soldier held the car door open for me, waving me over.

"Thank you!" I said, genuinely feeling gratitude even while thinking I would still miss the NIRC deadline.

"Bailey, Private First," said the soldier, adding "Good luck!" Private First Bailey extended his hand for a quick but firm handshake as I took my seat.

"Farrell. Connor Farrell. Thank you again!" I said as he closed the car door. I pronounced the NIRC address loudly with the best enunciation I could muster, and the car's self-driving system displayed that address on a screen for me as the car quickly pulled out of the boarding zone onto a loop that had signs pointing to exits for various routes. The screen now also showed "PASSENGER: CONNOR T. FARRELL", confirming that the charges for the ride would be automatically handled via my smarts.

"Any chance we can get there really fast?" I asked, not expecting any response. The car actually did speed up at that moment, and we moved along about as fast as anyone could have, navigating the ramps and highways with a fairly heavy amount of traffic. As the time flipped to 5:00 PM, I was somewhere in or near the Navy Yard, but I couldn't tell how much farther it was to NIRC.

It was 5:01 PM when I saw a sign for the National Institute for Resolve and Confidence on a building to the left. The car pulled up to the curb in front of the building. I popped out as fast as I could, shouting "wait here!" to direct the car to remain there at the curb.

As I began to run toward the building entrance, someone called out behind me, "Young man! May I use your car?"

I turned to see an elderly man in a long, gray overcoat, leaning on a cane and pulling a wheeled travel bag. He appeared very anxious and stressed. Before I could respond, he spoke again.

"I'm late for my flight! Please! You asked your car to wait. Can you please release it and just call another one for yourself?"

"Yes," I said and walked over to the car in order to release it via voice command. I placed my hand on the door handle to unlock it, then held it open for the man. He seemed unsteady and faltering as he tried to step inside, so I offered to handle the travel bag.

"Thank you. Sorry," he said, sounding embarrassed.

I held his arm to steady him as he slowly seated himself in the back. He then slid over to make room for the bag, and I placed it on the floor next to him. Looking at him, I noticed he was tagged as R. T. Ross on my smarts.

"I think I'm good now. Thanks again for your help," the man said.

I wished him a good flight, waved and closed the door. Then I turned and dashed back toward the NIRC building.

As I reached the glass door at the building's entrance, I noticed the car had not yet pulled away. I felt there was a chance that something went wrong ... maybe his payment account identity didn't clear or maybe ... ?

I took a breath and pushed aside my sense of urgency about the ACE delivery, deciding to go back to see if R. T. Ross needed help. As I took the first step toward the car it began to pull away from the curb. All was well, I thought, thank goodness.

Upon entering the building's lobby, I noticed an electronic directory display off to one side whose first line read "NIRC submissions to guard at desk." I ran to the far corner of the lobby where a man in uniform stood behind a desk, looking at me. My anxieties returned and pumped my stress level to its maximum. I began breathing rapidly as though there was not enough oxygen in the lobby air to support life.

There was an office directory board on the wall behind the guard, along with a huge, old-fashioned clock with ornate, bronze-colored hour and minute hands. I reached the counter noisily, flopping my hands on the top, panting. The guard stood calmly, smiling at me.

"Please tell me," I gasped, "where I go ... for the NIRC ... submissions ... due today."

The guard did not react for several seconds. It was difficult for me to just stand there, waiting and panting, but there really wasn't much else I could do at the time. Finally, the guard slowly turned around toward the clock on the wall. I noticed the clock displayed the time as between 5:02 and 5:03, as accurately as one could tell from the position of the minute hand. He kept his face pointed at the clock for several seconds, then turned back to me, still smiling.

Then, bizarrely, he turned slowly back toward the clock. I looked up at the clock again too, just in time to see the minute hand, which was nearly two feet long, glide over to cover the next minute mark on the dial. I began to feel some anger and frustration. Was this just his way to amuse himself at my expense?

I contemplated expressing my annoyance, managing to contain myself as the guard turned slowly back to face me ... still smiling! He said, in a slow, nonchalant manner, "So, this here is where you would drop off all that NIRC stuff ... those tech submissions. Now, they all had to be here no later than five today, you understand."

Not sure how to respond, I just stood there making eye contact and beginning to breathe more normally, noticing that the guard's smile had disappeared. He then raised his left arm, pulling his sleeve up a bit to reveal an old wristwatch, perhaps an antique that belonged to his father or grandfather, and he studied the watch intensely for a moment.

"You know," he said, as though reaching some conclusion, "I think that ol' clock on the wall was set a little fast this morning. Just to keep it all fair and honest and ... you know ... avoid any disenchantment with our procedures, I'm going to sign you in here as arriving at 5:00PM exactly."

With that, the guard pulled an old clipboard out from under the counter, and he proceeded to fill in the time and "NIRC" on the first blank line of the sheet of paper on the clipboard. "Name of your company or institution?" he asked.

"The Fifth Dentist," I replied.

"And your name?"

"Connor Tierney Farrell," which I spelled for him as I placed my backpack on the desk.

"Okay Mr. Farrell, you're all set, and thanks for helpin' that gentleman with his bag out there," said the guard, smiling and pointing toward the glass entrance door, adding "he's my uncle."

I turned to look at the door, noticing that the guard would have been able to watch my interaction with R. T. Ross from behind the desk. Turning back, I noticed "ROSS" sewn into guard's shirt pocket flap.

After thanking the guard profusely, I requested a car via my smarts. The car arrived in less than two minutes, and I felt much relief. As I entered the car it felt like my "mission" was completed. Without giving it any thought, I asked it to return to the airport, but on the way I thought about the heller ride from New York and decided it would be best to return by train, avoiding any type of air travel. The car dropped me at Union Station, where I caught a train about an hour later, eventually arriving at Penn Station in Manhattan. I walked from there to the hotel, tuning out traffic noises and other pedestrians, noticing only the cold wind, finally getting into my suite just before midnight. It felt so good to be there. It wasn't really "home," but it felt like a safe haven for me at the time.

Out of habit, I started checking work messages and emails. I noticed an email from Melinda and displayed it on my smarts.

Subject: your question

You asked: What would you say to Jason if he were somehow able to come back and ask what life would have been like growing up with you?

My answer: I would say, Jason, my sweet one, I remember when you slept in my room at night when you were frightened by a dream, but you did have a room of your own, with rocking horse wallpaper and the sun shining throughout upon airplanes, toy puppies and little wooden people colored like flowers. Your first steps were toward me. You grew faster than I expected. As you grew older, you would have stood in lines beside me. Your learnings in school would give birth to ideas that would charm me or dazzle me. You would be called away with seeming recklessness to adventures I would not completely understand. You would visit home on a break from college, and we would sit on the porch and reminisce about our times together at the beach, the park, the playground. At Commons playground we would have spun and rolled and bounced, laughed our lungs empty of breath, became make-believe knights and princesses or pirates, like in the stories I read to you. We would have feigned death with innocence ... and a margin of safety.

Awaiting harmony,
Melinda

I would have sent her a thank-you message, but her status showed as DND on my smarts, most likely, I thought, because she was asleep or traveling or both. I decided to stop checking messages at that point and turned off all my day-start alerts and prodware before getting into the bed.

I had a good night's sleep, waking up late in the morning. I took a leisurely shower, dressed and was about to make a cheese toasty in the kitchenette when there came a loud knock at the door. I opened it to find Burke and a uniformed officer standing in the hallway. Burke asked me to come with them. He said they needed to ask me a few questions.

CHAPTER 31

Learning by Interrogation

After we arrived at the police station, two uniformed officers led me down a hallway to the interrogation room. It was a fairly small space, with a rectangular table in the middle, made of synthetic wood, each leg bolted to the floor with a metal bracket. There were three plain-looking wooden chairs, each had one leg chained to a metal loop in the floor. The chairs could be moved a bit, I surmised, but not hurled across the room at someone. There was a mirror on one wall. I assumed it was a two-way mirror which would allow anyone in the room next door to observe what was going on in the interrogation room. There were likely hidden microphones, so that whatever we said could be monitored and recorded.

The walls were a medium gray, unadorned except for the mirror, a clock and a small whiteboard behind where I assumed the witness or suspect would sit. One of the officers had directed me to sit in that chair, which was across the table from the other two chairs. The floor was rough, apparently concrete, with some shallow grooves here and there, and it was painted a dark gray. The ceiling was hard to see because of the brightness of the LED array hanging above the table, but it looked white-ish.

They left me alone in there for a few minutes, during which it was difficult not to be anxious about what might happen next. In spite of my efforts to breath slowly and deeply, visualizing things that normally would lead me to a state of calmness, my heart raced. My body had a good dose of adrenaline running through it. I found looking at the clock on the wall helped. It was an old-style clock like the one at NIRC but much smaller. As I gazed at it, I came to realize that the expression of time via the relative positions of two pointers or "hands" of different lengths came with a strong sense ... a poetic sense ... of the passage of time, the apportionment of time, the potential of time, the infinity of time. No mere display of numbers, no digital timepiece, could have been so evocative.

Finally, Detective Burke entered.

"Alright," Burke said as he walked to a seat opposite me and sat down. "You okay? Need a drink? We have ice water. Flat or fizzy."

"I think I'm good, for now," I said.

"So ... I have you as Connor Tierney Farrell. Is that correct?" Burke's questioning began.

"Yes."

"And you are in New York City temporarily on business?"

"Yes."

"And normally you reside in … ?"

"Cupertino, California."

"And you work for TFD?"

"Yes."

"How long you been there?"

"With TFD? About seven years."

"You been there a long time. You like working there?"

"Mostly. Well, I did up until recently."

"Why don't you tell me about that. Tell me what happened recently that changed your opinion about TFD. And tell me how you wound up taking that … what is it? … ACE? … that ACE thing over to the NIRC guys." Burke then pulled a small paper notepad and a pen out of his pocket.

It took me nearly a half a minute to get my thoughts organized enough to start to answer. I recall being surprised at the time that Burke did not try to prompt me in any way. He just sat there looking at his notepad. Finally, I told the story of my growing disillusionment with TFD's integrity.

"First of all, in my first years with TFD … the first five or six years … the corporate character was profoundly ethical. I mean, everything TFD did was handled with the highest level of integrity and honesty. We strove to be trusted and believed, and we did that by our own example. Our behavior as a business and as individual employees was exemplary. And we used that … the history of our integrity and impartiality in our processes and the work output of our consultancy ... we used that as evidence of our trustworthiness and objectivity.

"But then, as TFD grew, we brought in more people from other companies, including some of the executive team. That's when I began to see things, ... like a strange spin put on results of a project ... exaggerating or misrepresenting the findings ... things that made me uncomfortable. I rationalized at the time that no work environment was perfect, that no corporation was perfect. Some had higher goals, higher ideals than others, perhaps, but none were perfect. Best to hope for was to work for a corporation that was responsible enough to correct an error they had made. So I guess I shifted my criteria a bit to be comfortable working in a responsible corporation, as opposed to one with perfect integrity."

"Sounds like you adapted. You were still comfortable there," Burke said.

"But then," I went on, "two things happened. First, shortly after shifting TFD's corporate messaging toward being 'the source of certainty' in the consulting realm, Ansell Beckmann, who was our CEO at the time, asked us to look into certainty. We did a study to plant a realistic stake in the ground on just how close to absolute certainty we could get in any judgement or decision."

"Then what?" Burke asked.

"We were pretty confident that there was no basis to think that absolute certainty was achievable in any way, in any area. Humans were not designed to get there."

"Okay. So what did Beckmann have to say?"

"We were asked to review it first with senior TFD execs. One of them told us to bury it. We were told not to let Ansell see the study."

"Who asked you to bury it?"

"Robert Svarog, who is now the CEO at TFD," I said. I felt there was no need to mention my leaving a copy for Ansell.

"Gotcha. Okay, so is that why you took the ACE to NIRC?"

Burke asked.

"No. The Gravity Train project prompted that. It became clear to me as we … a small team of TFD research people and myself … we began to dig deep into the background work leading to the GT proposal. It started to look like the Gravity Train was just intended to be a news-grabbing distraction. But a distraction from what? Then we found some shady stuff being planned with mind control. Thought control of millions of people by a just a few. And the best way to prevent it … to guard against it ... appeared to be mass-replication the ACE device. Taking it to NIRC was a way to get it to the team in Norway that would do the replication of it and distribute wherever it was needed to counteract the thought control scheme," I said.

"So, you stole ACE to save the world?" Burke asked.

"I didn't steal ACE. It was entered by the TFD Research people into the NIRC competition."

"Oh, okay. Sorry," said Burke. Then he asked me how I transported the ACE device to NIRC.

I described the experience in the helicopter, including the warnings from air traffic control, me being dropped off in the field, the military van ride to the airport, the car ride to the Navy Yard and, finally, carrying the ACE into the NIRC building lobby. Burke then suggested we take a short break. He left me alone in the interrogation room again.

I thought about my predicament. It seemed that they thought I broke some law by taking ACE to NIRC. Or maybe I was somehow linked to the terrorist threat received just as we were approaching the Washington metro area. After about ten minutes Burke returned, accompanied by someone else.

"Mr. Farrell, this is Detective Mallory Bruce. She's gonna join us for a bit. Got a few more questions," said Burke as he gestured for her to sit where he sat previously. Burke stood leaning against a wall.

"Hey, Connor, nice to meet you. You can call me Lori," she said while placing a paper notepad on the table. "Want to make sure we have our facts straight. So, when you landed at the airport, what color was the car you took?"

"It was blue, I think ... yes, a light sort of grayish blue," I said.

"So you landed at the airport?" Lori gave me an incredulous look.

"Yes. I mean, no. Randall, the heller pilot, was told to land in a field. Not far from the airport, but I had to ride in that military van for a few minutes to actually get to the airport," I explained, realizing that I needed to pay close attention to the wording of any question.

"Who told the pilot to land in a field?"

"Someone in Air Traffic Control. It was because of the terrorist threat they ..."

"Got it," Lori interrupted. "How do you know it was Air Traffic Control?"

"I was wearing a headset, and I could hear Randall communicating with them. At least, until he decided to turn off my headset. I think Randall was afraid I'd get freaked out by the warnings they were giving him."

"Warnings?"

"About us being shot down if we didn't follow their instructions."

"Okay. That's okay. Got it. So, it was a greenish blue car?" she asked.

"Yes. I mean no. It was *grayish* blue," I corrected, starting to feel vulnerable.

"So, grayish blue then? Okay. So, you mentioned that the TFD Research team entered ACE into the NIRC competition. Who specifically authorized that?" Lori asked.

"I don't know exactly. I worked with a couple of people from the Research team to determine whether it should be entered. They enter their prototypes into various competitions and trade shows fairly frequently. I just assumed it went through the normal process," I said. I took a risk there in answering that way, since I did not know for sure if anyone at TFD had actually authorized taking the ACE device to NIRC. It had not occurred to me to check on that before taking it.

"Got some bad news," said Lori, "no one authorized it. Got that from your CEO, Svarog."

"Sorry, but I assumed it went through the normal process," I said. I felt like an idiot.

"So, how did you get back to New York?" asked Lori.

"Well, I told the car to wait outside NIRC. But someone else needed it, so I let him have it, and then I just got another car when I left. Anyway, I started heading to the airport but decided to go to the train station instead. Union Station. I came back by train."

"Why train?" she asked.

"With all the drama in the sky about possibly being shot down … you know … I didn't feel up to flying anywhere else just then."

"I totally understand. So, you came in to Grand Central?"

"Ah, no. I came into Penn Station."

"Did you see anyone you knew on the subway?"

"I didn't take the subway. I just walked from Penn Station." I wondered why she thought I took the subway.

"Did you walk anywhere along Lexington? Near 53rd maybe?" she asked.

"No, I just went straight to 3rd Avenue, then up that to the hotel, near 47th," I said.

"Are you sure? Because it was such a beautiful evening. I love to take walks around midtown on an evening like that," Lori said, looking at me wistfully.

"Well, I do too, sometimes. And, I mean, I did walk over a mile, I think, to get to the hotel. That evening I really just wanted to get back to my room and lie down and process the day a bit," I said.

"So, tell me about after you got to the hotel up until Detective Burke here came knockin' at your door this morning," said Lori.

"Okay. Well, I messaged someone on my team about dropping the ACE off, checked a few work-related incoming and then went to bed. It was pretty late, and I was exhausted. In the morning I barely had a chance to shower and dress before the detective showed up," I said.

"Really. But Detective Burke didn't show up till 11:25. Don't you work during the day?"

"Yes. And I was planning to work today, but I slept in late. I was just really tired and needed the sleep. My hours are somewhat flexible, not exactly, you know, eight or nine hours a day every day. A little more or a little less as required. It all evens out though. I do work full-time," I said.

"Do you know a man by the name of Mars Janssen, by any chance?" Lori asked, unexpectedly.

"Yes. He used to work for TFD. Years ago. I didn't know him that well," I responded cautiously.

"But you've contacted him since, right? You've gotten together with him. In person. Socially. Since he left TFD, right?" Lori then turned to Burke, prompting a response from him.

"Yeah, I saw you guys together twice in the past couple weeks," Burke said, "at your hotel and at that bar near Gyre Ventures. You guys are besties. Or you *were* anyway."

It never occurred to me that we were being watched at the bar the evening Mars suggested taking the ACE to NIRC. I didn't notice Burke there, but I didn't think to look for him either. Burke's use of the word "besties" was strange too. I wondered if it were possible he was able to eavesdrop on my conversation with Melinda just before I decided to take the heller to NIRC. It just seemed too much of a coincidence. Lori turned back toward me.

"Would you say you were on friendly terms with Mr. Janssen?" she asked.

"Not really. My recent connection was initiated by Mars. He wanted to tell me about some suspicions he had about a project … the Gravity Train project we were starting to work on in TFD."

"Are you aware of Janssen being investigated for tampering with a medical experiment in Europe?" she asked.

"I became aware of that when Mars caught me in the breakfast area of the hotel. Detective Burke came by and mentioned a possible indictment coming soon. Although it wasn't until later that I learned specifics of what Mars had done … or had allegedly done," I said.

"Do you know anyone who was directly harmed by Janssen's actions?" Lori asked, then slapped her notepad down on the table.

I related what Mars told me in terms of justification for his actions, his "doing a bad thing to stop something worse" storyline. Then I revealed what I later learned from Melinda and her father, including the story of Melinda's memory implant of having a son who died suddenly as a child. As I spoke, Lori retrieved her notepad and took notes, looking up at me now and then with different facial expressions suggesting disbelief, horror, sympathy and anger. When I reached the end of my narrative, she slapped her notepad down again and began shouting and gesticulating.

"What a contemptible son-of-a-bitch! That guy, Mars. My point of view? That son-of-a-bitch should die! He should be executed! He should be a victim in our homicide files!" After turning to look at Burke for a moment, she turned back toward me, slapped her forehead and added, "What am I saying? He *is* in our files! Homicide victim! Dead right there! Fuckin' butchered!"

Burke suggested we take another break.

◊　　◊　　◊

That break was longer than the first one. During my time alone, I replayed the interrogation so far in my head, trying to figure out what they thought I did and what they hoped to get me to say.

Apparently Mars had been killed, or at least, they wanted me to *think* he had been. But why would they want me to think it if weren't true, I wondered. Or did they think he had been killed by *me*? I struggled with that for quite a while. Finally, I shifted to thinking about what information I could provide toward establishing my innocence.

The "theft" of the ACE device was tricky. I had assumed the Research team had officially entered it into NIRC's competition, but why did I assume that? I had not discussed it with Kenton or anyone else. A huge oversight on my part. About all I could do was claim negligence and admit to removing the device without permission from Svarog or Dr. Reddy or other proper authorization.

The possible murder of Mars Janssen was not as worrisome to me at the time. My thought simply was that I did not kill Mars ... or anyone else for that matter. So, not being guilty of murder, I did not expect it would be difficult to prove my innocence.

Based on the wall clock, it was a little over a half-hour before Detectives Burke and Bruce returned. The door opened and they marched in quickly. This time, Burke sat in the seat across from me. Lori paced around the area by the wall, staring intimidatingly at me.

"Okay, Connor. I think we're getting close here. Close to wrapping up," said Burke. "Just need to get a couple things straight. First off, you said you did *not* leave the hotel at all this morning until I showed up?"

"Yes. Well, actually what I said was that I slept in late. But of course, if I were sleeping, I wouldn't have been out anywhere. I mean, I wouldn't have left the hotel." I wanted to be precise.

"If you were sleeping."

"Right."

"If. Why did you say 'if'?" Burke asked.

"I said 'if' in the sense that … I mean, I was explaining why I didn't explicitly say I didn't leave the hotel. Because I said I had been sleeping. I slept in late because I was tired," I said.

"Were you outside the hotel at any time between 2:30 AM and 5:00 AM this morning?" Lori asked in an exasperated tone.

"No," I said, firmly.

Burke just sat and stared at me while Lori resumed pacing. I decided to ask a question of my own.

"Was Janssen killed?" I asked.

"Why do you ask?" Burke inquired.

"Detective Bruce mentioned Mars was a victim of homicide before our last break," I explained.

"That the first you heard it?" asked Lori, looking toward the mirror.

"Yes," I said.

"Okay, let's move on," Burke continued. "Yesterday, you were out in front of Gyre Ventures. Around noon. And some guys assaulted you. And a maintenance worker for that building intervened. He may have saved your life. Do you recall that?"

"Yes, of course I recall that." Did he actually think I would have forgotten?

"Don't get snippy. Just trying to get you to think about it and however much you can recall."

"I remember it pretty well," I said.

"How many guys assaulted you?" Burke asked.

"Two."

"Just two?"

"I'm pretty sure there were only two."

"Did you recognize either of them?"

"No."

"You had smarts on, right? Were their tags blocked?"

"Yes. Blocked."

"Was your tag blocked?"

"Yes."

"Did you know the maintenance guy?"

"Yes. His name was Wally. Wally Packer." I said.

"How do you know him?"

"We just met randomly in an elevator at Gyre about two weeks ago. The morning of the TFD quarterly meeting."

"That would have been Tuesday, February 22nd. Correct?" Burke asked after flipping a few pages back on his notepad.

"Yes."

"So, tell me about your relationship with Packer."

"Well, it was really just a minute or two in that elevator. He had seen me being confronted by some protesters outside on my way in. He said something about that, and we just started talking."

"So, random bullshit in the elevator for one minute. And you know his full name. And he risks his life … *lost* his life … to protect you two weeks later? Give me a break." Burke leaned back in his chair and folded his arms.

"Wait," I said, "did you say 'lost his life'? He was alive when they took him to the hospital."

"DOA," said Burke, "Dead on arrival."

I covered my face. I wanted to be somewhere else. Wally gave his life for me. I didn't deserve that sacrifice, I thought, and he didn't deserve to die.

"Okay, Connor. Give us something here. What else did you guys talk about in the elevator?" Lori asked. As I looked at her, she leaned over and rested both hands on the table.

"He talked about surfing and his girlfriend. Well, he asked me if I was from around here and I said no, from the west coast. And he started talking about a recent trip he made there with his girlfriend. He told me about a big decision he had been struggling with for a long time. He loved his girlfriend ... Rita ... and wanted to marry her, but he didn't think he was good enough for her. That he wouldn't be a good husband. He also said she wanted to move to California, and it seemed like he wasn't comfortable with that. Anyway, I remembered some advice my grandfather gave me that seemed relevant, so I quoted my grandpa. Somehow, that was exactly the right thing. Wally made up his mind right there to ask Rita to marry him that day. He even said they'd move to California."

"How did that conversation end? Did you guys plan to get together or something?" Burke asked.

"No, but Wally offered to help me if I ran into more problems with the protesters outside."

"Hey, Connor, what was the advice your grandfather gave you?" Lori asked.

"Basically, important decisions in life are made with your heart. Not your brain. So, if you're struggling with some big decision that could change your life ... well ... you may already have the best answer in your heart."

"I like that," Lori said as she moved away from the table to pace around a bit more.

"Do you know a guy by the name of Harper Golly?" Burke then asked.

"I know who he is. The executive assistant to our CEO, Robert

Svarog."

"Didja ever meet him? Talk to him?" Burke asked.

"No."

"Ever notice he looks a hell of a lot like you?" Lori asked. "He's your effin' doppelganger!"

"Yes, I noticed that," I recalled the first time I saw Harper at the New Q kick-off.

"Alright. Ever see them before?" Lori asked as she dropped two mug shots on the table in front of me. One I recognized as one of the two men who had assaulted me. The other might have been the other assailant, but I wasn't sure. I never got a good look at him. I explained that to the detectives. They then asked me to confirm that the man I recognized in the picture labeled "N. Cranshaw" was one of the assailants.

"We have those two in custody," said Burke, "on account of they killed Harper Golly yesterday evening as he left Gyre Ventures."

I was stunned to hear that. "Oh my God! Did they kill him by mistake? Were they looking for me?" I had trouble breathing. I looked back and forth between Burke and Lori. They looked at each other. Finally, Lori spoke.

"I had a fascinating conversation with those scumbags earlier today," she said, "in which they had no problem admitting that Harper was the target. The *original* target. So that day Wally saved you? They thought you were Harper. You looked just like his picture, they said."

"Oh my God," I said. That made it all seem worse, somehow. Wally was killed because of a mistake, because of my resemblance to an assassin's target.

Just then there was a knock on the door. A middle-aged man took one step into the room, wearing a shirt with rolled up sleeves, a loose necktie and a shoulder holster with a gun.

"Sorry to interrupt," he said, "Need to talk to you two for a minute. Just come down to my office."

"Will do," said Burke as the man left. Burke and Lori quickly gathered their notepads and some folders and left me there without saying a word. I assumed they would return at some point.

◊   ◊   ◊

That time they were gone for about twenty minutes, which was a relief. For some reason, I imagined each break might be several times longer that the previous one, escalating to them leaving me there over night. Both Burke and Lori returned and sat across from me at the table.

"Well, we got a lot to cover here," said Burke. My heart sank as I assumed that would mean hours of further questions. I began to contemplate whether I should refuse to cooperate further until I spoke to a lawyer.

"So, Mr. Farrell, we picked you up this morning for questioning about your trip to NIRC, your possible theft of the ACE prototype. Also we thought you might be linked to the murder of Mars Janssen," Burke said, adding, "and we also thought you could shed light on the Wally Packer and Harper Golly murders, but we learned something new about that in the last twenty minutes."

"Svarog was behind the Golly murder," said Lori. "We got evidence he hired those two guys in the mug shots I showed you, through a third party. Hired them to kill his executive assistant."

Apparently noticing my shock and confusion, Lori asked, "Do you need a minute?"

"Ah. No. You can go on," I answered.

"Okay. Mars Janssen. Coroner and Forensics did their thing," Lori said, "and the conclusion is that it was accidental. No evidence of homicide. No evidence pointing to suicide either, but we might find something later on that. It's possible. Most likely? Just an accident. Stood on the edge of the station platform and lost his footing just as the train was pulling in."

"And we got something on ACE!" Burke announced melodramatically. "Turns out you didn't steal it after all. It was approved for submission to NIRC by TFD's research director. Guy named Reddy."

"Svarog was the one who told us it was *not* approved. He told us you stole his important corporate research asset," said Lori. "Had we known at the time that he recently hired contract killers, we might have checked his story before grabbing you in your hotel room."

"So, now what?" I asked. At that moment, I really did not know what to expect. It did seem like there were no remaining crimes to which I might be a suspect. Perhaps, I thought, I would still be a "person of interest" … a potential witness or source of other useful information.

"Appreciate your cooperation Mr. Farrell. We may need to ask you some more questions as we get further into the pile of stuff on our plate here," said Burke, "but for now, no wants. You're free to go."

Both Burke and Lori politely shook my hand, and Lori pointed me to a uniformed officer down the hall who would drive me back to the hotel if I wanted. I thanked her and took the ride.

CHAPTER 32

Demise of Mars

Checking for messages upon returning to my suite, I found none from Melinda but several from Brendan, Kenton and Nilima asking me where I was and suggesting I watch Melinda's early morning interview. They were all surprised, as I was, that Melinda did that interview without giving us a heads-up on it.

I dubblinked on the "Today – Wednesday" banner at the top of the field of view and found the interview, tagged as *Research scientist leaves TFD – calls co-worker hero.*

Since I hadn't eaten anything since breakfast the previous day, I decided to wave up some breaded chicken strips in the kitchenette. After settling in on the couch with those, plus some honey mustard sauce and a beer, I transferred Melinda's interview video to the large flat-screen on the wall. I watched the entire interview several times and bookmarked it for future reference.

Liz Fedorova conducted the interview, but before Melinda was introduced, Liz summarized a few recent developments on the Gravity Train, including the indefinite postponement of a TFD executive review of our team's analysis, more protests against the GT, as well as growing dissent in the U.S. Congress on funding allocation and commitment. Liz then referred to the previous interview with Melinda, wherein she had stated that the Gravity Train was only being considered to distract everyone from a dark plot to take over the world with mind control. The view then changed to show Melinda standing to the left of Liz.

"We have with us again Melinda Beckmann, formerly with The Fifth Dentist," Liz began, "Melinda, thank you so much for talking with us again. I understand there have now been two attempts on the life of your co-worker Connor Farrell. First, can you tell us anything about Connor's trip to NIRC headquarters yesterday?"

Liz mentioning two attempts on my life confused me for a moment, but I realized that it was due to earlier incorrect or speculative reporting that Harper had been killed by mistake because he looked like me. Detective Mallory Bruce cleared that up this morning while interrogating the killers, and it was corrected in news reports later in the day.

"Yes," Melinda paused briefly, then continued, "we found a way, we think, to put a safety net in place."

"A safety net?" Liz asked.

"Yes. We wanted to distribute a technology that could be used to undo any effort toward manipulation of human brains ... of human thought ... on a global scale."

"And that's what the trip to NIRC was about?" Liz prompted.

"Yes. There was a way to get the prototype technology

replicated quickly using NIRC resources and distributed worldwide." Melinda appeared distracted at this point in the interview, turning away from Liz.

"A man by the name of Mars Janssen … I hope I got that right … has been mentioned as a key figure in clandestine efforts to assist you in your effort to get a technology … a *deflection* technology, as it's being labeled on some social media venues … out to every country that might need it," Liz spoke, placing her hand on Melinda's shoulder, appearing to squeeze it to try to hold her attention.

"We thought he was helping us," said Melinda, still looking away from Liz, "but it turned out he wasn't. He was trying to set us up for failure."

"Sorry. Did you say Mars was trying to set you up? How so?" Liz asked.

Melinda turned to look at Liz again. "He had … he has his own view of right and wrong. But we succeeded anyway, so it doesn't matter now. Mars doesn't matter now."

Suddenly, several people could be seen running in the background. A few faint screams could be heard, and both Liz and Melinda turned away from the camera. It was at that point on my first viewing of the interview that I noticed they were not near Gyre Ventures. There were some buildings I didn't recognize in the background and a sign indicating an entrance to the subway. Melinda was watching that subway entrance.

Liz turned to face the camera, saying "we appear to have some kind of emergency in the subway station. We're at 53rd and Lexington. Several police officers are running toward the steps. Can we get a shot?"

The camera then turned to show and zoom in on the subway entrance. The officers had just reached the top of the staircase and quickly descended until we couldn't see them. There was a man in a beige raincoat with them, whom I assumed was also with the police. A few people came up out of the entrance.

"While we wait to hear what the trouble is there, can you please tell us, Melinda, about your departure from TFD, The Fifth Dentist? Did you choose to leave? Do you have plans?" Liz asked.

"I chose to leave," said Melinda, "and yes, I do have plans. Leaving today for Norway, where I hope to find meaningful employment working to help the mentally and physically disabled."

"Given your background, will you focus on augmented reality?" asked Liz.

Melinda closed her eyes for a moment before she answered. "It's about implants and connections between people," she said. "It's about connections between many people at some level ... maybe just sharing some feelings or joys or fears ... something basic ... but something that ties us together. Something that helps humanity be humane. Not just a large collection of individual organisms that share some common DNA. I think there are real possibilities there. Some meaningful work I could do."

"So, a lot of changes in your life right now. Any regrets?" Liz prompted.

"No regrets, Ms. Fedorova," Melinda said, "I'm satisfied to have been part of a small team who decided to take action, risking their own careers to try to protect many people from manipulation and exploitation. Connor Farrell is a hero for what he did yesterday. I'll miss working with him."

Just then, several people in the background who had been standing in a semi-circle looking down the subway steps began to take a few steps back, spreading out a bit. Next, the man wearing the raincoat walked up and out of the staircase, waving the crowd back further. Then, appearing surprised or angry to notice Liz and the news camera, he jogged toward the camera.

"Detective, do you have a moment?" Liz called out, pointing her microphone at the man as he drew near. I recognized him as Detective Burke.

"No way! We're busy here! Clear the area! Move back!" Burke shouted angrily, then pushed the camera to the side. "I said *back*!" Burke's voice could still be heard clearly, although the camera view shifted randomly between the pavement and the sky as Burke added, "We got a possible homicide here! The perp could still be here! I said back the hell up!"

That was the end of the Melinda interview. The program then switched back to the news anchor at his desk, who promised "more on that story in just a bit," before cutting to an advertisement.

I replayed that interview on the flat-screen perhaps twenty times over the next hour. Each time, I paid close attention to Melinda's face and tone of voice. I observed her face as she spoke, as well as the visible part of her face as she turned back toward the subway entrance. As she spoke to Liz, she seemed relieved, spinning down out of some extreme anxiety, until the first time she turned back toward the subway. From then on, Melinda appeared as though she felt she had forgotten something important, but she couldn't decide whether to complete the interview or go back for what she forgot ... or maybe just run away. The glimpse of

Melinda's face that could be seen just before Burke grabbed the camera was too brief in real time to assess. I watched that portion of the video in slow motion several times, then frame by frame, concluding that Melinda had been compelled to feel shock or fear in that moment.

Was she afraid of Burke? Why was she being interviewed near the subway entrance? She never rode the subway, or so she had told me.

After dinner, I invoked Don Dander on the flat screen to see if there were any updates on the Janssen death. Instead, Don was interviewing Dr. Brenna Halvorsen, NIRC's Director of Origination Infusion. In reaction to Melinda's earlier warnings of widespread mind control, Dr. Halvorsen offered some speculative comments concerning what she defined as "pandemic affected cognitive regulatory acceptance", subsequently pronouncing its acronym, PACRA, to streamline the conversation. She said she had suspected for some time that there were several PACRA mind-control schemes being researched in various parts of the world, with some prototypes already being tested. She said we should be "watchful" to avoid evil intent, adding that the NIRC organization itself was "philosophically opposed to involuntary relinquishment of independent thought."

◊   ◊   ◊

After the interview, there was an update to the subway station news story. Mars Janssen had been found dead on the tracks. The incident as that point was still being treated as a possible homicide. No official determination had been made as yet. It was reported that Mars' own fingerprints had been lifted from the track-facing side of the pillar at the edge of the platform near where his body had been found. The cause of death was determined to be severe physical trauma caused by being run over by a subway train. The latter point on cause had been verified by the presence of human blood found on the wheels and undercarriage of one of the trains passing on that route within the time of death window. Several theories on the fingerprints had been tossed about, including the idea that he had tried to grab onto something while being pushed off the platform. I only watched that update twice before getting a news alert on yet another update.

I watched that new update on the flat-screen as well. It was just read by the anchor reporter while images of the subway station were displayed on the right. The manner of Mars' death had been determined. There was consensus that Mars simply stood too close to the edge of the platform, beyond the yellow safety line, lost his footing and desperately tried to grab onto the pillar with one hand as he fell. The pillar was cylindrical, fourteen inches in diameter with a smooth surface. No other fingerprints of interest or clues were found. Finding no evidence to suggest homicide or suicide, his death was determined to be accidental. It was just as Detective Bruce had said.

CHAPTER 33

Cadence 2.0

While lying in bed that night, I spent some time contemplating several theories on the death of Mars, but I was having trouble processing them. I even found it hard to simply articulate to myself what each theory was and why it could potentially be what actually transpired. I wanted to process and understand what was going on in Melinda's head during that interview with Liz and when Burke approached them.

I decided to follow Melinda's earlier advice on stepping outside myself to get out of my own way. I decided to switch to DND mode on my smarts for the next day or two. I would let Walter Winterwonderland tackle writing a fictional version, perhaps an allegorical version, of the death of Mars. I would start that in the morning, rather than trying to work on it that night. I really needed to get some sleep.

That night I had a dream about Melinda, about our last conversation before we left. In the dream it went more like I would have preferred, with more touching and promises for our future.

"When we met, you said you were looking for meaningful work," I said to her in the dream as we stood on the Gyre Ventures roof near the helicopter, rotors already spinning, "Melinda, I really hope you've found it this time. I do wish you all the best." I gently stroked her hair, curling my fingers around her ponytail, jiggling it a bit while adding, "I will miss you terribly. Ponytail reality."

"Connor, my dear, this is temporary," Melinda assured me, her voice sounding lovelier than ever, "please know that we'll be together again soon. It's inevitable. It's certain."

"I wish I could believe in certainty," I said, as the rotor noise began to increase.

"I wish I could make you feel certain," she said, raising her voice over the noise, "your dear love, Cadence, may have had some natural abilities along those lines. It's too bad she's not still around. I think I would have enjoyed getting to know her."

"Yes, I think you would have liked Cadence," I shouted over a deafening roar.

I awoke at that point, partially opening my eyes to verify that I was in bed in my Manhattan suite. The room was dark, but there was still enough visible to confirm my location. For some reason, I reached for my smarts to check the time, which displayed as 2:53 AM. I was about to take them off and put them back on the nightstand when I noticed something in the room. It was like a shadow of a person, moving about, barely visible in the dark room.

"Connor," a voice said, and I froze. "Connor, can you hear me?" the voice asked.

The voice sounded a little like Cadence's, but it was different than her digital avatar voice. It occurred to me then that I must have said "Cadence" out loud while dreaming, invoking the DA app in my smarts. The app may have been trying to simulate how Cadence would appear in her darkened bedroom and how she would have sounded having just been awakened from a deep sleep. In any case, I decided I would just invoke her avatar in the morning instead and try to get back to sleep. I quiesced the app and removed my smarts, placing them back on the nightstand.

I closed my eyes and rested on my back, hoping to drop off to sleep again quickly. As I reclined there, I focused on the sound of my own breathing, which in the past had often helped me get to sleep faster. After doing that for a minute or two, I reached up to the side of my head to smooth out the pillow. It felt like the pillow was bunched up and pressing on the side of my head, but when I reached up, the pillow was not pressing on me. Nothing was, but yet *something* was. It was an odd feeling.

"Having trouble sleeping?"

The voice startled me, and I sat up quickly to look around. My movement caused a lamp near the entryway to switch on, and I could see what appeared to be Cadence, lying on her side across the mattress at the foot of the bed, facing me, her arm bent at the elbow and her head propped up by her hand.

I reached to pull off my smarts and realized I was not wearing them.

"From time to time, we might discover meaningful purpose while we sleep," said the apparition.

Still feeling the pressure on my head, I whispered in astonishment, "Cadence!"

CHAPTER 34

Thursday vs. Friday

"Doubt is not a pleasant condition, but certainty is absurd." — *Voltaire*

"Doubt is the origin of wisdom." — *René Descartes*

Brendan and I agreed to meet for dinner on Friday. I spent most of that day thinking about Melinda and checking my travel arrangements. I had planned to return home to Cupertino the following day, but was that really my next best action? There were several key issues that I felt must be carefully considered.

First, our executive review on the Gravity Train had still not been rescheduled, but with Svarog removed, it was unlikely that The Fifth Dentist would officially support the project. Extremely unlikely, in fact, since the Board of Directors had named Astrid Ekland our new CEO that Friday morning. There was a rumor that the Board had considered acquiring an artificial intelligence algorithm that could take the role of a corporate CEO. While fewer than twenty businesses in the United States and Canada had appointed an AI CEO, several of those doing so published highly favorable reports of their experience, some citing that nuance and sarcasm were absent from their interactions with the AI CEO.

However, after much debate, the Board decided to go with Astrid, since she consistently garnered heartfelt praise every time she made a public presentation. Astrid's first official communication to employees referred to our corporation several times as The Fifth Dentist. She never liked the acronym.

I figured I could participate via video conference for the Gravity Train review. Afterward, we would still face the challenge of getting certain world leaders to abandon the project. I had a feeling that, with Astrid's help, we could get an overwhelming majority of citizens on our side.

In any event, the Gravity Train was not a reason for me to stay in New York City.

Next, there was ADADA. Phase two had not been completed, but there likely would be no advantage to my staying in Manhattan for that. While at home in Cupertino, I could do secondary research and propose new primary research if needed, including surveying respondents in our corporate market intelligence database, in order to discover potential benign uses of elective brain implants for ADADA phase two across various parts of the world. We just needed to stay ahead of those PACRA mind-control projects NIRC's Dr. Halvorsen mentioned. I worried that our ACE technology might not be able to shield us against all of them. I was glad to hear Dr. Halvorsen say in her interview that

NIRC was (publicly, at least) philosophically opposed to mind control.

Then, I considered my personal relationships. Cadence's ghostly visitation on Wednesday night had not been repeated. On Thursday morning, I was convinced it had been a dream, a product of my own brain's manufacture. I attributed it to a subconscious longing to be home. I should really return to Cupertino, I thought.

On Friday morning, I began to suspect that labeling the Cadence visit a dream was a deflection on my part, so that I wouldn't feel compelled to go any deeper into it. By Friday afternoon, I had gone deep enough to believe Cadence's presence was real. I concluded her spirit visit was purposeful, and that it helped me understand that my own memories of our relationship and my sense of how Cadence might react to challenges would be more useful, more cherished, than a digital avatar in my life ahead. Hence, there was no need for the DA app in my smarts. I uninstalled it that afternoon.

"I will never forget you, my love," I said out loud, as the task progress indicator advanced.

In a way, my "Entanglement" story may have connected more to my relationship with the Cadence avatar than with Cadence herself. I recalled Melinda's comment about the characters being stuck, endlessly looping and repeating their initial encounter, never progressing or maturing. I accepted that the Cadence digital avatar had been an homage. It was an on-going re-enactment of pleasant highlights of our past relationship. There was no movement forward. There couldn't be.

Finally, there was the issue of Melinda moving to Norway.

On Thursday, I theorized about non-accidental scenarios

regarding the death of Mars Janssen. As Walter Winterwonderland, I wrote a few scenes of a play portraying one of those scenarios. I used a penny with a star-shaped sticker on it to symbolize the brain implant, so I appropriately entitled the play *Star Penny*. An evil character, Pogo, had given the penny to an unmarried professional woman, Britt, which somehow caused her to remember having a son whom she may have accidentally killed when he was three years old. In the opening scene, Britt describes to a friend how she unintentionally caused Pogo to fall off a subway platform. She moves about the stage as though reliving the experience.

Britt wondered why Pogo stood at the very edge of the subway platform, near a support pillar, beyond the painted line and bumpy tactile bricks that indicate the limit of the safe area to stand. He leaned out beyond the platform and looked down the dark tunnel to the left. Britt supposed Pogo thought he might be aware of the train's approach a few moments sooner by seeing the headlight's glow reflected on the rails at the edge of visibility. She supposed he thought that it was fine to violate safety regulations and laws, in order to achieve what he believed was a benefit or positive outcome, no matter what the risk, no matter what collateral damage might result. Britt declared she would never need to cross the safety line until there was a train stopped at the platform with its doors open for her to board.

Then she saw Pogo turn and stare at her.

"Why was he looking at me? It must have been his way of assessing the damage ... learning the extent of my pain and the affect of his tampering with my life," said Britt.

Her monolog continued: *The train was now audible. Surely he heard it, but he still stared at me. For some reason, I clenched my fists tightly and lunged forward, my arms raised as if to grab or tear something away. Pogo's expression changed in an instant to perplexed, then to startled, then to afraid. He took one step back away from me. Only one. Stepping into the air above the track in a space still unoccupied by tons of moving metal and plastic. I remember his arms lunging forward. His right hand slapping against the pillar. He was falling. Then there was the visual shock of the train's leading edge cutting through the air in the space beyond the platform's edge. Beyond the margin of safety.*

I saw the train's driver or conductor. Just for a fraction of a second. Just long enough to see that he was not looking ahead but toward the opposite platform. Toward two young women standing there, I assumed. As the train decelerated, with fewer wheels per second violating Pogo's remains, I realized that no one but me had seen Pogo fall.

Britt's monolog represented my theory about Mars Janssen's death on Thursday.

On Friday, as I viewed Melinda's final interview with Liz yet again, it seemed there was no specific connection, other than the interview location, that caused me to think she was present when Mars died. Her reaction to Burke approaching seemed normal, even if she had not just caused or witnessed a tragedy on the subway platform. Any adult would have reacted the same way, I thought, to Burke running up and shouting the way he did. I scrapped the *Star Penny* project, which seemed like a contrivance anyway, and I switched off DND mode on my smarts.

My conclusion on Friday was that Melinda had absolutely nothing to do with the demise of Mars. I very much wanted to talk with her, but she was still in DND mode. On my way to meet Brendan, I wondered if I should look into changing my flight to a different destination.

◊   ◊   ◊

"Can't believe you're heading out tomorrow!" Brendan said while we ate. "We been too bloody busy. Sorry we didn't get to hang out more outside of work."

"I know," I said, "it's been pretty stressful. Workload was definitely a *part* of it."

"Ah, right! Here I am complaining, and nobody even tried to kill me," he said, laughing.

"Well, not yet anyway," I said, trying to be funny.

"Rather not think about that," he said. "Speaking of murder, did you hear about Harper? I heard on the news they suspect Svarog hired some guys to kill him."

"Yes," I said, "I heard that too."

"Why would he?"

"That may come out after further investigation, but I suspect it was because Harper knew too much."

"Too much about what?"

"He may have found evidence related to Svarog secretly promising to 'prove' the Gravity Train was a safe and beneficial investment, or maybe he found evidence of collusion with foreign powers to use ADADA phase two for malicious purposes."

"And Svarog knew Harper had evidence?"

"Maybe Harper had already contacted federal investigators, promising them something ... maybe a collection of incriminating documents … and Svarog found out somehow," I surmised.

"Right. Guess we'll just have to wait and see."

After dinner we speculated on when, if ever, we would present our GT work to the exec team. Then we each shared some memories related to previous projects we'd worked on together.

"I wonder if I'll still fantasize about 'pervasive certainty' at career day events," I said.

Brendan laughed, then leaned back and stretched, saying, "well, this has been fun, but time to get home to the missus."

"Oh dear," I said, "I hope I haven't gotten you in trouble by keeping you here too long."

"Nah. I should get there by 10:00 PM on the regional. Didn't promise earlier."

We stood and shook hands. I knew I would miss his companionship.

"Brendan, I'm so glad you found time for dinner. Thank you so much, and please thank your wife for me too."

"Glad to see you off, me old friend," he said, "and good to work with you again. Maybe next time 'round it'll be a bit less horrific."

"If only we could be certain," I said with a smile.

"Or just accept it as good, whatever it is," he said, giving me a little slap on the shoulder.

I took a fairly long walk through midtown and lower Manhattan, finally looping back into the general area of my hotel suite, at which point I decided to go to the Snegurochka pub. I was pretty sure Pru worked on Friday nights. She'd likely still be there, as it was around 10:30 on my smarts. "Around 10:30" was as accurate as I could be, since I had changed the clock display on my smarts to a tiny classic clock face with no numbers. It was hard to estimate the positions of the hour and minute hands with accuracy, and that felt good to me.

In a few minutes I arrived at the pub, took a deep breath and walked inside. Pru, who had been looking downward at something behind the little reception desk, became aware that someone entered. She looked up and began to deliver the standard greeting before recognizing me, "Welcome to Snegurochka's! We ... oh. Hi! Nice to see you again, Connor!"

"Hi Pru. How are you doing?" It felt good to see Pru again. She wore ammu tears that dripped one at a time from each eye, each appearing to shiver a bit before blowing off her cheeks sideways.

"Good. Been following the news, so I won't ask how *you're* doing."

"Right," I said, faking a chuckle, "I was wondering if you'd like to meet for a drink or something when you get off work tonight."

Pru stared at me for a moment, then let out a little laugh. "So, you're asking me at, like, 10:45 on a Friday night, if I would go on a date with you that same Friday night? Seriously?"

"I guess it is a bit presumptuous of me ... but ...," I spoke while looking down at my feet, tilting my head from side to side.

"I'll meet you at Lacey's in about a half-hour. Okay?" Pru sounded as though she were smiling.

"Thank you, Pru," I said, looking up to see her smile.

◊   ◊   ◊

Later, we were sitting at a small table at Lacey's, each with a glass of wine.

"You did the right thing, Connor. You've got to believe that." Pru sounded earnest, placing her hand on mine as she spoke. "When will she be back?"

"Melinda? I think she plans to stay in Norway," I said.

"You and Melinda ... you get mentioned a lot in the news about the tunnel and hacked brain implants. She called you a hero. You were more than just co-workers. Right?"

"I guess," I shrugged, disappointed in myself for not saying more while my head spun within a cloud of uncertainties.

"I *admire* her," Pru said emphatically, "I like her attitude and what she stands for. Good for her! Right? Good for you too!"

"Nothing is certain in life," I opined.

"Tell me, what are you thinking about right now?" Pru asked.

"The fact that you need to ask is part of the problem," I said.

"Explain," said Pru, as she tilted her head to one side and folded her arms.

"Well, I mean, I could meet someone in a cafe like this one. We could see each other a few times. I could write a poem and leave it for her at work. Unsigned, because that feels romantic to me. When I see her the next day, she doesn't mention the poem, but it's clear to me by the way she looks at me that I have touched her very deeply. I'm thinking that *she's* thinking that there will be many more poems ... a *future* for us."

Pru nodded and may have been about to say something, but I felt compelled to continue.

"During the next few days, she is both nearby and distant. She's present in the air I breathe, and her spirit levitates among the stars in the night sky. I imagine we both bask in the warm energizing glow of our souls drawing closer, our hearts making more room. A week later, as we're chatting back at the cafe, I quote an *a propo* couplet from that very poem ... the one I left for her at work, unsigned. She takes a beat and gasps, 'that was *you*?'"

Pru gave me a puzzled look. I think I may have been channeling Walter.

"Or maybe I meet someone in that cafe, and we start dating," I went on. "One evening over dinner, after we've been dating for several weeks, she seems unsettled and strangely nervous. Over dessert, she manages to admit that she's fallen in love with someone else. At that moment, the cafe owner walks up and asks if he can take our picture to use in an advertisement because, he explains, we look so charming together."

"Okay, I think I get it," said Pru. "We can't count on anything in relationships. We make assumptions. We go with what feels right. We think we know what other people are thinking, but we really don't. Future events are often surprising or oddly ironic, not what we assumed would happen, no matter how much we've thought about or agonized over the possibilities. Connor, you should learn to adore life as a blend. A blend of the expected and the unexpected. A blend of disappointment and fulfillment. But we grow with all of it, right? We become who we will be."

"Yes, in tech journal interviews in the past, I said we might achieve 'pervasive certainty' through new technologies soon. I don't believe that anymore, and I've been thinking today that relationships between people are the core of the uncertainties we face every day," I said, somehow missing Pru's key point in that moment.

Pru nodded, looking at me with a sympathetic expression, and she sighed before speaking.

"Maybe what we need is not so much 'pervasive certainty' but analogy or allegory. We need help grasping the meaning of things we see or hear or feel. Each of us could use some help understanding our own lives. Right?"

As she spoke, I watched her ammu tears, which then seemed to be turning into tiny birds that flew happily off toward her ears before they disappeared.

"There's so much," I said, "so much to see, to hear, to feel." My eyes began to well with real tears.

"Okay. Listen, I'm off to the ladies' room. While I'm gone, you might decide to go on a little journey of your own. Like maybe across the Atlantic? Hey, I promise I won't think ill of you."

"Please, tell me your full name."

"Pruven Valeriya Kowalczyk. I won't be at Sneg's much longer, by the way. Finishing up some post-grad work to get cert'ed for Occupational Therapy. My new career! Woohoo!"

"That's tremendous, Pru! You have my best wishes!"

"I plan to stay in the area though, so, I mean ... look, if you do decide to leave for Norway, I really hope it all works out for you. But then, if you decide to come back and start over around here somewhere ... well, you have my permission to look me up. I mean, we'll see. Right?"

"You're so sweet. Thank you."

Pru then stood, placed her hand on mine again and said, "If you're still sitting here when I get back, let's go for a walk or something. Okay?"

"Sounds lovely. Thank you, Pru."

Pru turned and walked away, still looking fairy-like to me, even without wearing her fairy work costume. I moved my glass randomly around the table surface for a while, staring intently at its slightly convex base. I lifted the glass, watching the sparkling flecks beneath it return to their previous appointments in space and time. Then I swirled the glass, nearly enabling the wine to overcome gravity to escape the confines of the paraboloid glass structure around it, before bringing the last of the grenache and syrah blend to my lips.

I recalled sitting with Melinda at her father's house, looking out over the pond as a swirling leaf came into view. The leaf had suggested human ballet, which somehow evoked the entire universe ... at least as much of it as my brain could imagine ... the spinning, the looping, the gravity-powered dancing of planets and solar systems and galaxies and galaxy clusters, stretching to infinity, yet compressed into one image, one thought. I thought about the entire history of the universe being presented to us in one instant, with all objects and their movements having their information relayed through electromagnetic waves whose speed is astoundingly fast, yet not infinitely fast, not instantaneous. By the laws of physics, not all information is allowed to be current.

We see the moon as it was a little more than one second ago. We see our sun as it was a few minutes earlier. Objects further away might be seen as they were months ago, years ago, billions of years ago. The vast spectrum of time is neatly compacted into each moment for us as we look at the heavens, as we contemplate the universe. Every moment is all-inclusive, I thought, with active participation of every elementary particle, every form of energy across all space and time.

The little clock in my smarts showed it was near midnight, and as I looked at it, there was a status change for one of my favorite contacts. Melinda was no longer in DND mode, and there was a message from her waiting for me: *You are in my head. Am I in yours?*

I stood and walked out of Lacey's, pausing just outside the doorway. The stars appeared as close to me as the streetlights, as the lights on passing cars. Faraway things seem closer when you focus on them, I thought. I decided to begin a journey at that moment. I anticipated meaningful employment in discovering secret rooms within the home of Melinda's mind. Soon we would explore together, I imagined, all the while attending the partitions between our lives, awaiting notes resigned to harmony, making decisions, moving forward, searching for a secret passage of our own, through walls of cold, solid stone.

Made in the USA
Middletown, DE
20 February 2020